BIRD OF PREY

Now, in her office, she found herself wearying of all the detail. All she really wanted to do was build the Jade Falcons back up to strength in order to head back to the Inner Sphere and finish off what the Clans had begun with the first invasion. While there, she would not mind asserting Falcon supremacy over the Vipers, who shared their corridor. After all that had happened since she had assumed the role of Khan, she had no desire to share glory with the Vipers.

She leaned back in her desk chair and pressed her fingers against her eyes. The pleasurable dots of light appeared, sliding side to side, blending with each other, looking like galactic clusters in a dark universe.

I will show them all what a Jade Falcon Khan can do. They will grovel at—but is not that arrogance? Very well, I am arrogant. I want them all—Khans, the Inner Sphere, all—at my feet. . . .

**Don't miss the other exciting chapters in the
Twilight of the Clans series!**

BATTLETECH®

Twilight of the Clans VIII:
FALCON RISING

Robert Thurston

A ROC BOOK

ROC
Published by the Penguin Group
Penguin Putnam Inc., 375 Hudson Street,
New York, New York 10014, U.S.A.
Penguin Books Ltd, 27 Wrights Lane,
London W8 5TZ, England
Penguin Books Australia Ltd, Ringwood,
Victoria, Australia
Penguin Books Canada Ltd, 10 Alcorn Avenue,
Toronto, Ontario, Canada M4V 3B2
Penguin Books (N.Z.) Ltd, 182–190 Wairau Road,
Auckland 10, New Zealand

Penguin Books Ltd, Registered Offices:
Harmondsworth, Middlesex, England

First published by Roc, an imprint of Dutton NAL,
a member of Penguin Putnam Inc.

First Printing, March, 1999
10   9   8   7   6   5   4   3

Series Editor: Donna Ippolito
Mechanical Drawings: Duane Loose and the FASA art department
Cover art by Doug Chaffee

Round up all the usual suspects, plus a special thanks to Donna Ippolito, Chris Hartford and Bryan Nystul for their help in working out narrative and background problems for me, and to Annalise for frequently brightening up my day with her e-mails from FASA. As always, thanks to Sir Drokk Darkblade (a.k.a., Eugene McCrohan) for his willingness to brainstorm BattleTech matters with me.

And, of course, to Rosemary and Charlotte.

Prologue

Steel Viper Hall
Hall of the Khans, near Katyusha
Strana Mechty
Kerensky Cluster, Clan Space
28 December 3059

Natalie Breen often sat in the dark, here in the Hall of the Khans on Strana Mechty. Once she had been one of those Khans that gave this place its name. Now, all that had changed. Eight years had passed since Tukayyid, eight years since she had stepped down in shame after being forced to withdraw from that bloody battle. Yet, here on Strana Mechty, here among her own kind, she felt like an exile.

Khans did not step down. They died in battle, like any good warrior. Once she had commanded the whole of Clan Steel Viper. Now she served as sometime advisor to her successor, Perigard Zalman. Natalie Breen would have preferred being sent off to a cave in the deepest jungle of Arcadia. Instead, Zalman had given her this out-of-the-way office in the Steel Viper wing of the Hall of the Khans.

In the rare times she went out among the Steel Vipers, she was treated with the respect due her former position, but she felt like an outcast anyway. She knew there were enemies among her own Clan who wished to toss her into the refuse heap of some solahma unit. She knew, too, that others in the Clans viewed her as disgraced.

Before shutting off the office lights through voice command, she had been working on her memoirs again. Memoirs were not often written by Clan warriors, but there were some precedents. Usually a memoir analyzed battles, so that readers, usually officers in charge of combat units or cadets seeking to deepen their understanding of Clan ways and history, could learn from past achievements and mistakes.

Breen had abruptly commanded the lights to shut off because again, for the umpteenth time, she had fallen into morbid thoughts about her failures as Khan. Thoughts of how she had been forced to stand by as the Steel Vipers were consigned to reserve status instead of taking their rightful place among the original invading Clans. Of how she and every other Viper warrior had rejoiced when the ilKhan finally activated the Steel Vipers, assigning them a portion of the Jade Falcon invasion corridor. More rejoicing followed when Viper victories placed the Clan at the front of the invasion line. Then came Tukayyid. Flushed with their successes, the Steel Vipers could never have dreamed what awaited them on that cursed world, in the grim terrain known as Devil's Bath.

That had been a dark time, and even darker ones followed. Natalie Breen had resigned, only to wonder too many times to count whether she should have ignored the shame and soldiered on. She had believed her sacrifice would help dispel the cloud of humiliation that hung over the Vipers' forced withdrawal from Tukayyid. And perhaps it had. With a new Khan at the helm, the Clan had gone on to capture several worlds from the Jade Falcons in the aftermath. And in the years that followed they had gobbled up even more.

She shuddered to think what might have happened to the Steel Vipers had she not given the order to withdraw from the bloodbath on Tukayyid. She had preserved her Clan, but it had taken every ounce of warrior spirit she possessed to resign as Khan. Instead of a glorious death, she had ended up consigned to a kind of nothingness. But the Vipers had survived, and that was all that counted. Too late now to re-fight old battles. It was all coolant streams under a 'Mech's toes, or however the old saying went.

There was a knock on her office door.

She stared at the door for a moment. "Come in, Khan Zalman," she said finally.

The door opened and she saw Perigard Zalman in silhouette. Tall and not a gram heavier since his days as a young warrior, he looked like a stick figure in the dim light.

"You knew it was me, Khan Natalie?" He always addressed her by her former title. She did not discourage him.

"It is always you. No one else comes here. You and sometimes your saKhan, who never comes alone. So, when I hear a knock, it is almost certainly you."

He paused in the doorway. "You are sitting in the dark, Khan Natalie?"

"My eyes hurt. Lights . . . on."

The room was suddenly flooded with light. Zalman himself had to squint from the sudden pain. "What brings you here, my Khan?" she asked, thinking he had come to inquire about the military report he wanted her to compile.

"It is the Jade Falcons again," he said, his homely face taking on a look of gloom.

Breen shook her head in disgust. "The Falcons. They are a thorn in our side, have been since long before I was Khan. Their hatred of us goes back to the days of the revered Khan Mercer. That, and the fact that we have defeated them too often in battle."

Zalman drew himself up to his considerable height and clasped his hands behind his back. "Aye, and now the Falcon Khan seems determined to win by politics what she cannot accomplish through honorable combat. Marthe Pryde is once again carping and complaining about sharing the invasion corridor with us." He gave a short laugh. "You would think she would hate us less for not picking her clean while she was busy attacking Coventry."

Breen smiled. She had a broad smile that generally suggested sarcasm. Still, it was the one attractive feature in an otherwise hawklike and heavy-browed face. Her eyes were as pale as her skin, as light as her hair.

"Typical Jade Falcon scheming," she muttered. "For all their heroic airs, they certainly do bitch a lot. But they cannot undo our invasion corridor victories so easily. This new Khan of theirs, this Marthe Pryde, she seems edgy. Too cunning, too arrogant."

"Funny you should say that. They call us arrogant."

"We are, *quiaff*? One of our main virtues. So, tell me, Perigard, what are the Falcons up to now?"

"They are bragging about their gains in the Harvest Trials. Marthe Pryde has the gall to mock our lesser wins in speeches to the Grand Council, and tries to shame us by claiming that some of our own Viper warriors defected to other Clans to be sure of a place in the new invasion. This, she argues, is cause enough to remove us altogether from the invasion corridor."

Natalie Breen could not hide her surprise. "That is un-Clanlike. I never thought this Marthe Pryde was one to play politics. She portrays herself so much as the warrior-hero. You know, thrust by circumstance into the Khan role."

"She does not seem devious, true, but nevertheless our intelligence reports that she and her Clan continue to plot against us. Our world of Jabuka puts us too close to Terra. That could easily make us the next target of this phony new Star League, now that it has driven the Jaguars out of the Inner Sphere. Until we see what those freebirths are up to, I do not want the Vipers warring with the Falcons over occupied worlds. I seek your advice, Khan Natalie."

"As always, I am at your service."

If only Zalman knew how difficult it was for her to say that, to be courteous to this man who had once been her saKhan, a minion she had at times bossed around mercilessly.

"I need to find an excuse to challenge Marthe Pryde," he said. "To make her fear us, so that she will not dare to attack before we are ready."

"A bold intention," Breen said. "I approve."

"But, in our present state, with the Clans poised to strike

once more at the Inner Sphere, challenges are discouraged. I need a reason for the challenge beyond the old bickerings between our two Clans. When the invasion resumes, I do not want the Falcons holding a knife to our back."

Breen nodded. The worlds of the occupation zone were so intermingled that Clan infighting could seriously weaken the Vipers. "Marthe Pryde originated in the same sibko as the famed Jade Falcon hero, Aidan Pryde, *quiaff*?"

"Aff."

"An over-rated warrior, if there ever was one. Hero of the Battle of Tukayyid, indeed. I was there, and I know what a bloodbath that operation was."

Perigard nodded, and Breen wondered if he were thinking the same thing she was. She and Aidan Pryde had both fought valiantly at Tukayyid, but Aidan had been acclaimed a hero while Natalie had ended up resigning in shame. He had died, and Natalie Breen often wondered why she had been denied the same death. But, if Zalman was thinking such thoughts, she knew he would never voice them here.

The one difference between Perigard Zalman and Natalie Breen, whom he had served so loyally, was that he did not mind occasionally dirtying his hands with political maneuvering. Like most Clan warriors, he despised dishonorable behavior. But as Khan of the Steel Vipers, and saKhan before that, he knew that the only thing that mattered was victory. That had ever been the way of the Clans.

"I know something of this Aidan Pryde," Natalie Breen said. "I have studied his history, and a complex and repellent history it is. Did you know, for example, that he failed his Trial of Position as a cadet—was outmaneuvered, in fact, by Marthe Pryde—and that he took a *second* Trial disguised as someone else?"

"No, I did not know that."

"Perhaps you should," Breen said dryly. "At any rate, Aidan Pryde then posed as a freebirth and fought his second Trial in that guise. He became a warrior, but think what this reveals about the Jade Falcons. It is vile that a trueborn would stoop to pretend to be freeborn, for even a moment.

This hero spent the next years of his life continuing to pose as a freeborn. He took on freebirth assignments, fraternized with freebirths exclusively, and only revealed his trueborn status after some heroic deed or other on a backwater planet. And why reveal it? So he could compete for a bloodname. For a bloodname! Does your stomach not turn at all the implications of this perverted history, Khan Zalman?"

Though she was sure he agreed, Natalie Breen could see that Zalman, always pragmatic, felt no disgust over the oddities of another Clan's history. To him it was probably best to let her, living mostly now in darkness and with the company of few others, have her say.

"He should have been vilified," Zalman commented.

"Oh, he was, I suppose, but the Jade Falcons always manage to justify their demented ways. Still, Aidan Pryde won the bloodname, and others let it happen. I do not deny that some of his acts were valiant, but the freebirth taint permeates his whole history, and the honor that the Jade Falcons gave this warrior is sickening."

Perigard nodded. Again she wondered if he really agreed. After all, any warrior in any of the Clans would have wished to become known as the kind of hero Aidan Pryde was in Jade Falcon annals, even with the freebirth taint.

"Aidan Pryde was rash," Breen continued. "He was given to impulsive risk-taking that only succeeded by sheer luck. But he was known as one willing to risk his life for any win. Now, this Marthe Pryde is from the same sibko and she shows symptoms of the same illness. She is sometimes rash and seems prone to phenomenal risks. You have not heard the latest?"

Zalman shook his head.

"She is allowing a freebirth to compete for a bloodname! Using the justification that the warrior is the spawn of this same Aidan Pryde and some other trueborn who was willing to bear a freeborn child." Natalie Breen took a deep breath in order to control her emotion. "I cannot imagine any trueborn, even one who has failed her warrior training and been relegated to another caste, so much as considering the idea of child-bearing. Much less that it would be a freeborn." Zalman grimaced at her words. It was distasteful for a warrior to even think about the state of freeborn pregnancy, much less talk about it. "And now this freebirth bastard could become a bloodnamed warrior in the Jade Falcon Clan! If, as Khan of the Falcons, Marthe Pryde does allow such a travesty to take place, she is taking a foolish risk, emulating this revered Aidan Pryde. That is the weakness you can take advantage of, Perigard. Do you see?"

"Aye," said Zalman.

"Prod Marthe Pryde," Breen said. "In the Grand Council. Whatever you can say, do, or insulate with sarcastic looks that the rest of the Council will see—work on her, get to her core and cause a meltdown. Use this freeborn bloodname issue to bring down scorn on her and her Clan. Get her angry enough to make the challenge herself. Then you will be—politically—in the right and you will have her set up."

Zalman grinned, looking pleased with himself. "I knew you would be able to counsel me in this. That is why I came here, why I always know you will see a way out of any problem."

Natalie Breen stared at him coldly for a moment. "You are saying that when you need someone to be devious you come to me?" she hissed. "Being devious is not the way of a Clan warrior. I know I have fallen from grace, but I have not fallen as far as that."

Perigard Zalman did not even flinch at her tirade. He had gained in confidence, she realized. Soon he would no longer be finding his way to this dark office to consult with her.

After he left, Breen called out again for darkness and sat for a long while, wondering who she had been and who she was now.

PART I

THE HOMEWORLDS

December 3059

1

Jade Falcon Hall
Hall of the Khans, near Katyusha
Strana Mechty
Kerensky Cluster, Clan Space
31 December 3059

"**W**ell, Horse, you are the last person I thought to see tonight," Khan Marthe Pryde said, as Horse opened the door of her office. "Have you come to help me welcome the new year in?" She beckoned for him to approach.

"You said we should talk," Horse said. "I thought you might be less busy tonight."

"True. The holiday occupies many who would normally be demanding my attention. But I have not seen you since your return from Huntress—when was that, three or four months ago?"

"August."

"That long? Well, how have you been occupying yourself?"

Marthe smiled, but Horse saw that her posture was straighter than ever, more than ever the look of command. He glanced around the office, a rather small one for a Khan, and noted its austerity. There was a plain, standard-issue desk and an obviously old, standard-issue desk chair behind it. For that matter, the rest of the room seemed standard-issue, even the bland landscape prints, one on each wall. At Marthe's gesture to sit, he chose a standard-issue chair, the kind in most offices, wooden and stiff-backed with a faded thin cushion screwed to the wooden seat. Marthe pulled up a similar chair and leaned toward Horse as he began to talk.

"As you ordered," he began, "I have brought my Trinary back up to strength. We have replaced 'Mechs, supplies, and personnel lost on Huntress."

"I have read all your reports, Horse. You had a tough situation there. That Galaxy Commander, Russou Howell, must have been mad to play those games with you. But you handled yourself like a true Jade Falcon."

"True or trueborn?"

Marthe waved her hand impatiently. "Enough of this true/free sarcasm, Horse. It is not one of your best traits. Accept the way of the Clans or join the Inner Sphere. I do not have time to debate genetics. The best I can say for you is that you are freeborn and that means genetically inferior. But you are a fine warrior, as skilled as any trueborn, and you have earned respect not only from me but from many other Jade Falcons."

"But I am still free—"

"Enough! That is a Khan's order. Some day we will straighten out this true/free matter, but the Jade Falcons have other concerns before us now. What is the readiness of your Trinary?"

"Training is proceeding well."

"Good, good. I do not have to tell you that rebuilding our ranks has been my principal concern since becoming Khan. The blooding of many new warriors on Coventry and our successes in the Harvest Trials have gone a long way to restoring our strength. The Snow Ravens alone yielded us two Clusters, and we have also culled warriors from the Fire Mandrills, the Ice Hellions, and the Star Adders. Now that the Smoke Jaguars have been driven from the Inner Sphere, the Jade Falcons again enjoy preeminence among the Clans."

"And so it should be," said Horse. The Jaguars had become the most powerful Clan after the Wolves and the Falcons had nearly destroyed each other in the Refusal War, but now they had been brought low. Lincoln Osis was still ilKhan, but he presided over a Clan that seemed all but dead.

Marthe studied him with her cool, unreadable blue eyes. "I have also been working closely with our merchant caste to replace second-line 'Mechs and materiel with top-of-the-line equipment. That has been another priority. The new invasion of the Inner Sphere was seriously delayed by the Burrock Absorption and other matters, but very little now stands in the way. Have no doubt that your Trinary is prominent in my plans for the next phase of the war against the Inner Sphere."

Horse could not help but grin at her words. "That day cannot come too soon for me, my Khan, but there will be those who would question such a decision, *quiaff*?"

"All things must change, Horse. We Falcons are devoted to tradition, but we cannot survive if we cling to the past. We have risen to many challenges, but even greater ones lie ahead. We must adapt or die."

Horse thought how much Marthe herself had changed since Coventry, how she had begun to change almost from the moment she became Khan. "I hear stories that the Steel Vipers are trying to stir up trouble for us."

Marthe made a sound of derision. "They are as self-serving as ever."

Horse thought about what had brought him here at this hour. "There is also the controversy over MechWarrior Diana's right to fight for a bloodname, *quiaff*?"

"Aff," Marthe said. "Perigard Zalman is opposed to it, as are others among the Khans. However, that is a matter for me to resolve. What I need from you now is for your Trinary to be prepared for combat."

"We are ready at any time to serve you and the Clan, my Khan," Horse said. "With your permission, I have come to speak with you about another matter."

Marthe looked at him sharply, then nodded for him to continue.

"I have a request, my Khan. A small one." He waited as Marthe continued to study him with those cool blue eyes.

"Permission to speak," she said finally.

"If I may be detached from my Trinary, I would like to

travel to Ironhold and assist in training MechWarrior Diana. This has nothing to do with the freeborn matters we just—"

Marthe waved away his words. "I know that. As Aidan Pryde's closest ally and friend, it is only natural for you to want to help. You were a member of Aidan's own training team when he won the Pryde bloodname. I will grant your request, Horse, but have patience. I may yet need your help here on Strana Mechty. I cannot explain right now, but—"

"I am at your service, my Khan. Ever."

Marthe smiled. "How—I do not know the best word— *knightlike* perhaps. Yes, how knightlike of you, Horse. I am pleased."

Horse began pulling at the side of his beard, as he often did when he was amused and did not want to show it.

Outside the Jade Falcon edifice there was a sudden series of explosions and gunfire coming from beyond the park surrounding the Hall of Khans complex. Horse stood up abruptly, and put his body between Marthe and the door, to protect his Khan should attackers suddenly burst in.

Marthe laughed loudly. She stood up and placed one hand on Horse's arm.

"No need for protection, Horse, though your action does show a loyalty I already knew was there." There were more explosions, more gunfire. "You have forgotten what night this is. They are celebrating the new year here on Strana Mechty. It is 3060, at least according to the Universal Calendar. Apparently, it is the one thing we and the Inner Sphere have ever agreed upon. Think, Horse, a thousand light years from here, people on the worlds of the Inner Sphere are carrying out their own versions of celebrating the start of another year. It is time to look forward to the future."

Horse shrugged. "I do not find it satisfying to contemplate the future. Or the past, although that is unavoidable, it seems."

Marthe reached out and gave his arm a gentle squeeze, and Horse did not know what to think. It was rare enough for a trueborn to be even mildly friendly in gesture or touch, but for a Khan such an act seemed, well, unsuitable.

"We are of a similar mind, Horse. But, unfortunately, I *must* think of the future. Every Khan must, if only to anticipate the actions of other Khans. Sometimes I would rather be surrounded by attacking 'Mechs than the Khans in Grand Council. But that is no matter. I thank you for your loyalty, Horse, and we will speak again."

Horse stood up and bowed slightly after her subtle dismissal and, following a ritual parting, walked rapidly to the door and out of the room.

Even after Horse was gone, Marthe could still feel his presence in the room. Reflecting on their talk, she realized that she never thought of him as freeborn any more, unless he brought it up. If anything, he was, in her mind, Aidan Pryde's comrade.

But it was precisely his freeborn origin that she needed now, both personally and for matters of policy. Some Clans, Jade Falcons among them, permitted freeborns to become warriors, though only in second-line and garrison roles. Times, however, had changed, and Marthe knew she needed every experienced warrior she could get. Samantha Clees, her saKhan, continued to quietly advise Marthe against being soft on freeborns and risking too much of her position on them. Samantha meant well, but Marthe knew this was a risk that must be run.

The times were more precarious than ever. She had blooded many young warriors on Coventry, had harvested warriors from other Clans in Trials across the homeworlds, and was bloodnaming many who would become senior officers in her touman. But a powerful military needed experience as well as numbers. Was it not better to use freeborn warriors who were skilled and experienced rather than depend too much on young or newly acquired warriors? Samantha would never agree, but Marthe had come to see that being true to the way of the Clan meant daring to find a new way when the Clan's very existence was at stake. The Falcons were ready for war, ready to destroy any enemy in their path and to take their place at the head of the Clans in liberating Terra.

She smiled to herself. More and more these days, thoughts would come into her mind that surprised and even shocked her. She had never pictured herself as a savior of the Clan but, once the idea was thought, she saw how accurate it was. All of her recent command actions, her policies, her daring risks had been at the service of a single goal—to preserve the Jade Falcon Clan and to restore its former glory. No, not simply to restore but to go beyond what the Falcons had ever been. To allow no other Clan—not the Vipers, not the Wolves, not any other Clan—to interfere with the rise of the Jade Falcons to a pinnacle higher than any before achieved. She had to do that. She would do that.

She could imagine herself as a visionary leader only at the onset of the new year, with the echoes of the celebrations outside beginning to fade, before the morning-after mood of reality would undoubtedly set in. Perhaps, though, she was on a track that was part of a destiny she could not possibly see. It had once had something to do with the Marthe Pryde who had been a cadet in the same sibko with Aidan Pryde, and that was all she wanted to know about it. Ever.

2

Sibko Training Center 111
Kerensky Forest, Ironhold
Kerensky Cluster, Clan Space
3 January 3060

"**S**top smiling at me!" Naiad growled.

"Was not smiling at you," Andi replied calmly. "Just smiling is all."

"You lie, stravag."

"Never lie, ugly stravag yourself."

"You call me stravag!"

"You are a stravag and anyway you called me stravag first!"

"Called me stravag again! All of you heard that?"

She turned to address the rest of the sibko, most of whom were tired out from their morning's training session and resting on their cots. Idania, Andi's closest friend in the sibko, said, "Stop fighting, you two."

"You freebirth, Idania!" Naiad yelled.

Idania, who had been sitting on the edge of her bunk, suddenly sprang up and charged at Naiad, but Andi intervened his body between the two.

"I am going to fight her, Idania," Andi said.

"No. Me!"

The others in the sibko grumbled but took no part in what was just another squabble among many.

Andi calmed Idania, a talent only he had, and he turned back to Naiad, who shifted around on her feet restlessly, an eagerness to get on with it clear in her gray eyes, eyes the exact duplicate of his own, just as most of Naiad's features resembled his and the rest of the sibko.

"Okay, Naiad," he said. "Fight then, you and me!"

As he spoke, his smile broadened. Naiad hated Andi and his insulting cheerfulness. He smiled much too much, especially now as he formally accepted her challenge to tussle within the Circle of Equals outside the sibko's barracks.

Naiad did not know how to smile. In her early days out of the vat, when she was just an infant and did not know any better, she might have smiled fairly often. She had vague memories of being tended to by an old hag who took no delight in her charges. Well-trained, this canister nanny, as she was sarcastically termed, had been efficient at supplying their nutritional needs and teaching them motor skills.

They had been taken away from the canister nanny early and transferred to this training center, under the supervision of a sibparent, Octavian, a former warrior who was now spending the latter part of his military career in charge of a warrior-training sibko. Sibparents built up the sibko's physical skills and instructed it in what it meant for a true-born to be a member of the Clan and a warrior, the pinnacle of Clan society. Eventually the sibko would be turned over to falconers, who would formally train the cadets in warrior skills.

Another thing that annoyed Naiad about Andi was that he was already at least a centimeter taller than she was. Naiad, already first in intelligence tests and physical ability, intended to be first in *everything,* so she did not want anyone in the sibko to be taller either. Or broader-shouldered (Daniel threatened to beat her there), or a faster runner (Nadia still managed to beat out Naiad in sprints, though never in longer races), or one who could wield a weapon with skill and grace, something that Adrian did so well that there were times when Naiad despaired of ever catching up with him. However, Naiad was near the top in most training skills. When the time came for her to test out as a warrior, she intended to wipe out every opponent. She was going to be the best and the sibko would have to deal with it.

From opposite sides Naiad and Andi crossed the line into the Circle of Equals. Andi not only kept the infuriating smile on his face, but he managed a sarcastic bow. The bow caused a burst of gleeful laughter from Idania, the only member of the sibko who had come out of the barracks to watch this tussle.

"Take care of you later, freebirth," Naiad screamed at Idania. Again Idania threatened a fight and Andi waved her away.

Within the warrior caste the epithet *freebirth* was the deepest insult. The name referred to freeborns, those Clanspeople who were born from human wombs. They were looked down upon by the trueborns like Naiad and her sibmates, who were all genetically engineered, born in laboratories and birthed from vats called iron wombs.

Even though Naiad knew that most freeborns were needed to do tasks that a trueborn would have found a waste of time—and Clanspeople, especially those in Clan Jade Falcon, deplored waste—she hated freeborns anyway. To her, trueborns were the highest rung of the evolutionary ladder, and the freeborns were human freaks who belonged several rungs down, necessary as a caste to support the trueborns but otherwise to be regarded with scorn. She had been around few freeborns so far in her short existence, and avoided the frees who came into the training center to execute their menial duties.

After the bow, Andi kept his head down and rushed Naiad. The charge made Naiad furious, since she always wanted to make the first move, strike the first blow. Andi knew that, and his preemptive strike only enraged her more.

She brought up her elbow to knock Andi aside. Twirling with a near-balletic motion, she brought her foot around to kick him in the side before he could recover. He fell and she jumped on him.

With some of the sibko members, that would have been enough. Naiad could have held them down until she had forced them to cry uncle. But the sibko physical training was extensive, even though they were all still so young, and Andi was no easy match. He had the arm and leg strength to resist being pinned, and forced Naiad away from him.

Losing all sense of balance, she rolled away and accidentally knocked her head on a large rock that, it seemed to her, had not been there before. She looked up toward Idania, still standing at the border of the Circle of Equals, but with the kind of mischievously satisfied look in her gray eyes that suggested she had rolled the rock into the path of Naiad's head. Naiad, however, had no time to contemplate revenge as she sensed Andi coming at her. He was scrambling like a crab across the dusty ground, making himself just another target for her talented elbow, as she pivoted her body to give force to the subsequent blow.

Andi's eyes closed as he fell suddenly at her side, blood streaming from his nose. Naiad began to get up. Before she stood comfortably, however, Andi suddenly opened his eyes and grabbed her ankles, one with each hand, and tipped her over again. Now he was the one on top, his arms reaching to pin her.

"Fat chance, freebirth," she shouted as she flat-palmed him right in his Adam's apple. The punch was more annoying than effective, but it allowed her to squirm out from beneath him and, with one of those wonderfully athletic moves she was already famous for in the sibko, leap to her feet, ready to finish Andi off. She knew she could win this fight, but fate intervened.

"Stop this, children," Octavian said as he seemed to materialize from out of nowhere and cross into the Circle of Equals.

The three sibmates seethed inside at Octavian's using the insult *children*. To them children were freeborn offspring, while those who emerged from vats were properly called sibkin until they began their warrior training, and sometimes the term was used even then.

Octavian's long legs carried him to the two battlers in a couple of strides. He seized the collar of Naiad's tunic and grabbed Andi by the shoulder.

What made the sibko fear Octavian was the impressive strength he had in an otherwise slight physique. That, and the fire in his eyes. And the scars all over his face and body, all remnants of his warrior days when he had been an expert BattleMech pilot.

Naiad often challenged this powerful former warrior to fights. Even she knew she would have lost such fights if he had accepted her challenges. But she did not fear him. She was determined not to fear anybody, ever.

"You crossed the line of the Circle of Equals, Octavian," she screamed. "Not right to do that!"

Octavian smiled, a smile unlike Andi's. It was mean and it was contemptuous and nobody liked to see it.

"You are a pretend-warrior, Naiad. Do not forget that. All of you are mere children, and do not forget that either."

He now addressed the whole sibko. Those in the barracks had scrambled out at the sound of his voice.

"You may call this a Circle of Equals, if in your babyish ways you choose to. But this is not a Circle of Equals and never will be, not while you are under my tutelage. When you go into training to be a warrior, then you may do as you like, fight when you like, get yourselves killed as you like. But here you are just children, children who act like babies. What was this little tussle about?"

"He smiled at me," Naiad shouted, pointing at Andi.

"You challenged over just a smile?"

"Yes!" Naiad shouted defiantly.

"Wasteful. Get back in your barracks, all of you. If you think your morning was difficult, you will all probably be dead before nightfall. Get what rest you can."

As the sibko filed into the barracks, Octavian asked Naiad to stay a moment. When they were alone, Octavian said: "So this fight was over a mere smile, *quiaff*?"

"Aff."

"Stupid of you, Naiad. You think yourself a warrior ahead of time. You are not a warrior until you are a warrior. While in the sibko, before your Trial of Position, you are a mere child. Dismissed."

As she walked to the barracks, Octavian said calmly: "A warrior ahead of time—but, on the other hand, I expect you *will* be a warrior, Naiad."

She watched him stride away. When he was out of sight, she ran swiftly to the border of the encampment, to an open field near some abandoned barracks located near the border fence. There she began to exercise fiercely so she could be better at tomorrow's exercises.

As she performed a long set of jumping jacks, she looked past the fence and saw some movement in the hillside beyond. There was someone behind a bush, she was sure. She gave the area sidelong glances while taking care not to interrupt the steady rhythm of the exercise.

After a while, she was certain someone was out there, spying. She detested spies, but she was also thrilled that she might discover one, so she began to make her plans.

3

Sibko Training Center 111
Kerensky Forest, Ironhold
Kerensky Cluster, Clan Space
3 January 3060

From her hiding place behind a patch of flowery bushes, Peri Watson studied the girl doing jumping jacks on the other side of the tangled wire fence. Although clearly about six or seven years old, the child was tall for her age and a healthy specimen, taut muscles on her thin body, a graceful agility in her performance of the aerobic regimen. She looked much like any sibko child in the early stages preceding the even more intense training of the cadet stage.

But the girl's physical attributes seemed meaningless when Peri looked closely at her face. The face was identical to someone Peri had known when she, herself, was a child. This girl looked exactly like Aidan Pryde as he had been then. Not just a resemblance, not just some identical features, but entirely like him. If she had not known better, Peri would have thought she was watching Aidan Pryde, returned from the dead as a young boy ready to do battle with the world again. Even the way the girl performed the exercise, rapidly and with a concentrated precision, and the way she held and moved her body, reminded Peri of the fallen hero, Aidan Pryde.

Peri had come to the training center because of suspicions that Clan scientists were conducting a secret genetic project. As a scientist herself, and one fairly high in the caste hierarchy, she had nevertheless been kept in the dark about these projects, a condition heightened by her exile to the Jade Falcon scientific outpost of Falcon Eyrie on the Smoke Jaguar home planet, Huntress. There she had discovered that copies of the Aidan Pryde genetic materials had been preserved not only in the Falcon Eyrie genetic labs but also, shockingly, in a dark corner of the Smoke Jaguar genetics repository in the city of Lootera. One of the ironies of the discovery was that news of it had been brought to her by Aidan Pryde's freeborn friend, Horse.

Because of the mystery of Aidan Pryde genetic copies existing outside the Jade Falcon Clan, she had returned to Ironhold where the governing body of the Clan's scientist caste, led by the Scientist-General, a weaselly man named Etienne Balzac, had its offices in the capital, Ironhold City. But her investigation soon stalled as she came up against various bureaucratic roadblocks. The official line was that there were no secret programs going on and, even if there were, she had no right to inquire about them. She asked did that mean then that there were secret programs, after all. They constructed new roadblocks. She requested meetings with the Scientist-General. Each time, the crafty man provided an excuse not to meet. Even when she confronted him on his daily walk, he told her he could not talk then, but would meet with her soon.

Peri's search might have ended in this tangle of red tape if she had not decided to go out one night to wander the city in a dark mood.

Sitting at a bar in one of the dark but clean tech taverns, Peri sipped at a version of a fusionnaire, the favorite warrior drink. This one had more taste than anything she had drunk in a warrior rec room, another virtue of drinking among the frees. In most Clan cities, the best booze was found in the tech district. Only the techs really cared. Warriors and scientists, on the other hand, usually did not distinguish the quality of what they drank. In the rare times when she had to muddle her busy mind with a calming drink, she always went to the nearest tech quarter.

Someone came up and sat on the stool beside her. While she was aware of his presence, she did not look at him. She knew that it was a man and, based on the smell of age that drifted toward her, probably an old man.

"You're drinking a fusionnaire," the man said in a surprisingly strong voice. "Very unusual for a freeborn to drink warrior drinks."

Peri chose not to look at the man.

"I was a warrior once, almost a warrior. Flushed out. Too bad for me." She felt the fusionnaire going to her head already.

"Lucky for you, you mean. Warriors are barely human. All that rigor and military folderol."

"I would not push it, fellow. I respect warriors, and so should you."

"You're trueborn, I'm not."

The drink made her overlook his use of contractions, a normal freeborn habit anyway. In the long subsequent silence Peri listened intently for sounds of her unwelcome companion leaving, but the old-age smell remained.

"Funny," he said suddenly. "In this light, or near lack of it, you look like someone I used to know. Know well, in fact."

"Then stop looking at me, the feeling will go away."

The fusionnaire was making her uncharacteristically sarcastic.

"Okay. But you look like a hero. Thought you might like to know that."

"Hero?"

"Name of Aidan Pryde. I'm sure you've—"

Peri had to look. What she saw was, indeed, an old man. In his face, there were wrinkles on wrinkles on wrinkles. For a moment, a wave of revulsion almost made her choke. While it was common for trueborns to react that way to anybody old, that was merely *somewhat* old, *solahma* old. This man looked ancient, like a mummy with the wrappings off. Yet the face underneath that repulsive accumulation of age seemed familiar.

"You knew Aidan Pryde?" Peri said.

"Yes. And, now that you're looking at me, I know why

you reminded me of him. You were in his sibko. Your name is Peri, and I think I last saw you on the planet Tokasha when we, Commander Joanna and I, captured that scamp of an Aidan to bring him back to Ironhold."

"You were the bastard with that stravag?"

"Yes."

Tokasha. So long ago. Staring at the ancient man, Peri took years off his wrinkled face.

"You . . . you are Nomad?"

"Congratulations! What a memory you have."

"I am a scientist. We organize, classify, define. I remember everyone I ever knew. I remember the anger I felt when you and Joanna wrecked my world for a time. I heard you were dead."

"There was a story going around . . ."

For the next hour, Peri and Nomad exchanged memories of Aidan, and their own histories, as people who met again after a long period often did. Peri found out that Nomad had been relieved of his job on a team of 'Mech techs when arthritis, a congenital condition among those who specialized in BattleMech repair, had crippled his hands.

"Quickly proved myself useless in several other jobs because of the pain. Finally, I was reassigned to the sanitation caste. Even hands in pain can push a broom."

"A waste of your talents."

"Arguable."

Eventually Nomad asked her why she was prowling the city's back streets and, because she had had too many fusionnaires, she told him. It felt good, venting her anger against Balzac. When she mentioned the hidden projects to Nomad, he nodded his head.

"You know something, Nomad."

"I always know something. A specialty."

"Dump the cryptic remarks. Tell me."

Nomad, in his direct but occasionally embellished style, described a wilderness camp run by the scientists. Rumor had it that the place was well-guarded by some surly thugs, pretending to be warriors, dressed in military uniforms of some past era. People said they were actually from the bandit caste, captured and pressed into service as Balzac's elite guards.

"Most folks are steering clear of the place," Nomad said. "In some circles there are stories of ghosts and goblins, the usual thing."

"You know more than that."

"Of course. I hear there are constant visits by Balzac and his minions, who apparently are especially concerned with the project. I know a lot, but I don't know what the project is."

In another few minutes both Peri and Nomad had drunk too many fusionnaires and could not communicate coherently. She had dozed for a moment and woke up to find Nomad gone. She wondered if she had dreamed him, especially after she tried to locate him within the sanitation caste and nobody there knew of his existence.

Nomad had given Peri just enough information to help her find the camp and slip through its guard ranks into this spying nook. While she had been dredging up the memories, the child had ended her exercises and disappeared around a barracks building.

Nothing much happened for a while, until suddenly Peri heard a slight sound behind her. Before she could turn, there was a tap on her shoulder.

She turned and saw the child. She almost gasped for breath when she saw how much, up close, this child looked like Aidan Pryde.

"You look real surprised," the child said.

"I am."

"Why?"

Peri did not want to discuss the resemblance with the child, so she said, "You sneaked up on me, surprised me."

The child stared into Peri's eyes. "You lie," she said, "But no matter. You are afraid because I captured you."

Even though Peri realized she could easily escape from this child, her curiosity made her stay put.

"Are you going to turn me in and get some reward for it?"

The child shrugged. "Not yet. You look like me. Why? Not telling? You are my prisoner, spy stravag. I will torture you if I have to. Come with me."

"Why go anywhere? You can interrogate me here."

"And you looking for a way to get away. Neg, spy stravag. I have a place, a secret place. We go there. Get up."

To Peri, it seemed like a good idea to play along with this child's fantasy. Even if she led her to one of Balzac's minions it would not be hard for her, with her rank within the scientist caste, to talk her way out of any situation here. The worst that could happen was a trip back to Ironhold City to be reprimanded by the Scientist-General.

The child led her through some greenery to a spot by the fence, where she was able to lift a section that would allow both of them into the camp.

"Disabled the alarm here long ago," the girl said. "Good at that kind of thing, I am. Allows me to sneak out. Figure some day I may see something. Name is Naiad."

"Peri."

"You are beautiful, Peri. Like me."

It was a tight squeeze but Peri got through the opening in the fence and followed Naiad to the nearest building, an unused barracks.

"Go in there," Naiad said, indicating the barracks door. "Got to go back soon, so we must talk quickly. You talk, spy stravag, maybe I will not turn you in."

4

Peri had not been inside a barracks since she was a cadet several years ago. The last time had been the day she'd flushed out of training, on her way to a quick exit off Ironhold to the Jade Falcon planet Tokasha, where she began her scientist caste apprenticeship. After the apprenticeship she had become a full-fledged member of the caste, and had even won the labname of Watson.

The surnames of the scientist caste annoyed warriors. For warriors, surnames—bloodnames—were fairly rare and only won through difficult competitions where the eventual winner had to defeat thirty-two other unbloodnamed warriors in a series of encounters. Warriors did not like that the higher-ranked scientists had such casually awarded surnames, even though they were careful not to use them outside the caste. Of course, it helped that the scientist surnames duplicated none of the traditional bloodnames and their utterance held little traditional weight.

Bloodnames were originally the names of those warriors who had fled the Inner Sphere with Alexandr Kerensky. When Nicholas Kerensky created the Clans and originated the concept of bloodnames for the best warriors, it had seemed natural that those surnames be drawn from those who had been loyal to Nicholas. Scientists, however, took their surnames from well-known Terran scientists of history, although occasionally a surname would have originated elsewhere, as in the current Scientist-General's name, Balzac. Peri had heard that Etienne had chosen that name because he felt that some ancient author had dissected society with the skill and thoroughness of a scientist. Since she already considered Etienne Balzac a pretentious fool, the story did not surprise Peri.

She shut her eyes as she entered the barracks and encountered the traditional smell of barracks sweat. Opening her eyes, she saw debris that clearly indicated this building had been abandoned some time ago. She assumed that its emptiness had something to do with the general rebuilding that, she had heard, was going on in all the crash camps on Ironhold, part of the acceleration of the training process to produce new warriors to fill out the depleted invasion forces and be ready when the invasion of the Inner Sphere resumed. In addition to the warriors coming out of the accelerated training, on Strana Mechty, the so-called "harvest wars" were taking place, with units from the Clans left behind during the initial invasion getting the opportunity to win Trials that would allow their warriors to join one of the invading Clans.

She had heard that veteran warriors condemned the new buildings, saying that the whole cadet training process had become softer. Rumor had it that the high command wanted more cadets to qualify and that some of the rules regarding training had been simplified. Whatever was true and whatever was based on traditional warrior resentment, the fact was that—as the current war effort increased—more cadets *were* passing their Trials of Position. Training officers claimed that the new facilities and methods of training had brought out the best in the cadets themselves. Soon the Clans would resume the invasion, truce or no truce. And this time they were determined to win.

There must be layers of warrior sweat ingrained into the wood of the walls, Peri thought as she walked further into the large room. *I seem to recall that the barracks where*

Aidan Pryde and I trained smelled exactly the same. And Marthe Pryde. What would you say about her now, Aidan? You died before she became Khan of the Jade Falcons, but perhaps we knew that was her destiny, even then. Forget her. I do not want to think of her. When we were cadets, she turned on you, Aidan, and you forgave her for it. This damn warrior philosophy with its acceptance of any deed done in the name of the Clan!

Marthe and Aidan had taken their Trial of Position at the same time. Marthe took out two 'Mechs, one of which was Aidan's, during her Trial, driven by her ambition to enter the Clan ranks as a Star Commander.

Ah, well, that is all coolant under a 'Mech foot. Marthe is Khan, I am a scientist, and Aidan is dead. One way or another we all served the Clan, and two of us still do. In a way Aidan's memory still serves the Clan well. The younger warriors revere him. But, Aidan, if you and Marthe realized how much mockery of the Clan was spoken in private among the scientists, you would probably take swords to us and arrange a little massacre. Or you would have laughed and said what did warriors care about what a lower caste thought? That is more likely.

From behind Naiad gave her a little push in the small of her back.

"Keep moving, spy stravag."

As she smiled and picked up her pace, Peri glanced around the room. Beds overturned and rusting. A couple of thin mattresses clearly ripped in a purposeful way. And dust, layers and layers of dust. She wondered why she had not smelled that rather than warrior sweat.

Naiad found an intact bed and turned it upright.

"Sit here, freebirth scum."

"I do not know that it matters my protesting this, but I am trueborn. And I know barracks like this better than you do, kestrel."

Naiad seemed surprised, but was clearly determined not to show any emotion. Reaching down, she picked up an abandoned, ruined mattress and threw it on the bed. At

Naiad's comically imperious gesture, Peri sat down. Not surprisingly, the perspiration aroma was stronger here, as if rising from the mattress like a morning mist. She lowered her right hand to the mattress surface, touching its rough material with the tips of her fingers. The feel of it was one she recalled clearly in all the years since her cadet days.

By odd coincidence, Naiad had set up the bed in the approximate position where Peri's own bunk had been in her original barracks. Viewing the room from this position, it somehow seemed more familiar. Squinting her eyes, she could call up a foggy visual memory—of herself sitting in a similar bunk, looking up from some instructional sheet or other, filled with the confidence of a cadet and dreaming of the day when she would take the field as a warrior—looking up and seeing the others also intent on their nighttime cramming. Aidan with an eagerness in his eyes and worry-lines indicating he was puzzled by what he read, Rena (who would die in training after Peri left) working her mouth from side to side as she read, Bret looking bored with the material, Marthe reading calmly with that supreme confidence she always had.

For a moment she longed for this room to turn into a time machine to take her back to that time, give her a second chance and—no, even with all she knew now, she would never have the warrior skills. She was an almost-warrior, one blessed with many of the skills, but somehow always not getting a detail right, reacting a nanosecond too slow, being castigated by Falconer Joanna and glanced at with disapproval by the overall commanding officer, Ter Roshak, a mean officer if there ever was one.

"What are you doing here, spy stravag?"

Peri identified herself as a scientist, which made Naiad's eyebrows go up in surprise.

"Then, why spy? Could you not just come in the front gate?"

"My credentials would have been denied. You may not be aware, but you and your sibkin are a secret project."

"I am aware," Naiad said, but Peri could see in her perplexed eyes that she was lying.

"Then tell me what the point of it is, kestrel, because I have somehow missed it in my research."

"Do not call me kestrel."

"It is not really an insult, child,"

"Not child either, stravag."

"Tell me the point of all this, all this secret project."

"It is secret. That is why I cannot say."

"Do you know that you are genetically linked to the Jade Falcon hero named Aidan Pryde?"

"Of course." This time it was hard to tell if she was merely playing along.

"Would it impress you to know that I come from the same sibko as Aidan Pryde?"

In Naiad's eyes there was new confusion, and then a light seemed to dawn. "Of course. That is why you look so much like us."

"And that means?"

"I cannot say. Secret."

"From what fine Jade Falcon warrior is your matrilineal line developed?"

Apparently confused, Naiad looked to her left, then her right, then back at Peri.

"None of your business, spy stravag."

"Let me tell you what I believe. There is no matrilineal line in your genetic materials. You and your sibkin are entirely offshoots of Aidan Pryde genes. I am not sure how or why it was done, but it is a sort of Clan version of parthenogenesis, one that goes against the Clan way."

Peri stopped talking as she saw complete befuddlement in the child's eyes.

"Are you following all this, Naiad?"

"Of course I am," the girl lied, and with a great anger in her voice. Naiad's stubbornness amused Peri, and it reminded her very much of Aidan.

Peri had gone beyond anything the child understood. Naiad merely stared at her, open-mouthed. Even if Naiad did not understand, Peri knew she should not reveal any more to her. She might understand just enough to tip off anyone who interrogated her about this conversation.

I wish I could find out more from her. I still do not grasp why this genetic experimentation is going on, even with the Clan expecting to produce warriors who represent the best of what has gone before. After all, for centuries we have been looking for what is best in one ancestral warrior and mating it with all that is best in another, to produce the most efficient and skilled warriors possible. Theoretically. But that has not happened as much as hoped. No matter how much genetic tinkering we do, the human result turns out to be just that: human. If old quirks are engineered out, new ones emerge. Somehow we cannot stop warriors from having tendencies toward certain emotions, like rage or sullenness, or govern their sense of humor or make them even-tempered. Sometimes the new generation found in a sibko is significantly a throwback or does not display the kind of Clan ideal planned for. So we scientists continue to tinker. Clan warriors are still the best history has to offer, but can be improved on.

As a scientist, it is not the tinkering with genetic materials that Balzac and his crew are doing that offends me. That is, after all, legitimate research. It is the political implications that frighten me. I do not like other Clan scientists having access to Jade Falcon genetic materials, and presumably to the research of our scientist caste. If scientists from several Clans are sharing information, what will be the result? What of Falcon warriors birthed with some insertion of genes from Clan Wolf? This has been done. Eventually, all the Clans might be diminished by all this infernal experimentation. But I cannot tell any of these thoughts to Naiad.

There was the sound of young voices in the distance. Naiad reacted to it.

"Have to train. Octavian does not like it when we are late. Guess I will have to take you to him, spy stravag. He is real mean."

Peri feigned an acceptance of Naiad's judgment, but she knew she could not submit. She had to return to Ironhold City, get to the bottom of this Aidan sibko phenomenon.

She stood up. Momentarily glancing around, she remembered her last day in a barracks like this one. Joanna had awakened her in the dead of night and informed her that she was finished with warrior training and would receive her new assignment at the Training Center. Joanna's voice, usually invested with anger or at least sternness, was uncharacteristically soft when she told Peri with some pride that Peri would become a scientist caste apprentice. For a flushed-out warrior, Joanna said, the scientists were the best reassignment available and it was to Peri's credit that she had been chosen.

Sad and angry, but knowing that the decision of the training officers was correct, that she was not sufficiently skilled to be a warrior, she had lain in bed until the early morning light creeping in through barracks cracks allowed her to gather her things to leave. It was tradition for the flushed-out cadet to leave silently, to steal off into the night, and she did not intend to display her failure to the quartet of cadets she was leaving behind, all members of a sibko she had spent her whole life with and would now, she thought incorrectly, leave behind her forever.

Just as she was about to take one last look and depart, a voice interrupted from across the room. It was Aidan.

"Who is it? . . . . It is Peri, is it not?"

"I am leaving. Please do not speak louder. I do not want to display my humiliation to others."

"It is not humiliation, it is—"

"I know. It is part of the whole damn noble goal we all seek. Only now I am out of it." She had not wanted to express her thoughts, but she had always been close to Aidan. Not as close as Marthe, but close. "Think of how it feels. All this time spent in training, only to be flushed out and told you now belong to another caste. Well, I do not *belong* to any other caste. Wherever I am, people will look at me and the thought will cross their minds that once I was in warrior training. It is like a brand mark on my forehead. I am a warrior and will remain so all my life. All my life."

It had been quite a speech for her, she remembered, especially for one who spoke rarely and then only briefly. But, as she looked into Aidan's concerned face, she had been comforted.

He asked where she was being sent and she told him the scientist caste. He said that sounded important and, for a while, they discussed genetics and how their sibko, in spite of sharing the same genetic sources, had displayed so much difference in their abilities and personalities. In a strange way, that conversation had induced in her a need to concentrate on what made a warrior like Aidan and what made failures like herself.

Naiad gestured toward her to go in front of her out of the barracks. The child had such confidence. Still, she was just a child and Peri could escape from her. Just as she was about to act, however, a thin, dark form blocked the daylight of the open barracks doorway.

"Just what is going on here?" the man bellowed.

Naiad whirled around. Was that a flash of annoyance Peri had seen on her face?

"Octavian! I—uh, I just captured this spy stravag."

Octavian laughed heartily and stepped into the room.

"You children do insist on playing your games."

He brushed back Naiad and came to Peri. Standing over her, he did not seem all that formidable. But Peri was cautious. Octavian had once been a warrior, and nothing could be taken for granted.

"So you are a spy then?" Octavian said.

Peri shrugged. "I was taking a look at your facility when I, uh, met Naiad. But I am not a spy. I belong to the Falcon scientist caste and have every right to inspect a facility such as this."

"Scientist? I do not recall you ever visiting us before, nor do I know your name. You are not on my list of those who may be admitted to this camp. So—how did you get here?"

Peri glanced at Naiad, who looked a bit apprehensive.

She assumed the child would not like her hole in the fence to be revealed.

"I entered by the front gate."

"Security would not allow you to—"

"Better check your security. No one tried to stop me at the front gate. I just strolled in."

"That is impossible."

Peri stood up and pretended to straighten out the bed, putting her hands on either side of the mattress.

"Nevertheless, the gate might just as well have had a welcome mat in front of it."

"You are lying."

Her back was now turned to him. Apparently, that annoyed him sufficiently to clamp his hand on her shoulder. She could feel his strength. She would have to move fast and efficiently.

"I am a scientist," she said, with as much officiousness as she could manage. "You may not treat me so roughly, even if you were once a warrior."

Her bluff apparently worked. He removed his hand. Before he could think of his next move, Peri lifted the mattress and whirled around with it, catching Octavian in the stomach and knocking him backward. *Thank goodness,* she thought, *that warriors, in their toughening process, have to use such stiff mattresses.*

As Octavian straightened up, Peri called up her vivid memories of hand-to-hand combat training and, in an underhand sweep, palm-struck him in his throat, then crouched down and head-butted him in his stomach. She was tempted to try a third blow, but did not trust her luck or her training memories.

Instead, she made a direct run for the barracks door.

Naiad tried to step into her path, but Peri elbowed her out of the way. Naiad banged her head against the barracks wall and became dizzy for a short time.

When Octavian got his wind back and Naiad's vision cleared, they rushed out of the barracks after their intruder.

Their quarry was on the other side of the fence, running up the hill. She had evidently squirmed through the hole Naiad had made in the fence. Its location would probably be found, but Naiad did not mind. The disabling of the fence would be blamed on the intruder and, anyway, Naiad could merely disable another section for her forays into the outside world.

Octavian raged for a moment, clearly angry that he had let Peri get away. Naiad was strangely glad that she had escaped. She had been impressed by the scientist's quick moves and the fact they had been directed at Octavian.

She had a new hero now.

As for Peri, as she cleared the hill and eased past the lines of security around the camp, she could not stop feeling exhilarated at having employed warrior skills that she had thought were long forgotten. She was able to run through the forest beyond the camp at a much higher speed than she had managed in a long time.

5

Grand Council Chamber
Hall of the Khans, near Katyusha
Strana Mechty
Kerensky Cluster, Clan Space
17 January 3060

Sometimes, even when you were prepared for a fight, even when the gloves were off and the rage in the back of the throat was engaged, there was still a moment of dread when the fight actually came. Khan Marthe Pryde of the Jade Falcons knew the moment had arrived when the ritually costumed Khan of the Steel Vipers, Perigard Zalman, stood up, half-turned around, and aimed the steely glare of his deep-set eyes up toward the high tier where Marthe sat.

Never had the sculpted granite seat beneath her seemed so rock-hard. Never had the large marble-top desk in front of her seemed so icy cold. There was even an ominous ripple in the cloth banner at the front of her desk, the banner that denoted Clan Jade Falcon, with the magnificently conceived and stylized view of the falcon in flight. Never had she more wanted to reach down and put on again the beautifully enameled Khan mask that would have hidden her reactions to the famously mean tactics of Perigard Zalman. A curious buzz of excitement among the Khans seemed amplified by the acoustics of this spacious, echoing chamber that was their meeting hall.

As she glared down at the sharply chiseled, unattractive features of the Steel Viper Khan, she wished he had his mask on too, so that the paralinguistic subtleties in his face would not add to her anger.

I know what Zalman is up to, she thought, *I almost know what he is going to say, I have thought about it all for weeks, and I have even planned my responses. That is politics, I guess, but at least the anger I will show has stayed permanently in my craw and will erupt honestly. I am so angry at this moment that I could just skip the ritual of listening to the Steel Viper savrashi's speech and just blast him with invective right now. But custom calls for me to wait patiently while the ugly bastard makes his oily statements.*

In the seat next to Marthe, saKhan Samantha Clees squirmed nervously. Samantha's jitteriness was her one difficult trait. The woman could pace from here to the Inner Sphere without stopping.

Unlike Marthe, Samantha had virtually no memorable physical traits. Marthe found herself glancing toward Samantha every once in a while, merely to recall her appearance. Of medium height and build, Samantha was a bit overweight by the standards of the village, but quite right for a warrior. Much of the extra weight was in her strong arms and muscular legs, the legs that drove her pacing sometimes to a frantic pace. The size of her head was proportional to her body and framed by close-cropped hair that made its medium-brown color almost unnoticeable. (Most people who knew her, even some who knew her well, could not easily specify the color of her hair when they were asked.)

Her face blended with the rest of her. No scars of battle deformed it and no marks of beauty enhanced it. Her features were average, except perhaps for the softness of her light brown eyes. That was the one feature people *did* remember—her eyes. She was most like Marthe in that respect. There was an appealing gentleness in Samantha's eyes at most times, and only those whose actions or words drove her to immediate anger knew how fiery they could become. If they encountered it, her temper was the other part most people remembered about her. Her rages were rare, but when they came they were like sudden tempests, hurricanes even, and they tended to reduce everything in their path to rubble.

Though people rarely took note of her appearance, all knew of her prowess in a BattleMech and her skills in combat. Samantha had survived the Refusal War and been commander of Gyrfalcon Galaxy for a decade. She was a logical choice to become saKhan when Marthe was suddenly thrust into the role of Khan. Marthe was well pleased to have Samantha Clees at her side. They had fought together at Coventry, and continued to stand shoulder to shoulder on all matters of importance

Before speaking, Perigard Zalman glanced around the dark, semi-circular tiered chamber. The great hall had been built to seat the original forty Khans, but that number had now dropped to thirty-two. All were assembled here today, though Marthe knew that Zalman's only real ally was his saKhan. Her eyes traveled down toward the center of the dim chamber, where that strange miracle of prosthetic engineering, Kael Pershaw, stood on the rotating podium. Next to him was the ilKhan, the Elemental Lincoln Osis, who took his seat and gestured for Loremaster Pershaw to begin.

Once a warrior, the mysterious Pershaw now served as Loremaster of the Grand Council. Though he had not seen battle since the early days of the invasion, he continued to hold the rank of Star Colonel and was respected among the Khans. The deformed old warrior, with his fake limbs and a mask hiding what must be irredeemably damaged features, was also head of The Watch, the Falcon spying arm. Though Marthe considered spying much too devious to be worthy of honor, as Khan she had come to realize the importance of Pershaw's meticulously gathered intelligence, especially with her fellow Khans engaged in scheming more characteristic of the Inner Sphere than the Clan homeworlds. The man's deformities, his half-face with its one visible eye, were disconcerting. A trio of deep scars ran from the edge of the half-mask, over his nose and across his cheek, disappearing into his hairline.

Perigard formally requested of Loremaster Pershaw that he be given the floor. Permission was granted with a stiff wave of Pershaw's metal arm.

"IlKhan Osis, Loremaster Pershaw, my fellow Khans," Perigard began, "I address you today concerning a stain on the Kerensky heritage, a blemish on Clan history, an insult to the ideals that all Clans, in spite of our differences, unanimously stand for."

Samantha leaned toward Marthe and whispered, "First missile locked on and ready." Marthe nodded and, for a moment, felt all the weight of the ceremonial robes a Khan had to wear in council. She would have sold her BattleMech for the chance to be in light fatigues for the coming attack.

"I will not mince words here," Perigard continued. "The issue I wish to address is the Jade Falcon Khan's decision to allow a freeborn warrior to compete for the renowned and celebrated bloodname, Pryde. You all recall the heroism of Aidan Pryde in the Battle of Tukayyid. All Clans, in spite of our differences, praised the heroism of that Jade Falcon warrior and, with a near unanimity, applauded the acceptance of the Aidan Pryde genetic materials into the Falcon gene pool, a reward for heroism that was not only unprecedented but appropriate to the valorous warrior's acts."

"He does love his own rhetoric, *quiaff*?" Samantha whispered. Marthe knew that another of Samantha's failings was that she could not abide Clan conclaves, or any kind of formality, for that matter. Steel Vipers were as rigid as Smoke Jaguars in their adherence to Clan ways and beliefs, and beat the Jags when it came to annoying tenacity.

Zalman paused briefly and glanced up toward Marthe, clearly a ploy to invite her to interrupt him with an angry protest. Any outburst would have been condemned by the Loremaster, since Zalman had requested the floor and must not be interrupted until he was done. Marthe decided not to be drawn in by the trick, even though Zalman was right about her wanting to protest angrily. Every fiber of her being cried out to jump over the marble-topped desktop and swoop down on the Steel Viper Khan like a powerful falcon.

An odd thought. In these heavy robes I could barely crawl onto the table, much less leap over it!

Zalman must have seen in the thin, set line of her lips that she would not erupt, so he resumed. Opening his arms as if to gather all the Khans into his views, he said, "I move that the Grand Council censure Khan Marthe Pryde for her violation of Clan traditions in permitting the freeborn warrior, MechWarrior Diana, to compete for a bloodname."

The uproar that followed from Warden and Crusader Khans alike indicated that more of them approved than disapproved of Zalman's motion. Samantha jumped up and screamed, her strong voice soaring over the noise of the assembled Khans. "Stravags! It is the right of the Jade Falcon Clan—"

Marthe grabbed Samantha's arm and pulled her back into her seat. Samantha, her eyes blazing, leaned over to Marthe and said, "Why did you do that?"

"You were about to say that the only way another Clan could reject our decision regarding Diana was to challenge us to a Trial."

"Of course I was. And it is so."

"But not opportune right now. They want us to issue the challenge so that we will look weak and in the wrong. We must bide our time." Marthe knew that the day for fighting the Steel Vipers would come. But it would be on the field of battle, not in a Circle of Equals. And only when she was good and ready.

As the uproar subsided, Loremaster Pershaw spoke. His tone was formal, but the sound was almost disembodied, his voice emanating from some sort of replacement apparatus within his throat. Pershaw asked if Khan Zalman wished to yield the floor to any of the Khans now clamoring for attention.

Perigard yielded and Marthe sat quietly and listened as one Khan after another expressed either distaste for Marthe's coddling of freeborns or supported her efforts to strengthen the Jade Falcons through any means, orthodox or unorthodox. The only Khan to remain silent was Vlad Ward of the Wolves. Marthe was not sure why he was sitting this one out, then realized he probably felt equally vulnerable on this issue. Many years ago, an Inner Sphere bondsman named Phelan Kell actually succeeded in earning a blood-name in spite of being a freeborn. Not only had the bondsman become Phelan Ward, but also Khan of Clan Wolf.

Now Phelan Ward had returned to the Inner Sphere, a traitor in Clan eyes for breaking up the Wolves and taking so many with him that it nearly destroyed the Clan. It had taken much strategy and brokering of power for Vlad Ward to reinstate Clan Wolf. He could not afford to be attacked for seeming to favor Diana's bid for a bloodname, yet he had also established himself in Marthe's political life, as her quondam ally, and in her personal life, as her lover. They did not couple often—only, Marthe suspected, when the contact was somehow politically useful to Vlad. She did not mind the infrequency, and even enjoyed trying to figure out just what political motive her occasional lover was pursuing beneath his desire to couple.

Yes, it is probably a good thing that Vlad keeps his trap shut. With a friend like him, as the old Terran saying goes, I do not need enemies. I have too many enemies as it is. But whoever said the job of Khan was easy?

The heated discussion of the Khans became so chaotic that Osis gestured to Pershaw to put an end to it, which the freakish-looking Loremaster did with a wide sweep of his mechanical hand. A whispered exchange took place between Pershaw and Osis. Pershaw looked up at Marthe and said loudly in that odd, staticky electronic voice, "Does the esteemed Khan of the Jade Falcons wish to speak?"

Marthe nodded and stood. "Annihilate them, my Khan," Samantha whispered.

"I have indeed approved MechWarrior Diana's pursuit of a bloodname," she said. "She was duly sponsored by a Star Colonel of House Pryde. I heard the arguments and decided in favor of the seeker."

That, of course, was not entirely true. Marthe herself had arranged for Ravill Pryde to sponsor Diana. He had protested, but a Khan could be most convincing when necessary. Diana had been persistent in asserting her right to seek a bloodname and she had argued well for it. She was, after all, the daughter of the revered Aidan Pryde, whose name Perigard Zalman had so skillfully invoked.

On Coventry, Marthe had deployed warriors fresh out of sibkos who had yet to fight their Trials. It was not the way of the Clans, but Marthe knew only that she must rebuild the Falcons to keep them from being Absorbed. Once she had broken one rule, what was to stop her from breaking others? She knew as well as anyone that freeborns did not compete for bloodnames, but this warrior was not just any freeborn. She was skilled and experienced, and she was in a direct genetic line with Aidan Pryde. Once Marthe began to consider the possibility that Diana's claim might have some merit, she had decided the experiment was worth it. Succeed or fail, a warrior with a claim like Diana's was not likely to come along again soon anyway.

Back on Coventry, Marthe had finally given in to Diana's incessant pleas. She had even strong-armed Ravill Pryde into sponsoring her. Having gone that far, she was not about to back down now, not even to a Grand Council of Khans.

Anyway, for all Diana's ability, I do not believe she can succeed. She looks like Aidan Pryde and anyone can see she's got a good dose of him in her, but I do not think I could ever believe that a mere freeborn could win a bloodname within the Jade Falcons. When she fails, this furor will be over. And, in the unlikely event she succeeds, then I will have made a point. No one will dictate what I will or will not do to rebuild the Jade Falcons, even if it means departing from the way of the Clans.

"As Khan of the Jade Falcons, I have the right to make policy for my own Clan. In wartime especially, many decisions are dictated by the demands of the moment, and this is one of them. I am fully accountable for it. I regret that some of my fellow Khans disapprove, but the way of the Clans has always permitted each one to govern itself. I praise the outspokenness of all of you, but the jade falcon soars alone. It lives by its wits as well as its fearlessness, and none may command where the falcon will fly, or when, or where, or how. And so it must be among the Jade Falcons.

"Thus do I stand by my decision to allow this kin of Aidan Pryde to compete for a bloodname. It is well known that some Clans do not permit freeborns into their warrior ranks, but the Jade Falcons do recognize the value of freeborns strategically placed within combat units. We have even had freeborn heroes. The value of freeborn warriors has been proven, especially in the Inner Sphere invasion. I will say no more. The bloodname competitions proceed apace on the planet Ironhold. I invite you all to travel there and perhaps you will see what you wish, a freeborn humiliated. Then again, perhaps not. I thank you, Loremaster, for the opportunity to address the Council."

Marthe sat down and waited for the next round of protests. There was some muttering, had been all during her speech, but at a sign from the ebon-skinned Osis, relayed by the Loremaster, the debate was, for the moment, closed. When Pershaw announced that there would be no further discussion, Perigard Zalman went into a hasty and heated conversation with his saKhan, the impressive and broad-shouldered Brett Andrews. Andrews seemed to be urging Zalman to continue, but Zalman shook his head. The ilKhan clearly meant to block any further interruptions by the Steel Viper Khan, and Zalman was silenced for now. Marthe was amused by the failure of his little game.

"There are other matters before the Council," the Lore-master said. "Most specifically, the Harvest Trials and deci-sions affecting our final readiness to resume the invasion of the Inner Sphere."

During the ensuing discussion, as Samantha fretted in boredom beside her, Marthe rather enjoyed the display of data scrolling across the computer screen of her desk. It showed, among other things, how dismally the Steel Vipers had done in the Harvest Wars.

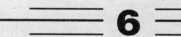

6

Falcon Caverns, near village of Falconpit
Ironhold
Kerensky Cluster, Clan Space
28 January 3060

Diana had known that, inside the famous cavern, it would be cold, but she was not prepared for the intensity of it. She felt the cold, it seemed, down to her bones. She imagined herself turning into an ice statue and being chipped into pieces by curious tourists.

Falcon Caverns was that rare phenomenon of Jade Falcon society—a tourist attraction. Not that it attracted crowds of tourists. She and Joanna had seen only a few others in their travels through the long, dark tunnels, the way lit by torches placed just far enough apart to keep the traveler from being plunged into total darkness. Diana often felt uncharacteristically delicate as she watched her step across the uneven surfaces of the tunnel floors, strewn as they were with loose rocks and sudden shallow depressions.

"So this is your idea of a break from training," Star Commander Joanna said from behind Diana. She had been silent for a long while, unusual for her, as they trudged through the tunnels, following the signs underneath the torches directing them to the central cavern, the famous Firefalcon Cavern. Firefalcon was not the only large cavern in this massive, networked cave system, but it was said to be the most dramatic. It had taken hours to convince Joanna, who cared little about natural wonders, to accompany Diana here.

"They should have given us our own torches."

"It was in the brochure. Light has to be carefully regulated for preservation of the site."

Joanna grunted. "That is just pap for freeborns. Trueborns need no such regulations."

"You forget that I am freeborn."

For a moment Joanna stopped walking and glared at Diana. "I *never* forget that, whelp!"

Diana chose not to respond. One could easily get entangled in fruitless haggling with Joanna over trueborn/freeborn matters. She could, in fact, be incredibly stupid, Diana thought. On the other hand, there were few trueborn warriors who, while complaining vehemently about freebirths, actually maintained close associations with them, as Joanna did with both Diana and Horse. In fact, Joanna was rarely seen with trueborns. Her advanced age apparently made warriors shun her. She decided to change the subject, or at least return to the previous one.

"Are you not impressed, then, with Ironhold's famous natural wonder?" Diana asked.

"Frankly, no. It is just a lot of darkness, dampness, and confinement. I like open spaces, fresh air, light."

"Light? With you and your dark moods?"

"Outside I can yell. Here I am afraid of rocks being dislodged at the slightest sound."

"Your anger could dislodge rocks, I agree."

"Is that sarcasm?"

"I would not know a sarcasm if I said one."

Joanna grunted. She did not want to tell Diana the truth, that this place or any enclosure reminded her too much of that pass back on Twycross. In her first time in the pass, she had been a participant in the Falcon Guards' greatest and most shameful defeat, and she and her 'Mech had been buried under tons of rock. She still had nightmares of being trapped in her cockpit and digging her way out. Her second time in the pass she had fought and defeated the famous Wolf Clan warrior, Natasha Kerensky, known throughout the Clans as the Black Widow.

The victory had won Joanna a place in Jade Falcon historic annals, but all she could remember was the time she was down, again seemingly trapped in a 'Mech cockpit, about to be the victim of the Black Widow. Even though she had fought back successfully from her prone position, incinerating the Black Widow in her cockpit, she still had vivid memories of lying in her 'Mech on the ground in that narrow pass, with its canyon walls reaching upward on either side of her. For her, trapped feelings accompanied any foray through a geologic phenomenon, and she could do without them. As she strode through the dark tunnels, she felt back in one of the nightmares, even though these walls were not high and this was not Twycross and she was not facing anyone in a BattleMech.

"Look at this," Diana said as they rounded a curve in the tunnel and were faced with a sudden brightness, illuminated by several wall torches. "Takes your breath away, *quiaff*?"

Joanna did not reply. She was struggling not to be impressed by the complex and colorful arrangement of dripstone, deposits left behind by the water that had eroded out this tunnel and, for that matter, the rest of the entire Falcon Caverns complex. The light caught the variegated dripstone surfaces and, in its flickering dance, formed more abstract patterns than what were already provided by the geologic erosion. The separate dripstone formations were themselves of varied shapes and thicknesses. The whole effect was something like ice on the side of a cliff, except that the ice, eroded by the sun's rays, changed constantly and here the dripstone was a permanent feature, left eons ago for all the latter-day Falcon Caverns tourists to stop at and be impressed by, just as Diana and (reluctantly) Joanna were at this moment.

"Imagine," Diana commented, "this formation has been here since long before our ancestors came to Clan space from the Inner Sphere. I mean, *long* before, in geologic time. Centuries, millennia . . ."

"And it has stayed right here for all that time. All that time. I think I prefer our short lives and our combats and . . ."

"And you complain about them on a daily basis."

"Sarcastic stravag. Let us get on with this little excursion. I am anxious to get back to training and working you until your body is scarred with its own erosion."

Following signs, they made their way to Falconfire Cavern. At first, as they stepped out of the dark tunnel, the flickering firelight and immensity of the cavern itself distorted their vision. Torches were placed at distant points along the impossibly high walls that stretched toward a ceiling that could be discerned only as an immense shadow hanging over the scene. The light itself danced off the varied and sometimes impressive formations, creating a massive, abstract creation in which all kinds of sights could be briefly glimpsed, depending on the notions of the observer. The sight could be a nightmare or a beatific vision or a remembrance of a nearly forgotten ancestor.

The floor of the cavern was crowded with people wandering along the precisely marked paths going toward the enormous pool at the center. Diana had read the brochure and knew that the pool was named Styx, named apparently after a river rather than a lake. The brochure had said the pool was more oil than water, an odd, useless type of oil found only on Ironhold. It was not useful as a fuel source or a lubricant, but it had one peculiar property. It sent up occasional geyserlike shoots of flame, apparently set off by some internal fire or from some intense heat deeper underground. Some scientists had studied the phenomenon, but nobody had been able to come up with anything more than theory. Nobody wanted to investigate further and, besides, the substance itself had no practical use for domestic or wartime functions. With no reason to find out more about the mystery, even scientists could cheerfully leave it as an unexplained phenomenon.

Strangely, with all the fire, in the pool and on the walls, there was no heat in the cavern. It was even chillier than the tunnels, and the two warriors could feel a wafting, frigid breeze on their skin.

"Let us get moving," Joanna muttered. "The sooner we get away from here and back to warmth, the happier I will be."

"What about all that cold-weather combat you talk about?"

"There is a difference between experiencing cold during a battle inside a cockpit and walking through caves. I do not remember my feet ever turning to ice inside a 'Mech cockpit."

Diana smiled and walked to one of the paths. There was no reason to deal further with Joanna and her complaints. Joanna, she had long ago decided, got her kicks from being angry and complaining loudly. Why destroy her happiness?

"Lot more people here," Diana noted, as they set foot on the path. The surface beneath their feet was harder than she expected, perhaps a smoothness caused by generations of tourists to the cavern. "I guess this is more of a tourist attraction than I had believed a moment ago."

"Your life is a tourist attraction, Diana."

Every once in a while Joanna said something puzzling like that. Often Diana did not bother to question her, but this remark was too provocative.

"Tourist attraction? What do you mean?"

"Maybe circus is more the word. Or spectacle. I have never seen bloodname competitions like these. Maybe it is the result of having to run so many so close together."

Diana knew what she meant. So many bloodnamed warriors had been lost in the invasion of the Inner Sphere that there were many bloodnames now available. The depleted strength of Clan military units during this truce period demanded that more positions be filled with bloodnamed warriors.

"Yes, circus," Joanna went on, "especially with all the sideshow attractions. There were always some marketplaces set up during the bloodname contests, and occasionally there would be shows based on Clan history—and some of them good spectacles, too. But this time it seems like half the damned freeborns on the planet have come to Ironhold City to profit from the contests. I mean, Diana, I see more greed and profiteering than valor and skill. Sometimes the bloodname contests seem more the sideshow and the sideshows are the main attraction. And then there is you . . . ."

"Me? What are you saying?"

"You are one of the main attractions. A freeborn actually competing for a bloodname. You are one of the sideshow freaks. Something unnatural, deformed by nature—"

"I thought you were in support of my participation in the contest, Joanna. Back on Coventry you—"

"Stop. I am in support of you. But not because you are a freeborn, but because the Khan has accepted your claim to be genetically valid as the daughter of Aidan Pryde. I do not like that you are not trueborn, but I know you as a warrior and you have proven yourself worthy in that. I do not even know my own reasons. But, in a world where I should be solahma and continue as a warrior despite that, the daughter of Aidan Pryde may go for a bloodname. Do not expect me to explain more. If I understood my reasons, I would state them."

This was the first time Joanna had spoken on this subject since they took the DropShip away from Coventry. In all the time on Ironhold, most of her conversation had been devoted to matters of training and physical conditioning. Oh, she would display her general anger at everything with predictable regularity, but she had stayed off the subject of Diana's eligibility for some time.

"Well, I may be a tourist attraction now, but I will show them later," Diana said.

"You had better. I think Marthe Pryde may have given her enemies ammunition by approving your claim. Any misstep and—"

"Yes, yes, Joanna. I know all that. I think about it every day. It is with me when I go to sleep at night."

They walked on in silence. Eventually, they came to a cordoned-off area overlooking the fiery pool. On stands small plaques told the story of the caverns. Diana read them, Joanna did not. Most of the plaques, Diana found out, merely restated what she had already read in the brochure.

Still, Diana found that looking at the pool close up like this was impressive. She jumped, along with most of the other tourists, when a tall burst of flame shot upward quite near the pool's shore. This pillar of flame was followed quickly by another. One of the tourists, a short, overweight man with stubby legs, was apparently too startled by the sudden apparition, and he fell backward against Joanna. Joanna also stumbled back as the chubby man fell to the ground. She nearly regained her balance, but one of the stands tripped her up and she fell, too.

Diana struggled not to laugh as Joanna sprawled out helplessly on the ground for a brief moment. She recovered quickly and sprang to her feet, looking around to see how many people had seen her clumsy pratfall.

Diana noticed that many tourists had indeed noticed and, like her, were struggling to hold back their amusement, but in their cases failing. That was not good, Diana saw, as she watched rage redden Joanna's face.

"You are amused, eh," Joanna shouted. At the same time, she offered her hand to the fallen man. He stood up, with a running stream of abject apology. Joanna nodded and, with disdain, shoved the chubby man away. He nearly stumbled and fell again.

"Be amused then," she shouted. "But remember this: I walk out of this damned place a trueborn warrior, and tomorrow I will still be a trueborn warrior. And you all will be filthy freebirth scum. Just remember that."

Collecting herself, she began to walk away from the pool, down a path whose sign denoted the way to the exit.

For a moment Diana watched Joanna stride down the path, wondering if she should go after her or just stay here. She enjoyed this cavern and would not have minded staying a while and contemplating its grandeur.

At the same time she was furious with Joanna, who ultimately was a trueborn warrior and did not care that anything she said about freeborns also applied to Diana.

Diana looked around at the stunned tourists, all of whom were indeed freeborns. In a way, she belonged with them, even though her acceptance years ago as a warrior had separated her from them. She was more aware than ever of her isolation within the Jade Falcons. Neither trueborn warrior, nor othercaste freeborn, she was an anomaly—as Joanna had said, something of a sideshow freak. She could not just blend with this crowd of freeborns and feel comfortable there, nor could she travel within trueborn circles and not see that her comrades saw her as a freebirth no matter what her considerable exploits as a warrior might prove.

This was her life, but it was a life that she could change by winning the bloodname. But could the bloodname resolve her feelings of isolation from both trueborns and freeborns? That would remain the mystery, a mystery as puzzling as the fires leaping from this pool. A new pillar rose up a couple of meters away.

Diana shrugged and started after Joanna, who had, with her quick pace, proceeded halfway down the long path. In spite of her superb conditioning, the result of Joanna's intense and brutal training, Diana had to struggle to catch up.

7

Jade Falcon Hall
Hall of the Khans, near Katyusha
Strana Mechty
Kerensky Cluster, Clan Space
30 January 3060

The knock at the door of Marthe's private quarters was discreet. The only person who knocked quite in that way was Marthe's aide, a clerical tech named Rhonell. Marthe had been up and working at her small, battered desk for hours.

"Enter," she called, looking up.

Rhonell, a tall man, taller even than Marthe, came into the room briskly, an almost military stiffness in his bearing. Rhonell's face suited his job. His eyes were as devoid of emotion as a column of figures; the rest of his features were like dull documents of his personality.

"Yes, Rhonell?"

"Khan Clees to see you."

"I will meet with her in my office within the hour," Marthe said crisply, then turned back to the papers spread out in front of her.

Rhonell cleared his throat, his way of informing Marthe of an unsuspected complication.

"Yes, Rhonell? Out with it."

"The saKhan requests an interview that is private."

"Well, what could be more private than this?" Marthe spread her arms to take in her small quarters. "Show her in."

"Aye, my Khan."

Rhonell left quickly and with a deferential nod, the perfect bureaucrat, courteous, efficient, and humorless.

Marthe stood and gave herself a quick once-over in the clouded mirror that someone had long ago attached to the back of the door. First she inspected her clothing. As always when there was no ritual need for command uniforms, she wore the standard emerald-green jumpsuit of the off-duty Jade Falcon officer, simple and properly tapered in the legs, seams coming to swordlike straight lines leading down to highly polished boots, low-heeled and knee-high. The sheen of the boots caught the room's light and seemed to send off rays every time she moved.

On the right-chest area of the jumpsuit, she wore the soaring falcon insignia of the Jade Falcon Khan. Marthe always opted for the simplest, even in her choice of ceremonial dress. Too much garish color, too many resplendent feathers, too ornate a cape—such display disgusted her.

Evidently her appearance did set standards. She had noticed that the extra decorations on warrior uniforms had been significantly reduced after she had become Khan. Earlier, as a Star Colonel, those in her Command Cluster had simplified not only their uniforms but all manner in which they presented themselves, even down to the way they conducted themselves at meetings or dealt with her in oral and written reports. This was a definite consequence of her leadership, then and now, and she was damn proud of it.

Satisfied that her garb was in order, Marthe almost inadvertently gave the rest of her appearance a glance. She did this rarely, since she did not care much how she looked, as long as it was command-proper and signaled authority. As ever, her body was muscular and toned, revealed by the short sleeves of her uniform. The muscles of her arms showed sharply etched striations, suggesting a wiry but strong and properly warrior-toned physical appearance.

She tried to resist inspecting her face, but lately she could hardly help it. Clan warriors detested signs of age. As Khan, Marthe did not face the shame of ending her life as solahma, any warrior considered too old for combat and whose only salvation was to die for the Clan as cannon fodder, if he or she were lucky. But Marthe was shrewd enough to know that lines in her face or a weakening of her bodily appearance would be viewed aslant by other Clan warriors, even her fellow Khans in the Grand Council, many of whom were themselves showing serious signs of age. Marthe did not much think about it, but now that she had reached late forties, there were definite signs. Not many, but definite. Lines rayed out from her slightly bloodshot eyes. The eyes themselves—cool blue, yet piercing—were still strong.

She had heard that many of the elite in the Inner Sphere used cosmetic surgery to ward off signs of age, as well as to make themselves better-looking. The thought brought out her signature abrupt laugh, though of course there was no one to hear her. A true Jade Falcon, she would never allow anyone to surgically alter her looks; it was a detestable procedure. Nor could she use traditional cosmetics, as some Clanspeople did, to hide the age-signs. She believed that a warrior who hid anything, who deceived with words or powders and paint, was not worth the honor of the name.

While Marthe had been told by some that she was beautiful, her ice-blue eyes set off dramatically by her high forehead, full lips, and narrow chin, the idea of beauty had no significance for her. Even now, Vlad's occasional comment on it, usually invoked in the throes of his rather animalistic lovemaking, only amused her.

Sighing audibly, she turned away from the mirror and glanced around the room, knowing that she need exert no effort to straighten it up. Attendant techs would come in later and take care of it. She had not made a bed or neatened up a room in several years.

Like any good Clan warrior Marthe had no interest in the look of any room. Her private quarters, as well as her offices, were spare and sparsely furnished. This, her sleeping room, was undecorated—no pictures on the walls, pale shades with no curtains on the windows. Except for the bed, the only other furniture was the old desk and a couple of chairs, complete with computer and, in appropriate containers, disks and datachips. In a tray next to an ancient printer were a few pages of hard copy, consisting mainly of various schedules and documents that required frequent consultation. Her file records were maintained by Rhonell in his cubicle adjoining her command office.

Another knock at the door cleared Marthe's thoughts, but this time the knock was firm and decisive.

"Enter," she called.

The door opened to reveal saKhan Samantha Clees, who entered Marthe's small private room with the kind of decisive movement so characteristic of her. The moment she stopped moving, however, Samantha stood there awkwardly. She never seemed to know what to do with her body when at rest. Marthe gestured for her to be at ease, and Samantha seemed to relax. Even the seriousness of her face softened, although Samantha Clees rarely displayed any expression of humor, rarely laughed.

The quintessential warrior, Marthe thought. *She does not even seem conscious of any behavior that would be the least bit unClanlike. Maybe it is the genes, after all. The genetically engineered genes of a trueborn warrior.*

"Rhonell said you wished a private meeting, Samantha. Well, here we are, so what is on your mind?"

"The debates in the Grand Council," Samantha said, without preamble. "All that insulting invective from the Steel Vipers. What are they up to? And why did you hold me back?"

"This is more than rhetoric or old rivalries, Samantha. The Vipers hope to use their protests to intimidate us. With the Clans ready to return to the Inner Sphere, they would like to get our invasion corridor all to themselves. Perhaps they are mad enough to believe they can destroy our Clan. We do not have to do much about it, except make sure they do not succeed."

"We are Jade Falcon," Samantha said. "We can do that."

"Aye, Samantha. The Vipers would drive us from the corridor tomorrow, if they could. Just as surely as we would drive them out. But war with the Inner Sphere could resume at any moment. Now that their forces have smashed the Smoke Jaguars, our corridor might be next. Even Kael Pershaw and his operatives in the Watch have been unable to penetrate the enemy's secrets. The only sure thing is that they can be counted on to be devious, and we must be ready for whatever comes."

"We cannot be certain what the Vipers will do either," Samantha said. "They are as erratic as ever. What if they go over to the Inner Sphere, like the cowardly Nova Cats?"

"They are capable of anything. We must be prepared."

"Aye," said Samantha. "It is maddening."

"What else can we expect from the Vipers? But they too must watch and wait for now. They could just as easily be a target of the Inner Sphere as we Falcons. Meanwhile, Samantha, we will not lose sight of other important tasks before us."

Samantha nodded. "Aye, the need for warriors and materiel, and only of the finest quality."

"I know you are weary of deskwork and Council sessions," Marthe said. "I have been thinking that it might refresh your mind to travel to Ironhold to review the war effort. While there you could also verify that training has been made more streamlined and efficient, as I have ordered. The moment for returning to the Inner Sphere is near, and we will need warriors more skilled and fearless than ever. This time the Falcons will fulfill our destiny."

"Aye, my Khan. The Falcons must be ready."

Marthe nodded. "So it is. If the Steel Vipers want a fight with us, they will get it, but on our terms, *quiaff*?"

"Aff."

Marthe studied Samantha for a moment. She had come to know her well. "But there is something else, Samantha. I sense something else on your mind."

"Aye, Marthe. I am concerned about this bloodname contest the Steel Viper Khan uses to mock us in the Council. While I am on Ironhold, I wish to see for myself that everything is conducted properly. The events on Ironhold could have overwhelming implications for our Clan."

"I agree, but I am not sure that you need to—"

Samantha held up her hand. "I know what is on paper," she said, "but in delicate circumstances like this not everything is conveyed on paper. Your permission, my Khan?"

"Go ahead, but be brief."

Samantha began to pace. It was common for her to pace while she worked out her thoughts. Marthe did not sit down, but leaned against the wall with arms crossed as she watched Samantha walk and talk.

"This Falcon Guard warrior, MechWarrior Diana, will participate in the Trial of Bloodright. Though freeborn, she believes herself to be technically eligible to compete for a bloodname because she is the daughter of the great hero Aidan Pryde. This Diana's mother—" Samantha swallowed hard at having to use the word *mother,* a term that made genetically engineered trueborns, born from vats, quite uncomfortable—"is a woman of the scientist caste named Peri, once a sibmate of yours and Aidan Pryde's, but one who failed in her training. All this is correct, *quiaff*?"

Samantha stopped her pacing, or really just paused it, but Marthe nodded for her to continue. How bizarre the circumstances sounded when put in Samantha's concise and matter-of-fact way.

"Her claim is based on the fact that both parents were genetically engineered warriors. Therefore, while her birth was—" Samantha struggled again briefly over the word "—*natural,* she claims to be genetically eligible for a bloodname. Such natural births among warriors are rare, and most of those are illegitimate births that the warrior, who has gone on to greater experiences, is rarely even aware of."

Marthe nodded. "Aidan Pryde, in fact, did not know that Diana was his daughter until just before his heroic death."

"Warriors do not need reminders of their useless spawn,"

Samantha said irritably. "The only babies who count are birthed from the vat in sibkos of a hundred or more. Single births from a female womb are wasteful by any Clan standard. Why opt for single births that may have innumerable genetic flaws when you may birth a hundred with identical, nearly flawless genetics? Were it not for the need to staff the tech and service castes, all freebirthing would be forbidden, *quiaff*?"

"Your views are perhaps a bit harsh, but traditional and quite reasonable."

"I believe that this Ravill Pryde is sponsoring Diana at your suggestion—at your very strong suggestion, *quiaff*?"

"Aff, Samantha. Do you wish to question me on this issue?"

Samantha stopped pacing. "Just one question. Why, when given the choice of allowing this freeborn warrior's quest or forbidding it, did you allow it?"

Marthe walked past Samantha to the window while Samantha resumed her pacing. Pulling back the shade and gazing out at the park surrounding the Hall of Khans, she saw the same slice of Strana Mechty she always did from this vantage point. The city itself lay in the distance, but the trees and shrubs of the park were vibrant in the bright sunshine. Not far from the hall of each Clan were the bloodname chapels where were stored the genetic samples that supplied the eugenics program.

"My official reason is that Diana's genetic arguments must be tested. We are, after all, severely drained of skilled warriors and have lost many bloodnamed to both the Wolves in the Refusal War and the Inner Sphere on Coventry. The Clans are uneasy now. You see that in the Grand Council meetings you complain of so accurately. The Falcons have done well in the Harvest Wars. Have we not won two Clusters from the Snow Ravens, and enough warriors from other Clans to make up still a third? The Steel Vipers have performed abysmally. That, I believe, is the main reason for their current attacks on us. They seek to weaken us on every front, military and political."

"I agree."

"We must return to the Inner Sphere with as much military might as possible. The more warriors, the better. But only warriors of the highest skill. The need to replace blooded warriors does help to justify Diana's quest. Few believe she can win the bloodname anyway, but I am curious to see how she will do. Her argument may be specious, but. . . . well, there is another reason, one harder to explain—an unofficial reason."

Dropping the shade, Marthe turned away from the window. Samantha was pacing slowly, deliberately, her head down as she listened intently. Her arms barely swung as she moved.

"To speak of the unofficial reason, I must speak of Aidan Pryde and my connections with him. His story, set down in *The Remembrance,* is one that takes on mythic dimensions for our Clan. After he failed his Trial of Position, which I took with him and won—"

"Sufficiently to enter the ranks as a Star Commander, as I recall."

"That is irrelevant, at least to what I am saying now."

Samantha showed no reaction to the edginess in Marthe's voice.

"After he failed the Trial, he was reduced to the tech caste, but even that could not make him anything but a warrior. I think I knew that even after he had failed the first Trial and I had turned my back on him. We had once been close within the sibko, but I scorned him afterward. That is, after all, the way of the Clans.

"I knew that Aidan would never take easily to a tech role, but I believed that his adaptability and resourcefulness would gain him reasonable success in a lower caste. Instead, as it is recorded, he fled, then returned under the name of Jorge. It was the doing of training commander Ter Roshak, who gave Aidan the chance to qualify as a warrior in the disguise of a freeborn."

"Freebirth," Samantha muttered. It was the uglier version of the term *freeborn* and often served as a vile curse-word in the Clans. Marthe realized that some of this story must be a shock to Samantha, for certain details had remained secret all these years.

"After becoming a warrior, Aidan vowed to Ter Roshak that he would not reveal the circumstances of his second Trial. So he played the role of freeborn warrior for several years before he was pushed into a situation where he had to break that vow. At that time there was strenuous protest against Aidan competing as a trueborn in the Trial of Blood-right. He fought and won a Trial of Refusal, then entered the grand melee to qualify for the competition. He won the melee and later the bloodname, doing it with an unorthodox ploy, utilized after it looked as if his opponent had defeated him.

"In fact, had his opponent not insisted on a fight to the death, Aidan would have lost and been long forgotten. Instead, he won and became a full-fledged warrior and eventually commander of a unit as tainted as he was, the Falcon Guards. He restored the reputation of the Guards, whose status was later cemented by Joanna's defeat of Natasha Kerensky, the infamous Black Widow. But by then, Aidan had died valiantly on Tukayyid. He held off hordes of attacking BattleMechs so that the rest of the Falcon Guards might lift off the planet without further casualties. Except, of course, for himself.

"Ironically, one of the warriors whose lives he saved was this very Diana."

Samantha stopped pacing for a moment to say, dispassionately, "Dramatically put, Marthe. Some of this I had not known before."

"I merely present these details to support my view that Diana's claim is valid for me subjectively. Her demand to be allowed to compete for a bloodname is analogous to the unorthodox tactics of Aidan Pryde."

"How can you compare the two?"

"If there is any chance that Diana, as the offspring"— Marthe almost smiled as she noticed Samantha's wince at the word *offspring*—"of the courageous and resourceful Aidan Pryde, can earn a bloodname, I am willing to risk the disapproval of our entire Clan to allow her the opportunity to prove herself. Frankly, I, too, have my doubts that she can succeed, but then I think of Aidan Pryde and all the obstacles he overcame and I am not so sure. That is why, Samantha, I went against the tide and approved her candidacy and pressured Ravill Pryde to be her official sponsor. He was furious, but he is a good Jade Falcon warrior and an intelligent strategist who could see the worth of my contentions, as I am sure you do now, *quiaff*?"

For a moment it looked as if Samantha would disagree, but instead she spoke the ritual *aff,* then resumed her pacing.

"Many Falcon warriors oppose you on this decision, just as do many Khans in council."

Marthe swallowed hard. "It is true, I am afraid. But we will get past all that, and I will need your help, saKhan Samantha."

"I am at your service. Always."

For a moment, as her pacing picked up speed, it looked as if Samantha was going to crash into the wall. But she stopped abruptly and whirled to face Marthe.

"I have to say I cannot endure the catfights in council," she said, her voice calm but her mood clearly urgent. "Jade Falcons were not meant for this eternal palaver. We are becoming just like those Inner Sphere surats, with all our talks and maneuverings to maintain our own increasingly complicated political units and you—Marthe Pryde—are right there in the thick of it. You and the Wolf Khan Vlad Ward and—"

"Shut up, Samantha. Even if we are both Khans, there are limits to what we may say to each other. You are heading toward views that could be the basis for a Circle of Equals being drawn for us. And it is essential that we must not fight with each other, *quiaff*?"

Samantha nodded and started pacing again. Silently. She

was clearly marshaling her thoughts for the next rush of words.

"At any rate," she finally said, "it is in my nature to be useful to the Clan at all times. Sitting in council and maneuvering through the bureaucracy are not much part of my personal arsenal. Inspecting troops and munitions and training units are more to my taste. I will always be more useful in the field than in the council chamber. While on Ironhold, I will report to you on this bloodname contest, too."

She stopped walking and her body relaxed as she looked to Marthe for comment. Marthe paused a moment to collect her thoughts.

"One more thing, Samantha. There is another matter on Ironhold that you could usefully attend to. The mother of Diana, the scientist Peri, has just arrived onplanet. She claims to be there to support Diana, but she is nosing around, and I hear that she is asking embarrassing questions about the scientist caste. The scientists are so secretive, so absorbed with their own concerns rather than the fulfillment of Clan goals, that—"

"I have often wondered why you, and the other Khans, allow the caste to carry on in such secrecy. It seems to me that—"

"I know what you are going to say, Samantha, and I partially agree with you. The scientists' hermetic leanings must be broken. At any rate, they have accomplished some impressive genetic advances, and I am sure they will produce even more to come. For now, I must find a reason to change the situation and I do not have one."

"As Khan you do not need one."

"But I do need one. It is important to be fair, Samantha. We depend on the scientists for genetic research that will provide us even more powerful warriors. I intend for the Jade Falcons to be the *most* powerful of all the Clans."

Samantha stopped in her tracks and turned to Marthe. "In that we are one, my Khan. We know that only the Falcons are the keepers of Kerensky's vision. That is what has let us overcome every obstacle, every defeat, every challenge."

"Aye, Samantha," said Marthe. "We are unstoppable. We are Jade Falcons."

Samantha turned to go, and with a sigh Marthe resumed her seat at the desk and the mountain of paperwork before her.

As she walked down the corridor away from Marthe's quarters, Samantha Clees wondered if she had over-stepped in her conversation with Khan Marthe. She had become saKhan after a distinguished career, but believed that Marthe's achievements were greater. Sometimes she wondered if she should even open her mouth before such a daunting Clan hero. She had never wished for the high position she now held. It was for her merely a step in a career that was totally imbued with the values of the Clan.

Could I be Khan of the Jade Falcons? Samantha wondered. *Probably not. But, if I were to achieve it, I would try to serve with the skill and firmness that Marthe Pryde displays. If only her mind did not sometimes take too political a turn. That is my only worry.*

8

Grand Council Chamber
Hall of the Khans, near Katyusha
Strana Mechty
Kerensky Cluster, Clan Space
31 January 3060

Perigard Zalman, standing at the Grand Council Chamber entrance, surveyed the large room. He was generally one of the first to arrive for a Grand Council meeting, and today was no exception. But today he was more confident than ever. Today he would get to Marthe Pryde.

A half-hour earlier he had been to see Natalie Breen in her small office. Heading there, he'd experienced one of his sudden headaches caused by the shift from intense outdoor sunlight to the serious and gloomy darkness of the Hall of Khans.

The headache was throbbing as he stopped at Natalie Breen's door and made the usual polite knock. The erstwhile Khan's equally polite response came loud and clear from the other side of the heavy door. Entering quickly into the darkened room, Zalman got right to the point.

"This Marthe Pryde is unflappable. She is the Clan version of an ice sculpture. I provoke. She stays calm. If anything, I am the one who gets agitated."

"She gets under your skin, *quiaff*?"

"Aff."

"She did not become Khan until after I resigned, but long ago I knew her slightly. I can see her getting under anyone's skin."

Zalman described his efforts to provoke Marthe. "It seems as if she sees through me."

"A smart politician."

"For a politician, she complains about politics a great deal."

Natalie Breen laughed. "That is probably her best political tactic. Deny, then do what you deny."

Zalman shook his head. "That would not be the way of the Clans."

"Perhaps, or perhaps it is simply a facet of being a Khan. I suggest that, instead of hammering on the bloodname issue, you invoke the matter of the freeborn warrior, Horse, and his outfit."

The words surprised Zalman. "That would mean revealing information collected by our intelligence unit."

"It is your choice, Khan Zalman. I have no better advice for you than that which I have already given. Perseverance is the key. All warriors are humans, even Khans. There is a weak spot. I am confident you will find it."

When he left Natalie's office after discussing further strategy, Zalman was surprised to find that his headache had subsided.

While he appreciated Natalie Breen's faith in him, Perigard Zalman wished he could be as confident as she had suggested.

"Excuse me, honored Khan," said a voice behind him, and Zalman realized he was blocking the doorway. As he turned to clear the way, he discovered that the words had come from the individual he had been thinking about so intently, Marthe Pryde.

She nodded courteously as she passed by him and headed for her seat. Zalman felt vaguely insulted. Her courtesy had been too pleasant, much too pleasant.

When he had settled himself alongside Brett Andrews, he noted that Marthe Pryde sat alone at the Jade Falcon place. According to his last information, Samantha Clees was inspecting munitions and BattleMech factories on Ironhold.

Marthe seemed tall even when seated. It was the way she held her back straight, as if she did not enjoy the comfort of a chair. That was not strange among warriors, who often were uncomfortable sitting anywhere but in the cockpit of their BattleMechs.

After the Loremaster and the ilKhan had entered the chamber, the Khans donned their masks and performed their pre-meeting rituals. Then the session began and most of the masks were removed and set on the ornate desktops before them. Next began the usual debates, most of them concerning the final preparations for the Inner Sphere invasion. Sometimes the speeches were formal and repetitious, and even the normally intense Viper saKhan, Brett Andrews, seemed about to doze. Zalman stood up, interrupting the officious commentary of the Ice Hellion Khan, Asa Taney.

"We are like ants arguing at the edge of a puddle, one side

wanting to skirt the shore of the puddle and take the long way around, while the other side wants to plunge in and take the risk of drowning on the way to the other side."

Zalman was gratified to see that Marthe Pryde was among the several Khans who sprang up angrily, and that it was she whom Loremaster Pershaw allowed to speak.

"The esteemed Steel Viper Khan dishonors all of us in his demeaning comparison to ants. Perhaps he should devote his time to the study of imagery."

Her remarks were perfunctory, Zalman thought, spoken by rote. A typical response, the kind he hated. Suddenly he saw a way to use it. Perhaps, as Natalie Breen had suggested, Marthe Pryde could be provoked, if you came at her sideways.

"I am not surprised, Khan Marthe, that you should complain about imagery. It is the kind of remark that wastes the time of the Khans gathered in this chamber, the kind of waste so typical of the Jade Falcon Clan."

Zalman knew that, while all Clans abhorred waste, the Jade Falcons made something of a fetish of it. Marthe Pryde could not allow his remark, mild as it was, to pass by.

"Typical? Jade Falcons waste little. Everything is used. Several times. The Steel Viper Khan should retract his statement. I demand it, in fact."

And there it was, in simple terms, the opening. A small, almost trivial remark regarding Clan honor. Zalman's heart was beating faster as he spoke even more calmly.

"Steel Vipers do not lie; there can be no retraction."

"In this chamber you must prove your assertions, Khan Zalman, *quiaff*?"

"Aff."

"I await your proof."

Marthe Pryde looked so confident, so sure that she was merely defending her Clan on a small matter of honor, that she would never perceive the ambush in it.

"You waste warriors, Khan Marthe. Warriors die more because of your Clan's policies than their lack of prowess. It is a heroism bought at high cost, a wasteful heroism."

The sudden fire in Marthe Pryde's normally icy eyes thrilled Perigard Zalman. Famed for her coolness in all situations, this hint of emotion encouraged him to continue.

The other Khans, who usually at least muttered in commentary as a conflict escalated within the chamber, sat quietly in their seats, watching the two Khans as if they were BattleMechs circling each other in combat. Brett Andrews, who had apparently divined his Khan's strategy, whispered encouragement.

"I believe that the Khan of the Steel Vipers has been afflicted with a momentary madness," Marthe continued. "Please explain yourself, Khan Zalman."

"It is simple, really. The Jade Falcon policy of not only accepting freeborns into their ranks, but of actually allowing one to compete for a bloodname is one of the most wasteful policies to be found in *any* Clan."

"We have given our reasons for the freeborn in the present contest at—"

"Waste. You train freeborns to fight as warriors. In their inferiority they endanger all the trueborns in the units. Many have died due to the actions of free—"

"More have been saved by the actions of freeborn warriors. Jade Falcons have shown that, while respecting their trueborn warriors, they have utilized their freeborns intelligently, without waste."

"With respect, Khan Marthe, your words are unconvincing. We Clans who maintain strict control over the freeborns of our warrior caste know that better than you who do not."

"You only think you do!" shouted a new voice. Khan Vlad Ward of Clan Wolf. No surprise there, Zalman thought. The Wolf and the Falcon had somehow become allied of late, and the Wolves' record of using freeborns as warriors was even more shocking than the Falcons'.

"I need no help here, Khan Ward," Marthe said. Vlad sat down, but he was clearly irritated.

Zalman, pleased at creating even a slight rift between Vlad and Marthe, continued. "Recently we of the Steel

Vipers have discovered that Khan Marthe Pryde authorized, while still with her forces on Coventry, the formation of a Trinary *entirely* composed of freeborn warriors. *That,* my fellow Khans, is the honor our esteemed Jade Falcon Khan wastes on the filthy freebirths in her—"

The other Khans protested loudly. Many of them shook their fists as they leaned over their council places. Others pounded on the desks. The commotion stopped at the raising of ilKhan Lincoln Osis' hand. The giant, black-skinned Elemental stood up and, while he spoke, kept his eyes firmly on Marthe Pryde.

"Khan Marthe Pryde of the Jade Falcons," Osis began in his impressively stentorian tone, "a serious accusation has just been lodged against you and your entire Clan. You wish to respond, *quiaff*?"

Marthe did not speak angrily, as Zalman had hoped, but in a low voice that resembled the rumbling of a volcano. Even amid the muttering of the Khans all around her, her voice carried through clearly.

"The Grand Council is no forum for your social views, Khan Zalman."

"Social views? Khan Marthe, that is a mild description for the expression of—"

"I apologize for using polite language to counter the muck that came out of your mouth, Khan Zalman."

Inside, Zalman was pleased. He felt confident now, in charge of the situation.

"I think my eminent colleague is not at this moment in a position to defend Jade Falcon policies."

"The policies of Clan Jade Falcon are consistent."

"Agreed. We are not just discussing the use of freeborns to fill out the ranks of units, especially support and garrison units. Sometimes that may be necessary, particularly in Clans who cannot produce sufficient trueborns to—"

Vlad stood up, but remained silent as Marthe interrupted Zalman.

"The distinguished Steel Viper Khan wishes to insult our trueborns as well as our freeborns. I would remind him that

Jade Falcons can provide proof that both genetic types performed valiantly in—"

"We do not mean to denigrate your Clan's heroism. It is in the extent of freeborn involvement where we part company, you and I."

Zalman glanced around the chamber, making sure he had the attention of all the other Khans. He did. Good. Time to heat up the rhetoric, score more hits against Marthe's protective armor.

"I say that any Clan that allows freebirths to rise in their ranks, that allows freebirths to compete for bloodnames, that forms freebirths into Trinaries and, worse, has them commanded by a near-renegade piece of freebirth scum, is to be—"

"Star Commander Horse is not scum! He is a Jade Falcon hero! *The Remembrance* celebrates his bravery in—"

"Bravery or not, he is freebirth and, as such, he is scum, filth—"

"The great hero Aidan Pryde did not endorse such—"

He had been waiting for her to mention Aidan Pryde, hoped for it.

"Ah! Your Great Hero! Your hero so valiant his genetic materials were accepted into the gene pool ahead of their destined time. And I agree. In my study of this fine warrior's life, the main flaw seems to be his bizarre connections with freebirths. Recall that he failed in his Trial when he was a trueborn cadet, defeated, incidentally, through the shrewd tactics of my honored fellow Khan, Marthe Pryde. Recall that he played a role in order to obtain the unprecedented second chance at a Trial—he actually posed as freebirth scum and toiled for years in a garrison unit with many freeborn warriors. He lived with them, ate with them, fought and played with them, associated with them on every level. What kind of life was that for a trueborn? Is a trueborn warrior in freeborn clothing really a trueborn? Is—"

"The Steel Viper Khan's portrayal is distorted! I do not claim to support the decisions that led to these incidents nor do I endorse the policies that allowed Aidan Pryde to continue in that role. However, whatever is ugly in the past of Aidan Pryde was more than made up for by—"

"Was it? Was it really? Recall that Aidan Pryde never did shake the freeborn taint that colored his career. Even after his questionable victory in a bloodname contest that drew similar criticisms as the present one involving his freebirth daughter—and I will not even bring up again the ugliness of that distortion of Clan ideals—after he received his bloodname, your Clan showed contempt for him by placing him in command of a unit as tainted as he. The Falcon Guards."

"The Falcon Guards redeemed themselves at Twycross."

"I do not deny the accidents in the career of your celebrated Jade Falcon hero. What I claim is that Aidan Pryde represents the debasement that has adulterated and demoralized the formerly great Jade Falcon Clan. It is no wonder that freebirth scum can rise to power, to become commanding officers with their own units of genetically debased warriors."

Zalman took a breath. He wondered why Marthe Pryde had suddenly gone silent. She should be leaping over her desk, flying toward him.

"Recall that Aidan Pryde's heroism in the Battle of Tukayyid, where he did indeed save uncounted lives and many 'Mechs as well, occurred as he protected the body of his fallen daughter. His daughter. This hero fought valiantly, true, but for what? To save the life of a filthy freebirth. And yet the Jade Falcons honor him. With this kind of history it is no surprise that the Falcons have brought warriors into battle before they have passed their Trials, have given freebirths command, have become so—so tolerant of the freebirths in their ranks that they are no longer the Clan that could win a Tukayyid battle. Their losses to our Clan in the invasion corridor serve as further proof of the decline of this Clan. We should reprimand—"

"Give it up, Khan Zalman," Marthe said finally. "You make a fool of yourself."

Zalman spread his arms. "Fool? Look around you, Khan Marthe, at our fellow Khans."

The other Khans, with only a few exceptions, escalated

their agreement with Zalman through loud protests and angry gestures. Marthe held up her hand and the response diminished.

"Khan Zalman," she said, "you have spoken well, for a Viper. This council is certainly a forum for the airing of opinions, no matter how clouded logically they may be. The Jade Falcons share your views on trueborn superiority. What we cannot abide is your demeaning of a Jade Falcon hero. Aidan Pryde's achievements, worthy of a long passage in our *Remembrance,* are actions to be admired not only within our Clan, but among all Clans."

The hubbub in the chamber was dying down, Zalman noted. Her words were having their desired effect. He was losing his advantage. He had to jump in and destroy her.

"It is not surprising, Khan Marthe, that you cannot see the deterioration of your own Clan's genetic strains. Further, it is possible you do not see the harm you do your own Clan by elevation of freebirths to power within the Clan or your willingness to deny a trueborn a bloodname so that a freeborn might win it. And it is clear that in your own Clan mythology you have obscured the fact that the greatest of your own heroes was himself an aberration, an abomination, who was indeed something of a sham hero in his—"

Zalman did not have to go on. Even as he was speaking, Marthe had started to descend from her tier down toward the Steel Viper place in the council. He tensed.

"You vile stravag!" Marthe shouted. "Your lies foul the air! Your accusations are the lowest use of politics I have heard in this chamber. It is you, Perigard Zalman, who is the filthy freebirth, and I challenge you to a Trial!"

Marthe's eruption shocked everyone. No one expected it from her, not the cool, reserved Marthe Pryde. Zalman wondered if Natalie Breen, no doubt monitoring the council meeting in her dark room, was nodding her head at the success of the strategy the two of them had concocted.

"I accept your challenge, Khan Marthe," he said calmly.

Loremaster Kael Pershaw yelled for the two Khans to stop. They both looked toward him. He had raised both of his arms. Zalman could not remember which arm was the prosthetic one.

"The ilKhan will speak," Pershaw said.

As she returned to her place, Marthe began to curse herself for being maneuvered into a challenge.

But I could not allow him to go any further. In a way, the challenge was his. It was just that he needed me to break. Well, I set myself up, quiaff? I knew I would get griping and grumbling in council, but I did not expect that the Vipers would take it this far. Especially the Vipers. They want something more. Either to destroy me or to make a move against the Jade Falcons as a whole. I must tread carefully from here on. The Steel Vipers cannot win this. I will destroy them before that can happen.

The ilKhan glanced around the room before speaking. The Khans understood his fierce look well and they became silent.

"I regard the Jade Falcon Khan's challenge as legitimate, as well as judge the words of the Steel Viper Khan that provoked it to be worthy of Grand Council consideration. However, it should be clear to all present that two Khans may not enter the field of battle, no matter how justified their desire for honor. It is fine that, as Khans, we do not forget our origins as warriors."

Many of the Khans muttered agreement, though Vlad Ward did not speak or show more than cynical interest in the proceedings.

"As you know, we discourage combat between Khans, a rule I endorse, especially since the last time it occurred."

Several of the onlookers briefly switched their attention to Vlad, who had not only beaten ilKhan Elias Crichell in a Trial, but had fought him to the death. Vlad glanced smugly around the room.

"It is enough," Osis continued, "that we are free to disagree so vehemently within this chamber. I would not like seeing Khans kill each other off. We represent the strength of the Clans, all the Clans.

"I also do not approve the use of a Trial to settle this particular matter. Although its theoretical implications are profound, especially in the matter of freeborn warriors competing for bloodnames, I say that a fight between representatives of the disputing parties will satisfy this challenge. An honor duel between two BattleMechs, if the esteemed Khans agree, *quiaff?*"

Both Marthe Pryde and Perigard Zalman signified their consent.

"Good," Osis said. "As is traditional, each Khan must select a warrior to represent his or her Clan in this honor duel. Loremaster, conduct the proper ceremony."

Kael Pershaw gave both Khans the chance to invoke *surkai,* the Clan rite of forgiveness that allowed the accused party to admit wrongdoing and accept the consequences, in this case consequences prescribed by the Grand Council. Each Khan was given the option of invoking *surkai,* since in the dispute each had offended the other. Marthe wondered if the wily head of the Watch was hinting that the two Khans would be allowed to agree to back down. However, Zalman's rejection of the offer was just as vehement as Marthe's.

The Loremaster allowed Marthe to repeat her challenge in formal language and state the reasons for it. Perigard Zalman was then allowed to present his side. He gave in cool summary what he had earlier spoken so emotionally.

"In olden days," Pershaw said, "it was common to call a warrior who represented his leader a champion. For this situation I choose to revive the term. As challenged party, Khan Perigard Zalman, you may name your champion first."

"I will disappoint many fine warriors who, I am certain, would be eager to do battle with any Jade Falcon. I choose, however, Star Colonel Ivan Sinclair, the grand hero of the Trial of Possession with the Jade Falcons for the right to invade Twycross during the invasion. The Star Colonel was even more a hero in the taking of Schreuder Heights, the deciding battle that forced the Ninth Federated Commonwealth RCT to flee Twycross in utter defeat."

Zalman's allies in the chamber nodded approvingly at this choice. It was clear that they relished his shrewdness in sending out as his champion an heroic warrior who had already bested Jade Falcons in a conflict. Zalman noted with satisfaction that Marthe's lips grew tighter, the only indication that she was impressed by his choice.

"As challenger, Khan Marthe Pryde, you may now name your champion."

"Well, of course it is difficult to choose a champion from such an abundance of valiant Jade Falcon warriors, but I note that Khan Zalman has chosen a warrior who is peculiarly appropriate to the situation. I should do the same. Since the issue is the worth of the freeborn warrior, I nominate one of the Jade Falcon's toughest and most heroic warriors, a warrior whose tenacity and skill have won him acclaim within the Clan. I choose Star Captain Horse of Trinary—"

The uproar Marthe expected was even more violent than she had anticipated.

It is probably good that Samantha Clees is not here. She might be right up there with the protesters. For that matter, many Jade Falcon warriors will be against me on this one. It is a risk, but one I want to take. Horse is a fine warrior, freeborn or not. He will make the point that has to be made.

As she waited for the deafening noise to subside, Marthe continued to stare at Perigard Zalman. The puzzlement in his eyes pleased her. In the chess game that he had started, she had him currently in check. Now, the game only awaited Horse's checkmate.

She sensed a presence behind her. Turning her head she saw that Vlad had walked over to her, a strange smile on his face.

"Congratulations," he said, "you have just become the most hated Khan of all the Khans."

"Horse will win."

"In that case, you will be the most hated warrior of all warriors."

"Would that fit into your political agenda, Vlad?"

Vlad winced slightly, as he did when one of her barbs got too close. She suspected he always liked to think that he had the upper hand in all matters, even in his relationship with her.

"Allowing me a political agenda is giving me too much credit, Marthe. If I had one, hating you would not be part of it. I support you in this. You have a way of doing the right thing and, for the moment, I think humiliation of the Steel Vipers could be useful for both of us."

Marthe shrugged and returned to her place, leaving Vlad standing there, smiling his usual enigmatic smile.

9

Holovid Arena
Warrior Sector, Ironhold City
Ironhold
Kerensky Cluster, Clan Space
2 February 3060

Sometimes a holovid recording of BattleMech combat was so frustrating that Diana wanted to reach over the low border of the holovid display table and, the way she did in her occasional chess games with Horse when she was losing, rearrange all the figures in the way she would have them had she been doing the fighting.

But I guess you can't change history like you can move chessmen, she thought. *On this table is the depiction of my father's last bloodname battle, recorded with all its flaws. I would have liked him to perform different maneuvers, at-*

tack in a different way, be more heroic. He was a hero, after all. The great hero Aidan Pryde. Let's run it again.

She reactivated the holovid program and watched again the miniature ships arrive at Rhea, the Ironhold moon. At first the field of the table seemed to have infinite depth with the spinning moon at its center, the planet beyond it, and the sun and stars beyond the planet. The DropShip came into view from behind the moon, and from it the two Battle-Mechs dropped in an arc that seemed too slow but, given the accuracy of the recording chips, was probably played off in real-time. Aidan had been in a *Summoner,* and the opponent—named Megasa—in a *Mad Dog.* Each 'Mech landed in an area of Rhea sufficiently far apart to keep their pilots from view of each other.

Touching the controls that let her choose which vantage points and aspects of the battle she wanted to see, Diana shifted the landscape to view where the holographic Aidan, whose miniaturized reproduction could sometimes be seen in a cutaway version of the 'Mech, if the player so wished, waited in his *Summoner.* In real-time each had been given an hour to acclimate to Rhea's gravity, but a running strip to one side of the scene noted that the wait was being skipped. There was a sudden adjustment and Aidan's BattleMech seemed to disappear from one place and reappear quickly a short distance away. He must have moved to that point in real-time.

What did Joanna say? Something about Aidan Pryde never having fought in a low-gravity environment before and his tech, unaccustomed to the needs of a low-gravity situation, being unsure how to compensate for the differences in general BattleMech adjustments to the weapons and control systems. Nor had Joanna and Horse, his coaches, known much about what to do. They had all consulted manuals and hoped for the best.

The battle began. Aidan's *Summoner* leaped up, and came down again, more slowly than it had risen.

Of course. The relative lack of gravity makes each move more pronounced. I wonder what he felt like at that moment.

*I have no idea what it must be like traveling in a heavy
'Mech that feels light as air. Was he afraid or did his famous
coolness prevail? I would really like to know. I suppose I
should not be interested in him just because he was my father, but I cannot help it.*

Always dissatisfied with holovid miniaturization, Diana
readjusted the perspective so that Aidan's 'Mech seemed to
grow a bit while the landscape contracted. As a result she
missed the entrance of Megasa in his *Mad Dog* onto the
scene. What she saw were some laser pulses materializing
suddenly and heading toward her father's 'Mech before it
took cover. The pulses passed out of the scene, seeming to
disappear into the holovid table's protective panel.

The *Summoner*'s response was quick. A line of LRMs
arced toward the *Mad Dog* as it now moved into the scene.
They went over its head. Apparently Aidan had not completely adjusted for the change in ballistic characteristics
within low gravity. The LRMs landed just beyond the *Mad
Dog,* near the edge of the holovid table. The effect was one
of half-explosions abruptly cut off by the table edge, plus a
little bit of dust being stirred up.

Diana sensed someone watching her. She was getting
good at that. Lately she had suffered the rude remarks and
challenges to fight of several trueborns who resented her
seeking a bloodname. The incidents had made her more
alert.

She considered pausing the holovid battle and turning
around, but instead she kept her focus on the miniature
'Mechs maneuvering on the holovid table. The *Mad Dog*'s
approach was determined, its volleys of fire continuous.
Because of the low gravity, it appeared to be quite agile, an
impression no one would get from a *Mad Dog* in normal
gravity. Tiny, almost indiscernible in miniature, pieces of
armor were flying off the *Summoner* as the *Mad Dog*'s fire
hit home with regularity. A missile impacted the *Summoner*
near its shoulder, and the low gravity sent it spinning wildly,
turning it around, making it vulnerable to the *Mad Dog*
from the back. Diana almost shouted "Watch out!" then re-

membered she was watching a holovid of a battle fought many years ago.

She was startled by a whisper behind her, near her ear. "Filthy freebirth," the speaker said.

Diana whirled around and almost collided with a beefy but rather short Jade Falcon warrior. His breath reeked of fusionnaires, the favorite drink of most Jade Falcon warriors, those who bothered with drinking anyway. Diana did not like them much, since they smelled like BattleMech oil, and the blast of fusionnaire aroma coming from this warrior's mouth made her gag. His eyes, which could not have expressed much intelligence even when he was sober, were cloudy with the alcohol and there were streaks of dirt near his mouth, no doubt places where he had wiped his mouth with his dirty hands following a good gulp of the potent liquid. The insignia on his fatigues showed him to be a Mech-Warrior of the 109th Striker Cluster—Star Colonel Heston Shu-li's unit, which had something of a reputation for rough behavior.

Joanna had mentioned this Cluster to Diana a couple of times. Having been left behind in the homeworlds while other Falcon units were assigned to the invasion, they were full of anger. Shu-li himself was a fierce-tempered officer who sometimes exacted punishment in extreme ways. The result, Joanna claimed, was that the warriors of the unit, the trueborn ones at least, tended to be a brawling, contentious lot.

Shu-li was known for overlooking his warriors' sometimes unClanlike actions as long as they fought fiercely. When called to account by high command, Shu-li—whose physical largeness and booming voice were impressive to all—claimed that his warriors fought better in combat if they fought often in noncombat situations. Since his unit's combat record was erratic, with his warriors fond of taking chances that sometimes led to disaster but just as often to victory characterized by an overwhelming display of 'Mech power, Shu-li had merely been reprimanded. However, his skills and the proven worth of the 109th Striker Cluster had kept him in command.

"Before I ask you what you said to me, MechWarrior . . ." Diana said in a cool voice, still watching the holo of her father's battle out of the corner of her eyes. This was a moment she especially enjoyed, when Aidan emerged from a dust cloud created by a relentless missile attack from Megasa. ". . . I will ask you to reconsider it, as you are obviously somewhat the worse for wear, and substitute something . . . well, more complimentary, than your previous oath."

The MechWarrior seemed confused by her rather formal speech. When she reverted to formality, she found it gave her an advantage that her attackers never suspected. Words bought time, words gave you time to think of other words—the words of strategy—or at least gave you an edge to attack from.

The MechWarrior had some difficulty focusing his eyes. He blinked several times. Then he tried to talk, but all that came out were unintelligible syllables.

"Should we reason together?" Diana said, more to buy time than to encourage dialogue. What she wanted to do was keep track of the miniaturized battle, and this boorish warrior was merely an intrusion, a speck of dirt in the eye. She caught the moment when the *Summoner*'s leg came down hard on the moon's surface and snapped off at the knee. The broken-off piece dropped gently to the surface, bouncing low-grav all over the place, while Aidan's 'Mech rushed forward on momentum and fell into a pit that had not been at all obvious from the view Diana had set up.

The MechWarrior muttered something about a lot of damnfool talk, then collected himself and said, louder this time, "Filthy freebirth!"

Giving the man only a cursory glance, Diana tried to delay him by holding her open-palmed hand up, while she maneuvered the holovid scene with her other hand. She moved the landscape to a point where she, like Megasa's 'Mech, seemed to stare right down into the hole, where the *Summoner* lay. This was the point where Megasa had made his mistake. He could have proclaimed himself victor of the match and earned the bloodname for himself, but earlier—

in a pact agreed on by all the warriors who had made it to the latter stages of the contest—he had vowed that the match would not be over until the impostor Aidan, the freebirth at heart who had insulted the entire bloodname tradition by going after a bloodname, was dead. If he claimed victory at that moment, Aidan would have been rescued and the vow unfulfilled.

"Filthy freebirth!" the MechWarrior muttered again and jostled Diana. She tapped a button to put the scene on pause, then turned to the drunken warrior and quickly decked him with a solid left to the cheekbone. The blow hurt her knuckles, but she smiled through the pain as she watched her attacker fall to the floor comically.

Touching the pause button to reactivate the scene, she quickly expanded the viewing size to its largest so that Megasa's *Mad Dog* was the size of a small animal and the pit it looked down into had widened to fill more than half of the holovid table's field.

Some analysts of this part of the battle had stated that Aidan's bloodname was tainted because he was given that second chance by Megasa's obtuseness about the vow. They noted that Aidan was, during the time that the rather slow-witted Megasa had taken to come to the conclusion that Aidan must be killed, a sitting duck. He could not eject into the vacuum that was Rhea's atmosphere, and he could not right the fallen and somewhat crumpled *Summoner*. All Megasa had to do was fire any of the weapons he had left into the pit, and Aidan was finished. The only reason Megasa delayed was, apparently, to gloat.

She tensed a bit as she awaited her father's counterattack, then suddenly a thick pair of hands landed on her shoulders like a 'Mech on its jump-jet way down, and pulled her roughly away from the holovid table. As it happened, her hand accidentally brushed against the repeat button, which started the whole sequence all over again, and she knew that she had missed the climax, missed her father's success. That made her furious.

Her attacker this time was also a member of the 109th

Striker, a fact she noticed as he flung her backward toward another of Shu-li's warriors, a woman who caught her by the shoulders and pushed her back toward the holovid table, where the bloodname holographic figures were now settling again onto Rhea, this time with the ships and figures much larger. Diana stumbled against the side of the table with such force that, were its legs not securely fastened to the floor, the impact would probably have toppled the table. The two attackers tended to verify the reputation of Shu-li's warriors. They were clearly strong and brutal. Their faces were twisted into what seemed like the same cruel expression, and their stances indicated they were warriors experienced in aggression of all sorts.

Diana's hand brushed against the control panel, activating a button that accelerated the action of the holovid field. Speeded-up 'Mech-walks became brisker, as if taking advantage of the low-gravity state to fulfill their aerobic needs.

The male warrior grabbed Diana's right arm and pulled her closer to him. Inadvertently inhaling as she came close to his face, she realized that this one had been tossing off a few drinks, too. But his eyes were clearer and, for that matter, meaner. He looked like a warrior who was not satisfied unless he maimed or killed another human being each day. However, since warriors rarely drank to excess, she felt his drunkenness gave her an advantage.

The woman came up behind him, in firm strides that showed she was not drunk like her companions. Her face became visible over his shoulder. She was an ugly one, her leather-skinned and hard-featured face bringing no credit to Clan genetics. (Horse had told her long ago that there was no DNA programming for beauty in Clan warriors, although it often turned out that they were superb physical specimens. Diana had no care about beauty, her own—which was considerable—or that of any other warrior. But the one staring cruelly over the other's shoulder was one grotesque individual.)

"Freebirth scum have no right to Clan warriors' holovid

arenas," the man said, his speech slow and a bit slurred. "We will let you walk out of here without dishonor. Start walking now."

He let her go as the other warrior came around him, and both confronted Diana.

"I am a Clan warrior," Diana said, smoothing out her uniform where it had been roughed up. She noticed that their uniforms were a bit scruffy—dirty and torn from what no doubt were other fights they had picked. "I, like you, am Jade Falcon."

"We know who you are. You are the filthy freebirth who has the gall to compete for a bloodname with warriors more worthy than yourself. You have no right to a bloodname. You have no—"

"I get your point."

"Will you leave or should we kick you out?"

"Before I do anything, I must know the names of true-borns who would exert authority over me."

The two glanced at each other and apparently decided to grant her request. As they spoke, the drunk who had first attacked her, now off the floor, joined them, shaking his head to clear it either from Diana's blows or from the lingering effects of the booze. He did not look like much of a threat, even at his best.

"I am Selor Malthus."

"I am Janora Malthus."

"And your semi-conscious colleague here?"

"He is Rodrigo."

Diana raised her eyebrows. "What, no bloodname?"

"He will begin his bloodname competition tomorrow."

Diana smiled at the warrior as he swayed. "Seems well-conditioned for it," she commented. "I wish he was in my line. I would be happy to draw him first, so I could know I had at least one step won."

She glanced over her shoulder. The speeded-up fight between Aidan and Megasa was nearing its finale. At the fast rate it was proceeding, the tiny *Mad Dog* would shoot off the *Summoner*'s leg in seconds. She had to move quickly.

Selor was clearly about to issue his final challenge. She decided not to wait for it.

Seizing Selor's rumpled collar with her right hand and Janora's with her left, she pulled both warriors close to her, then past her—first Selor, then Janora. Caught by surprise, with Selor at least slowed by indulgence, neither offered much resistance.

Releasing her hold on the clothing, she whirled around to watch the pair of warriors collide with the holovid table, each at an awkward angle. Janora slid to the floor. Diana noticed that her foot was held at an odd angle, perhaps sprained. Selor, who was taller, bounced off the side of the table, then appeared dazed and fell backward, right into the hologram field, on top of the spot where the figure of the *Mad Dog* stood at the edge of the pit, about to be demolished by Aidan's last-gasp maneuver. The head of the *Mad Dog* materialized on the surface of Selor's stomach. Before Selor moved to extricate himself, there were some tiny fragments of Megasa's cockpit appearing to emerge out of Selor's stomach, then the miniature holographic body of Megasa briefly visible before it, like the unseen cockpit, exploded in the vacuum above Rhea.

Missed the ending again! I'll never get it right.

She sensed Rodrigo's attack, braced for it, elbowed him in the stomach, then flung him into the holovid table. She sensed others coming at her, officials of the Holovid Arena clearly wanting no more damage to their equipment. To help them out, Diana assisted Rodrigo and Selor off the holovid table, somewhere in the middle of which she kicked the stirring Janora in the side of her grotesque face.

Stepping over the unconscious Selor, she glanced down at the clearly dizzy but conscious Rodrigo.

"Good luck on your bloodname match tomorrow," she said, smiling down at him.

"Good. . . . good. . . . good *luck*?"

"You will need it. You have about as much chance of getting a bloodname as I have of discovering that I am trueborn, after all. I considered killing you to spare you the effort, but I am told our forces are still understrength and we need warriors nowadays."

Rodrigo tried to sit up and attack Diana, but she pushed him down again with her foot and strode toward the holovid arena's exit.

Near the door a warrior in Jade Falcon fatigues stepped abruptly in front of her. Although he smiled, it was not necessarily the smile of a friend.

Diana sighed. *I'm getting tired of this. Do I have to exhaust myself on every two-bit trueborn who wants to challenge me?*

The man evidently read her thoughts through her disgusted facial expression, for he held up his hands, palms out, and said, "No challenge, freeborn. If anything, admiration. You handle yourself well. That was a mean trio of warriors you just wiped the floor with. Two of them, anyway."

He was about her height, but broader, with wide shoulders. She stared straight into his affable eyes. His skin was smooth, and he looked quite young. He stood calmly.

Diana squinted at him. "Thanks, I think," she said. "But what business is it of yours?"

He shrugged. "None, far as I can tell. Like you, I am here amusing myself with holovids."

"Amusing is a funny word for it."

His eyes narrowed. "Well, actually, like you I was studying classic battles to see what I could learn from them. I think you are the famous Diana, *quiaff*?"

"I do not know about famous, but my name is Diana."

"Oh, you are famous all right. Notorious. We are all supposed to resent you deeply for being the freeborn stravag who is trying to steal what we deserve."

"We?"

"I am competing for a bloodname, too. The same as you. The same competition, in fact."

"And you say you do not resent me?"

"Not at all. I saw now that you are a fine warrior, freeborn or not. May the best warrior win, I say. I do not care about your origins."

"That is certainly rare, so rare I wonder if you are being truthful."

"Ease up, warrior. I am content right now, but that does not mean I cannot be riled. I am not deceitful, I assure you."

"I will believe you. For the moment. What is your name, warrior?"

"Leif."

"Never heard of that name."

"You know how it is back in the nurseries. Canister nannies pick names out of hats or mythology texts or lists of Clan heroes. I do not know how mine came up with Leif. Would you like to walk? I am tired of the stale air in this place and could use some exercise."

"Lead on, Leif."

The street outside was a dirt one, common among the kind of makeshift training camps that sprang up for blood-name competitions. Although warriors did not believe in waste, they did not have much time or concern for it either, especially when there was the training to concentrate on. As a result the streetbed was unusually littered. Castaway food, shreds of crumpled paper, metal pieces, and materials not easy to define were visible in the moonlit dimness of the street. There was not a lot of debris, but its rarity made it seem cluttered.

They walked slowly. Clearly Leif had adjusted his pace to accommodate her own slowness. The fight had caused her to strain a thigh muscle, and her walk was just a bit off-kilter.

Leif glanced at Diana from time to time, but evidently did not intend to initiate any conversation.

They passed an alley, and the sounds emerging from it caused Diana to look over, although Leif showed no interest. In the darkness of the alley, two people, at least one of them no doubt a warrior, were coupling energetically. Looking at the sexual silhouette, Diana was, as always, struck by how strange and unwarriorlike coupling was when viewed from a distance. Also as always, she wondered why she did not have much need for it. Some of her reluctance to follow even her occasional urges had to do with the fact she was a freeborn and could not easily approach a trueborn. There was an unwritten set of customs that tended to discourage freeborns from making the first move, while allowing it for trueborns. A freeborn warrior could easily couple with another freeborn, but unfortunately for Diana she had too much sense of herself as somebody other than either trueborn or freeborn, and she had few urges. They passed the alley and she turned her head toward Leif, who was smiling.

"What is the smile about, surat?"

It left abruptly, there was a moment of anger in his eyes, and then his face became calm again. "Nothing much," he said, "I just find it strange to be strolling along a street with another warrior who, in a few days, may be my opponent."

"You intend to reach the finals?"

"Certainly."

"Then I will be there to fight you. And I will regret having to force a fine warrior such as yourself to endure the shame of defeat at the hands of a freeborn."

A sharp spasm in her leg nearly made her stumble. She knew she should treat the pain, but somehow she did not want to leave this warrior yet.

"You are confident," Leif said. "I will give you that."

"Are you not confident?"

"Supremely. I will hate to beat you, but what is to be, must be."

Diana laughed and said, "I like you, warrior."

"And I, you, warrior."

They walked on a while, often laughing at each other's words. At one point Leif stopped walking and, resting the back of his hand on her upper arm, he stopped Diana, too.

"Your fight back there, in the arena. It was fierce. I would have jumped in to help, but it was clear you were in command from the first attack. You are tenacious, really."

Diana's turn to shrug. "I was taught by a good teacher, one with more rage in her than a dozen of us could hope for. Star Commander Joanna, perhaps you have heard of her?"

"The conqueror of the Black Widow, *quiaff*?"

"Aff. She is my coach for the Trial of Bloodright. If it ever comes, what with all the delays. Anyway, she is putting me through the hell of training for the bloodname matches. I am not sure I need the training any more. I have been ready for weeks, it seems."

When Diana and Joanna had first arrived on Ironhold, Diana had been immediately assailed by challenges from the many enraged warriors already there, warriors who resented the presence of a freeborn competitor. But the head of House Pryde, Risa Pryde, and the leaders of the other Blood Houses quickly stifled any official Trials on the grounds that they were too wasteful at a time when the Clans were trying to rebuild their invincible might. According to Risa Pryde, the outcome of bloodname competition itself would provide sufficient proof of Diana's claim. She would have no undestined fatalities.

Still, if there had been no official Trials, there had been plenty of unofficial ones, mostly brawls like the one in the holovid arena.

"I think I saw this Star Commander Joanna this morning," Leif said. "She looked ready to devour a dozen warriors before breakfast."

"If that was the look, then Joanna was the one you saw."

When they came to the training barracks, she told Leif that Joanna had scheduled an especially early session in the use of whips, a skill that had eluded Diana. Leif said he had a training session early in the morning also.

In the barracks she described part of her conversation with Leif to Joanna, who laughed mockingly. "Do you not see what he was doing with all that friendliness and no-it-is-all-right-you-are-freeborn bilge? He was trying to confuse you. He found out you were deficient in the use of whips, *quiaff*? A small thing, since it is unlikely to be a weapon in your matches. Still, he could use the knowledge against you, if a chance to use whips came up. I know the basic tactic he is employing. Get into an opponent's mind and find a weakness. Ignore this Leif, and stay out of his way."

"You are wrong about him, Joanna."

Joanna's aging face, itself an object of repulsion to younger warriors who despised any signs of age, any step on the road toward becoming solahma, screwed itself up into an angry map of disapproval. "Listen to me, Diana. You have only one goal, to earn the bloodname. I will train you to the best of my ability, the best of my considerable ability, I might add, but finally it is you in the cockpit of the Battle-Mech, you who must beat your opponent. I will not allow you to consider anything that could divert you from the goal. Forget this Leif's words. You must forget all that he said, *quiaff*?"

"Aff," Diana responded, but she was positive Leif had been open and honest. The memory of her conversation with Leif remained with her in spite of Joanna's urgings, even though it was some time before she spoke to the young man again.

10

West Scar
Strana Mechty
Kerensky Cluster, Clan Space
4 February 3060

West Scar, named for its location on the Scar River and not for physical signs of warrior injuries, was a village whose inhabitants and their families worked in the capital city, Katyusha, mostly as techs for the various Clans. In Katyusha the Clans met in a free-city atmosphere to administer aspects of Clan government, conduct a bit of commerce, and obtain some occasional entertainment. The unusual aspect of West Scar, and its companion village, East Scar, across the wide river and a few kilometers south, was that Clan affiliation was less significant. When villagers worked in the city, they stayed within Clan groupings for their proper duties, but out here in West Scar, they mingled socially and cooperated in a municipal government.

West Scar made trueborns, especially warriors, uneasy. They did not like to observe the breakdown of Clan barriers in neutral zones, so they avoided both Scars.

As in villages throughout the Clans, West Scar was built around a town square, with main streets going out in spokes around a marketplace area. The West Scar marketplace contained an outdoor tavern, where—several moments before a number of the villagers would face death—Marthe Pryde's aide, Rhonell, sat with several villagers who were mainly family-members of techs or were off-duty. Rhonell, who had no family, had often noted that *family* was another of those words that made trueborns react with disgust. Rhonell, who had absorbed many warrior views, nevertheless found something oddly pleasant in families, or at least in the idea of families. But he definitely preferred serving warriors to living with frees. Marthe had given Rhonell the day off. He did not much like days off, nor did he like sitting in the village and trying to drink. He did not drink much and did not much care for the stuff. But he did like sitting quietly and observing the villagers.

Although he sat with them, he rarely talked with them. Part of that was due to his preference for warriors, but another part was caused by the fact that he never talked much anyway, and then usually in cryptic terms. Since he rarely came to the village, the villagers did not know the tall, imposing tech with the emotionless eyes. His lack of personality worked in his favor, allowing people to easily forget he was there. This made him more useful to Marthe, who frequently quizzed him about the views of other castes.

He sipped at his fusionnaire and listened to the techs at the next table talk. Much of the buzz in the town this day was about Marthe Pryde's choosing a *freeborn* warrior to represent her Clan against a Steel Viper *trueborn* hero, especially since they knew the challenge was being settled on a plain a few kilometers away. Rhonell, preferring to hear their opinions, did not reveal his connection to the events. He could have told them that the Pryde line always took risks and that was what he admired about Aidan and why he was so happy to serve Marthe. On the other hand, he was aware that the Jade Falcon Clan, his Clan after all, put itself too often in danger, lost too many lives in battle, and suffered from that exact daring that he so admired.

One of the villagers, an Ice Hellion sci-tech named Flute, was talking to Susanna, whose tech role within the Fire Mandrills was unknown to Rhonell. Susanna seemed to think that Marthe had made a courageous move, while Flute called it a foolish one.

"Putting so much that is on the line in the hands of a freeborn is too risky."

"Excuse me, I thought you were one of us," Susanna replied. "A freeborn."

"You know I am. Don't you think this Horse'll lose and the Jade Falcon Khan may resign as a consequence?"

"Marthe Pryde does not appear to be the quitting type to me."

The discussion was clearly escalating into an argument, maybe even a fist-fight, when some shouting people hurried into the town square to tell the citizens that the Viper-Falcon challenge duel had strayed into the area near West Scar. The drinking area cleared swiftly, as the villagers, eager for anything to relieve the monotony of village life, headed for this new excitement, leaving for a short time Rhonell still in his seat, finishing the drink he did not much care for. Then he followed the villagers to the city limits to watch the spectacle of two titans in the meadow.

The force of the water of the Scar River Rapids, as it roiled around the feet of Horse's *Summoner,* could be felt all the way into the cockpit. He had chosen to jump to Scar

River because the *Summoner*'s heat was rising to dangerous levels. He had needed the quick cool-down the icy waters of the river would furnish.

This battle had been going on so long that he was starting to feel seriously fatigued. The 'Mech's legs were his legs, and they could barely move as the force of the water raged against them. If he relaxed, allowed himself a moment to re-group and rejuvenate, the *Summoner* would no doubt fall, face first, into the waters, and that would be the end. The Steel Vipers would win their point, and Horse would have proven to Jade Falcons that he was, after all, no better than any other freeborn.

Ahead of him, the *Stormcrow* of the tenacious Steel Viper Star Colonel, Ivan Sinclair, appeared to be negotiating the surging rapids with efficiency. Horse could see, though, that his own assault had done more damage than he had sus-pected. As often happened with persistent warriors, they sometimes drew more damage than they inflicted, simply because daring countered skill with the significant hit that ended the conflict, no matter how far down the warrior had seemed, no matter how ill-advised and asinine the winning strategy might have been. Horse noted, though, that the *Stormcrow* torso had lost an abundance of armor. Good. Something to fix on as a target.

Glancing at his secondary display, Horse saw that he might be mistaken as to which combatant's 'Mech had suf-fered more damage. The *Summoner*'s right arm was slow to respond; the charge on the lasers was way down. Its small laser had been blown off in a particularly lucky shot from Sinclair. He had more than half his short-range missiles left. Along with his autocannon, the SRMs had been particularly effective in causing the *Stormcrow*'s torso damage. Sinclair was in only marginally better shape. In spite of the severe torso damage, his missile rack had more missiles; his lasers were still a danger to Horse.

Well, I suppose just standing here and letting the river de-stroy me, or waiting for Sinclair to get back in range, are poor options. Have to make it to shore.

Thinking it and making it possible were two different things. Lifting one leg, he took a step toward shore and his 'Mech's foot landed in deeper water. The *Summoner* tilted forward and nearly did fall, but Horse was able to regain balance and swing the right foot around. This time he found firm footing. Working that way, step by step, he found the rise to the river bank and picked up speed. Sinclair had gained some, but was now making his own way to the river bank. A good tactic on his part, since firing from a firm footing on shore had better potential than standing and swaying in a swirling river.

At first the mud of the bank, very soft and apparently deep, made Horse's 'Mech flounder a bit, but he adjusted to the new obstacle and quickly freed himself of the muddy part of the shore to stand on dry land and turn to face Sinclair.

Oddly, Sinclair and his *Stormcrow* were not coming at him. The Viper Star Colonel had set his 'Mech running in a wide arc around Horse. He passed Horse's *Summoner* before slowing down and pointing his *Stormcrow* toward Horse.

Horse laboriously executed a turn to face Sinclair and saw a surprise behind the Viper warrior. Sinclair and his *Stormcrow* stood just outside a small village. Checking his map screen in a quick, flicking eye movement, Horse saw that it was the village of West Scar. Although he knew it could be fatal to interrupt a contest like this one, Horse had to talk to Sinclair on the commline.

When the Star Colonel's voice came on the line, Horse noted its dispassionate coolness and the fact that no tiredness showed in it. It was alarming to hear that your enemy was not even out of breath after this long, bitterly fought combat. Horse felt his own words coming out between heavy breaths that he struggled to control.

"I request a repositioning of our 'Mechs, Star Colonel Sinclair. There is a village in the line of fire. We should not endanger civilians."

The arrogance in Sinclair's voice was chilling. Even for a Clan warrior. Even for a *Steel Viper* warrior. Viper warriors were renowned for their aloofness, which was much greater than the aloofness of the other Clan trueborns, and Sinclair sounded like he'd provided the mold they were made from.

"My opponent has qualms about the death of a few bystanders, *quiaff*?"

In all their communications, Sinclair had not called Horse by name or even rank. He did not even curse him as a freebirth. In a curious display of Clan courtesy, he always used phrases like my opponent or fellow warrior.

"Aff. Who would not?"

"I, for one, would not. Oh, I would not deliberately seek to kill bystanders, but it is of no consequence to me. Besides, repositioning is to your advantage, buys you time. No, I will make my stand here. If a few villagers die, then so be it. Anyway, they are only freebirths. You are freebirth scum yourself. You worry about them!"

If Sinclair had intended to enrage Horse, the strategy succeeded beyond his expectations. Rage surged through Horse's body like heat shooting into the red zone. He put his own *Summoner* into a run now, straight at Sinclair's *Stormcrow*.

Sinclair started firing all he had at Horse. Laser fire streaked over an intensely green meadow. Many of the beams hit, and pieces of armor slagged off in every direction. A missile from the *Stormcrow* just missed its target due to a quick dodge on Horse's part.

In the back of his mind, somewhere beneath the rage, Horse knew that he could fail Marthe Pryde and bring deep shame upon the both of them, their Clan, and the freeborn caste. In another, also rational, part of his mind, he knew that trueborn warriors detested physical attack from another 'Mech and that anticipating such an attack could enrage Sinclair and throw his judgment off-balance. It would also be dangerous to Horse, since he would be vulnerable to the *Stormcrow*'s close-in firepower.

To the rear of Sinclair's *Stormcrow,* Horse saw the people of West Scar rushing out of the village, looking to get a good view of the action. They seemed tiny. How could they be this foolish, placing themselves in such danger, as if to verify Sinclair's judgment of them as worthless?

But to Horse they were not worthless. They were human beings. Yes, their origins were low, as Horse's had been. Yes, the loss of a few would not be significant. They could be pins on a map knocked off by a careless hand. Yes, the other freeborns would applaud the reckless bravery of their comrades. Yet their deaths would be a waste. Horse could not allow it to happen.

He slowed his *Summoner* and quickly calibrated its jump-jet system for a leap that would bring him down on the other side of Sinclair's *Stormcrow,* then he could mount a rapid attack on Sinclair from the rear, force him to move farther away from the city to fight Horse. Unless they came into the perimeter of battle, the villagers would be safe. If they did cross that perimeter, then their fate was in their own hands.

As he was about to make the leap, the rectangular red warning box appeared on his monitor screen. The jump jets were disabled, the result of a hit from Sinclair that Horse had not previously noticed or felt. He could not leap.

All of the curses he had learned as a child in his own village, a cadet in training, seemed to go through his mind in a wild rush. At the same time the curses were underscored by a series of direct hits from the *Stormcrow* on the *Summoner.* The *Summoner* began to sway. Its left leg was now severely weakened.

No matter, Horse thought. This *is my fight to win*.

More villagers had emerged from the village limits. Sinclair maneuvered his *Stormcrow* a step backward and to the side, closer to the villagers. It seemed an obvious strategic move to Horse. The stravag was deliberately forcing Horse to make a choice between continuing the assault and putting the villagers in danger and sacrificing the battle with any move to protect the villagers.

In the meantime Sinclair continued his fierce assault on Horse.

The bad part about piloting a severely damaged 'Mech

was the emotions the warrior had to endure while still struggling to win in spite of knowing the damage to the 'Mech. A pilot had to reach within to summon the strength to make a damaged 'Mech function amazingly in a battle.

Horse felt the effort of every step as, much slower now, he advanced his 'Mech toward Sinclair's. He held his fire even as he came closer to defeat. His laser weapons had been damaged more by Sinclair's attack. It seemed to Horse that the rest of his own attack was reduced to using his autocannon and his SRMs. He did not want to use them until he had achieved the most effective distance. Even in his anger, he calculated the moment while keeping a steady eye on his monitor, where continually changing arc lines showed probable results of a launch at each second.

Horse almost waited too long. Laserfire from Sinclair narrowly missed the *Summoner* missile rack. He had to start firing them soon or lose all strategic advantage they could provide.

First, though, he aimed his autocannon at the damaged *Stormcrow* torso and thumbed the trigger. All he needed was a hit in the right place. And he got it. The torso was laid open by a stream of autocannon fire. Horse could be mistaken, but the recoiling motion of the *Stormcrow* appeared to be caused by more than just the torso hits. He had to have hit the gyro. He had a chance to lay out the *Stormcrow* completely, if he could zero in on the gyro, but right now Sinclair's counterattack was too ferocious to accomplish it.

He let off half his SRMs in two firings, all aimed for the lower legs of the *Stormcrow*. The first hit the left leg just above what would have been an ankle if a 'Mech had ankles. The second hit just a bit higher on the right leg. In both cases clumps of myomer fiber underneath were revealed in large, gaping holes. The *Stormcrow* swayed more.

Horse knew Sinclair was too skilled a pilot to lose control yet. He could keep the *Stormcrow* upright. So Horse let off the second half of his missiles. The first cluster of this barrage struck the *Stormcrow*'s left leg, just where Horse had intended, right at the knee joint.

However, unexpectedly, the *Stormcrow*'s right leg had begun to buckle just before the missile-firing and the missiles hit too high, at upper-thigh level. Horse saw that the left leg was about to collapse in a slow but inevitable fall that, with the other leg successfully disabled, would have sent the *Stormcrow* forward, away from the villagers. However, the thigh-hit sent the *Stormcrow* in a countermove toward them, especially after Sinclair managed the single step he was able to accomplish with that leg. Sinclair's efforts were not directed against the villagers. It was merely a desperate attempt to keep his 'Mech upright for long enough to send all the artillery he had at the suddenly vulnerable *Summoner*. The effort was not successful. Horse responded with more autocannon fire, working the *Stormcrow* away from the villagers. A shell evidently hit its gyro and disabled it, for the *Stormcrow* suddenly seemed to go limp, and it began to fall again toward the villagers.

Horse did not have time to realize that he had won the challenge as he raced his *Summoner* toward the *Stormcrow*. If he could reach it in time, as it now swayed right before the final collapse and Sinclair's last-ditch firing went skyward, he could nudge it just enough to miss the clump of villagers who were now realizing their danger and beginning to scatter.

It seemed as if he could reach out and deflect the Stormcrow *just enough, but there had been too many hits on the* Summoner*'s own legs and its speed had been diminished just enough and perhaps there had never been enough time.*

Before he reached the *Stormcrow,* he saw three things. First, Sinclair ejecting out of his cockpit, his ejection seat taking an odd straight line over the villagers and toward a flat roof on a building just within the city limits. Second, the *Stormcrow* torso making an unfortunate unexpected turn that allowed the right leg to be a sort of pivot that directed the heavy torso right down onto the clump of villagers. Third, the *Stormcrow*'s agonizingly slow fall, its right leg twisting into a mass of metal and myomer to allow the torso to land flat upon the screaming villagers.

After, with the *Summoner* stopped (and with only a moment for him to notice that Sinclair's skill had patterned his last shots so well that it would have taken only moments to defeat Horse), Horse climbed out of the 'Mech, ran to the remains of the *Stormcrow,* and tried frantically to extricate some of the villagers from the wreckage. Those he did manage to free died soon after anyway.

Rhonell, who had stayed at the city limits, raced to the scene to help. Like Horse, he and the others were able to save no one. Rhonell, with a sick pain at the pit of his stomach, saw the corpses of Flute and Susanna mingled together, two villagers from different Clans in final embrace. There was a moment when Horse looked over at Rhonell with mixed anger and sadness in his eyes. Rhonell saw his own emotions reflected on the other man's face.

Later, as Rhonell made his way through the village street, his mood dark, his eyes still filled with tears, he came upon a fight in one of West Scar's alleys. At first it just seemed like a village brawl, some drunken disagreement. Then he saw that one of the combatants was Horse. The other wore the remnants of what Rhonell could identify as a Steel Viper uniform—undoubtedly the other pilot. What had they said his name was? Sinclair.

Sinclair seemed to be unconscious, but Horse did not seem to care. He kept propping the man up against the alley wall and hitting him again. Rhonell had a momentary urge to help Horse, but saw that the warrior needed no help, especially from a clerical tech. Rhonell watched until Horse, too, collapsed and the two warriors did not look much better than the 'Mechs they had left behind on the battlefield.

"They say it will be a long time before Sinclair returns to duty," Marthe Pryde said, as she stared at Horse. The freeborn warrior's outfit was apparently new. He himself stood as stiffly as his sharply creased trousers. A week had passed since the Trial, some of which Horse had spent in a med-center being treated for injuries. They were officially listed as incurred during the battle, but Marthe knew they were the result of the alley brawl with Sinclair afterward. A couple of facial bruises on the left side of his face were only now disappearing.

"I am sorry I did not kill him."

"I know. I would have killed the son of a bitch myself."

Horse's eyes widened. Son of a bitch was an epithet rarely used within the Clans, ancient as it was in Terran history. There was something about the double insult of it, with the designation of genetic origin and genetic role, that made Clan warriors reserve it for the worst kind of human being.

"You look startled, Horse."

"I did not know that the Khan's support of freeborns in combat units extended to sympathy for the deaths of a few freeborn villagers."

Marthe winced. Horse could really get to the heart of a matter. It made him the fine warrior he was, the trustworthy ally he had become for her, and one of the most annoying people she had ever dealt with. *Though not as annoying as Aidan Pryde could be sometimes.*

"Do not make some kind of paragon of tenderness and compassion out of me, Horse. I believe in the superiority of the genetically engineered warrior caste. But that does not mean I will not use freeborns in ways most beneficial to the Clan or that I would not regret the death of freeborn villagers, some of them techs, whose loss is as wasteful as the destruction of tools and machinery. Do not mistake pragmatism for, as you say, sympathy."

"You say you regret the deaths of useful techs. It is wasteful. As it happens, none of the dead were of the Jade Falcons. Ironically, the Clan most represented in death was the Steel Vipers."

"Points taken, Horse. Now, I think it will be best to get you away from here for a while. Let me cope with the benefits of your victory. I have arranged for your passage to Ironhold. You will leave early tomorrow morning and, as you requested, help in the preparations for MechWarrior Diana's bloodname battles, *quiaff?*"

"Aff, my Khan."

Horse turned to leave.

"Horse."

"Yes?"

"The Clan takes pride at your victory. Why the grimace?"

"I wish I could share in such pride, but the memory of corpses is—"

"Enough! Never mention that to me, again!"

"Yes, my Khan."

After Horse had left, Marthe stared at the door for some time. Earlier in the day she had encountered Vlad Ward. He had congratulated her on the Falcon victory, saying that she had properly humiliated the Vipers.

"You will have to take this challenge further, though," he said. "The Vipers will push you to the wall now. Perigard Zalman cannot afford not to. Only the fact that the Clans are up to their necks in final preparations for the new invasion prevents the Vipers from moving against you. That, and the ilKhan's inclination toward more peaceful solutions of conflicts among Khans. After we prevail against the Inner Sphere, you will have to face the Vipers in war."

"I know that. I am expecting it. I am, in fact, planning on it."

"Your political savvy grows by the minute, Marthe Pryde. I will have to watch my own back."

"I would suggest that, Vlad Ward."

Vlad gave her a smile that made his scarred face look even more wolfish. "Marthe, with this victory you may not be the most hated Khan of all. On the other hand, because of this victory, you may be."

Marthe waited till he was gone to add softly, and to herself, "Then again, with this victory I may be on the way to being the most powerful Khan of all."

11

Training Field 17
Warrior Sector, Ironhold City
Ironhold
Kerensky Cluster, Clan Space
13 February 3060

Joanna opened her eyes suddenly. She had been in some dream or other about combat. She often dreamed of combat. At least this one did not revive her battle with the Black Widow.

She had fallen asleep in her fatigues, as she often did. Driving herself to exhaustion, she would become too tired to bother changing clothes at night.

Glancing at her chronometer, which she had left as always on the bedside table, she saw that it was already six in the morning, a fact she verified by glancing out at the gray dawn of Ironhold.

She sat up quickly. Normally she was up by four and out on the training field with Diana within the half-hour. She had overslept. She had actually overslept for the first time in years.

Starting for the door, she realized she could not appear in public in these wrinkled fatigues. Rapidly she pulled out her last clean fatigues from a drawer.

She looked around the room. Messy as usual. Joanna had always neglected all the quarters assigned to her during her long military career.

After dressing quickly, she gathered up the dirty clothes

that were in piles around the room—on the floor, on the chest of drawers, on her work-desk—and, as she sped out of the room, dumped them in the bin for a tech to pick up later. By nightfall the clothes would be returned to the room—clean, pressed, and piled neatly on her bed—and, for a brief moment, would be the only orderly looking feature of the room.

Joanna found Diana at the training field, going through her regular weapons drill, firing charged-down laser rifles at a distant target. The shots, Joanna noted approvingly, were clustered at the center of the target. She discovered this on the monitor that reported hits. Her deteriorating eyesight would not allow her to make out anything on the target itself.

"Why did you not wake me?" Joanna asked.

"I did try a bit," Diana responded. "But, believe me, you were out of it. Your snores were like the whoops of a sick surat. You looked so exhausted that I thought you could use a couple extra hours of sleep."

"That is insulting. You imply that I cannot keep up with you. That I am too old."

"I did not mean to imply it. But, if the combat boot fits . . ."

Joanna knew she should be angry at Diana's remark, but found herself amused. *What is wrong with me?* she wondered.

"You are improving in at least one respect. Your arrogance."

Diana smiled at Joanna. "Learned that from a master."

"Keep your mind off the smart remarks and on the target, eyass."

Diana's body relaxed and she turned to address Joanna. "I am ready, Joanna. If it were not for all these delays that have kept us in the homeworlds much longer than expected, I would be through with the Trial of Bloodright and on my way back to one of our Inner Sphere outposts. Instead, all I do from day to day is train. I need no more training. I need a battle before I forget how to think in one."

"I agree. The talk is that your Trial will begin soon, in a matter of days."

"They have been saying that for—"

"Wait. Look who has come to visit. Risa Pryde."

Star Colonel Risa Pryde had been the leader of House Pryde for many years and had, in fact, been the House Leader when Aidan Pryde competed for his bloodname. Although Risa Pryde was a small woman, Joanna thought she looked tinier than ever as she approached the two warriors. Thinner, too. Definitely thinner.

But she was as businesslike as ever.

"Your competition will begin in a week. Its date has been moved up because the saKhan has arrived on Ironhold for an inspection of various military production facilities. She will be in Ironhold City next week, and she wishes to observe the bloodname contests. Any that MechWarrior Diana participates in was her specific request. Be ready."

Joanna could sense Diana smiling, but she did not care to see it, so she did not turn around. Besides, there was a distraction. Over Risa's right shoulder Joanna saw a figure running toward them.

At first she thought it might be an attacker of some sort, although reason told her no one would start anything with someone as important as Risa Pryde here. Then she saw, by the pumping of his short legs, that it was Ravill Pryde.

"The Grand Melee will take place a week from today, so your first match will be a couple of days later. All is clear, *quiaff*?"

"Clear, aff," Joanna said. "House Leader Pryde, may I ask something?"

"Naturally."

Joanna looked into Risa Pryde's eyes. They seemed very tired, as though she were even more exhausted than Joanna herself.

"This information would normally come through regular channels. It is not usually delivered by the House Leader herself."

Risa Pryde frowned and sighed. "You are right. I am here

for another reason. You see, I anticipate a wave of protests at one of the Khans observing Diana's bloodname combat. Many of the warriors already take her participation as an insult, as you know. That is why I have strictly forbidden challenges and honor duels. Hard for me to prevent private brawls, though."

Her pointed glance at Diana displayed her knowledge of the fight in the holovid arena.

"Adding the saKhan to the mix will simply accelerate bad feeling. You know that I have been opposed to this from the beginning. I filed a formal protest with the Khan, which she has overruled. I have no choice but to accept her decision and make sure that the Trials proceed in a fair and honorable manner. Others, however, will not be so cooperative. I am here today to caution you to proceed with even more care. Nothing must mar the competition itself, no matter what the others do or say. I am sure Khan Marthe would say the same to you. You understand, *quiaff*?"

"Fully. I vow as a Jade Falcon officer that I will see to it that we do or say nothing that would bring shame to the way of the Clans."

Risa Pryde's brow furrowed. "I guess I will have to accept that although there is a certain ambiguity in it. Who can judge shame and who can say what action would precipitate it? But I trust you, Star Commander Joanna. Your record as a warrior and your heroism at the second battle of Twycross have won my admiration. Just see to it that your words do not backfire on you."

"I will, House Pryde Leader."

Joanna, as always, was fascinated by the formality of Risa Pryde's speech and wondered if she ever let herself go in order to have a good time with other warriors. As far as Joanna knew, Risa Pryde devoted her life to House Pryde.

Risa Pryde seemed ready to leave as Ravill Pryde came rushing up. Next to the short Risa Pryde, Ravill did not look quite so short, although he was a few centimeters shorter than Risa.

"I see, Risa Pryde, that you have preceded me with the news, *quiaff*?"

"Aff. Excuse my abrupt leave-taking, Star Colonel, but I have duties . . ."

"Of course."

Risa Pryde left them. Joanna noted that she did not walk like one hurrying off to attend to other matters.

Ravill Pryde stared at both Joanna and Diana for a long while before speaking. "Well, the flag is up, *quiaff*?"

There was a sarcasm in his voice that Joanna found difficult to interpret. Of course, she usually found any of his attempts at sarcasm obscure. Much of what he said was understood only by him. His actions, too, often lacked a sense that Joanna could discern. But on Twycross he had proven himself to be a fine Jade Falcon warrior, skilled at both combat and command, so she had stopped wishing for him to meet a bad end.

"I suppose the flag is up," Joanna said.

He turned toward Diana. "I cannot persuade you to give up this ambition for a bloodname?"

"What are you saying?" Joanna interrupted in a loud voice. "You are her sponsor! It is bad luck for a sponsor to speak so discouragingly!"

"Joanna," Diana said, "it is all right. Ravill Pryde is a reluctant sponsor of my candidacy, and I can live with that."

Ravill's tone turned icy. "But I do not know if I can. Daily I feel the shame of being your sponsor. I see the judgment against me in the eyes of others. I would have had several fights over it if Risa Pryde had not put a ban on them. I would never have sponsored you under normal conditions, and I regret that it became necessary. But I am not allowed to withdraw my sponsorship. Only you, Diana, may withdraw, and I ask you to do just that."

"Surat!" Joanna shouted. "How can you call yourself Jade Falcon? Clan warriors must stick by their words."

"You were not listening, Star Commander. I have no intention of interfering with Diana's candidacy now. I just think it would be better if she saw that her pursuit of this goal demeans our Clan and—"

"That is cowardly!" Joanna said.

"Cowardly? Perhaps in some lights, but it would be easily forgotten. Once Diana withdrew, someone would replace her and the Trials would go on. Her withdrawal would be seen by most as an honorable act."

"I meant that you are the coward, Ravill Pryde."

Ravill jumped at Joanna. The jump was necessary for him to attempt to punch the tall warrior in her face. The blow missed, and Joanna pivoted to land an elbow on the side of his cheek. He reeled sideways, then crouched to make the next assault.

But Diana stepped in between the two warriors.

"Stop! Risa Pryde has not even vacated the field and you two are breaking her law. At this moment, that would be disgraceful, *quiaff*?"

Both warriors relaxed. With the back of his hand, Ravill Pryde rubbed at the side of his face where Joanna's blow had landed.

"I must tell you, Star Colonel," Diana said calmly, "that there is nothing that would make me back away from, as you call it, my bloodname quest. I think you know that, *quiaff*?"

"Aff. But I want to make sure you know the dimensions of the damage you are causing, not just to yourself, but to the Clan overall. This is no mere adventure. Whether you win or not, your involvement in this Trial of Bloodright has severely shaken the Jade Falcons, and I do fear for its effects on all Clans, if we allow our bloodlines to be so diminished."

Ravill Pryde whirled around and began striding away.

Both visitors caused the angry Joanna to accelerate the day's training and Diana to push herself even more. Risa, because the imminence of the actual contest made Joanna wonder if Diana was as ready as she had claimed to be just moments ago. Ravill Pryde, because he made Joanna seethe and, as Diana's coach, led her to work her charge all the harder.

Diana was exhausted by the time they returned to the barracks. For a moment she did not even notice a familiar figure lounging beside the barracks doorway.

"You two surely look like the butt end of a surat," Horse said affably.

Diana ran to Horse and embraced him. It would have been difficult to decide who of the three warriors was most shocked by the act. Although some Clan warriors could be a bit demonstrative, such emotion was rare among the Jade Falcons. Horse looked uncomfortable in the tight grip of Diana's arms, Joanna was angry at a disgusting act that could only occur between a couple of freeborns, and Diana—who knew that she was glad to see Horse again after so long—was astonished by the spontaneity of her response to seeing him again.

They quickly parted and Diana backed away awkwardly. Horse grinned, which drew a responding smile from Diana. *Freeborns,* Joanna thought with distaste.

The next hour was taken up with Horse energetically telling them of his adventures in the long period since they had seen each other last. For Diana the story was invigorating. It rid her of the edginess she had felt right before Horse had arrived. Tales were like that for her. It did not matter whether Horse's report was meticulously accurate or exaggerated. She responded to the story itself. She asked Horse several questions during the narrative, made him go over an adventurous part again. Joanna, on the other hand, criticized Horse's actions mercilessly, telling him he should have acted sooner on this or that occasion. Horse managed to keep Diana fascinated while fending off Joanna's criticisms with the sort of skill he regularly showed piloting 'Mechs.

After Horse was done catching them up, the two women told Horse some of what they had been doing all this time, too. As Diana said, "It has been more waiting than anything else. Waiting, and Joanna making me work like a demon."

Horse glanced at Joanna and said, "I can well believe that."

Joanna merely grunted. Horse turned to Diana.

"Well, Diana, your training is about to become even more hellish. The Khan has assigned me to your training team."

Diana seemed happy, and Joanna resented her happiness. But there was no time for little resentments, she thought, not when there was so much to be accomplished to keep up Diana's edge. And, anyway, the training was getting to her, although she would not have admitted that to anyone. Her legs ached, then ached even more when she stubbornly refused to rest. Her eyes sometimes could not focus easily within short distances, and she made some judgments based on blurs. Sometimes she felt she must stop and rest, and so she ran an extra couple of kilometers.

Even she knew it was age catching up with her. But this was no time to let it. No time was a good time to let it.

12

Jade Falcon Tower
Ironhold City, Ironhold
Kerensky Cluster, Clan Space
18 February 3060

Formalities bored Samantha Clees. After being welcomed by the highest-ranking warriors on Ironhold, then conducted on an inspection of a munitions factory, followed by the grand tour of Ironhold City, she was glad to be alone in her room in the Falcon Tower. She felt as exhausted as if she had just battled with a trio of *Mad Dog*s on the edge of a high cliff.

If she had not been so tired she might have worked up enough energy to hate the room assigned to her.

I guess they think being at the top of a high tower, one of the few in the entire Kerensky Cluster, is considered to be exalted treatment for a saKhan. Scattering a few plush pieces of furniture and putting some OmniMech holos on the wall is supposed to accord me some kind of honor. A bed with wooden posts carved into a melange of intertwined falcons—falcons in flight, falcons attacking, falcons at rest—is supposed to make me feel at home. Well, the intention is good, but I feel better with undecorated rooms, plain furniture, a cot as hard as a rock, and an uncluttered floor that I can walk around on.

Samantha started to pace, as if measuring the workable parameters of the room.

The room was unimportant. She had to think out this part of her mission: the Diana quest for a bloodname. Dull as inspections were, she would rather have been watching the production line in a factory than considering this issue.

She paced in her usual scattershot pattern. For a while she merely walked back and forth. When she had had enough of walking back and forth, she strode toward the door of the room and paced to and from it for a while. Another variation in pattern occurred when she deliberately walked to the wall near the door, where the OmniMech holo hung, slightly atilt. She touched the wall with the tips of her fingers to push herself back, whirled around, and walked to a point on the opposite wall where a set of hooks for hanging clothes had been placed. She touched one of the hooks with the tips of her fingers, pushed herself back, whirled around, and went back to the wall containing the 'Mech holo. She could not keep her pacing on a regular and straightforward basis but had to keep changing directions, length of step, rate.

A firm knock on the door. She opened it and saw Grelev, the MechWarrior who had been assigned as her aide. Tall with dark features and dark hair, there was—as she had noticed earlier—the hint of a smile playing around his lips, even while his deep voice spoke with certainty and somberness.

"Star Colonel Ravill Pryde is here. You summoned him?"

"He came right away. A good sign, Grelev, *quiaff*?"

A twinkle in Grelev's eyes suggested that he was pleased to be asked his opinion by a saKhan.

"Aff, my Khan."

"Usher this Star Colonel in please."

"Right away."

Samantha took a deep breath, glad to get started with this thing.

Although she had consulted paperwork on this Star Colonel, the actual appearance of the man surprised her. His small stature was uncommon among Jade Falcon warriors, who ran to large and muscular. This short fellow was a Star Colonel even though he looked barely out of the vat. In spite of fairly even features on his small face, he reminded her of some kind of animal. Something rodentlike. Adding to this impression, she noted, were his small feet. However, all reports said that he was a good officer, disciplined and smart.

He came into the room and looked around slowly, as if he planned to inhabit it some day. Even the look he gave her was somewhat imperious.

Samantha took an instant dislike to Ravill Pryde. She suspected people often did.

After they went through the normal formalities of an officer reporting to his saKhan, they got down to business. Samantha was not much for small talk and neither, apparently, was Ravill Pryde.

"Star Colonel," she said. "It is odd to find you here on Ironhold, with your Falcon Guards still assigned to the Inner Sphere."

"I am only here as sponsor of the Falcon Guard Mech-Warrior Diana who will compete for the Pryde line bloodname. And, yes, I am eager to return to my command as soon as this is over with. Inaction is frustrating for a warrior, as such a fine one as yourself knows."

"I will ignore your last comment. Flattery is an ugly trait in a warrior."

"No flattery. Just stating facts."

Although Ravill Pryde stared at Samantha wide-eyed, the eyes were closed to her, denying her clues to the meanings of what he said.

"A sponsor does not have to actually attend the Trial of Bloodright, Star Colonel."

"My reasons are not exactly in accordance with Clan traditions," he said uneasily, "but they are, I feel, justified."

Samantha nodded. "As part of my current tour of Ironhold, I am overseeing the progress of the bloodname trials for Marthe Pryde. I would be most interested in your honest opinion."

Ravill cleared his throat before speaking. "I felt it was in my own interests to observe this Trial of Bloodright. I assume you know the circumstances surrounding the event."

Samantha nodded for him to continue.

"To sponsor a freeborn warrior for a bloodname reflects ultimately on me and my command role. I may always be associated with this folly. Still, the Khan—"

"I caution you to take care what you say about Khan Marthe Pryde."

"You requested honesty!" There was an edge of anger in Ravill Pryde's voice.

"All right, Star Colonel. Honesty."

"All I meant to say is that I acted at the request of the Khan to sponsor Diana. I registered my disapproval at the time."

"Yes, I have seen the record. I know that Khan Marthe is pleased by your loyalty and cooperation."

"I feel I must protect my interests here. I hope to one day rise further in the Clan hierarchy and—"

"That is obvious, Star Colonel. I applaud your ambitions."

Ravill clearly did not know how to take Samantha's

words. "This . . . this quest of Diana's could impede my progress, so I wish to know fully what happens here."

"If I had been brought into the formative stages of this decision," Samantha commented, "I would have discouraged this Diana from even dreaming of a bloodname for herself."

Ravill Pryde's grunt was, Samantha supposed, his way of laughing. "You do not know MechWarrior Diana," he said. "She is as stubborn as . . . as stubborn as—"

"As stubborn as Star Colonel Ravill Pryde, perhaps?"

She meant the comment in a friendly, conversational way, but—like many of her attempts at affability—it fell flat. Ravill Pryde was obviously irritated by her suggestion.

"She is stubborn, that is all," he said lamely.

"Star Colonel, in your opinion why did not Diana's free-born status disqualify her from the competition?"

"I believe that data has been misconstrued. Khan Marthe seems to think that Diana's heritage, as Aidan Pryde's daughter, makes her special. I do not agree, but she does have the Khan's support, and somehow this ugly Star Commander named Joanna is involved. I tell you, Khan Samantha, that this Joanna has been a—"

"I would suggest, Star Colonel, that you refrain from indulging your dislike of this warrior in my presence. Work out any bad feelings in a Circle of Equals. That is what the circle is for. Anger left to fester, well—"

"Anger? You do not know what anger is, until you have met Star Commander Joanna!"

Ravill Pryde stood in place and hardly moved, while Samantha fidgeted somewhat. She felt a need to pace, go back toward that wall with the uneven OmniMech holo and straighten it. But instead she tried to stand still, too.

"In the matter of Diana's bid for a bloodname, it will occur and there is no way I or Khan Marthe could stop it now, even if we wanted to."

Ravill Pryde slammed one fist into the open palm of the other. "The Steel Vipers are complaining incessantly about our Clan's soft treatment of freeborns. It has happened at least once before that a freebirth has won a bloodname, but no true Clansman can condone it. Personally, I believe there should be a formal ban on any freeborn laying claim to a bloodname, then we would not have the arrogant surats looking to raise themselves beyond their caste."

Even I have broader views than this narrow-minded, brain-frozen Star Colonel. But, brain-frozen or not, he is a ristar, and his beliefs may become the majority view. He is obviously ruthless. His record as a command officer is admirable, especially distinguished when you consider his heroic actions at the second battle of Twycross, but he does not instill confidence, not in me, at least. Kerensky forbid he could become a Khan of the Falcons. I have little ambition for myself, but whatever else I do I will have to stay ahead of this runt. You are on my surat list, Ravill Pryde. Forever.

She dismissed him and watched him walk crisply out of the office. A moment after the door closed, it opened again and Grelev took a step into the room, asking Samantha if there was anything more he could do. She said to summon Star Commander Joanna to her.

As she awaited Joanna's arrival, Samantha Clees reflected on her interview with Ravill Pryde.

Dealing with the Star Colonel brings back my feelings against all male warriors. I thought I had beaten that.

At one time Samantha had resented all Jade Falcon men. She had gone around with a chip on her shoulder, abusive to all and often insolent with male superior officers, actions that definitely held her back. After being bested in a Trial by a fellow female warrior, she had to listen to her opponent claim that Samantha had lost because she had no discipline. The other warrior said that resentment colored all her actions. The words had gotten to Samantha, and thereafter she worked on mastering both discipline and her emotions, and the self-training had led to her becoming a much better officer, eventually Galaxy Commander of the Gyrfalcon Falcons. Even now, though, when she encountered a man like

Ravill Pryde, the old anti-male feelings rose briefly within her.

Grelev brought in Joanna, who did not look as if she wanted to have this interview. She greeted Samantha according to custom, then stood silently at attention as she waited for Samantha to speak. Samantha told her to relax, but even the other warrior's at-ease stance looked pretty stiff. Samantha offered her a seat, in order to encourage informality, but Joanna refused. She positioned herself behind the piece of furniture, often putting her hands on the back of the chair, sometimes using it as a pivot when with her other hand she gestured to support her statements, and sometimes as a focus of punishment as she battered the back of it with her fist.

Joanna's reputation for rising to anger easily apparently was justified. It exploded almost instantly. And with the most logical question.

"Do you believe that you do the Clan a disservice by remaining a warrior when you are past the usual solahma age?" Samantha asked.

Joanna's eyes blazed. "I serve the Clan."

"But, when Star Colonel Ravill Pryde wanted to reassign you to homeworld duty, you protested."

"And I still protest! I am a warrior, and that is that. I trained Marthe Pryde and I will not bow down to her any more than I will bow down to you! You cannot question my codex and you know it! If you tried to reassign me now, I would protest and, more than that—"

"Do not say it. We do not question your courage or your loyalty, Star Commander Joanna," Samantha said, with more control than she thought herself capable. "In this, well, delicate situation, you have taken on a great responsibility as the coach of MechWarrior Diana."

"Do you find my role in Diana's training team inappropriate, because of my advanced age?"

"I am not concerned with your age, Star Commander, but there may be others who believe that having a Clan hero as coach perhaps distorts the warrior's claim. And in this case it is especially important to—"

"Examine my codex before you start making such claims! My ratings as a training officer for sibkos is enough justification for my ability to train any warrior, free or true."

Samantha sighed. "Your ability is not in question. I am referring to a volatile situation that has already caused brawls and challenges for Trials of Refusal."

"Trials that should have been allowed to proceed, but for Risa Pryde's intrusions."

This Joanna could certainly rattle the most patient of listeners, and Samantha did not consider herself patient.

"Star Commander, do I understand you to say that the turmoil you and your group have created during your current stay here on Ironhold is beneficial to your cause?"

"I think I meant that, yes."

"Explain, please."

Both of Joanna's hands grasped the back of the chair as she clearly tried to speak without her characteristic anger. "I believe in turmoil. When I was a falconer, I always kept my charges off-balance. I punished them more severely than they deserved, withheld deserved praise. I used punishment liberally and never felt a day was a success unless I saw blood on at least one cadet face. To me, right now, MechWarrior Diana is the equivalent of one of those cadets. I mean to make her life more miserable day to day. I intend for her to be undistracted by any weakness, always ready to cut a throat if it means victory."

Samantha agreed that the methods Joanna described were necessary, even admirable, for warrior training. She had just never heard them expressed so baldly.

Joanna talked on without interruption for another minute or so, finishing with, "So you see, I cannot regret any turmoil we have caused here on Ironhold. We have our goal, the bloodname. Anyone who gets hurt, or even killed, on our way to it is not significant to me."

"Not significant?" Samantha said, this time feeling her

own anger "Even if they are trueborn and your charge is freeborn?"

Joanna's rage left her suddenly. Her gray eyes went cold. She looked more dangerous than she had when shouting with anger. She spoke in a detached, colder-than-her-eyes voice.

"I am Jade Falcon. Forever. I grew up in a sibko of brawling warriors who were taught the ways of killing even before we were cadets. Although many flushed out of training, several passed their Trials of Position. Unlike me, most won their bloodnames when they competed, usually on the first try."

Although Joanna maintained her detachment, Samantha thought she detected a slight vocal interruption, a gasp or an emotion threatening to interfere but failing, during her comment about her own failure to get a bloodname. Samantha suddenly imagined what it must have been like all these years for this warrior without a bloodname and without the glory of an honorable death.

Distracted by her thoughts, she missed the next section of Joanna's speech. Her concentration returned as Joanna said, in a slightly stronger voice: ". . . saKhan or not, you have no right to suggest that my support of a freeborn warrior in any way changes my loyalty toward the Clan or trueborns. I merely believe that, at a time when we need all our warriors to continue the cause, it is not inappropriate to allow a proven warrior of whatever origin to seek the bloodname."

"Well-argued, Star Commander," Samantha said. "I will take your words into account. Dismissed."

Samantha's abrupt dismissal caused a flicker of surprise to cross Joanna's face but, in fine warrior fashion, she wheeled around and exited the room. After she was gone, Samantha took a moment to regain her calm.

This warrior could rattle anyone. On the other hand, the anger in her is quite similar to what I felt early in my career. Stravag! Joanna is the warrior I might have become if I had not turned my career around. I do not enjoy thinking of that.

Samantha began to pace again. To the door, back to the room's single window.

If we were Smoke Jaguars, or even Steel Vipers, this problem would not exist. They do not allow freeborns to be warriors. Perhaps a better policy, certainly a less complicated one. But I would not wish to be either a Jaguar or a Viper. As Joanna put it, I am Jade Falcon—to the core.

Since we allow freeborns to be warriors and have gained by using them in roles where trueborns would be wasted, we have established the dilemma of what to do with those freeborns who are extraordinary warriors. Mostly, our freeborns are not in circumstances where they would make any claim to deserve a bloodname. But . . . Aidan Pryde was a hero and his daughter is not only a warrior with an outstanding codex but her genetics are untainted, except for the circumstances of her birth itself.

The fact is that she is a freeborn, however, no matter what heroic matter is in her blood or her cursed codex. As I have told Marthe, she has unsettled our Clan merely by opening the possibility of a freebirth winning a bloodname.

Samantha stopped pacing. She stood at the room's single window and stared down at the streets below. Far below, from this vantage point. As a leader, she had been raised above Jade Falcon warriors, perhaps too far, perhaps from a height like this top floor of the Jade Falcon Tower. She whirled around and began to walk more slowly across the room's thick rug.

This Joanna is our conscience, an angry warrior, capable of responding to challenge fully and without doubt, the kind of warrior we think we are but do not regularly succeed at being. No subtleties, no secrets, no deceptions. If anyone can push MechWarrior Diana to the bloodname, Star Commander Joanna can do it. And there is a part of me that irrationally believes that she will. Perhaps Marthe has finally convinced me. A part of me sees Diana's situation as a grand experiment, and I am most anxious to learn the outcome.

Samantha stopped pacing again and her eyes scanned the

room. The surroundings still made her uneasy. But she felt better when she went to the crooked OmniMech holo and finally straightened it.

13

Jade Falcon Headquarters
Warrior Sector, Ironhold City
Ironhold
Kerensky Cluster, Clan Space
19 February 3060

"**E**nter, but be ready to have your legs shot off for the interruption," Ravill Pryde shouted rudely.

Samantha smiled before entering. Clearly, he was not expecting a visit from his saKhan. Who would?

When he saw it was Samantha, his face reddened slightly, but he did not get flustered. He merely stood up and said in a laconic voice, "I was expecting a subordinate."

"It is my duty, Star Colonel Ravill Pryde, to inform you that Khan Marthe Pryde—in her capacity as a senior member of House Pryde—has appointed you acting Leader of House Pryde for the current Trials of Bloodright. Although other higher-ranking officers are present on Ironhold, they are involved in vital war preparation activities. You are here, by your own admission, to observe the bloodname contests as an interested party. Your have no other official military duties to prevent you from attending to this post. As the commander of the Falcon Guards, you are the logical choice. You will hold the post of House Leader until the formal election, which will be held when a quorum of representatives of House Pryde can be assembled for the vote."

"House Leader?" Ravill Pryde said, clearly astonished. "But Risa Pryde is the—"

"Risa Pryde is dead. The Grand Melee must be postponed a few more days. Since there have already been too many delays, it is necessary for you to take over immediately. You must learn your duties as Oathmaster with all possible haste. You are known to be a quick study, after all. Khan Marthe Pryde wishes the bloodname Trials to resume as soon as you are ready. Of course it will be necessary for you to supervise all the aspects of the Trials."

Samantha stopped and indicated he could respond now.

"Did someone kill Risa Pryde, assassinate her? Did she lose her life in an honor duel? Was—"

"Risa Pryde simply died. The medexaminer used some term like cardiac arrest. A rare death but not impossible. Warriors die. It happens."

"But Risa Pryde was not ailing," Ravill Pryde insisted. "Someone must have wished her harm."

"Our medtechs assure me that the body was fully examined. There was no foul play, no sign of a fight. Risa Pryde merely died. Her heart stopped. Why do you smile, Ravill Pryde?"

"Was I smiling? I did not realize. I was just thinking, how shamed Risa Pryde must be, wherever she is. If there is any afterlife, she must be cursing up a storm."

"Afterlife? Who cares about an afterlife? What is now is what is important. The Trial must take place. Within the hour you will receive all the information you will need regarding the role of House Leader. Please arrange for the ceremonial robes and familiarize yourself with the Bloodright coin ritual. I have instructed my aide, Grelev, to see to it that everything is properly done. He will also be here within the hour."

"I do not wish an aide. I can—"

"You will accept the gift of Grelev with grace and dignity, Ravill Pryde, *quiaff*?"

"Aff."

Samantha turned and abruptly left. As she walked back to
Jade Falcon Tower, she was conscious of the many people
in the broad boulevard that bisected Ironhold City who
pointed or nodded surreptitiously toward her, obviously
noting the presence of the saKhan among them.

*What will this mean, Risa Pryde's death? There will be
some reaction, I think. As Ravill Pryde said, warriors simply do not die in bed—although Risa Pryde died at her desk.*

Samantha had been summoned to Risa Pryde's office after it happened. She had looked down at the older warrior's
head resting on the desktop. *How peaceful she looked. Not
sad, as Ravill might have expected. It was as if she had
merely gotten tired and put her head down for a doze. Perhaps she never knew she was not dying a warrior's death.
She would never have had a thought about it. And why
should there be an afterlife? Life is enough. Warriors die
before the battle is won, leaders die before their goals are
achieved, Khans die in flames. There cannot be an afterlife
for warriors. How could it satisfy them?*

Grelev handed Ravill Pryde a rather thick sheaf of bound
papers.

"What are these?"

"That is the manual for the Leader of House Pryde."

"I have to read all this?"

"I have marked the relevant passages you need now. You
can absorb the rest at your leisure."

"What leisure?"

"I will help. I am proficient at scheduling."

"You are proficient at scheduling. You think highly of
yourself."

"I am as good at scheduling as I am at combat skills."

"I do not like you, Grelev, and I do not need your help."

"The saKhan's orders, Star Colonel."

"Stay out of my way."

"I will wrap myself in the background shadows, sir."

Grelev paused. "*After* I provide your daily schedule and indicate where in the manual you can find—"

"Oh, shut up, Grelev! I might be stuck with you, but you may be dead before our relationship is terminated."

"One of us may be dead, sir."

At first Ravill was angered by the apparent insubordination, then he laughed. "This begins an ugly relationship, Grelev, *quiaff*?"

"Aff."

"One more delay and, I swear, I am going to give all this up and just return to the ranks, a normal, content, everyday warrior. Without a bloodname!"

Diana was rankling at the postponement of the competition for another few days. Joanna, seeing that the edge was already off for Diana, vowed to push her all the harder.

It might have been better if Diana could vent her rage with a few fist-fights or honor duels within the Circle of Equals. But saKhan Clees had endorsed the banning of them by the late House Leader. In a meeting the day before, Samantha Clees made it clear that Diana's behavior would be closely observed.

Joanna did not care much for Samantha Clees. But there were so many other Jade Falcons that Joanna despised that a mild dislike for any person in authority did not matter much to her.

As they were walking away from the saKhan's quarters, Diana had muttered that she felt as if she would spend the rest of her life waiting for this competition to begin. They had been waiting for months already, as the preceding competitions dragged on. Due to the plethora of bloodnames available, the sheer number of bloodname contests here and on Strana Mechty and elsewhere had become unwieldy and created a spectacle that had drawn hordes of merchants and opportunists to the periphery of the contests themselves.

Joanna detested the delays, too. They seemed to sap Diana's energy, make her irritable, and even affect her focus in training. Horse's joining the training team about two weeks ago had not seemed to improve matters. Today, in the training field, Joanna had had to put Diana through hell just to perform simple routines. In the simulator Diana had been defeated twice by inferior BattleMechs, something that rarely happened with a MechWarrior as sharp, experienced, and well-trained as Diana.

And she *was* well-trained. Joanna had poured all the skill of her many years as a falconer into the training of Diana. She had never put any cadet through the hell she had created for Diana, even cadets whom she had deeply hated. And she did not even hate Diana. Over the years she had come to— what was the word?—*like* Diana? Well, for Joanna, like might be too strong a word. She could not imagine actually liking anybody. But she *almost* liked Diana. And Horse.

Sometimes she wondered if she had liked Aidan Pryde. He had interested her, that was certain. But liking him would have been too hard. She could not have liked him. It was curious, though, in all her years of coupling with various Jade Falcons, the only memories of the experience she ever recalled were her few nights with Aidan Pryde when he was a cadet. She had forced him to come to her, and he had not wanted to be there. His subdued defiance had been clear to her and had become part of the coupling itself. For a moment or two, as she remained in control but threatened, she had even liked coupling, an activity that was usually just a release of edginess for her.

Now, it seemed, Diana could not stop her threats to abandon the bloodname contest. It was becoming more annoying.

"You give up now and you know what will happen," Joanna said, with a rare calmness.

"You will kill me."

"Diana, you can bet on it."

"Fighting you would at least give me something to aspire to. This waiting around, without a real fight, does strange things to my mind. I cannot concentrate. I can hardly even think. I just want to go somewhere and, I do not know, beat up a tree or a concrete building or something."

Joanna nodded. "I know the feeling, Diana. I have lived with it for most of my warrior life."

"Another insult. Now you seem to say I am becoming like you."

Joanna shrugged. "If you wish to think so."

"Would you be honored—if I was like you, I mean?"

"Hardly."

"Nobody could be like Star Commander Joanna," came a new voice. Both women turned toward the doorway, where they saw the thick-bearded, thick-bodied Horse leaning against the doorway. "To be like her, Diana, you would have to be a paragon of rage. It would be harder than winning a bloodname, believe me."

"I know. I am just a bit rattled. It has been the waiting more than anything else that makes me edgy. Waiting and Joanna making me work like a demon."

Horse glanced at Joanna and said, "I can well believe that."

Joanna merely grunted.

"Ravill Pryde has been appointed Leader of House Pryde by the saKhan," she said after a long pause.

Horse's eyes widened. "Ravill Pryde House Leader? How—I mean, what about Risa Pryde?"

"She is dead. Died a natural death, actually, if you believe that."

"You mean, she just died? Died like that? Not in a battle or a fight or accident or—"

"Just died. Went to sleep, did not wake up."

"It happens, I guess. But I thought only solahmas died natural deaths, and then only rarely."

"Freeborns die naturally, I hear."

"Well, yes. I only meant warriors." Horse seemed disturbed. "I guess it means that we need another war."

"Good idea. Go create one, Horse."

Joanna, who had come as close to liking Risa Pryde as she came to liking anybody, recalled that she had noticed that the House Leader looked particularly tired during her training field visit and wondered if that had been a clue to her coming fate, an omen.

After a pause, Horse said, "Ravill Pryde will preside over the Trials of Bloodright? Specifically, at Diana's?"

"True."

"Hard to believe."

"Hard."

"I hope it is not an omen."

"Of what?"

"I don't know, but not anything good."

"Stop the contractions. You know I cannot stand them. Especially when we are threatened."

"Threatened? What about?"

"I am not sure. I guess I am the one thinking about omens now."

The news of Risa Pryde's death spread rapidly through Ironhold. Jade Falcons in all castes stopped to wonder how such a thing as a natural death to a warrior could even happen. They had to conclude that, once in a while, a disease slipped by all the preventives of Clan medical science or a heart simply stopped without any weaponry involved.

Nomad, drunk in a tech sector bar, delighted in the irony of the demise. Samantha, who had barely known Risa Pryde, was annoyed at the inconvenience of the warrior's passing. Back on Strana Mechty, Marthe Pryde found she did not remember Risa Pryde well.

After Samantha had left his quarters, Ravill Pryde realized that, ambitious as he was, he felt uncomfortable with the rise in position afforded him by Risa's death. This was not an honor, but a detour on his way up. As the saKhan had indicated, he would not hold the job long. He sincerely hoped that proved true.

But everyone got through the day with their occasional reflections on the passing of Risa Pryde and, the next day, only a few even thought of her. Even Ravill Pryde was too busy to care who had been responsible for thrusting him into the quagmire of his new Jade Falcon role.

14

Science Research and Education Center
Ironhold City, Ironhold
Kerensky Cluster, Clan Space
19 February 3060

Etienne Balzac never raised his voice. As Scientist-General of the Jade Falcon scientist caste, he did not have to. He had subordinates who could do that for him. As he leaned toward Peri Watson, she thought she could detect a faint odor on his breath. A faint, chemical odor.

"Those children are not your concern," he said. "Nor is any other project to which you are not assigned."

The man had grown more bloated since she had last seen him. His complexion was paler than ever, perhaps due to his not leaving the Science Research and Education Center very often. He remained in this office and his own quarters nearby most of the time, studying all the projects going on within the scientist caste, while looking for more ways to consolidate his power.

"With all due respect, Scientist-General, I believe it is my concern. The genetics of Aidan Pryde must not be misused, and I believe that—"

"That is sufficient, Peri Watson. I do not know why you see conspiracies everywhere you look. There is no cooperation in some chain of secret projects among the scientists of different Clans. We barely communicate and then only to exchange useful information in open conferences, diplomatic missions at best. Anything we discover that is useful to *all* Clans is readily available to all. Jade Falcon scientists work for the good of the Clan and all Clans, that is all, *quiaff*? I take your silence as an act of insubordination."

He takes this general role too seriously, Peri thought. *Even his office reflects that. Everything in its place. Materials on desktop neatly arranged in geometric pattern. The proper Clan history holos on the wall. Furniture suitable more to the stark demands of warriors.*

"I am not insubordinate, Scientist-General. If I were not loyal to my Clan, I would not be here. As a scientist I wish to continue serving the Clan. I am currently between assignments, on research leave, and so I request formally to be assigned to Sibko Training Center 111."

Balzac turned away, returning to his neat and polished desk. "Request denied. Dismissed."

Peri noted the militaristic style of address. The man was too pompous for words.

"What assignment do you suggest?"

"You know the proper channels. Use them."

"I thought that you—"

"You were mistaken. I repeat, dismissed. The next time I say it, you will leave with a guard escort, Peri Watson."

"Very well," Peri said, knowing she had no other choice.

After she had left, Balzac thought for a long time, while staring at a painting of the battle of Tukayyid that he had positioned beside his desk. The artist's conception was intended to depict Aidan Pryde's final moments in that battle, the final event in the series that led to his enshrinement as a Jade Falcon hero. Balzac doubted that the real battle looked anything like this artist's version, with Pryde in his *Timber Wolf,* blue fire shooting from his lasers, enemy 'Mechs falling around him, Aidan's 'Mech itself a mountain towering over the action. Something about the *Timber Wolf* was off. It was a bit too tall, its width a bit too broad. Artist's license, Balzac decided, as he switched on his intercom and summoned the head of his guards, Olan.

* * *

The tall and thin Olan stood at ease before Balzac. Even in starched fatigues, the man looked disreputable. Well, he had been a bandit for some time.

"You will need to perform another elimination, Olan. I would like you to choose two of your best people for the job."

Olan nodded. He never talked much and when he did, it was only in a few words. "The target?" was what he now said.

"Named Peri Watson."

"The one who just left."

"Yes. But, remember, I cannot be connected to the deed, nor should the scientist caste be. I do not want you carrying any ID in case anything goes wrong."

"Naturally."

"Plan well, but do it soon."

"My duty."

"Dismissed."

Olan, expressionless, bowed and left the room. For a second or two Balzac regretted the necessity of the elimination. But soon he returned to his routine, intensely examining reports, commenting on progress, calling in various scientists working on various projects. Work was always his best palliative and, by the end of the day, he had forgotten about Peri Watson.

Keeping matters in compartments was his best qualification as Scientist-General. It had helped in his scheming to gain the office and it would continue to aid him in doing what few of his predecessors had accomplished, staying in office alive. He had seen early that, within the scientist caste, intrigue created success, and he had become skilled at intrigue. He was so skilled at it that few ever caught him doing it. It was clear, however, that Peri Watson had and, when he saw that, her fate was sealed.

=== 15 ===

Bloodname Plains
Ironhold
Kerensky Cluster, Clan Space
26 February 3060

Joanna, perturbed as ever, watched the tail end of the
Grand Melee. She found the melee uninteresting, but she
had no choice about being there. The Grand Melee was
the beginning of the House Pryde bloodname Trials, after
all. It was unlikely, but still possible, that Diana might have
to face the winner of the melee somewhere along the way,
and Joanna believed in knowing the most you can about
your competition.

Generally, the Grand Melee sounded better than it turned
out to be, at least to trained eyes like Joanna's. As a former
falconer she could trace nearly all mistakes through simple
observation. It was as if the BattleMech, the armored fighting machine that, with its limbs and at least the suggestion
of a head, had a body language similar to its human pilot.
What she saw in this sloppy Grand Melee was a pack of
'Mech pilots who, while they might be sturdy warriors in
the heat of combat, had lost too much edge to compete well
in a rule-bound trial. In such a contest she merely noted
poor training, bad habits, eroded skills. Perhaps that was no
more than could reasonably be expected. After all, these
were the warriors no regular warrior wanted to sponsor and
so did not represent the best of the breed.

For this melee she could not even pick a winner. Whoever

survived among the many who competed, that warrior would almost certainly be defeated in the next round.

Standing next to Joanna now, as the Grand Melee wore down to a quartet of contestants almost blindly searching for each other across the ravaged plain, was Ravill Pryde. Ever since his appointment as House Leader, Ravill had looked even more surly and uncomfortable than ever.

She had felt Ravill's steady gaze on her even while not looking his way. She wondered what he saw—a wreck of a face under ever-graying hair?

Some of the younger warriors regularly exhibited their disgust at Joanna's age, and she had taught several of them painful lessons. However, as most other warriors noticed, she rarely showed her age in her walk or in the way she stood. At those times she could be mistaken for a much younger warrior. Her status as the hero-conquerer of the Wolf Clan legend, Natasha Kerensky, added to her image among the younger warriors and, she had heard, there were even a few who had formed a kind of cult that secretly honored her. She found that hard to accept and figured they must be other outcasts among warriors.

Suddenly Joanna was aware that Ravill had just addressed her.

"I am sorry, Oathmaster, my mind was elsewhere." She enjoyed addressing him as Oathmaster. It seemed to make the little ferret even more uneasy.

Ravill surprised her by grinning. "I merely observed that this melee's warriors could use a crash course from you in basic training."

"I have not trained a sibko in a decade."

Ravill nodded. "I know, but here on Ironhold your reputation as a falconer and combat hero is quite formidable, I have observed."

"I am honored, Oathmaster."

As she resumed her observation of the melee, watching the final pair of contestants maneuver their BattleMechs clumsily, almost as if their pilots realized that who won did not matter, Joanna thought, as she often did, of her anomalous position among warriors. She had proven herself as the best among unblooded warriors and longed for this long Trial of Bloodright to be over so she could return to a combat unit.

Marthe Pryde had promised her that, if she returned to the homeworlds for Diana's contest, she would not lose her position as a combat officer in the Jade Falcon occupation force. They had promised not to reassign her to a solahma unit in the homeworlds, but every day she spent away from the front lines made her more uneasy. Especially with Ravill Pryde here on Ironhold and now head of House Pryde. He wanted Joanna out of the Falcon Guards, his command, and he made no secret of that. Had she not ended up a hero in the second Twycross battle, she would have been shipped out long ago, reassigned to some shameful role.

"Well, that is over," Ravill said suddenly, and Joanna realized she had missed the whole finish of the Grand Melee. One of the warriors, the loser, was being carried away on a stretcher. From what Joanna could see, the warrior's leg was severely injured. A gaping wound revealed the mess inside, and Joanna could not help thinking how much uglier than the inside of a 'Mech leg, where a mass of twisted myomer fiber was usually the most inartistic damage.

"What did you think, Joanna?"

"A desultory display, not worthy of Jade Falcons."

Ravill nodded. "I agree. I hope to see better from here on in."

Joanna wondered if the carefully planned Clan eugenics program had somehow resulted in ever weakened generations of warriors. And the proof of that now stood before her. Ravill Pryde, a sort of genetic mutation as Jade Falcons went, with his mixture of Falcon and Wolf genes, was a brave enough warrior, but he seemed corrupted in some way she had never quite been able to define. There was definitely something different about him. Yet most others did not seem to see it. She wondered if the good warriors were being produced at the old rate. Why was she seeing fewer Aidan Prydes and more Ravills?

A few years back, the head of the Watch, Kael Pershaw, had sent her on a mission to investigate some genetic violations that his secret service had detected. Her spying had revealed that the scientist caste was regularly tampering with Clan genetics, sometimes even combining genes from different Clans.

When her mind dwelled on this subject, she decided that too many warriors had been killed in the costly and devastating battles that had been part of the Inner Sphere invasion. The ranks had, simply, been weakened. The genetic tamperings were irrelevant.

Diana would not have been allowed to compete but for the lack of eligible warriors. From Joanna's viewpoint, the current situation was pathetic. Had she encountered this same kind of field in her own days of competing, she would have strolled to a bloodname. Joanna *did* deserve a bloodname, and nobody knew that better than Joanna.

Forget the bloodname. All that matters now is to remain a warrior and to return to the battlefield. And I will get the chance when the invasion resumes.

Ravill Pryde was going on about something. Joanna had stopped listening to him. "I must go now, congratulate the Grand Melee winner. The win was so sloppy, the words will choke my throat."

The House Leader walked off abruptly. As soon as he was gone, Horse came to her side.

"Interesting rumors," he said.

"Oh?"

"They say that, on Strana Mechty, Marthe Pryde is fighting simulations of the invasion of the Inner Sphere, exercises designed to eliminate the mistakes of the first incursion. She is relentless about it, I hear, pushing everyone the way we push Diana. I am certain that Samantha Clees will be recalled at any moment."

"I will not miss her."

Joanna just wanted to get away from this place and force Diana to outdo herself, now that the bloodname Trials had finally started. She needed the new invasion. If there was

not something big soon, somebody might make another
move to retire her or reassign her to a solahma unit. She did
not plan to be solahma, ever. She had every intention of going down in flames in front-line combat.

"Diana will be competing tomorrow," she said. "We have
the rest of today to make her life hell."

===== **16** =====

Gyrfalcon Marketplace
Ironhold City, Ironhold
Kerensky Cluster, Clan Space
27 February 3060

Normally the business of the renowned Gyrfalcon Marketplace was a small daily event. Craftsmen showed their
handiwork, and people came because of the high quality of
the goods. But, with the extended string of bloodname combats going on in the city, new merchants peddled wares that
were sometimes not up to the standard of the market. As a
result, there had been a few clumsy skirmishes among the
merchants, usually with a permanent seller attacking one
of the intruders and trying to smash the inferior merchan-
dise. The intruding merchants had brought in bodyguards to
protect them. Some suspected that these bodyguards were
from the bandit caste, since they tended to disappear when
some authority figure came to browse in the marketplace.

Peri knew little of this as she fingered a gauzy shawl that
a merchant had draped over the side of his table. There was
not much pattern to it, but the weaving was close and it was
difficult to tell where the threads of a color blended into a

slightly different shade of the same color. The merchant started to quote her a price, but she released the cloth and walked away quickly. She did not much want to buy anything, but she liked walking through marketplaces. It was relaxing, and she enjoyed taking in all the sights, sounds, scents, and colors.

She stopped at a booth featuring wooden furniture in old-fashioned, reconstructed styles. For a long while she examined an oak desk that she would have liked for her office, except that she had no office now. With Etienne Balzac's hostility toward her and the scientist caste's tendency to isolate its recalcitrant, potentially rebellious members to backwater assignments, there would be no reason to possess even such a fine piece as this desk. And the word was that Balzac would again send her somewhere far from Ironhold on her next assignment. The desk was too expensive for her, anyway. Oak trees were rare on Clan worlds, having been transplanted so long ago from faraway Terra.

To avoid the haggling of the merchant, she glanced outward from the dim booth at the brightness outside. After blinking to focus, she saw a figure who seemed vaguely familiar to her. She took a step toward the edge of the booth and squinted to see better.

It was her daughter, Diana, idly browsing at an ancient weapons table.

Peri had known Diana was on Ironhold competing for the Pryde bloodname and had chosen not to distract her by making her presence known. She remembered Diana as a squalling pinch-faced baby and then as a bright, inquisitive child, one for whom Peri had foreseen a life as a scientist. But the genetic trait of Aidan Pryde, her father, had emerged instead. Nevertheless, as Diana's mother, even one whose trueborn heritage prevented her from any deep motherly feelings, Peri was proud of anything Diana achieved. Her heroism in battle was a mirror of the heroism of her father.

Peri admired her daughter's audacity and was pleased by how good a warrior she had become, but she was not comfortable with the idea of a freeborn acquiring a bloodname.

Peri held contradictory feelings on this subject. She did not believe Diana should be competing, yet she hoped Diana would win.

In case her own confusion might somehow affect Diana, hurt her, Peri thought it best not to see her until after the contest was over. She stood within the darkness of the booth until Diana had passed on, after skillfully bartering with the arms merchant for an ivory-handled knife.

How long had it been since she and Diana had had any communication? Over the years they had sent each other messages, but they had been as cold and emotionless as the screens on which they were displayed. Diana had looked well—tall and strong and beautiful. The light in her eyes was the same light that had shown from her father's eyes. It had always seemed to be there, contradicting his sadness or despair, even in his darkest moods. A light in the midst of the bleakest darkness.

I have to stop thinking like this. Too much stupid senti-mentality. All these ancient feelings. Feelings are much too dangerous.

When she had finished her tour of the marketplace, Peri decided to return to her temporary quarters, a building maintained by the scientist caste for its transitory personnel and official visitors. She had a tiny room there—she had asked for the smallest room available and the building concierge had been meticulous about accommodating her request.

Three or four blocks from the marketplace, she realized she had taken a wrong turn somewhere. She walked to a corner, looked down the intersecting street both ways and saw nothing she recognized. These streets and the street ahead looked bleak, and she did not recall ever being in this part of Ironhold City.

"You are lost, *quiaff*?" said a deep, almost gentle voice behind her.

Startled, she turned around to face a tall, thin man dressed in the uniform of a Jade Falcon warrior. His face was bland and his pale, nearly colorless eyes almost nonexistent. He was one of those men who regularly seemed in need of a shave. Why, she wondered, did they not just grow the full beards so popular among many male warriors of the Clans?

"Aff, I do not seem to know this sector," Peri said.

"This is a warehouse district. What do you look for?"

"The Scientist Residence Complex."

"Ah. Not far from here."

"Can you direct me?"

"I will take you there."

The man started walking abruptly, turning right at the intersection. Peri almost did not follow him, since she was so surprised by the quick way he moved on and the fact he did not look back to see if she was following. She ran to catch up with him, and he barely gave her a look. Noticing the patch on his sleeve, a swooping falcon (another surprise), she said, "You are with the Falcon Guards?"

"Aff."

"I heard that Ravill Pryde had been appointed House Leader, but I thought the Falcon Guards were still stationed in the Inner Sphere."

"They are," he said, without even glancing toward her.

"Are you part of the bloodright trials?"

"The trials? Yes, I am."

Something about the way he said it made her feel he did not know what she referred to.

"Are you part of MechWarrior Diana's team?"

"Diana. Yes, I am."

"What do you think about the controversy over her seeking the bloodname?"

"It does not concern me."

Not the response of a typical trueborn Falcon warrior. He could be on Diana's side or against her, but this diffidence was unusual.

"Do you think, as some do, that she is too short to be a bloodnamed warrior?"

"That does not concern me."

Peri stopped walking. "It does not concern you because you do not know what I am talking about."

"This is the way to your residence complex," he said, turning into an alleyway that she had not noticed before.

She had a moment of hesitation about following him, but her curiosity propelled her onward.

"You do not know who Diana is, *quiaff*?" she said as she entered the alleyway. The man walked on ahead of her, apparently indifferent to her.

"It does not matter," he said.

"You are wearing a Falcon Guard uniform, but you are not a Falcon Guard, *quiaff*?"

"It does not matter," he said and turned. Even in the dimness of the alleyway, Peri could see the man's hands curling into fists. Behind him she saw two other figures emerge from the shadows. If she was not mistaken, they too wore Falcon Guard uniforms.

She started backing away and stumbled. She fell against a wall and had to struggle to keep her footing.

The man seized her shoulders and lifted her off the ground. There was a strong smell coming from him, one that recalled to her the odors she had noticed in the area around Etienne Balzac's headquarters. For a moment she got to look into his eyes and saw nothing there. Then he threw her to the others, and they began striking her.

She took many blows—many brutal, painful blows—before she passed out.

=== 17 ===

"**D**iana, she may not open her eyes for days, weeks," Joanna said, her voice unusually soft, probably because hospitals seemed to demand lowered voices. "She may be in a coma, for Kerensky's sake."

Diana did not even look over her shoulder, but instead continued to stand by the suspension shell in which Peri's body seemed to float, even though it was clearly connected to a double bank of diagnostic and medicine-providing equipment. It looked eerie, especially with the complex of tubing around it, leading into the shell and then through narrower lines of tubing into various parts of Peri's body. Although dressed in a hospital gown that seemed draped on her, Peri's arms, legs, and face still showed the dark and purple bruises of her beating. A medtech had told them that the attack should have killed her. However, she had been improving slowly but steadily since her suspension in the transparent shell, where curatives were administered at intervals through tubes.

Joanna realized as she looked at the body in the shell that she had not thought of Peri in years. Peri had long ago flushed out of the same sibko that had produced Aidan and Marthe, when she and Joanna met again. Aidan had fled Ironhold, and Ter Roshak had sent Joanna and a peculiar tech named Nomad to seek him. When they finally found him, he was with Peri at a scientific outpost on the planet Tokasha. By that time, although neither Joanna nor Aidan would know of it until years later, Diana had been conceived and would be born a few months after Aidan's departure. Joanna felt sick to her stomach. She did not like to think of natural childbirth.

"Diana, your first bloodname trial is tomorrow. Hanging around this place is not going to—"

"Shut up, Joanna."

Normally Joanna would have reacted to the insolence, but this time her old falconer instincts kicked in and told her to allow Diana some latitude. She did not want anything to interfere with the edge Diana would need to win a bloodname.

What am I thinking? When all this started I did not really believe she could do it. Oh, I knew that as a Jade Falcon warrior and the daughter of Aidan Pryde she has all the instincts to fight well. And with that extra degree of fierceness that not every Clan warrior can claim. Horse says there were clans in Terran history that were called barbarians. They were famed for their cruelty, their savagery, their ability not only to pierce the skin with a knife but to twist it afterward. When she fights, Diana has that kind of quality. She is a true barbarian. But not a trueborn, that is the drawback. When this started, I really believed that her freeborn origin would work against her. Now it seems to be her advantage.

She can win, I believe that now. But not if she spends tonight hovering by her mother's bedside.

What kind of emotions was Diana feeling here, in this medical center treatment room? Joanna wondered. Concern for this damaged woman inside the medshell?

As if to answer the question, Diana suddenly spoke. "I have not seen her, my mother, for some time. Why is she here? I did not know she was here. We do not communicate much. Why did she not come to see me? My quest for a bloodname, does that mean anything to her? Would she not want to encourage me?"

Joanna turned away, a bit confused and offended for reasons she could not figure out. "I am trueborn," she said. "I do not know what mothers do."

Diana laughed quietly. "Of course. Trueborn. Freeborn. Freebirth. *Freebirth!*"

Joanna noted the contrasting and complicated intonations in the two utterings of the same word. The first was what trueborns called freeborns, the second was the angriest curse among the warrior caste. In some way, she thought, the words defined Diana herself. Caught between the idea of what she might be, a virtual trueborn of two trueborn parents who lived, thought, and fought like any warrior originating in a vat, and the fact of what she was, a freeborn from a human womb, a freebirth.

Thinking this, Joanna could not help but look at the body in the medshell. It was from this body that Diana had been born. Some hand had perhaps helped to make the emergence easier; some freeborn tech had tended to the infant, cleaning its body or removing the traces of the womb's interior; some arms had held the infant in some kind of complicated freeborn tenderness before placing it in the mother's embrace. Even thinking what little she knew about freeborn births, picturing images in ways she knew were probably distorted, like mythic monsters in children's nightmares, sent an intense wave of revulsion through her body, and suddenly she did not want to be in this medical facility room any more.

She took a step toward the door, then stopped. She could not leave Diana. Not just because of some lingering companionship, but because she could not let her lose the match tomorrow, the match for which Joanna had so meticulously and cruelly prepared her. She had to get Diana out of here, get her thoughts back on track toward the bloodname.

It was at that moment that Joanna finally understood her own complex emotions toward Diana. Diana would win the bloodname that Joanna could not. That was Joanna's need now. She had to take charge.

"Diana, we are leaving. Nothing good can be accomplished here."

"I wish to talk with—"

"And you should not. You will not. If I have to grab you by the throat and drag you out of here, I will. This is no place to—"

"All right, all right. I wish to go. You are right. Nothing can be accomplished here. This is just a woman in a medical shell. She is of no importance to me any more."

Diana strode past Joanna toward the door. "Her pain does not concern me, not in the least," Diana said and turned at the doorway to address Joanna. "But I do wish her well."

Joanna followed, shaking her head in confusion, deciding she would never understand this strange freeborn-trueborn warrior.

As soon as the two warriors had left, Peri's eyes opened. She had regained consciousness moments ago and heard the last words of Joanna and Diana.

I could have opened my eyes, let Diana know I was awake. I do not know why I did not. What I heard I like. She sounds like a trueborn warrior, something like Aidan Pryde when he was on a tear.

She did not remember the violence that had brought her into this medshell. She would find out soon enough, she knew.

Inside a medshell there was very little feeling, so she had no suspicion of the pain she would feel outside, the pain to which Diana had referred. She had a vague memory of being lost. And of a Jade Falcon warrior who was not a Jade Falcon warrior helping her, but she could not focus her mind sufficiently to recall the details.

Should I even attempt to see Diana again? I do not know. But I will see her compete for the bloodname. Win the bloodname. Yes.

18

Jade Falcon Training Area 14
Ironhold
Kerensky Cluster, Clan Space
1 March 3060

Samantha could sense many eyes on her as she sat in the holovid observation room watching the holovid version of the contest between MechWarrior Diana and her first-drawn opponent, a Star Commander from the Eighth Talon Cluster. Although the fight had just started, Samantha recognized that Diana would win this one. As she maneuvered her *Nova* across the narrow Blood Plateau, the venue choice of Star Commander Ethan, her superior piloting skills were obvious.

Coming near the edge of the plateau, Diana seemed unconcerned about the one-and-a-half-kilometer drop-off. In one stunning move, she pivoted the *Nova* to face her opponent's *Mad Dog* and triggered a PPC barrage that sent the armor boiling off both sides of the *Mad Dog*'s torso. As Diana moved sideways along the cliff edge, Samantha watched big hunks of the *Mad Dog*'s armor making the long, slow drop to the ground below.

In response, Ethan battered the torso of Diana's *Nova* with his large lasers. Though his fire did not seem to do much damage, the *Nova* seemed to sway and slip a bit toward the plateau rim. Most of those watching in the observation room gasped sharply, as they expected the *Nova* to follow the *Mad Dog*'s armor fragments on the long trip down to the ground.

Samantha watched more dispassionately than the rest, but she thought Diana had taken too much of a risk. Her tactics had allowed her to maneuver toward the side of the *Mad Dog* and get off the devastating previous shots, but she had made herself too vulnerable to the *Mad Dog*'s assault.

Now Diana moved away from the rim, which Samantha mentally applauded. Again, her control of the *Nova* was skillful. The *Nova* seemed almost to dance across the surface of the plateau, fearlessly facing the frantically firing large lasers and missiles of the *Mad Dog*. Diana held her own fire until in short range, ignoring the successful laser hits and using her anti-missile capability artfully against the *Mad Dog*'s missiles, then she launched about as devastating an onslaught as Samantha had seen in a bloodname contest. Firing wildly in intervals to lower her heat, she sidestepped and triggered her medium laser, the red bursts intensifying the previous damage inflicted on the *Mad Dog*'s torso.

This is more than a bloodname contest for her, Samantha thought. *She is proving something. A blow for the freeborn warrior as she mows down the trueborns. I would not have judged her to be this vindictive, yet what else can be the meaning of her actions? Perhaps it is something else. Something about her being the daughter of Aidan Pryde. What am I thinking? The woman can fight. She is a fierce warrior. And that is all. All!*

Suddenly a successful shot hit the *Mad Dog* ammo case, and an explosion that was impressive even in its miniaturized holovid version erupted from the *Mad Dog* torso—and the battle was over. Diana's hammering had disabled the *Mad Dog,* and it stood with arms down, still. Diana told her opponent to eject. He refused, adding the curse of "free-birth" to his defiance. He moved his 'Mech, which was clearly still ambulatory if a bit unsteady, toward the *Nova*. The observers chattered among themselves, wondering what damage, beyond kicking at the *Nova,* could possibly be accomplished by the disabled *Mad Dog*. Some speculated that physical infighting would at least show disrespect to the Star Commander's freeborn opponent.

But Star Commander Ethan's intentions would never be clear. Taking her *Nova* a step forward as if to meet the *Mad Dog* on its own insulting terms, Diana triggered another barrage, one that sent the *Mad Dog* toppling and sliding along a slight incline toward the edge of the plateau. At the edge its arm hooked onto the rigging that had been planted there to transmit holovid signals to the observing room where Samantha sat watching and to all the spectator stations on Ironhold and other Clan worlds in the Kerensky Cluster. The rigging held the *Mad Dog* back as its legs cleared the plateau edge. The metal of the rigging was too light to hold the 60-ton 'Mech for long. It began to bend.

Diana and Ethan had another exchange, one too garbled for those in the observation room to comprehend. Someone near Samantha yelled, "He is still refusing to give in to her!"

"Good for him," another spectator shouted.

"He will refuse to leave his cockpit," the first spectator yelled back. "She will have to shoot the *Mad Dog* over the edge to validate her win."

"Filthy freebirth!" someone else yelled. "If she does that, I will personally kill her!"

As they had all during the match, emotions ran high in the observation room.

It is truly strange, Samantha thought, *to watch these tiny figures, the two 'Mechs on a small version of a plateau that is really the highest point in this region—all looking like some toy version of a BattleMech battle. And to have the excitement rise as we watch. And then to realize that the real battle is taking place a few kilometers from here with a real Diana and a real Star Commander Ethan and both their 'Mechs. Truly strange.*

Before anyone in the holovid room had seen her do it, Diana had climbed out of her cockpit and scrambled down its side to the ground. The small holographic figure of Diana raced toward the *Mad Dog* as the rigging bent further and more of the 'Mech's legs protruded outward over the plateau rim.

As the tiny Diana ran, the Jade Falcon warriors in the room hurled epithets at her. But everyone went silent when Diana reached the *Mad Dog*. A noticeable crack had appeared on one side of the holovid rigging and the *Mad Dog*'s legs had cleared the rim.

"What in the name of Kerensky is she doing?"

"She is climbing onto the *Mad Dog*. What kind of a free-birth fool is this one?"

A brave one, apparently, Samantha thought.

The tiny Diana went to the diamond-shaped *Mad Dog* cockpit and climbed in. As the figure disappeared through the hatch, it seemed as if the crack in the rigging was growing and the top half of the restraining straps was about to snap off. The *Mad Dog* would fall before rescue teams could land on the plateau.

No one in the room spoke, and it seemed to Samantha that no one breathed, either.

The miniature Diana threw open the hatch and started to emerge from the cockpit, struggling. It became clear to all those in the room that she was dragging a miniature version of her opponent out of the cockpit. The body was limp. Star Commander Ethan had either passed out or, most likely (Samantha thought), had been knocked out by a solid punch from Diana.

After throwing her opponent off the *Mad Dog* torso and seeing to it that he landed on the ground without anything of his catching on his sharded and bent BattleMech, Diana looked toward the rigging, just in time to see its top half bend toward her in an almost formal bow. No doubt the real Diana felt the *Mad Dog* beneath her begin to shift as the weight of its legs began to drag it over the cliff edge.

All the heavy breathing in the room seemed to collect in a single, deafening gasp, as the spectators watched Diana begin a long race up the 'Mech's torso. At what seemed the last possible minute, she made a rather graceful leap off the

Mad Dog. Whether the thrust of her leap or some crazy urge in her caused it, she flipped once before landing unsteadily but securely on her feet.

Those on one side of the holovid plateau watched the *Mad Dog* seem to vanish over the far side of Blood Plateau, while those on the other side stared open-mouthed at the plummeting, graceless, miniature *Mad Dog.* Although the holovid could not possibly pick up all the destructive detail, the 'Mech seemed to explode into a hundred flying fragments when it hit the ground.

Back at the top of the plateau, the miniature Diana was dragging the miniature Ethan away from the plateau rim. After moving him a few meters, she stopped and arranged the apparently unconscious body of her opponent. Sitting down with, it seemed, weariness, the small figure signaled to a rescue copter to land and do its job.

Samantha's thought was, *I am glad I stayed on Ironhold the extra days. This will be an interesting contest, I think. And I also think maybe I like this Diana. Very much.*

Near her, the audience was getting back its energy and beginning to grumble angrily about what they had seen. They were furious that, not only had the freeborn won, but she had rescued her opponent. It was such a unique event in a bloodname fight that no one was sure what to make of it. But most clearly felt that, if this damn freeborn had done it, there must be something wrong about it.

Samantha smiled—well, inwardly. She was not one to show amusement in a public situation. But sometimes the acts of her fellow warriors were, she thought, amusing.

$$=== 19 ===$$

Jade Falcon Training Area 14
Ironhold
Kerensky Cluster, Clan Space
1 March 3060

As soon as she debarked from the copter and waved her thanks to the pilot, Diana heard the rushed and heavy footsteps of Joanna coming toward her. Timing her move perfectly, she turned to face Joanna just as she was about to holler her name.

Diana spoke first, her eyes mirthful. "You have something to say to me, Joanna?"

"You are stravaging right about that, cadet." Joanna often called her a cadet when she was particularly angry. "You look so satisfied with your little bit of useless heroism after the victory. What kind of a show were you performing up there? And for whom?"

Approaching more slowly, Horse smiled broadly.

"I did it for nobody," Diana said. "Or for myself. Who knows? I did not stop to think it all out, so I just reacted by—"

"You are damn right you did not think!"

"He had fought well. I had won. Why let him go over the cliff with his 'Mech?"

"I do not care about that savrashi. And I cannot see why you did. All he did was insult you from the beginning of the battle. Let his death be the final insult. Did it not enter your head, Diana, that you took too many risks? Anything could have happened inside that cockpit. He might have disabled you. You might have caught your foot on some wreckage. Too many things could have happened and then you would have gone over the cliff with that warrior and his *Mad Dog*. Your next opponent might have been grateful for the bye, but otherwise no good would have come of it. Too many risks, Diana."

"Yes, Diana," Horse said, "you keep taking risks like that and they might start comparing you to your father."

Joanna cursed Diana's laugh as she whirled to confront Horse.

"You approve her stupid heroism?"

"I am not sure," Horse replied. "But even you called it heroism."

"In a risk not worth taking. Let the stravag crash with his 'Mech."

"How unClanlike of you, Joanna. He would have died wastefully, and we abhor waste, we Jade Falcons. And let us not forget that Diana has efficiently countered his own attempt at humiliation of her by humiliating him with the rescue. I applaud that, Diana."

Joanna threw up her hands in disgust. "I give up on the pair of you. Freeborns sticking together. Just remember what I say about foolish risks."

"Joanna," Diana said, "is it not in the nature of risks that you cannot know whether or not they are foolish until after you have taken them? I mean—"

"I do not give a surat about what you mean. Just do not make a habit of pulling enemy pilots out of their cockpits, *quiaff*?"

"Neg. I will do as I wish."

"Horse is right. You are so like Aidan Pryde. Something to like, at least."

Joanna strode angrily away. Looking at Horse, Diana shrugged. He shrugged back.

"Did you mean the comparison to my father?" she asked.

"Yes. From some perspectives, his actions on Tukayyid were foolishly conceived, but he was hailed as a hero for them. Heroism depends on your luck in selecting your risks."

"That is too deep for me."

"Aff. For me, too."

Horse and Diana caught up to Joanna, and the three walked out of the training area together. At first they walked silently, then Horse began to analyze Diana's battle in technical terms. Joanna, her anger diminished, eagerly joined him in criticizing Diana's performance.

In the barracks complex, crowds had gathered. Each bloodname battle drew many spectators, but Diana's audience was, she estimated, at least double the normal showing.

It was hardly a sympathetic group. Surly was more the word for them. Even before she could hear any words from the assemblage, she saw that the crowd was angry—fists shaken, insulting gestures, incensed facial expressions. When she, Joanna, and Horse got closer, there was a definite rumbling sound, which gradually formed into discernible words, with the insult of "freebirth" dominating the crowd's reaction.

There were few physical threats, since the law stated that no attacks could be made on any warriors in competition. It was a rule formulated long ago when too many of the bloodname contests would take place outside the formal Trials. Further, many of the burlier techs had been temporarily reassigned to security duty, and they were stationed at intervals to hold the crowd back. Diana wondered, though, whether the security techs would be effective if a crowd this size decided to attack.

Although the warrior's unwritten code said to respond to any significant attack, custom decreed that warriors in bloodname competition should not respond to the jibes of spectators. So Diana and her two companions passed near the shouting and gesturing crowd without apparently seeing them. The echoes of their insults remained as the sounds began to fade.

* * *

Near her barracks Diana saw a familiar figure, standing casually, apparently waiting for her. For a moment she could not think of his name. Then she remembered meeting him back at the holovid arena. Leif. He was as relaxed and strong-looking as ever and, in the light of day, seemed even younger than he had on the dark night when they had first met.

As she came closer, she smiled. She was glad that Joanna was not here to see him. Joanna and Horse had gone to oversee repairs on her BattleMech.

"You did well," Leif said. "I watched on holovid."

"Cheering me on?"

His smile widened. "Well, cheering you on was not exactly popular in the holovid room. But I *silently* approved your victory."

"And were you appalled at my dragging the Star Commander out of his cockpit?"

"Not appalled. It was a risk I might not have taken, but I admired your courage. It was very . . . very trueborn."

The word made her laugh. "What kind of a joke is that?"

"No joke. I think I agree with your quest, if I may call it a quest. I do not want you to win, but not because you are technically freeborn, but because I intend to obtain this bloodname."

"I reviewed the holovid tape of your first round. A good match, if a bit short."

"I do not waste time."

"No, you do not."

"You realize that, since we are in different lines of the draw, it is likely we will only meet in the final match, *quiaff*?"

"It has occurred to me. I welcome your opposition. I would choose to obtain the bloodname from a worthy competitor."

"You are very courteous—for a Jade Falcon warrior."

"Some kind of genetic throwback, I suspect. I will rid myself of it as soon as I can."

"You do that. I will try to be courteous when I defeat you."

Leif merely smiled affably and bid her farewell. As he passed her, he touched her lower arm lightly. She stared after him. He did not look back. She could still feel the touch. That was no surprise. Warriors rarely touched each other so casually. What kind of warrior was this Leif?

20

Jade Falcon Hall
Hall of the Khans, near Katyusha
Strana Mechty
Kerensky Cluster, Clan Space
6 March 3060

Marthe seethed inside. There was only so much she could take from the other Khans in council meetings like the one just ended. All the restrictions placed upon a Khan made her long to be a simple warrior again, heading up a Galaxy or even a simple Star. Each step she had made up the ladder toward being Khan had felt like the loss of an important part of herself. Going from cadet to warrior she had forever altered a comradeship, the one with Aidan. In her first command, with her rigidity of belief and cool attitude, she had lost some of the usual camaraderie with other warriors. Each higher command position had taken her further from everyone, until now—alone and powerful—she had only herself to rely on.

On the other hand, have I not always separated myself from others? Deflected moves toward friendship, isolated

*myself in the shell of my own ideals, my own—in fact—
ambition?*

Marthe thought how she could use a chat with Vlad right
now, but he was occupied somewhere with his own duties
as Khan. And Samantha was still on Ironhold. Her last report had contained praise for Diana's first-round win. In a
few days the Trial of Bloodright would end and some of the
sniping in council would diminish. Marthe knew it was politically important for her to keep her cool.

Ever since Horse's victory against Ivan Sinclair, the Steel
Vipers had doubled their attacks in council. Marthe had
thought their humiliation might have silenced them, but it
only seemed to have enraged them further. The style of the
attack had changed, however. Perigard Zalman was allowing his saKhan, Brett Andrews, to deliver the snide comments, the sarcastic allusions to Diana's bloodname quest.

After Diana had successfully won the first round,
Andrews suggested that the whole bloodname contest be
canceled and begun all over again with only trueborns competing. He proclaimed the whole thing to be technically in
violation of Clan laws and traditions, especially since the
only previous instance of a freeborn competing for a bloodname had been that of Phelan Ward. "And what did he do?"
Andrews asked, sarcasm heavy in his voice. "Split the Wolf
Clan and defected to the Inner Sphere! There is no point in
favoring a freebirth, ever!"

Marthe, of course, had the advantage. Horse's victory
over Ivan Sinclair had convincingly validated Diana's
claim and refuted Andrews' objections, but Brett Andrews
still appeared to have much support among the other Khans.

Now, in her office, she found herself wearying of all the
intrigue. All she really wanted to do was rebuild the Jade
Falcons to their former strength in order to return to the Inner Sphere and finish off what the Clans had begun with the
first invasion. While there, she would not mind asserting
Falcon supremacy over the Vipers, who shared their corridor. After all that had happened since Marthe been thrust

into the role of Khan, she had no desire to share glory with the Vipers.

She leaned back in her chair and pressed her fingers against her eyes. The pleasurable dots of light appeared, sliding side to side, blending with each other, looking like galactic clusters in a dark universe.

I will show them all what a Jade Falcon Khan can do. They will grovel at—but is not that arrogance? Very well, I am arrogant. I want them all—Khans, the Inner Sphere, all—at my feet.

Moments later an aide came to inform her that Diana had won another bloodname battle, this time bringing down a *Hellbringer,* on a dry plain where the dust of combat had not, the aide said, settled. Perhaps he exaggerated, but Marthe was pleased to hear the news. She told the aide to bring her a holovid recording of the battle. She was eager to see it, she said.

21

Training Field Barracks
Ironhold
Kerensky Cluster, Clan Space
12 March 3060

"**D**id you think Diana would get this far, Horse?" Joanna said. "All the way to the final match?"

"Yes."

"No, I mean *really*."

"Really. Oh, don't get me wrong. I know the part genetics

plays in all these competitions. If allowed to compete, I would never have won a bloodname."

"I never thought I would ever say this, but I am not so sure of that, Horse."

"Then why did you doubt Diana's potential?"

"I did not so much doubt it as see all the odds against her. Would you like another fusionnaire? I know it is only homemade, but—"

Horse shook his head. "No, it is too potent. We probably should not be drinking on the eve of—"

"Forget it. I can drink a dozen of these, get sick, pass out, and still get up in the morning and fight three battles in a Circle of Equals."

"I do believe you can. Why did you think she could surmount the odds you spoke of?"

Joanna looked off in the distance. "I do not know what I thought. My job was to train her. I always train from the same point of view. I start with the assumption that the trainee is scum and I have to make her worthy. Well, of course Diana is not a trainee in the usual sense, she is a proven warrior, but I have to take the view that more has to be found inside the warrior, that there is a well from which apparent impossibilities have to be drawn."

"I have never been a falconer, as you have, but I wonder, wouldn't it be better to assume that the warrior you're training is going to go all the way and—"

"No, it is not. If I assumed that, I might miss something." She stood up and began to mix herself another fusionnaire at the low table where the three bottles that contributed the fusionnaire ingredients stood. She had had to brush off piles of clothes and paper onto the floor to make room for the bottles. The room itself now looked like any room Joanna had ever inhabited. Messy and cluttered—at least that was the way other people saw it. She herself knew that the piles of things were not as careless as they looked. She always knew where everything was.

"You know," Horse said, "it's odd, but your sour views probably are what have made you such a success."

Joanna turned, her eyes squinting as she took a sip of the fusionnaire. She must have made it particularly strong, because Horse noticed her shoulders shudder a bit from the impact of the drink. "What, Horse, do you precisely mean by your babble? I tell you, you are reading those books much too much. Or did something happen to you on Huntress? You seem somehow different."

"Something did happen to me there. I discovered that there was the possibility I could be beaten. Subdued."

She took another sip. "More of your babble. Tell me, what did you mean about my, what did you say, sour views?"

"I meant that, by taking the wrong side of the issue, you somehow wind up with the right side."

Joanna guffawed. A little of her drink spilled, and Horse could see that her eyes were slightly glazed.

"By assuming Diana had practically no chance, Joanna, you have gotten her to the last round of the bloodname trials. I like her choice of the caverns as venue."

This time Joanna took a big swig of the drink. "Do you? I despise it. I wish I had never let her visit them. This idea originated there, I can almost recall seeing it in her eyes without knowing what I was seeing."

"Now, who's babbling?"

"Maybe so. It is easy to do when I have to listen to your drivel, with all its contractions and words from books."

"What is wrong with the caverns, from your point of view? Do you agree with the others who say they should not be allowed as venue?"

Joanna snorted. "No, what do I care what *they* say? I meant the caverns themselves. Too confined, too many narrow passages, only a few areas where a BattleMech can maneuver well. Combat should be out in the open, not in small, confined areas."

Horse almost brought up the two times Joanna had been forced to fight in the Great Gap on Twycross. Even though she had gained a significant victory the second time, both experiences should have provided sufficient reason for her to distrust confined spaces.

"Well," he said, "I think the choice of the caverns is fine, especially each time I recall Ravill Pryde's furious reaction to it."

Ravill Pryde had indeed been furious. Even as House Leader serving as Oathmaster for the coin ceremony, where the warrior whose coin came out first from the gravity funnel called the Well of Decision got to choose the style of combat, while the one whose name was on the back of the second coin to emerge chose venue. Diana's coin had come out second, and there had been a trace of a smile on her face when she followed her opponent's choice of BattleMech combat with the choice of Falcon Caverns as venue.

Now, as he sat alone in his quarters, Ravill could not stop thinking of that moment. At the ceremony the room had suddenly been possessed by the angry reactions of those in the room. Diana had seemed pleased by their opposition. The audience had clearly agreed when Ravill pointed out that the caverns were an honored Ironhold tourist attraction. Sending BattleMechs into it, machines that could damage and even destroy age-old features, would be a desecration.

Diana had stood firm.

" 'Mechs will fit into the caverns, *quiaff*?" she asked calmly, ignoring the anger around her.

"Aff."

"And, in choice of venue, I may choose any site on Ironhold, even its moon, so long as the fight does not take place near settlements of people, *quiaff*?"

Her moon reference was, of course, to Rhea, the moon where her father had fought his final bloodname battle.

"Well, aff."

"Then, it appears I have fulfilled all the conditions. I choose Falcon Caverns as venue."

Ravill Pryde had been silent for a moment. He was unusually conscious of his shortness when facing the tall Diana. Even though freeborn, she had always exhibited the roughness and toughness of a trueborn Jade Falcon warrior. He had never seen her so confident. He did not like to think that this freeborn was one step away from a bloodname.

After holding a stare at Diana for a long while, Ravill Pryde said, "Very well. Falcon Caverns attracts mainly freeborns, so I suppose damage to it is no cause for regret."

The freeborn comment was calculated on Ravill Pryde's part. If the insult had found a target in Diana, she did not, however, show it.

Grelev had reported to him that disapproval of the choice of the Falcon Caverns site had swept Ironhold City.

"There will be few who will be sorry to see this Diana's defeat there," Grelev had said in his usual careful, well-thought-out way. As ever, the man made Ravill's skin crawl.

"I thought the fact she is freeborn is enough reason for the resentment of Diana," Ravill said.

"That, too," Grelev replied.

Grelev had then dutifully left the room, leaving Ravill alone with his thoughts.

I never thought it would get this far, her quest. My mistake. I should have realized her tenacity could work in her favor here, too. If she does pull off the miracle and actually win against this highly skilled warrior, I do not know if I can bear her victory. What should I do, though? What can I do?

At that moment a plan began to form in Ravill Pryde's mind.

Joanna's speech had become thick, but she remained coherent.

"Did you see Diana tonight, when I warned her against this Leif? She knows him, Horse. She seems to think he is, I do not know, a decent fellow or something like that. I hate that."

Horse nodded. "I agree. The less you know of your opponent, the better."

"She could see him as a friend and, at a key point, hold back. Try to defeat him without hurting him or be afraid to finish him off when the opportunity occurs."

"Look at it this way," Horse said. "If she is worthy of the bloodname, she will have to act as a warrior, in all the meanings and implication of that word."

"Stop with your precious learning from a book."

"This is from no book. It is from my own experiences. I believe a warrior does not, as you say, hold back. If Aidan Pryde had suddenly become my enemy, I would have killed him, simple as that. True warriors do not let subtleties of friendship and comradeship interfere with their duty."

"High-sounding words, Horse. If Diana could pull a stranger who had just tried to humiliate her out of his cockpit, then she is capable of easing up on this Leif because of her stupid emotions."

"I disagree, Joanna. I think her stupid emotions, as you call them, are her best weapon. Think of her father. She *is* Aidan Pryde in her ways, in her skills, in her willingness to take risks."

"I should detest you for saying that. It is a typically freeborn thought. Yet, I think I agree with you. There is not only the physical resemblance, there is the personality. With her, I have to remember Aidan Pryde much more than I want to. I cannot think any more. You are as difficult to talk to, Horse, as dealing with a trio of 'Mechs in combat—or Aidan Pryde. I have to sleep now."

Pushing aside a pile of fatigues, Joanna dropped onto the bed and was immediately asleep.

Delicately, trying not to disturb her, Horse transferred the bed debris onto a table and managed to get a blanket over Joanna with only a weak grunt from her.

I must get some sleep, too. Tomorrow is the day, the day when Diana proves her point or shows she is essentially a freeborn not fit to bear a bloodname. I wonder what Aidan Pryde would think? He would not support her as a father, since he only knew of her existence in the last minutes before he died, but I think he would support her as a warrior. After all, he posed as a freeborn for much of his military career, all part of the great legend. He understood freeborns better than any other trueborn. Yet at heart he remained trueborn. Well, it's a problem I can't resolve now, will probably never resolve. Best I get back to my former ways. Back then, I just settled into my natural freeborn resentment of trueborns and did not have to deal with the gray areas between the two. Stravag, I must get to sleep.

In his quarters, Horse duplicated Joanna's fall into bed, though it was a neater bed, with sheets and blankets tucked in military fashion.

22

Ironhold City, Ironhold
Kerensky Cluster, Clan Space
13 March 3060

In the hospital room to which she had been relocated after being taken off the shell, Peri had not even requested a chance to watch the bloodname contest. Some medtech would probably have told her she was still weak and should not subject herself to the excitement of viewing such an event. Medtechs reasoned that way.

She had vowed to escape from the hospital room in order to find a holovid room and watch Diana compete. In the interim, she had managed, during her exercise periods, to steal items of clothing from various sources. She could not believe that stealing could be so easy. Now, she could sneak out of the hospital. Since the clothes were mismatched, she would not be very fashionable, but she knew there were a lot of freeborns who traipsed about in strange get-ups. She was confident she could blend in.

After she had secreted a pair of pills beneath her tongue

during a medtech scheduled visit, she spit them out, then quickly donned the bizarre clothing. She found it strange that no one seemed to notice the woman in odd clothing walking unsteadily through the halls, past the administrative area and out the doors of the medical center.

Samantha Clees had arranged for holovid cameras to be placed all through the potential combat areas of the Falcon Caverns. Dark interiors were usually difficult for holovid transmission, and—should the combatants enter certain areas—the figures would vanish in the holovid field. However, the cameras were linked to a computer that constantly digitized the image, analyzing it carefully to locate and provide images that would not be visible to the individual cameras. The computer's memory base could often fill in the rest of the figure appropriately, in ways that sort of filled in the blanks. The result would not always be an accurate representation of the reality, but usually it came close enough for viewers to follow the action.

As she paced around the holovid table that had been set up in her Jade Falcon Tower quarters, Samantha watched the two miniature BattleMechs appear on the perimeter of the holographic field. She felt excitement building up in her. Any contest between 'Mechs thrilled her. A powerful machine and a pilot at one with it seemed to Samantha the essence of being a Clan warrior.

Diana showed mastery of her *Nova,* even though her former 'Mech of choice had been a *Warhawk.* She had probably made the change with the bloodname contest in mind. The lighter, more flexible *Nova* heightened her skills at maneuverability and quick reactions.

MechWarrior Leif used a *Black Lanner,* a 'Mech Samantha particularly admired. It had good range and excellent firepower. Even in battles the Falcons had lost, Leif had acquitted himself well in this 'Mech, with a particular talent for using its weapons wisely, with a cold calculation and mercilessness that was characteristic of the finest Jade Falcon warriors.

Samantha had to walk around the holovid field to view
the two BattleMechs about to enter their respective entrances. Each stood outside, out of sight of the other, awaiting the relayed signal from Oathmaster Ravill Pryde to
enter Falcon Caverns through the only two entrances large
enough to welcome a BattleMech into the interior. The
whole cave system had been checked and mapped over-
night for the two warriors. Accessible tunnels and caverns
had been discovered and placed into their 'Mechs' computer maps. Some accessible locations had been declared
off-limits at the order of the saKhan. Samantha had not
wanted destruction wrought on the particularly popular
and, she assumed without being able to analyze for herself,
beautiful attractions. Tracking information would warn
each pilot away from the off-limit locations and tunnels that
contained too many hazards.

Samantha heard a noise behind her. She turned around
and saw Grelev, standing in the shadows.

"Yes, Grelev."

"Ravill Pryde told me to stay out of his sight today. I had
no place to go but my quarters. I thought I would find a
place to watch the battle from instead. I still have my key-
card for this complex, so I came here. I hope you do not
mind. I will stay in the shadows here, remain silent."

Samantha laughed. Even Grelev must have noticed the
unusual phenomenon, for he stepped forward, as if to see if
there was anything he could do to cure this sudden malady.
Samantha held up her hand. "No, I am all right. I was just
startled, that is all. Sometimes your talent for understate-
ment catches me off-guard. You seem to have an unusual
sense of humor, Grelev. Warrior humor does not often have
the edge you put on your observations. Of course you may
stay. I could use someone to talk to, Grelev. Come forward.
Take a seat."

Grelev seemed pleased.

As he sat down, he pointed toward the holovid images.
"Look. The signal. It is starting."

While Grelev watched the holovid version of Diana's

Nova enter Falcon Caverns, Samantha saw MechWarrior Leif's *Black Lanner* manage to get through an opening whose real counterpart was massive, but was just wide enough for the 'Mech to clear both sides without angling its body. The field on the holovid table darkened as the interior cameras were engaged, and one saw the battle through a cutaway view of tunnels, a cutaway that changed whatever position the viewer took.

"I wish I could be there, riding on the shoulder of one of the 'Mechs," Grelev said suddenly. "This could be quite spectacular. I mean, not only with the battle itself, but there will be rocks flying, maybe a stalactite or two shot off and flying to the cave floor. This holovid will never capture the real thing."

"Some of the formations have been there for centuries. You wish to see them destroyed in a moment, Grelev?"

He shrugged. "What difference does that make? I cannot comprehend centuries. This is now. I mean, rock that has been on the wall for several centuries falls on the ground and stays there for several years and people of other times, after we are long dead, happen to kick some of the rocks around. We do not even know who they will be, so what about rocks? What difference will there be about some rock debris in centuries from now?"

"I do not know, Grelev. I do not truly know."

The light of the cavern interior seemed dimmer when viewed on a screen inside a 'Mech, Diana noted as she allowed the *Nova* to lumber slowly down the tunnel. If she had transferred the view to a rear camera, she would have seen the tunnel opening recede quickly with the long 'Mech strides. She sensed some movement above the 'Mech. Tentative, skittery movement. *Bats probably,* she thought. She knew there were clumps of them covering the cave ceiling near the opening. She had been told that at nightfall they flew out of the large cave mouth in a thick black cloud. Many of them toured the night sky, searching for insect prey, and often were sighted at a great distance from the cave. Somehow they made it back to Falcon Caverns each morning, though. Her informant, a freeborn who worked as a tour guide in the caverns, had told her that few dead bats had been found away from the caverns and, mysteriously, few bat corpses were found inside the tunnels.

She started studying the patterns discovered by her active probe system, which she had asked her techs to install for this contest, replacing the *Nova*'s anti-missile system that she felt would not be needed for this battle. She noticed the delicate handiwork of nature upon the cavern walls. In addition to the stalactite formations, varied in thickness and shape, there were many latticelike accumulations called boxwork. In some spots they looked like delicate lace. Warriors knew little about such things as lace, but Diana had been brought up as a freeborn and had actually fingered the delicate craftwork in some of the lower-caste freeborn households. Back in those childhood days, the skin of her fingertips had been sensitive and not the callused rough surface it was now. She could probably not even feel the cloth now, but her memories of touching the lace were still vivid.

Well, enough of foolish recollections. Time to find a way to the *Black Lanner* through the intricate network of the Falcon Cavern tunnels.

The active probe showed Leif to be quite far from her now. She wondered if he had detected her yet. Probes were variable underground. Mineral and ore deposits could distort signals, not to mention what might happen to them through mud and sludge.

He briefly flashed out of sight, no doubt due to some geological phenomenon. No matter. Plenty of time to work with. Leif had agreed that entering by different routes, aside from eliminating the problem of one 'Mech having to follow the other, also allowed for them to learn to maneuver in unaccustomed territory. Right now Diana felt a little resistance from her *Nova* at having to descend into the caverns along a rocky and sometimes steep path. She remembered the difficulty in merely walking through similar tunnels weeks ago and, for a moment, doubted whether her choice of this venue had been as clever as she thought—especially as she noted the *Black Lanner* come back on the probe screen, appearing to making its way through the tunnels with expertise.

At the moment she'd announced her choice, Leif had reacted with a strange smile. *Well, all smiles are strange in the coin ceremony, where everyone traditionally remains somber. But his smile was certainly unexpected. Before we left the ceremony, he whispered to me that the choice was inspired, he liked it, and he looked forward to meeting me in one of the large caverns. Stravag son of a bitch! Maybe Joanna is right. His pleasantness is merely his strategy. Since it makes me so edgy, maybe it is a good strategy. I can see him in his cockpit, cool and relaxed. Things would be easier if I did not like him. You are supposed to hate your opponent. That is easy in battle. Only in the Circle of Equals or a bloodname battle do you have to fight someone you might like.*

She just missed knocking her 'Mech's shoulder against a thick stalactite whose side gleamed with dampness. The movement nearly made the *Nova*'s left foot skid a bit, but Diana, expert pilot that she was, regained control and continued the dark descent.

Nomad, his usual drink in front of him, watched the match on a rather large holovid field that had been brought into the tech sector tavern. He did not know what he was drinking. He did not taste much any more. His drinking was a search for numbness, a chance to ignore the physical pain that age had bestowed upon him in so many places.

As he drank, he continued his commentary on the bloodname contest to a companion who had long ago fallen asleep, although Nomad was not aware of the man's comatose condition.

"These warriors don't think about an audience when they have their bloody matches. Look at that. Many meters deep underground searching around like crabs for each other. And look how the resolution goes in and out. You can't get a good signal from underground or, for that matter, undersea. Holovid's garbage anyway. Something to keep us lower castes and lowbirths diverted. We've forgotten all about revolution, you realize that? No, of course, you haven't; you're a damn freebirth after all.

"Still, they look good, these two warriors. Look. The *Black Lanner* just flashed out of sight. Prob'ly blocked by some ore or other. Or the damn camera can't keep up with it. Or the damn director doesn't know what he's doing. I could've worked in holovid, you know that? Almost did. But I wanted to do something more, don't know, useful to the cause or something. I could be sitting in some booth choosing holo images. Or I could've—who cares what I could've—"

It was now clear, even in the frequently hazy holovid form, that the two BattleMechs were finding each other.

"Looks to me as if the *Nova*'s leading the *Black Lanner* by its nose. I'm still always looking at these 'Mechs like they're real people. Nose. Head. Arms. You know. That *Black Lanner,* if it had a nose at all, it'd be a fish's nose. Does a fish have a nose? As for the *Nova,* that's a pug nose above a lantern jaw. You know? Any minute now they'll be going—" Nomad chuckled in a self-satisfied way "—be going nose to nose."

He nudged the sleeping companion beside him, who managed a grunt that Nomad took to be an assent.

Peri found Nomad in the tavern. Seeing that the seat next to him was occupied by a sleeping drunk, she strode up to the counter that surrounded the holovid field and pulled the comatose man off the stool. He seemed to wake for a moment, then gave it all up and collapsed to the floor. A couple of techs dragged him to a far wall and propped him up there. Peri took his place on the stool.

Nomad hazily looked at her. "You," he said.

"Me," she replied.

"How did you find me?"

"I knew that, if I wanted to find you, a bar is the best place to look."

"You insult me, *quiaff*?"

"Not really, I—"

"Stick with the story of insulting me. I like it better than any alternate you can offer."

"How is the battle going?"

"About to heat up. You here to root for your daughter?"

"You are one of the few people who could even say that to me."

Nomad nodded and returned his attention to the holovid battle. Peri ordered a fusionnaire but, as soon as she took a sip and felt the dizziness rush to her head accompanied by an intense chest pain, she decided she would not be able to drink it. She put it down on the counter, between two small puddles, and stared at the small screen.

Diana's *Nova* was now in a large cavern. A tiny picture placed on a screen in the corner of the holovid table showed the *Black Lanner* still in the tunnels somewhere. The torso of the *Nova* was twisting as if Diana was assessing the potential of the cavern as a confrontation point.

"What an ugly place," Peri muttered.

"It's a prime Ironhold tourist attraction."

"Do not think I would ever care about that. Look at it. It is like somebody's idea of hell. Fires coming out of pools and what is going on in the walls?"

"Streams. Waterfalls. Same stuff. Sometimes catches fire, too. Most of the time sets off sparks that cause the pools to catch fire."

"I do not know of any geological phenomenon like that."

"Only on Ironhold. Makes us unique."

"Unique or not, that is an ugly place."

"Your daughter chose it."

"Stop calling her my daughter. Use her name."

"You don't look well."

"I have been, well, sick."

"More than that."

"I was beat up."

"Good for you. Didn't know you had it in you. It must have been one serious attack."

"It was."

"You winced just then. Something hurt you."

"It did."

"Should you be in a hospital?"

"Just left one."

"Go back."

"I will. After this."

"You must be from a Pryde sibko. You're a fool."

Peri was about to reply, but that was the moment when the holovid depiction of the MechWarrior, in his *Black Lanner,* came out of the tunnel, lasers blazing. He encountered a swift response from Diana in her *Nova.*

23

Falcon Caverns
Ironhold
Kerensky Cluster, Clan Space
13 March 3060

It had not been too difficult to lure Leif into Falconfire Cavern. Diana had known he was tracking her with his own active probe, and she had used the map of the whole Falcon Caverns system—with which she had spent a couple of early morning hours—to lead him by the fish-nose of his *Black Lanner.* She apparently headed toward him only to divert into what must have seemed to him an unexpected tunnel.

She felt she was controlling the situation. Unless, of

course, it was part of Leif's strategy to be lured into this cavern of rising smoke and sudden flames, of oil leaking in waterfalls from the walls and pools with names like Styx.

Before coming into Falconfire Cavern, she had taken her 'Mech perilously close to a tunnel where Leif's 'Mech was proceeding slowly down a long, fairly steep descent. For a moment, standing in the intersection of two tunnels, she had seen the lower half of the *Black Lanner* in the distance. She could have sent a PPC blast at the legs and there was a chance she might have actually hit one, might have started a disablement that would have been finally fatal to the 'Mech. But she could not do it. She could not take a potshot, even for the bloodname. With all the taint that had accrued around her father's bloodname contest and other phases of his military career, she could not be even slightly dishonorable.

Would he have taken that shot? Joanna would probably say that he would. I do not think so. Anyway, it does not matter. My decision, not his.

Now, in the massive Falconfire Cavern, she awaited him. Her own probe had lost his whereabouts, perhaps due to interference in the air from the unusual geological activity. But she had led him along the center tunnel, and she expected him to emerge there, so she was surprised when he raced out of a tunnel to her right, fire shooting from his right-arm PPC and his left-arm medium lasers. Although much of the assault was apparently designed to surprise and rattle her, only some of it worked. The *Nova* vibrated from several minor hits, and a piece of armor fell into the pool called Styx, sending up a large sizzling geyser of its oily liquid. On the wall behind her, several chunks of rock fell and bounced along the cavern floor, one rolling quietly into the Styx, whose waters, if they could be called that, were barely stirred by it.

Diana responded with some rock-shattering fire of her own, concentrating on her left-torso medium pulse laser as she set the *Nova* on a path toward the *Black Lanner*.

* * *

Samantha nudged Grelev and said, "Well, there is a few hundred years of history going into the pool."

"With all due respect, Khan Samantha, they were just rocks. Think of it this way: someday they may excavate that pool, find that piece of armor that also went in, and try to figure out what it could possibly be or could indicate about the civilization that once lived here."

In spite of the flurry of activity between the combatants, Samantha glanced at Grelev with raised eyebrows. "Are you saying the Clans will vanish and become forgotten history?"

He shrugged. "Everything is transitory, *quiaff*?"

"I suggest you keep that particular idea to yourself. Some might see it as treasonous. The Clans are forever, remember that."

In the dark Ironhold City tavern, Peri found watching the contest difficult once the shooting started. She gasped at each hit against the torso of Diana's *Nova,* silently approved each of her successes against the *Black Lanner*. At the same time, the various pains in her body seemed to intensify.

"Are you all right?" Nomad asked.

"Of course I am. Why do you ask?"

"You look sick."

She gasped again as a blue PPC blast from the *Black Lanner* narrowly missed the *Nova*'s head.

"Or you're acting like a mother."

Diana kept edging her 'Mech sideways, causing Leif to counter her movements with shifts of his own. Leif maneuvered his vehicle very well. And why not? He was a Jade Falcon warrior, just as she was, well trained and fierce. The only real difference between them was, after all, the matter of birth. *Freebirth,* the derogatory name for a genetic type and the foulest Clan curse. Somebody had once said that nations could rise or fall on the strength of a single word. Whatever that meant, Diana thought, the lines and borders created by the word freebirth were considerable.

Even though Falconfire Cavern was huge, when a pair of battling BattleMechs inhabited it, it somehow seemed smaller. Where Diana had foreseen laser fire and charged-particle beams streaking across large distances, the combat was conducted at much closer range.

Diana had to swerve the *Nova* torso violently to escape a deadly arc of electrical and particle discharge coming right at it. Immediately after, the cockpit rocked from the force of the impact. *"Freebirth!"* she muttered, then laughed to herself at her own use of the foul word.

Another hit, and the cockpit seemed to reel in the other direction. For a moment she was dizzy, but she remained in control of the 'Mech. Knowing the way was clear behind her, she moved the 'Mech three steps backward, each step maneuvering a bit to the side in order to confuse Leif's aim.

Leif's voice came suddenly over her commline, loud and clear. "Retreating, Diana?"

"Regrouping, stravag."

The sound that came in next was perilously close to a sigh. A pilot did not hear many sighs through a commline. "Stravag, huh?" Leif said. "Do we need to go through the insult rituals just because we are pitted against each other? We are friends, Diana."

His voice sounded so warm, so—well—friendly.

Now she seemed to hear Joanna's voice through the commline. *Stop with that, idiot! Do you not see what he is up to? It is the strategy he has employed ever since the two of you met. I would not be surprised to find out that he planned the meeting, that he saw the possibility you would be his opponent in the final bloodname match, that he came to you to disconcert you with friendship. It is not friendship. It is a ploy, a vile ploy.* The words were so convincingly Joanna's that for a moment Diana, still fighting her way out of dizziness, thought she was really hearing her.

NO, damn, it is just your own voice telling you to shape up. It does not matter who is in the cockpit of that Black Lanner! *Whoever he is, he wants your behind on a platter. This is a bloodname we are fighting for. He may be sincere, he may be a liar, but he wants that bloodname just as much as I do. But there is a difference. I need it. I need it. I need it.*

She kept the phrase going as a mantra as she shook the dizziness out of her head and swung her 'Mech's torso around to go face to face with the *Black Lanner*.

Joanna and Horse watched the contest at a public holovid arena. It was like being a spy in an enemy camp. There was very little support for Diana among the unusually large audience jockeying for position, trying to see the best parts of the holovid broadcast.

Joanna always got the position she wanted by elbowing aside anyone who got in her way. Surprisingly, even those ready to fight the jostler changed their minds when they saw her wrathful eyes. Horse wondered why Joanna had even bothered to fight her battles in a 'Mech. Her stare alone could make a 95-tonner back off.

Joanna spoke over her shoulder to Horse. "I think she has forgotten most of what I taught her. She is fighting this Leif on his own terms. Look at her sidestep. And she was just retreating! Even if she gets the bloodname, I will wring her neck!"

"Demolish her, Leif! Melt her down!" yelled a warrior next to Joanna, and she knocked him out with a clip to his jaw.

Horse smiled briefly, then frowned when he saw in the holovid representation of Falconfire Cavern that Diana was in trouble.

Leif had nearly ruined her *Nova*'s left arm, and it felt to her as if the weight of the PPC itself would not allow the arm to raise, although it was also clear the arm was not disabled. She felt as if she were raising her own arm, a wounded arm wracked with pain, as she brought the 'Mech's arm level and started firing the PPC alone, wanting it to do as much damage as possible before another *Black Lanner* shot crippled the arm for good. Instead of losing the use of the limb, however, she made a couple of lucky hits on the *Black Lanner*'s right arm. What she hit she could not tell, but one of the medium pulse lasers there had become inoperative.

There was no intelligence in standing still and slugging it out while the heat in both 'Mechs rose to dangerous points or one 'Mech survived through sheer staying power. Anyway, if she moved to her left at this moment, Leif would likely counter by shifting to the right, and he would be close to the position she wanted.

"Makes for a nice fight," Grelev said. "All that debris bouncing around, all the sparks from the waterfalls, the fire from the pools."

"Do you often judge warfare by its aesthetics, Grelev?" Samantha asked.

"I just observe. I am easily entertained."

"I am not so impressed. It is just the sort of sloppy contest I would expect from the choice of venue. Open spaces, Grelev, that is the real test of a warrior."

"So you do not favor this freeborn's quest, *quiaff*?"

"I did not mean that. I do not take sides. I am only commenting on technique, that is all."

"I just like a good fight. For me, these two are good. Look at the way this Diana is edging the other toward that pool, the one called Styx. She is up to something."

"I wish I was sure."

"She is good, your Diana," Nomad was saying. "I am impressed by her skills. She reminds me very much of—"

He stopped talking as he looked over at Peri. Her brow was furrowed and her eyes hazy.

"Are you all right? You look—"

"I am fine. Must be . . . must be the drink."

Like most people who drank often to the point of drunkenness, Nomad was generally aware of the amount his companions had consumed. Peri had hardly touched the fusionnaire in front of her.

"Maybe you should—" he said.

"Stop! I have to see this out. I have to see the end."

She seemed to sway on the bar stool, Nomad noticed and began to pay more attention to Peri than to the holovid battle.

Although armor was flying off her *Nova,* Diana was relentless, not caring about her own damage. This was her chance at the bloodname, and she was willing even to die doing it. Therefore, she did not care how many hits Leif made against her 'Mech, did not care for the increasing damage or the rising heat. She realized now that, when it came to winning bloodnames, caution and intricate strategy were liabilities. It was possible that no one had ever won a bloodname logically. Her father, Aidan Pryde, certainly had not.

Each barrage she triggered, each stream of laserfire, appeared to hit somewhere on the *Black Lanner.* Leif's counterattack was effective enough, but time and position were working in Diana's favor. Her 'Mech was advancing on the *Black Lanner,* forcing it backward through the sheer impetus of her attack. Alongside the *Black Lanner,* an especially high geyser of flame erupted, almost to elbow-level of the 'Mech. Behind him, a new waterfall came down, opened up by the impact of a PPC hit. The liquid gushing out was particularly dark, darker than Styx, where the oily liquid was diluted with underground streams of water. The waterfall with little water in it sent up spray when it hit the cavern floor, then began to form a current that meandered toward Styx. It reached the pool quickly. Diana saw that it would not be long before it overflowed the pool's banks.

Even with her left arm hampered in its movements, Diana was able to keep its PPC firing. Raising it a bit more with a great deal of effort, she targeted the *Black Lanner*'s left arm in crossfire. She was not sure whether it was instinct or luck, but the arm with its PPC abruptly went limp. Behind him, her fire had apparently ignited the waterfall. A stream of fire appeared to travel down the stream of liquid, across the newly formed rivulet that had now reached the pool called Styx, which seemed to erupt in high flame. Fiery reflections painted a vast abstract pattern all over the surface of the *Black Lanner*.

"The fool!" Joanna shouted angrily. Since many in the holovid arena audience had gone silent, her words echoed around the spacious room. Several turned to look at her, some of them surely believing that Joanna must be on their side.

"What do you mean?" Horse asked, in a decidedly softer voice.

"She is going to get both of them killed. These damned Prydes, they—"

"You include Diana in that? You think she is winning the bloodname?"

"Of course she is. But she may have it for only seconds if she is not careful. Then she will be dead. With an earned bloodname, but dead."

"You are trembling," Nomad said as he touched Peri's arm. He had not seen any of the last few minutes in the bloodname match, but had kept his attention firmly on her face, which was deathly pale.

"I am all right. I will last. Any moment now this, this fight will be over. Diana will—Diana will—I do not know what this is all about. Why is she there? What is happening?"

"Come, hold my hand, I will walk you someplace, to someplace where they can help, to—"

"Get your bloody wrinkled solahma hands off me! I . . . I stay to the end!"

"I am not solahma. I am just old, freeborn."

"Who bloody cares? Look, Diana is attacking. The other one, what is wrong with the other one?"

This is my bloodname, damn it! I will have it.
The remaining active medium pulse laser on Leif's 'Mech was still firing, but inaccurately. The arm itself was wavering. She must have hit it somewhere. Her left-arm

PPC was inoperative, but the one on her right arm was still usable, as were the medium pulse lasers on her torso. Concentrating all still-active weapons on the *Black Lanner*'s right arm, she disabled it rapidly, then she activated her commline for transmission.

"MechWarrior Leif, I have you. You are disabled. You surrender, *quiaff*?"

"Neg," he responded calmly. "Tradition says you have to finish me off. Do it."

It seemed as if the entire surface of Styx was now on fire. The liquid had already begun to overflow the pool's banks, spreading the fire with it. It would soon accumulate around the feet of the *Black Lanner*.

"What has happened?" Peri asked blearily.

"Diana has won. The *Lanner* cannot respond, counterattack. It can't do much of anything but walk into her to knock her over, and I don't think any Jade Falcon warrior would end a bloodname match in that way."

"You are sure she has won?"

"Positive."

"I must get back."

"Get back where?"

"The hospital. I feel—"

She did not say what she felt, but merely stepped off the stool, gave a meek groan, and fell unconscious to the floor.

Feeling his age, Nomad stepped off his own stool and knelt by Peri. She was breathing heavily, with the choked gasp of someone injured.

There must be something internal, he thought. *Something reinjured maybe.*

Nobody else was paying attention to either of them. Most of the people in the bar were intent on the contest, and most of them looked drunker than Nomad.

It's up to me then, he thought and, leaning down, gathered up Peri into his arms with surprising agility. It would not only have surprised others, it astonished him.

A few steps outside the tavern and he thought he could

never make it. The trip meant carrying her through many streets. He managed several muscle-straining blocks, until the weight of Peri had made his ancient arms numb. He came to a complete stop, breathing heavily. There were no other people in the street. Peri's breathing had subsided. She was either better. Or dying.

He could not let her die. For Kerensky's sake. For Aidan Pryde's sake.

He started to get up.

Peri stirred and opened her eyes.

"What are we doing here?"

"You passed out. I think you are still hurt."

She grimaced. "I *know* I am. Must get to a hospital."

"I've been trying that. It's not easy when you're an old relic, believe me."

"I will try to walk."

She tried to put her legs onto the road. They collapsed immediately.

"My turn," Nomad said and picked her up. Her eyes were getting woozy again.

He felt stronger. The rest had helped.

Before she became unconscious again, Peri whispered, "Diana. The bloodname. She won?"

"I am sure she did."

"Sure? That is not enough. Take me back. I need to see her win."

"She won it. She is now Diana Pryde."

"That makes me strangely happy," she said and shut her eyes.

As Nomad carried her down the street, his pace picked up and he felt his heart beating with what seemed a new strength. He started thinking back to the days when he was Aidan Pryde's tech, and he forgot about the heavy burden he was carrying.

"Leif, I will back away. Let you take your 'Mech past me, away from the flames."

The flames were leaping higher now.

"Good idea perhaps. Unfortunately, my 'Mech will not move. I kept that a secret from you. Its legs were disabled even before you got the last arm. Good work, Diana. I hail you and your bloodname."

"Eject then. You might hit the ceiling, but at least it is worth the risk."

"Sorry. Mechanism jammed. No chance."

"Climb out of the cockpit. I will bring the *Nova* as close as I can. I can make a bridge with the 'Mech's arm. You can walk across to me on it, or I can get in as close as I can and you could jump across the gap or—"

"And have you humiliate me the way you did when you rescued that other warrior?"

"That was no humiliation. I saved a warrior to fight again."

"The old waste argument, eh? Do not waste a nut or a bolt or a 'Mech or a warrior."

The flames must have started to burn something inside the *Black Lanner*'s left leg. It began to tilt sideways, toward the mass of fire now on the surface of Styx.

"Get out, Leif! We can do something. Do you want to die?"

"It is honorable. This is the bloodname battle, after all."

"You want to die that way, as the victim of—of a *freebirth*?"

"You are a warrior, Diana. You have earned the bloodname."

Diana was about to move her *Nova* forward in some desperate attempt at a rescue, but the *Black Lanner* began to fall. She listened on the commline for Leif to scream, but he did not.

There would be a few jokes made later about the way this bloodmatch ended. The *Black Lanner* at first seemed to stretch across the pool, but there was a shift in the cavern floor as the 'Mech hit it heavily, then the *Black Lanner* shifted just enough for it to slip head-first into the pool, flames momentarily encircling it before most of the fire was stifled by the 'Mech's bulk. Only half of it became submerged, but of course that half contained the cockpit. On all the holovids there was a semi-comic scene that to some looked like the 'Mech had bent down for a drink, then fallen into the pool, leaving its legs pointing straight upward. From that picture the jokes were created. Some of them had to do with 'Mech stalagmites.

Samantha turned away from the holovid depiction in disgust and began to pace. Grelev, understanding her revulsion, quickly switched off the holovid. The small version of Falconfire Cavern flicked off in a crackle of static.

Grelev, rarely at a loss for words, could not speak. He knew he was not exactly a man of refined tastes, but the scene had been too grisly for him.

He did not have to speak, since there was a knock on the door.

"What is it?" Grelev shouted.

"Transmission from the Khan," a muffled voice replied.

Grelev opened the door and took the envelope from the messenger.

"Read it," Samantha said.

He opened the envelope and took out the half-sheet of paper.

"It is coded. I cannot read it."

Stopping her pacing, Samantha took the paper from him, spent some time reading it (apparently translating the code section by section), crumpled it and cast it away from her. Her revulsion had been replaced by anger.

"Dirty stravags!" she said.

"Who?"

"The Inner Sphere. Their troops are in Clan space. They are attacking the Smoke Jaguars on Huntress!"

"Dirty stravags," Grelev muttered, though the news seemed beyond comprehension.

"Clearly a new phase has begun in the war. I do not know how we will respond. But we are more ready than anybody believes. I saw that on my tour here. Come with me, Grelev.

We must arrange transport off Ironhold. I must get back to Strana Mechty."

She walked toward the door, then looked back, past Grelev at the now-imageless holovid field. "We still need more good warriors," she said. "Warriors like that one."

She gestured toward the field where, after all, Diana had been.

"Like Diana Pryde," she said and strode out of the room.

Airfield outside Ironhold City
Ironhold
Kerensky Cluster, Clan Space
13 March 3060

Diana came storming off the hovercraft that had transported her back to Ironhold City. A large number of silent spectators had come out to the airfield, looking like mourners at a funeral.

Probably trueborns here to jeer at me, resentful of my victory, here to hurl insults. I'll fight them if I have to. All of them at once!

But they were not all trueborns. A group of freeborns located somewhere in the middle of crowd began to cheer. It was unusual for freeborns to pay attention to a bloodname contest—it was just something trueborn warriors did—but the quest of a freeborn for the harshly fought-for surname had stirred their interest. After the first freeborns cheered, others in the crowd joined in and the acclaim for her surged to a deafening level. Trueborns among them vocalized their disapproval, but most of their grumbling was drowned out.

Diana paid them no heed, whether supporters or enemies. It was just noise to her. She was annoyed by both the praise and the disapproval. She started walking past them.

Coming through the crowd, creating their own path much as Diana was creating hers, Joanna and Horse hurried toward her.

Joanna started talking before they reached Diana. "That was some show, Diana. You violated most of what I told you. You ignored the strategy we discussed. And—"

Joanna had reached Diana now and she planted herself in front of her, stopping Diana's progress at the same time.

"And what, Joanna?"

"And you have the bloody bloodname, you wretched stravag. Congratulations!"

Then an extraordinary thing happened. Horse, watching from behind, said later he had not really believed it happened. *Joanna embraced Diana.* It was a brief embrace that ended abruptly, but it was a definite embrace.

"I would have done it all differently, of course," Joanna said, pulling away.

"Spoken like a warrior who could not herself win a bloodname," Horse said dryly. For a moment Joanna's eyes flashed in anger, then she realized Horse was merely chiding her, and she relaxed.

Turning toward Diana, Horse said, "I can see in your eyes you are upset."

Diana nodded. "He did not have to die. I was ready to rescue him. I offered—"

"That does not matter. The warrior made his choice. In old days, sea captains went down with their ships, soldiers fell on explosive devices, surrounded warriors fought till the last of them was killed."

"I know, but there is honor in what you say. What honor comes with a death as useless as that?"

"From some points of view, it was—"

"Look who is coming," Joanna interrupted. "The bantam surat. Strutting his heart out, as usual."

Horse and Diana looked where Joanna pointed. The approach of Ravill Pryde did indeed have a comic appearance. Each step was deliberate, accompanied by swings of his arms that advertised his arrogance.

He was still dressed in the Oathmaster's ceremonial uniform, which featured a long cape decorated with vari-colored falcon feathers. Since he was short, the cape kicked up dust behind him as it dragged along the ground. He did not speak until he had stopped in front of Diana. Even with a fairly high lift to his boots, he was a few centimeters shorter than Diana.

"MechWarrior Diana," he said in formal voice. "It is my duty to state that, in this Trial of Bloodright, you have officially won the Pryde bloodname and henceforth will be known as Diana Pryde."

Joanna's brows furrowed. This kind of speech usually came in a formal ceremony later. Why was Ravill Pryde saying it now? Was he so inept that he had not bothered to learn the proper formalities?

Oh, well, it does not matter. Risa Pryde is dead, long live Ravill Pryde.

She was immediately aware of the oddness of her thought. Although she had invoked a timeworn cliché, she realized how strange it was to apply it to warriors, who did not seek or expect long lives. Certainly, to stay a warrior and live as long as Joanna had was unusual among the Clans.

"I accept the bloodname with the full cognizance of the honor the Clan has afforded me," Diana said. It was a common ritual response that she had prepared some time ago.

Ravill Pryde was supposed to respond with some formula about how the warrior had earned the honor and was welcomed into the bloodnamed ranks, but instead he stared at Diana wordlessly for a long while. Then he spoke in a lowered voice. "This is a bleak day for Clan Jade Falcon, with a freebirth bringing dishonor to the bloodname she has won in as ugly a battle as I have ever seen. Diana Pryde, I accuse you of bringing dishonor to the Pryde bloodname with your absurd quest and your repellent victory and—"

The pause he took was clearly planned, perhaps in order to be dramatic, and he raised his voice to finish the sentence.

"—Diana Pryde, I challenge you to a Trial of Refusal on the issue of this tainted bloodname victory. It cannot be allowed. This bloodname to which so many Prydes have brought great honor cannot be borne by a freeborn warrior. It must be rejected, and I will do so at this Trial."

The challenge was so unexpected and unprecedented that nearby members of the crowd who heard it were stunned and quiet. The few who knew that Ravill Pryde had officially sponsored Diana were even more confused than the rest. A muttering started among those in the crowd, that soon spread among the entire group. Some responded with anger, at Ravill's audacity, while others cheered the chance that he could eliminate this upstart or at least deprive her of the now-tainted bloodname.

Joanna took a step toward Ravill, but Horse's strong grip on her arm held her back. He also whispered to her not to say a word.

Diana spoke quietly. "I accept your challenge, Star Colonel. I will be happy to defeat you in a Trial."

Ravill glared at Diana. There was a momentary flicker in his eyes that Joanna thought might have been admiration. What did he admire? she wondered. Her clear defiance, so characteristic of a Jade Falcon warrior? Her terse words, that reflected a warrior's no-nonsense ways? Or merely the fact that she had, quite honorably, not decorated her acceptance with useless, wasteful insults?

"Very well then. This is neither the time nor the place for further formalities. We will fight tomorrow at Jade Falcon headquarters, *quiaff*?"

"Aff."

"Your challenge will have to be postponed, Oathmaster,"

interrupted a new voice. All turned to see Grelev, the Mech-Warrior assigned by the saKhan to Ravill Pryde.

Since Ravill had never liked Grelev, he was livid at the interruption, and his face was growing red with anger as he whirled to face the arrogant young warrior. A cloud of dust rose from beneath the cape as it swung around a bit slower than Ravill.

"How dare you tell me what I—"

Grelev smiled slightly as he interrupted again. "By order of the saKhan. I have just received a dispatch from her summoning you and all other high command officers on Ironhold to a conclave at Jade Falcon Tower."

"What is this about?" Ravill demanded angrily.

"You will be informed, Star Colonel."

Ravill Pryde strode away, following Grelev, without any further words. The crowd slowly dispersed, leaving Joanna, Diana, and Horse alone and puzzled in the center of the airfield.

"I wonder what's up," Horse said.

"It is not for a freeborn like you to wonder about such things," Joanna told him. "Come, Diana. I can help you to beat Ravill Pryde. I beat him once already, did I not?"

"I would have taken him on right now," Diana muttered.

"And wound up with a bloodname for the shortest period in recorded history, kestrel."

They spent the next few hours discussing how to proceed with the unexpected challenge from Ravill Pryde. But the hours proved to be wasted. The next day came the announcement that all challenges, trials, and further bloodname contests had been suspended by the saKhan due to a surprise attack by the Inner Sphere against the Smoke Jaguar homeworld of Huntress. Horse was especially shocked, since he had so recently been there. Many of his thoughts were of Sentania Buhallin, the solahma warrior he had befriended there, and the Smoke Jaguar Galaxy Commander, Russou Howell, who had been his enemy.

25

For Peri it had been one of those times when reality and dreams intermingled and she could not tell one from the other. The rule of thumb for her was, if it was vivid, it must be a dream. Some of it was even fun. The image of Nomad inside a *Nova,* handling the controls with the expertise of a seasoned warrior but his small aged head looking ridiculous inside a neurohelmet. Diana attacking Etienne Balzac, twisting her fist into the skin of his face. Naiad standing on Peri's chest and shouting that she was victorious, she had won her bloodname, Naiad Pryde. Joanna singing stirring anthems in a choir.

Now, suddenly, she came awake and the shock of the reality was worse than a dream. Nomad stood next to her bed. And he was holding her hand. She pulled her hand quickly away. The act had no effect on Nomad. His ancient face remained relatively impassive, with only a hint of distaste for everything in his eyes.

"You should have died, but you are still here," Nomad said. "Everything else from here on in is a gain."

"I remember some of it. It was you, *quiaff*? You carried me from that place to here."

"Means nothing."

"Do you ever talk straight?"

"Rarely."

Peri put her head back and closed her eyes. She opened them again quickly as a new dream threatened to begin.

"And the bloodname. Diana really won it or was it just one of my dreams?"

"She won. She is a hero among the freeborn population. We talk about her a lot. The trueborns are not exactly thrilled, but they have accepted the reality in true warrior style. Except for Ravill Pryde. He challenged her to a Trial of Refusal against her bloodname victory."

"And did they fight?"

"No. The invasion interfered."

"Invasion?"

Nomad explained the Inner Sphere penetration into the homeworlds, and about the intense fighting now taking place on Huntress.

"The Khans of the other Clans have voted to stay out of this particular war, let the Smoke Jaguars defend their own neighborhood, so to speak."

"What about the Inner Sphere forces? Do not the other Clans fear they might be attacked next?"

"Perhaps. Some say that each Clan is confident it can defeat the Inner Sphere in any other incursion."

Nomad shrugged and clearly would not offer more.

"Was Diana here?" Peri finally asked.

"Once. She seemed distracted. It may be all the war effort."

"There is a war effort? I thought only the Jaguars were fighting."

"Even though Khan Marthe Pryde concurred that the Smoke Jaguars should fight their own battles, she has given orders for all Jade Falcon units to increase all drills, training maneuvers, simulations and other combat preparations. The bloodname contests have been suspended, and challenges and honor duels are strictly forbidden. She does not want to waste a single warrior. Makes a lot of the truebirths antsy. Like Ravill Pryde, who I am sure would like to embarrass your daughter. At any rate, Marthe seems to want the Falcons ready for war."

Peri's turn to nod. She had been in the same sibko with Marthe, after all, and remembered her well. Along with Aidan, Marthe was the best warrior among the cadets, but there was always a sense she was keeping something back. She did not seem to have changed over the years.

"Marthe Pryde may—no, will be—the salvation of the Jade Falcons."

"Salvation. A strange word. But then I have always thought scientists strange."

Peri tried to respond, but against her will her eyelids drooped and she was asleep. There may have been dreams, but they were not as vivid as before. When she awoke, Nomad was no longer there. Apparently he had assured himself that she was well now, for he did not return to the medical center.

She thought of Diana and wondered if she should make any effort to see her, if only to congratulate her on the victory. No, Diana was on a path to an unknown destiny, equipped with a Jade Falcon bloodname, and she needed no help from Peri.

She decided that she would not go to Diana.

Diana did not need her.

Instead, Peri turned her thoughts to Etienne Balzac and what she could do about him.

26

Jade Falcon Hall
Hall of the Khans, near Katyusha
Strana Mechty
Kerensky Cluster, Clan Space
6 May 3060

As it happened, things did not turn out as Marthe Pryde expected. Instead of being driven from the homeworlds, the Inner Sphere forces obliterated every trace of the Smoke Jaguars on Huntress. The destruction of a whole Clan was an unspeakable act that had happened only once before in Clan memory. That it should have come at the hands of an enemy the Clans believed to be inferior was an outrage.

Then Victor Steiner-Davion had proceeded to Strana Mechty with a challenge to all the Clans—a Trial of Refusal that would settle the invasion once and for all. When the Ghost Bears refused to participate, the Crusaders took up the challenge while the Nova Cats went over to the enemy. Each of the eight Clans would fight a separate Trial.

The battles took place in the mountains, on the plains, and in the valleys of Strana Mechty, and it was all over in a single day. At Zhaloba Mountain, Marthe and the Falcons smashed the ComStar forces, a victory especially sweet as payback for Tukayyid eight years before. If anyone still doubted whether the Falcons could hold their own, Zhaloba Mountain laid those doubts to rest.

The Star Adders were the only other Clan to win their Trial, while the Wolves fought the little-known St. Ives

Lancers to a draw. The Inner Sphere won all the rest, a total of five wins out of eight. The unthinkable had happened. The Crusaders were defeated, on the very soil of Strana Mechty, an outcome no less shocking than the destruction of the Smoke Jaguars and their homeworld.

The Clans were left stunned, and Marthe still wondered at the speed with which her whole universe had changed. There was no longer an ilKhan, the Wardens controlled the Grand Council, and the invasion of the Inner Sphere had come to an abrupt and humiliating end.

The Jaguars were destroyed, the Ghost Bears had relocated to the Inner Sphere, and the Nova Cats had defected. Bitter clashes immediately broke out over rival claims to the assets and worlds of all three. Trials of Possession now raged across the homeworlds, each series triggering another set of Refusals. The Clans were at war again, and it looked like it was going to last for some time.

The Falcons were in the thick of it. When word came that the Ghost Bears planned to gift Tokasha to the Diamond Sharks, Marthe immediately attacked, as did the Goliath Scorpions. The Diamond Sharks retreated, but that did not discourage the Hell's Horses from entering the fray. On other worlds, the Falcons were also fighting the Wolves over Eden, and the Diamond Sharks and Hellions over Barcella.

The situation was bloody and chaotic, and Marthe welcomed the constant action. She had spent too many months shut up in the Grand Council. Today, though, she was strangely pensive. Perhaps it was the day, the weather slightly overcast but uncomfortably warm. The humidity seemed to drip from the dull gray paint of her office walls. Though her desk was piled with disks and urgent hardcopy reports calling for her attention, Marthe sat back and let her mind drift for a moment.

She rarely dwelt on the past, but she would never forget the sight of Victor Davion strolling into the Grand Council two days after the fighting on Strana Mechty. He had uttered some pomposities about their two peoples learning to know each other, then had the gall to announce that the Clans were welcome to join his phony new Star League. Did the Inner Sphere leaders really believe that by throwing together some new alliances and employing the fancy rhetoric of a Victor Davion, they could somehow turn the tide of history? Only the descendants of the great Kerensky would restore the Star League.

Vlad had leapt instantly to his feet. He declared that because the Wolves had abstained from the vote, they were not bound by the Trial of Refusal. Then he warned the other Khans that any cooperation with the Inner Sphere would doom their way of life. Vowing to remain true to the vision of Kerensky, he turned and strode from the chamber. Marthe could not help but admire him.

And agree with him. Victor might think that the Inner Sphere had tamed the Clans, but he was wrong. The Jade Falcons would never join any sham Star League. Nor would she ever renounce her belief that the Falcons would one day take Terra and the whole Inner Sphere in the name of the great Kerensky.

The stravags had thought to teach the Clans a lesson about war by annihilating an entire Clan and every shred of its military might. Lincoln Osis himself had died at the hands of Victor Davion. But it was all done through trickery and deceit. Even the fact that the Inner Sphere had somehow discovered the location of the homeworlds could only have been bought through some treachery or other.

It is infuriating the way that infernal Victor Davion employed Clan rituals of combat against us. It was the only way he could hope to defeat us. It looked so honorable, but what a swindle it was.

Marthe remembered thinking that Davion was making a colossal mistake. The Inner Sphere could never hope to win a Trial of Refusal, not even with the limited battles he was proposing. The Clans had superior warriors, machines, and infinitely more courage and valor. Now she realized they should have known the sneaky little surat would have something up his sleeve. *I would like to grab his little neck and squeeze the life out of his little body. Not honorable, perhaps, but satisfying.*

Marthe's fingers curled into a strangling position. She raised her hands to where the short stravag's neck would have been and just then heard the sound of someone clearing his throat from her office doorway. She looked up to see Rhonell standing there patiently, apparently undisturbed by the fact that his Khan was strangling the air in front of her. He announced the arrival of Samantha Clees.

Marthe dropped her hands, feeling somewhat sheepish. "Send her in, Rhonell."

She leaned back and closed her eyes for a second. No good. The face of Victor Davion appeared before her. The invading Clans still held territory in the Inner Sphere. This phony new Star League concocted by the Inner Sphere might move against her there, to wipe out the advances made by the Falcons.

A slight tapping on the door broke her reverie, followed by Samantha's entrance into the room. Though she did not sit down, neither did she begin her usual pacing. "You sent for me, Marthe?"

Marthe noticed that Samantha's eyes were tired, with what looked like smudges beneath them. There were lines of tension emerging from the corners of her mouth. War was exhilarating but it also took its toll.

"Aye, Samantha. It is time for us to speak of urgent matters. The invasion is over, but that does not mean we shall not return to the Inner Sphere."

Samantha nodded. "We must press for our advantage there as we are doing here at home."

"Aye, Samantha, but we are not strong enough to resume the invasion on our own, and it will be some time before the Clans will unite behind such an operation again. For now let us focus on what we can do—take back possession of the invasion corridor and drive the viper from our midst."

Samantha frowned. "The Steel Vipers have tried our patience long enough, *quiaff?* It was a slap in the face when they made Andrews their saKhan. I have long hated the whole Clan, but I despise Brett Andrews."

Marthe nodded. "Aff, but your own report indicates that our military is still not fully staffed or trained. I want all routines and training regimens doubled, tripled. We will need the falcon screaming, raging for a fight. We will fight the Vipers in the invasion corridor, but armed with plans and strategies as well as 'Mechs. Brash courage will not be enough. This time we will take a lesson from the Inner Sphere. We will out-think the Steel Vipers and catch them where they are most vulnerable—in their arrogance and over-confidence. We will move against them. But only when we are ready."

"Are you not being too cautious, my Khan?" Marthe knew Samantha used the honorific to show that she meant no disrespect in disagreeing. She had come to rely on Samantha for both her loyalty and her frankness, and took no offense.

"Perhaps not cautious enough. Do not worry, Samantha. We will be in the field soon, and it will not be an easy fight. But we will win, I promise you that. Meanwhile, we will continue to sharpen our talons."

The two Khans of the Jade Falcons began then to discuss in earnest various possibilities for an assault against the Vipers, studying the holomap Marthe called up of the invasion corridor. As they spoke in voices that became increasingly spirited, Marthe felt more like her old self than she had in a long while. At one point she even picked up a pile of papers and flung them across the desk, pleased at the way they spread across the surface messily.

27

Ironhold Science Research and Education Center
Ironhold City, Ironhold
Kerensky Cluster, Clan Space
7 May 3060

As she sat tensely in the waiting room of Etienne Balzac's office, Peri kept going over her meeting with Marthe Pryde several days ago. She had been summoned to Strana Mechty by saKhan Samantha Clees, who had interviewed her briefly during her tour of Ironhold. The circumstances of that interview had resulted in the saKhan's bringing Peri's suspicions before the Khan.

Peri had left Marthe's office feeling less than confident about the way the interview had gone. She feared the risk she had agreed to take. She shut her eyes and recalled the meeting . . .

. . . She had been shocked when she walked into the office of the Khan to see the many changes in Marthe's face. Her emotionless eyes seemed weary. Her mouth was tight, and new thin lines were etched around them. Her skin, once so ruddy from the outdoor life, had paled, perhaps from too much indoor deskwork. She still stood tall and strong, though.

Since they were from the same sibko and therefore the same age, Peri was more than normally conscious of Marthe's years. She knew that age was obvious enough on her own face—those in lower castes tended to age less gracefully than warriors, even trueborns who had once been warriors—but she had not expected to see it in Marthe.

Samantha Clees was there too, and she sat quietly in a chair against the opposite wall, while Marthe and Peri talked.

Marthe's face softened a bit as she welcomed Peri. That shocked Peri almost as much as had the signs of age. She did not recall any moment from the past when Marthe had been friendly with her.

"Sit, Peri."

She indicated a chair to the left of her desk. Taking it, Peri noted that Marthe omitted the use of her labname. Warriors, resenting the scientists' adoption of surnames, could not abide that the names be spoken in their presence. After Peri sat, Marthe rose and walked around to the front of her desk. The setup, with the already taller Marthe looking down at her, made Peri even more aware of the fact she was talking to a Khan.

"Been a long time, Peri, *quiaff*?"

"Aff."

"We have not seen each other much over the years."

"Hardly at all."

"But of course I have kept track of your progress."

Peri did not know whether to believe that or not. What reason could a warrior ristar like Marthe, who had now become Khan, have for keeping track of someone like her? Peri knew she was just a small bureaucrat in an overly bureaucratic caste. Maybe Marthe was being obliquely sarcastic, knowing that Peri had been a cadet who'd flushed out of warrior training. Or maybe the Khan still harbored some sentiment toward one who had formerly been her sibkin.

Before Peri could further ponder that line of thought, Marthe went on to praise Peri's report on the LAMs, especially the unorthodox way she had used them in combat action on Huntress.

"Also, I am told you helped to save Horse, a warrior invaluable to me."

Then she began to speak of Diana's victory in the blood-name contest, commending her and noting several dramatic moments of the winning battle. Suddenly Marthe stopped talking and said, "What is wrong, Peri?"

"Frankly, my Khan, it is all this talk of Diana. You keep calling her 'my daughter' and referring to me as her mother."

"Do you deny that these are the facts?"

"Neg, my Khan. I am just not comfortable with them. Biologically, Diana Pryde is my daughter. When a child is little, there is no other choice but to act as her mother. One cares for a daughter in much the same way one has to keep laboratory animals healthy. But, you see, I was trueborn, and freeborns are, well, different when it comes to parents and children. Mothers, especially, give their children a lot of attention and become terribly emotional with them. But it was not our way, Diana's and mine. I was not only trueborn, I was a scientist who worked long hours."

"So you and Diana Pryde are not especially close."

"There is a tie. I am glad she has become the warrior she desired to be so ferociously, and she has regularly kept in touch with me. Well, not exactly regularly but often enough. And I was content when she won her bloodname."

Marthe's smile was sudden and disconcerting. "Content? You got out of a hospital bed, dragged yourself across half of Ironhold City, and nearly died because—in spite of your obvious pain—you would not leave the holovid broadcast until it was over and you had to be carried back across half the city."

"You know about that?"

"I am Khan. I have more sources than anyone."

"I suppose there was some, well, emotion in my need to know what happened to her. However, I suspect we are now through with the parts of our lives that intersect, and I wish her well. I have not seen her since."

"But she came to see you when you were still unconscious, *quiaff*?"

"How did you know that?"

Marthe spread her arms. "Khan, *quiaff*?"

"Aff. But I think that was courtesy, and there is no need for us to see each other again."

There was an uneasy pause, and Marthe moved away from the desk and walked over to where Samantha sat.

"SaKhan Clees has briefed me on the matter of the secret genetic experiments you have uncovered among your caste. Actually, Peri, this is not the first such report to reach my ears. We have undertaken other investigations that lend extra weight to your claims. One even involved a person from the past who still links us—Star Commander Joanna. She discovered evidence that helps to substantiate your claims that the conspiracy of scientists involves those from several Clans. The conspiracy is, in fact, so vast and so complicated that there is virtually nothing we can do about it."

"Nothing?"

"Peri, they are so organized they could form their own Clan. They even have their own mercenaries, mostly recruits from the bandit caste whom they use as bodyguards and, occasionally, as in your case, assassins."

"You are saying that the men who attacked me in the alley were assassins?"

"Most assuredly."

"How do you know that?"

"Some of it comes from Kael Pershaw and his Watch. Pershaw has learned to crack any information system, outwit any idiot with information. I do not favor clandestine activities, and saKhan Clees despises them, but we must have them, I am afraid. Anyway, he gave me not only the news about the attack on you, but the name of the assassins. The main one was a brute named Olan. In the bandit caste, he was known as the 'saint without mercy.' "

"Saint? The man was no saint!"

"Among bandits he is. I am not sure of the origin of the phrase."

"Well, I hope to see him dead some day. If I could kill him myself, I would consider it. But there is one drawback:

my memory of that evening is all a blur. I cannot recall what he looked like. I am glad to find out his name, at least."

"I wish I could arrange to have him killed for you, but even as Khan I draw the line at deliberate assassination and murder."

Peri was suddenly tired, a residual effect of the attack. Although she had been cured, there were still some pains and twitches that would probably remain with her to the end of her life.

"Can anything be done about Balzac and his murderers?"

"Not right now. Perhaps in the future. Right now, with disruption throughout the Clans, the scientists have an edge they never had before, an opportunity to conspire more freely. I sense they might accelerate their activities, thinking they are not being observed. I cannot have that, and for that reason I am going to ask you, Peri, to accept an assignment from me, one that will be of immeasurable value to the Jade Falcons."

Peri was flabbergasted by Marthe's words. She had expected merely to report and be dismissed. She had not even expected the Khan to take her seriously.

"This may cause you to violate your oath as a scientist. I do not like asking that of you, but this is my first chance to place an agent who is also a scientist within the caste ranks, and I am eager to take it."

"Spy? I do not know if I could—"

"Permission to speak," Samantha said.

"You always have that permission, saKhan."

Samantha stood and began to pace between the chair and the office door. "I know a lot about you, Peri. I have even examined the codex of your cadet days. You washed out of cadet training, but at heart a trueborn will always be a warrior. We need you as a warrior in the field, on a military mission under the orders of your Khan. I would think that loyalty to the Khan and the Clan outweighs simple caste loyalties. I suggest that the mission itself, especially if accepted in warrior spirit, releases you from caste secrecy. And anyway, if we do not act against this conspiracy of scientists, we will continue to dilute the genetics of our warriors. Therefore, any data we can assemble about these clandestine projects is useful to all castes."

Peri blinked. "That is all too metaphysical for me, but I accept your statement that the good of the Clan overrides caste loyalty."

"Then you agree to discover what you can," Marthe said. "For the Clan."

"And for you, Marthe Pryde. But I am not exactly in favor among Balzac and his scientists. What can I even do?"

"Return to favor," Samantha said. "There is nothing a fanatic likes better than to welcome a prodigal back into the fold."

"He arranged to have me murdered."

"Praise him for that, if it comes up."

Peri had left the office soon after that and returned to Ironhold, to these tense moments outside the Scientist-General's office.

Etienne Balzac did seem smugly satisfied at Peri's "conversion."

"I am pleased you came to see me," he said toward the end of their meeting. "It seemed to me that, in your apparent opposition, we were losing the benefit of one of the sharpest minds among Jade Falcon scientists. In volunteering for a new assignment, you show your true loyalty to the caste."

"Scientists are meant to seek answers, and I may question, but my loyalty should never be in question," Peri managed to say without choking on the words.

Balzac seemed pleased.

"Scientist-General, I have one request now."

"Make it, Peri Watson."

"Since I know about the sibko at Kerensky Forest, and since I am from the same sibko as Aidan Pryde, I believe I could do valuable work there. It would also return me to my specialty of genetic research. Work I carried out in my earliest assignments in the caste has been applied to the current experimentation, and I am certain I can continue to make a contribution to the Kerensky Forest station. I formally request reassignment there."

Balzac frowned and thought for a long moment. Finally, he said, "Very well. I see your logic and will approve your request."

After he had dismissed Peri, Balzac called in Olan, his captain of the guards. The tall, nearly emaciated Olan stood as usual, at calm, expressionless attention. As he spoke, Balzac's hands were busy on the desk surface, rearranging already neat piles of paper into other neat piles of paper.

"Peri Watson, whose elimination you and your cohorts did not achieve, will be reassigned to the Sibko Training Center at Kerensky Forest."

"You wish her eliminated there?"

"Not yet. She has, well, recanted and we must see if the recantation is genuine."

"Why not just kill her, then the doubts would be meaningless?"

"You still think like the bandit you were. Wastefully. She is a valuable tool, this Peri Watson, and I think we can use her abilities, especially in our experiment at the Sibko Training Center. Further, we might attribute one attack on her to street violence, but a second might draw too much attention to her. If we have reason to kill her, we will do so, but it must take place away from here. So the Training Center is a good place. Place two of your guards into the security crew there to monitor her activities."

"It is done, Scientist-General. Should they report any suspicious activity, I will travel there myself to deal with her."

"She has seen you. She knows who you are."

"I doubt that. We passed in the corridor. She looked at me without recognition."

"Nevertheless, stay out of her way for now. As always, I will use you when I need you."

"Very well."

Balzac sat at his desk a long while after Olan had departed. As he thought, he tapped his fingers on the surface of his desk. Then, as was his habit, he forgot the Peri problem and began to deal with the next item on his agenda. It was just this skill at compartmentalization that had been the key to his meteoric rise from lowly bureaucrat to commander of the whole scientist caste.

28

Steel Viper Hall
Hall of the Khans, near Katyusha
Strana Mechty
Kerensky Cluster, Clan Space
8 May 3060

"**N**ow is the time to destroy the Falcons," Natalie Breen said softly, her voice nevertheless filling the dark room.

Perigard Zalman nodded, then realized that she could not see a nod in the darkness. "Aye, Khan Natalie. It is what we have come to discuss."

Natalie's voice, coming out of the shadows, had an eerie quality. "The invasion corridor, that is where the fight must be engaged. We have been watching Marthe Pryde long enough now. We read her like a book. She most surely plans to move against us, but the Viper must strike first. Let us build up our strength in the Inner Sphere and take the Falcons by surprise."

"She is so full of herself these days," came the voice of the third person in the darkened room, that of Khan Brett Andrews. "So high and proud over her victory against the Inner Sphere. But she has her hands full. The Falcons are still not up to strength or readiness."

"Aye," Natalie said, for once in accord with Andrews. "The Falcons look good on paper, but we can best them. Many of her units are still short, despite what the rosters show. Our training is the truest and the harshest of all the Clans. No freebirth scum taints our touman. The Falcons cannot stop us, if we plan well. Let us seriously reinforce our personnel in the invasion corridor, then strike with the swiftness of the Viper. We can seize a swath of worlds before the Falcons even know what has hit them."

"Kael Pershaw's Watch is the best of all the Clans, except perhaps the Wolves," Andrews said. "They will take note of any extraordinary troop movements, or any other change in our normal procedures."

"Not if we take certain measures," Natalie said. "We can disguise our activities. Troop ships can appear to be something else. First, we increase the number of troops rotating to the Inner Sphere. By hiding this troop increase in plain view, we will certainly get the attention of The Watch. They will congratulate themselves on discovering the Steel Vipers' 'secret' agenda and will look no further for deception. After all the Vipers are *so* transparent." Natalie let scorn fill her voice with those words, then went on matter-of-factly. "At the same time we significantly increase the number of ships in use by the merchant caste. We will, of course, have to manipulate our shipping data, which is Pershaw's main source of intelligence. But thinking he knows what the Steel Vipers are up to, he will hardly notice."

She laughed softly. "Those additional DropShips will be transporting nothing but warriors to the Inner Sphere. We should employ only the largest ships available. It will strain our resources here, but the added space will drastically increase the number of troops and supplies we can put into place. We will not be able to keep up the deception for long, but it will be enough. By the time Pershaw and The Watch realize their mistake, it will be too late."

"Unacceptable," Andrews snorted. "You know how warriors feel about honorable combat. They will detest being part of such subterfuge."

"Rubbish. Our Vipers are just itching for a chance to fight the Jade Falcons. They will welcome the chance to catch them napping. What do you say, Khan Zalman?"

"There is merit in your plan, Khan Natalie. The Falcons outnumber us on the books, but Marthe still has many slots to fill and a long way to go before all her new troops form a unified fighting unit. As Brett says, she is preoccupied with manpower activities here at home and will not likely move against us yet. We still have time to gain the upper hand."

"I suggest we begin immediately. The time is right. My thought is to send in Delta Galaxy."

Brett Andrews made a sound in the back of his throat that was just audible to the others in the room. Zalman recognized it as a sign of disapproval. He understood his saKhan's concern, but the steel viper was known as much for its stealth as for its bite. Not a leaf or a branch or a stem of grass moved to reveal its passage through the jungle.

"Brett," he said, "I would like you to begin immediately working out the logistics of deploying troops into the invasion corridor. You should find Natalie Breen of great assistance in this. Her recent report on our military status was most thorough."

Brett was silent for a moment, then said quietly, "I will do as you ask, my Khan. Civil unrest on the occupied worlds kept us from cleaning up after the Refusal War. We will finish the job now."

"Good. I knew I could count on you. You and your Fourth Guards won us several Falcon worlds after Tukayyid. They have good reason to fear you."

After some further discussion of strategy and tactics, Zalman and Andrews bade Natalie Breen a ritual goodbye. As the two walked down the corridor away from her office, Brett grumbled a bit more in the back of his throat.

"SaKhan, you have been grumbling since we got here. Do you wish to speak what is on your mind?"

Andrews gave him a sideways glance and hesitated a beat that made him fall behind Zalman's pace. Catching up, he said, "What disturbs me is this—I do not know what to call it—this link between you and Natalie Breen. Even though she was once Khan, I do not see why you consult her so eagerly."

"I was her saKhan for some years. I saw how intelligently she could analyze a situation, be it military or political. I respected her so highly and for so long that I have never quite lost the feeling that I should bow to her wisdom."

"That is precisely what I am talking about! Excuse my bluntness, but with her you act like an apprentice to a master. You are the master now! Natalie Breen once held power, but no more. In freebirth life, when a master is retired, the apprentice takes over. He does not go running to the former master each time a nail is off center."

Zalman stopped walking and laid a hand on Brett's shoulder, halting his progress also.

"How do you know that? What do you even know of freebirth life?"

"Not much, I admit. But I do know that there is something wrong with your keeping Natalie Breen around and consulting her on significant matters. She is not Khan any more, for good reason! She failed. She accepted the failure and resigned. You should do what all that means. Put her out to pasture!"

Zalman smiled. "I suspect you do not know much about pastures either. Natalie Breen would die if she were sent away. Hers is one of the best military minds I have known. I use it the way I use any valuable tool, the way I use anyone who can help me achieve my goals—the way, in fact, I use you, Brett Andrews. You are the fire I need to make the Steel Vipers more powerful. I need your bluntness, your rage. In the same way I need Natalie Breen's coolness, so that we may attack with both fire and ice."

"You would drown and burn your enemies simultaneously?"

"Not a bad idea. In that way I get help from both of you. And anyone else I can employ to assert Steel Viper supremacy. The Clan is all, *quiaff*?"

Andrews nodded and repeated the ritual Steel Viper

maxim. "The Clan is all, my Khan." Then, "I still would advise my Khan that there is danger in permitting the meddling of the former Khan."

"What kind of danger?"

"Perhaps she would like to regain her seat as Khan."

"Natalie Breen knows that will never happen."

"I wish I could agree."

As the two resumed walking, Perigard Zalman sensed that, instead of convincing Brett Andrews, he had merely intensified the standoff. He would have to watch this man closely. Brett Andrews, so obviously ambitious, might be capable of anything.

In her room Natalie Breen thought about Brett Andrews for a few minutes, then decided she could handle any roadblock he could put in her path. Not that there was anywhere she wanted to go just now.

No, that was not quite true. There *was* someplace she wanted to go. Back into the cockpit of a 'Mech. Resigning as Khan had not been enough. She had to redeem her failure, and there was only one way she could do that. By piloting a 'Mech to heroic victory.

She knew Perigard Zalman would fulfill any reasonable request from her. Now she had one to make.

PART II

THE INVASION
CORRIDOR

June 3061

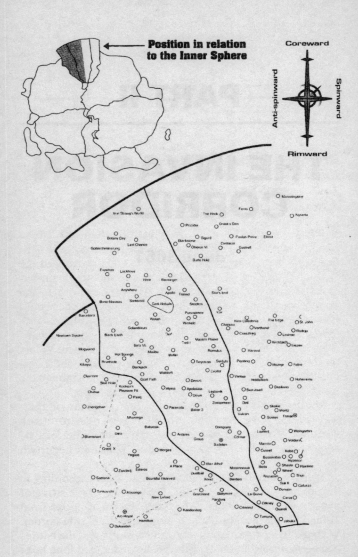

Position in relation to the Inner Sphere

Coreward

Anti-spinward

Spinward

Rimward

29

DropShip Turkina's Command
Inbound, Bensinger System
Jade Falcon-Steel Viper Occupation Zone
4 June 3061

It had been months since Marthe Pryde had left Strana Mechty, and she felt better than she had in a long time. Anticipating battles to come, her spirits soared. Aboard the DropShip there were no Grand Council meetings, no bureaucratic crises, no supervising war preparations to the point of readiness for just this moment, when she would first engage the Steel Vipers on the planet Bensinger.

Marthe was pleased with the thought of the battle awaiting her. The Falcons had been saddled with the Steel Vipers for too long. Now they would exterminate them like the vermin they were. She needed to consolidate her position in the Inner Sphere and that meant the Vipers had to go.

Marthe and a fleet of JumpShips were already on their way to the Inner Sphere with their own plan of attack when the Vipers had suddenly struck at a number of Falcon worlds in the invasion corridor. That had been two months ago.

The first wave of the Viper campaign, was—according to the reports—wildly successful. They took a whole string of planets with relative ease, forming a kind of noose from Toland all the way to Quarell along the Wolf-side border. With the Falcon garrisons weak and unprepared, the battles had been fierce but quick. Marthe, however, had long been expecting a move by the Vipers, and had put in place various contingency plans that would save as many troops as possible. Once the battles for those worlds became impossible to win, almost all of her forces had engaged in tactical repositioning, withdrawing to other Jade Falcon worlds.

Almost immediately the Vipers launched a second wave, trying to close the noose around another seven border worlds. It was a good plan with a fatal flaw. Believing the Falcons overwhelmed, the Vipers had left the coreward sector of the corridor poorly defended.

It was there that the Falcons would spring their surprise, with the help of the Wolves. Vlad had granted her ships safe passage, allowing the Falcon fleet to emerge undetected on the spinward side of the invasion corridor. Except for normal prebattle edginess, Marthe Pryde was happy. It felt so good to be on the attack again.

Truth be told, she had never really wanted anything else from life but to serve her Clan as a warrior who would one day die a glorious death in combat. For her, that was the way of the Clans. As a cadet, she used to think she would do anything to achieve her goal. How hard-nosed she had been then.

Thinking about her cadet days brought back, as always, the memory of her Trial of Position, when she had not only defeated the 'Mech that qualified her but also a second 'Mech piloted by Aidan. He later reproached her furiously, demanding to know why she had targeted him instead of one of the 'Mechs assigned to her as an opponent.

Marthe hardly knew the reason, then or now. It was the act of a warrior and she would do the same thing all over again. It was right; it was even destiny. By killing two 'Mechs she had entered the ranks as a Star Commander. That had spurred her onward, prodding her to develop command abilities from the first days of her life as a warrior.

She remembered the fury she had seen in Aidan's eyes after his defeat, when she had walked past him without speaking. For a moment she had wanted to turn around and wish him luck, but something held her tongue. She was young, just blooded. She was a warrior, while Aidan had become a tech. To this day, Marthe felt uncomfortable around other castes, especially freebirths. She wondered what Perigard Zalman would say if he knew that.

In some ways, she had never stopped being the newly blooded Marthe, thinking only of serving the Clan. No deed she had performed as warrior, no decision she had made as Khan, had applied only to her. Marthe could never think of herself as separate from the Clan. The well-worn phrase—*I am Jade Falcon*—fit her so well.

Yet the command process, from Star Commander to here, had chipped away at many of her beliefs. Learning to make decisions, learning to make compromises. Opponents had to be dealt with and problems had to be solved. And that is what she had done. Now she would deal with the Vipers, in her own way. Even as they tried to catch the Falcons off guard, they had sown the seeds of their own defeat. They had given her time to reflect, time to plan.

Over the centuries the Vipers had stuck in the craw of the Jade Falcons. That would change now. It would all end now.

On another DropShip, Samantha Clees was talking with Grelev in her quarters aboard the *Blue Jesses,* inbound to the planet Persistence. She had come to value his calm presence ever since he had first been assigned her aide on Ironhold. She felt nervous, and as always when that happened, began to pace.

"I have to admire the Vipers for their boldness. The way they went after a whole string of our worlds more or less simultaneously."

"Thirteen, eh?" Grelev said. "They are not superstitious, these Vipers."

"They are no Nova Cats at least. I doubt they even bothered to count."

"That will be their bad luck then. And now we will counter with our own wave of attacks, *quiaff*?"

"That is as the Khan would have it."

"You are not sure?"

"Strategy is strategy. I will fit myself and my unit into it."

"But there are doubts?"

"Just apprehensions. The Vipers got the jump on us here in the occupation zone. It allowed them to solidify their position. We start at a disadvantage. Not an insurmountable one, but still a disadvantage. We are Jade Falcon and can handle it, especially under the command of a Khan with the spirit of Marthe Pryde."

Samantha strode from one end of her tiny quarters to the other. "The Crusader cause died on Strana Mechty, but I say the Falcons are still crusaders. This time Marthe is leading us on a crusade of her own."

Grelev looked puzzled and asked what she meant.

"In ancient days a crusader would do anything for the cause," Samantha said. "He would go to any destination where he thought the object of the cause resided and slay anyone in his path. He would lay siege to the holy city as long as he could, he would level it to the ground if need be. That is what I mean by a crusade. Marthe Pryde intends to make the Jade Falcons mighty again and to take control of the invasion corridor. She will annihilate the Vipers, at least those in the corridor, with the same ruthlessness the Inner Sphere showed in demolishing the Smoke Jaguars."

"Take no prisoners, burn the harvest, and clutter the killing fields."

"Something like that, whatever you meant. At the moment the Vipers have the tactical advantages and think they are on the way to winning it all. They will not. They cannot. Not as long as we have Marthe Pryde's zeal. I am a crusader, too. I believe in our Khan, and I believe we will prevail, even if the odds against us are great. Marthe Pryde has the zeal in her eyes and that, oddly enough, is our advantage, Grelev."

Grelev nodded. "We will follow anywhere she leads."

"Aye," said Samantha. "The Vipers, now that they perceive their narrow slice of the corridor as firm, have made at least one mistake. In their overconfidence, they have let us slip in without resistance. They have no idea we are on the way, so they are not expecting any response from us. They also did not anticipate that Vlad Ward would grant us safe passage through the Wolf Zone. How could they?

"In less than twenty hours we will be making our batchall to the Viper commander on Persistence, while the Khan leads an attack on Bensinger. With those worlds as a base we can sweep down through the corridor, hitting them at Waldorff, Zoetermeer, Sudeten, and others."

"You are confident, Khan Samantha."

"I am Jade Falcon. Of course I am confident. We have seen difficult days since the Refusal War, but now we are on the rise. I assure you of that, Grelev. We are on the rise."

30

DropShip **Raptor**
Inbound, Bensinger System
Jade Falcon-Steel Viper Occupation Zone
4 June 3061

The spirits of Star Commander Joanna were also revived by the prospect of the invasion. Every day spent on the home-worlds and away from battle had been agony. Each night she had dreams in which she had finally grown too old, and that Marthe Pryde had reneged on her promise to allow her to return to the Inner Sphere as a warrior. When a warrior got as old as Joanna, not even the support of a Khan could ensure her warrior status. Even after she had beaten much younger opponents in training, Joanna still had the dreams, still feared there was a chance she would be left behind.

One of Horse's running jokes had been that Joanna could always defect to the Nova Cats, where age was something of an advantage. "You might even become a Nova Cat Khan," he used to say. When the Nova Cats turned coat and joined the Inner Sphere, Horse dropped the joke.

This campaign may be my last chance, she thought as she lay in her bunk. She could abide these quarters that were more suited to a rat than a human. What she could not abide was the way the bunk felt littered with unexploded land mines. *There are too many pains running up and down my arms and legs, too many neurohelmet glitches that give me such fierce headaches. If I were sensible, I would resign my commission gladly, but I am not sensible. If I have pain in every muscle of my body, if the blood coursing through my veins is being pumped erratically, if my head is enveloped in pain, I will go on fighting.*

She thought back to the time when Ravill Pryde had tried to get her reassinged to a sibko nursery as nanny for newly hatched sibkin. Only the intervention of Kael Perhsaw had saved her.

This time, though, I will prove myself so well, so fiercely, that they will not dare try to reassign me. If they do, they will have to tie me to the back of a DropShip and drag me away.

In the BattleMech bay of the DropShip *Starbird,* Horse stood at the tip of his *Summoner's* giant feet and looked up. He especially liked this view. The foreshortening gave the 'Mech a look of mightiness that made even Horse draw breath.

He watched some members of his Trinary mill about in the DropShip bay. They were edgy, it was clear. Edgy in a good sense. They were ready for battle, itching to prove that this unusual unit of theirs could justify the Khan's faith in them.

Horse had spent little time in his quarters during the six-month voyage. He preferred to be here among his warriors.

Marthe had designated them as "The Khan's Irregulars." The unit consisted entirely of freeborns, some of whom had been with Horse on Huntress and some who were replacements for those who had died on that mission. They were skilled warriors who might have been persecuted in other units or relegated to garrison or second-line duty. But not now.

"Star Captain?"

Marthe had assigned Horse the temporary rank of Star Captain when she'd sent him and the Trinary to Huntress to investigate activities at the Falcon Eyrie outpost. After she had decided to keep the special unit, he had fought a Trial to retain the rank. He had succeeded easily, and felt a thrill of pride knowing that freeborns rarely, if ever, achieved Star Captain.

The voice invoked his rank again, and he turned. It was Pegeen, commander of one of the Trinary's Stars. She was a short, meek-looking woman who, more than most warriors, had to prove her fierce warrior instincts on a regular basis.

"Yes, Star Commander?"

"You looked so deep in thought, I wondered if you needed someone to talk to."

Pegeen had gradually become his unofficial second in command since the Trinary was formed. Amiable and perceptive, she had become a valuable asset to Horse.

"I was thinking, Pegeen, that we must not fail in the coming battles. We have more to prove than any regular unit. You can bet the trueborns will never let us live down any little failing they perceive, any combat humiliation. They are quiet now, ever since the Khan ordered the official designation of our unit for this campaign."

"But it is a fine challenge for us, *quiaff*?"

"Aff. Since Diana won her bloodname, their grumbling and snide remarks seem to have diminished."

"True."

"And they will remain subdued—unless we fail. Then they will be on us like insulation on a myomer fiber."

"Diana herself is in the same boat, Horse. She has only won the bloodname. A significant achievement, to be sure, but her every action will be scrutinized minutely from here on."

"I know, even though she has proven herself in battle time and again in the past."

They paused, both of them staring up at the gleaming *Summoner*.

"Do you ever mind being freeborn, Horse?"

"How could I mind? It's what I am, *quiaff*?"

"Aff." Pegeen glanced away from the 'Mech. "I guess aff."

Another warrior ready for battle seethed in his cold and forbidding chamber on the *Raptor*. Ravill Pryde had tried to drink a fusionnaire to quiet his mind, but—like most drinks he had tried—it did little for him. He was not a warrior partial to drink. On the whole, few were.

My challenge to Diana's bloodname will never take place now, he thought. *She has Marthe Pryde on her side. The tide will turn for me if this damned Diana succeeds in battle. My challenge will be remembered. My ristar status may evaporate. I will be just another warrior among many. I cannot abide that. Dying in battle would be preferable.*

Not many Jade Falcon warriors thought in terms of ambition, but Ravill Pryde was not like most warriors. The anomaly was perhaps due to the injection of Wolf Clan genes into his sibko. The Wolves seemed to enjoy deviousness more than the Jade Falcons.

But Ravill knew he must accept whatever happened. If he had a chance to hurt Diana, outside of combat where they had to be allies, he would grab it. If he did not, if he were not to rise any further within the Clan, he would have to accept that also.

Sitting in one of the point-defense turrets that served as backup should the *Raptor*'s fire control system go down, Diana's meditations were similar to those of Horse and Pegeen. She stared out at dim planets she could just make out in the distance, at flickering stars, at the fearsome darkness of it all, and felt like exactly what she was at that moment, a lonely warrior small in a little pustule on the side of a ship that, in the breadth of the surroundings, was itself a small physical imperfection.

Diana closed her eyes, shutting out the universe with the

simple action. The tiny compartment was cold, since there was no need to heat it unless an attack developed, and probably not even then—the warrior who usually occupied the bubble would be too busy to care about personal comfort.

I can almost sense my father, the great Aidan Pryde, looking down at me from wherever in this stravag universe the spirits of heroes go.

She opened her eyes again. The universe was still out there, majestic and incommunicative. *Now that I have the bloodname, many think of me already as the heir to his heroism. Heroism was how much of your life, father?* She had only recently begun addressing his spirit in her mind as "father." *How much of your life in actual time? I mean, you spent many of your warrior days in garrison units, doing mop-up work and simple guard duty. There was heroism in the battle that made you reveal that you were a trueborn, after all. The admittedly tainted heroism of your bloodname victory. The quick thinking during the battle of Tukayyid. The last few minutes on Tukayyid. Maybe a couple of other events that do not come to mind. If you added up the time for these acts of heroism, how much time would that be? A few hours? Maybe under an hour? How much time do I have?*

In the part of the sky she examined, a star seemed to flare up. She wondered if it was an answer from her father, a mere random astronomical event, or only just an optical illusion.

31

Sibko Training Center 111
Kerensky Forest, Ironhold
Kerensky Cluster, Clan Space
27 June 3061

"Tell me more about the war."

Naiad's voice was shrill and urgent.

"I have told you the little I have heard," Peri said. "Not much news filters through to this sector, Naiad. The fighting is fierce and the Falcon reinforcements, led by the Khan, have won back a half-dozen planets. The Vipers were taken by surprise by the sudden appearance of the reinforcement army in the two-pronged assault on Bensinger and Persistence. The Falcon troops hit fast and took those worlds quickly, and with ease. The garrison troops the Vipers had left behind were not strong enough to defend against a Falcon attack. They were easy victories, causing minimal damage to the Jade Falcon forces."

Peri glanced around the abandoned barracks, where she and Naiad came to talk. Naiad was the only one of the sibko members who deigned to say much to Peri. Most of them resented her presence, as just another scientist picking them apart. On some of the visits here, Peri had straightened the bunks and swept the floor. Anything that was debris had been shoved into the general recycling unit a few meters away.

"And then?" Naiad asked eagerly. "Come on, Peri—and then?"

"Then the Khan won back our corridor capital of Sudeten,

a crushing blow to the Vipers. With all our command facilities still intact there, the Sudeten victory won not only a world but many strategic advantages. Losses there were somewhat higher, but overall relatively light. A couple of units are out of action. It is said that the freeborn unit, the Khan's Irregulars, will be a part of the next bid. It sounds as though many warriors are fearful about that, but I know the commander of the Irregulars, and it would be a mistake ever to underestimate him. That is about all I can remember from the dispatches that have come into Training Center headquarters. Details were scant. We are, after all, pretty low on the information food chain, Naiad."

"You saying we're not important?"

"Not at all. Merely that there is a certain secrecy attached to this place and what is sent here is carefully monitored. And, Naiad, easy on the contractions, *quiaff*?"

Naiad, who definitely did not like being criticized, frowned. "I'll say as many contractions as I want. When I'm around you anyway."

"But not around Octavian, *quiaff*?"

"Right. He'd rip my skin off."

"As any good sibparent would."

"Stravag! I wish I could be in this war!"

"Your time will come."

"When I'm a warrior, we'll prob'ly have peace. I want to go now."

Peri smiled. *How young this child is. And sometimes how old. I cannot remember Aidan at this age, but I am sure he was just as feisty, just as dramatic. The others are always reminding me of him also, but this Naiad is the most like him.*

"It is time for me to return," Naiad said. "Octavian is already angry enough at me for breaking Dania's arm."

"I can see why. But it is early. You have several minutes yet."

"Something I gotta do first."

Naiad left the barracks abruptly, waving goodbye.

Peri was glad the child had left so early. She had something on her mind anyway. The guards were used to her now, and she needed to take a look at some records while the other scientists were in the field or in the commissary for the midday meal. The offices would be empty now. She had searched the place three times before and become familiar with the general routines.

Naiad stayed in the shadows and watched Peri pass by. Tracking her was easier than any of the other people at the training center. Octavian was the hardest. He admitted to having eyes in the back of his head, although Naiad had never seen them. They had to be there, though. He saw too much.

She had already noted how Peri, who did not mingle much with the others, acted mysteriously from time to time. Naiad saw her going to the main building again, the same place to which she had followed her a week ago.

She's a nosy one, this one. But she's beautiful, the most beautiful person I've ever seen. Ever. Of course, I haven't seen many people. And she does look like me but older.

Peri was gradually accumulating information about the project at the Training Center. However, since Marthe Pryde was off at war, there was little she could do about it.

What if something happens to Marthe? If she is killed in this campaign, who else even knows my mission? Samantha Clees. What are the odds of both of them being killed in battle? It could happen. Then I am stuck here, a spy without a control to report to. I would still work against Etienne Balzac.

Colm Harvey, the silent geneticist who seemed to be the workhorse of the cadre assigned to the Training Center, had a cubicle on one side of the large room that served as the main office for the scientific team. In this room, the scientists often met, sitting around the enormous mahogany table in its center, to share their research, which centered around the sibko being studied here. Peri was not allowed into these meetings. Balzac had saddled her with a low security clearance, which he had called a mere protective measure that would be lifted after a short time. It was as if he knew the real reason she had requested this assignment and, like a game, intended to set traps to catch her. The low security clearance meant she would have to explain her presence in any wrong place, such as her current presence in Harvey's cubicle.

Harvey had left little behind on his desk or anywhere to indicate what he was working on. Not that his current research would be of much importance to her, anyway. The subject of most studies was the activities of the sibkin, and were irrelevant to her purpose. She sought the secrets behind the studies.

She switched on the computer set on one side of Harvey's desk. Searching the computers was, she knew, a particularly dangerous act. If anyone found her at someone else's computer display, she had no clever excuses for being there. For that reason, she had a small but long-bladed knife secreted behind her back in a spine-holster.

All of the computers had to be accessed through passwords. Peri had managed to get into parts of other scientists' files by cracking their passwords, but so far had failed at most and discovered little in the files she was able to enter. However, she had noticed that Colm Harvey had a tendency toward absent-mindedness. He forgot appointments, showed up late to meetings, often seemed distracted as he worked. A man like that would want a password he could remember easily. She tried both his names. No luck. Both names together did not work. She tried the name of the sibkin, and Aidan's. Still no access. She tried all the names backwards, the names and numbers of buildings in the complex, some common Clan words. Nothing.

She sat back in Harvey's swivel chair and thought about the labnames awarded to scientists within the caste. *Harvey. Who was Harvey? I wish I had paid more attention in the classes devoted to Terran scientific history. Harvey goes way back, almost prehistoric in science. Something to do with anatomy. Made discoveries in that field. Bones.* She typed in the word "bones" and received the message denying access. She tried the names of the bones she could remember. Nothing. *Not bones, then. Parts of the body?* She rapidly typed in the common parts of the body, got the same message. *No, it*

*was not that. What did Harvey study? Something about cir-
culation? Try blood.* She typed the word "blood."

The password worked and icons appeared all over the computer screen. *I was right. Harvey counters his forgetfulness
with an obvious password. Anyway, there is no reason not to
have obvious passwords. Who would expect a spy here?*

It only took moments for Peri to find and examine several
files. Most of them were not much different from files she
had already seen. In a shared network many of them *were*
files she had already seen.

She did not believe that the absent-minded Harvey would
not record everything that might be of value to his work.
There had to be something in his files she could use.

And then, almost accidentally, she found it. It was in a
file blandly titled "Strategics." A long, multi-paged and
coded file, with many cross-references to other files. The
thing that immediately caught her attention was that the
document had clearly come from the Scientist-General
himself. When she had quickly scrolled to the end, she
found a message that said not to print out the file and to
memorize it, then destroy it. Perhaps the message should
have been more specific for Harvey, telling him that if in his
absent-mindedness he could not memorize or assimilate the
information in it, he should destroy this file anyway.

Peri had discovered long ago that it was dangerous to
leave a scientist with an instruction or message that could
be taken literally. They would usually take it literally. In an
atmosphere like that of the center, where the scientists were
not particularly security-conscious, a person like Harvey
would just keep such a message on file until he had fulfilled
the instruction of memorizing it, never expecting anyone
else to break into the computer to read it.

The coding of the file was intricate and clever and it might
have put off a normal spy, but since Peri knew most of the
codes and had seen this one before, a series of keystrokes decoded it for her, as another series would send it back into its
coded state when she was done. The only problem after that
was the file's extreme length. She scrolled through it as best

she could, seeing many long, involved tables and lists of data. One thing the tables and data did indicate was that the sibko secreted in Training Center 111 was one of several. Many, actually. No specific locations were indicated, but apparently they were located all over the homeworlds.

This project is interClan then. We may have training enclaves put away in remote sections of planets involving most or all of the Clans. It is clear the genetic materials used are drawn from several sources, so Aidan is not the only hero whose genetic materials are being used. But, if I am right, his may be involved in several different secret projects the caste is running.

Nearly two years ago, when she had been assigned to the Falcon Eyrie station on Huntress, Peri had found that copies of Aidan Pryde's genetic materials were being kept in the labs of the Smoke Jaguar genetic repository in the capital city of Lootera. It had been a shock to discover that materials that should have been stored only in Jade Falcon facilities also sat on a shelf of the Smoke Jaguars. She had been appalled that a scientist of another Clan would work with Jade Falcon genetic materials.

She had left Huntress soon afterward and set herself on the long quest that had led up to this moment. She wondered what had happened to the Aidan Pryde materials, in the time the Inner Sphere controlled the planet. Huntress was now claimed by the Falcons, but it sickened her to think that Inner Sphere scum might have been at liberty to even touch the Aidan copies. That was what the secrecy and intrigue of her caste had caused. It had to be stopped.

Further into the file, she read a message that apparently came from Balzac himself. A long section, it clearly showed that sibkos like that of the Aidan sibko on Ironhold were not being developed to become Clan warriors. Balzac clearly stated that they would be at the service of the scientist caste. All the warrior personnel involved in their training would apparently be disposed of and the units would be shipped out to a location not mentioned in the message.

Balzac is assembling an army of his own! If I get this

right, he intends to form his own power base, a virtual scientist Clan that frees us from caste status. What would he call his Clan? The Devious Labrats? The scary part is that this might work. What can I do? I cannot print this, there is a lock against that. I have to take notes, memorize as much as I can. Have to go now, getting dangerous here.

Naiad watched Peri leave the building. Next time she would have to follow her in.

In the distance she heard her name being called. Sounded like Idania's voice. Naiad knew she was late for her class on warrior history. Octavian would kill her, she thought.

32

Daemon Beach, near the city of Daemon
Waldorff V
Jade Falcon-Steel Viper Occupation Zone
1 July 3061

Skyscrapers were an unusual phenomenon, at least to Clan eyes. In the homeworlds most buildings did not go beyond five or six stories, except for the occasional ornate and massive genetics repository or maybe an official building. Great height in a Clan city was generally limited to statues honoring Clan heroes. In statues was seen a rare instance of Clan social competition, as each Clan poured more resources into creating larger and larger ones. There was one statue of a Star Adder warrior whose exploits no one remembered, but whose stone likeness could be seen for kilometers around the city where it stood.

When she first walked her 'Mech onto Daemon Beach, Diana was struck by the long shadows cast on the sands by the gargantuan empty structures of the city of Daemon. With some of the roofs sheared off by BattleMech activity during the original Clan invasion and ragged walls still standing as battle scars, the shadows seemed abstract—gray things crawling along the sand.

Beyond the shadows the rough surf attacked the shore, high waves peaking for a moment that seemed unnaturally long, then capitulating to the beach, evening out and sliding up the sands, then retreating, taking layers of sand and other debris with it, while creating a kilometers-long terrace of hard, damp sand, a terrace becoming higher by the moment. Even while sitting high in her warm *Nova* cockpit, Diana could sense the frigid dampness outside. It must be very cold, she thought. The onshore breeze rocked the *Nova* as it lumbered forward.

Diana and her Star were on a flanking movement to attack the Viper 'Mechs now holding the city of Daemon, but she was having difficulty moving her *Nova* across these sands. Its massive metal feet did not grip securely. It felt like the 'Mech was slipping and sliding across the beach, with the sand doing its best to brake its speed. On either side of her, Diana sensed her fellow MechWarriors also struggling to maintain balance on the moving sands pushed by the strong breeze.

After following an arc along the beach, skirting the edge of the sand terrace, they headed for a gate that, at one time, had ushered vacationing Inner Sphere citizens onto the beach. At that time Daemon Beach had been a prime attraction for those with enough money to enjoy a respite from the stress of their daily lives. All that had ended eleven years ago when the Falcons had swooped down and taken the world of Waldorff during the invasion.

Everywhere one went on this planet, one saw scars of that time. Daemon and Daemon Beach had been abandoned long ago, casualties of some of the hot fighting that originally won the planet for the Falcons. The Falcon victory was short-lived, however. By order of ilKhan Kerensky, the

Falcons had been forced to turn Waldorff over to the Steel Vipers after they were assigned to share the corridor.

When the Falcons dropped insystem two days ago, bringing with them the Turkina Keshik, the Falcon Guards, and the Falcon Hussars from Gamma Galaxy, the First Falcon Striker Cluster and Seventh Talon Cluster of the Gyrfalcon Galaxy as well as the Khan's Irregulars, they had lost the surprise factor that had gained them their early triumphs. Waiting for them was the Viper Khan's Triasch Keshik, the most elite unit in the Steel Viper touman, reinforced by a number of other units.

The fighting had been formidable so far, and almost immediately a new kind of combat had erupted. Diana was not sure how it had happened, except for the age-old rivalry between the two Clans. At some point the Vipers had abandoned *zellbrigen,* the traditional one-on-one combat of the Clans, and the fighting had exploded into an all-out melee. As the battle grew fiercer, no one had tried to revert to tradition.

An earlier Viper assault had divided the Falcons into two forces—the Turkina Keshik with the First Falcon Cluster, the Seventh Talon Cluster, and the Falcon Hussars; and the Falcon Guards with the Khan's Irregulars—that were only a few kilometers apart, but with too many obstacles between for them to join up again easily, at least for now. Then the temporarily oversized Triasch Keshik had moved into nearby Daemon, knowing the city was empty. From there, they had managed to split the already besieged Falcon Guards and Irregulars into three disparate units, which were now desperately attempting to converge on the city, in hopes of linking up with their fellow units.

Diana was ready. Everything rechargeable in her *Nova* had been recharged, everything loadable reloaded, the heat that had risen fairly high now at low level, and the newly bloodnamed pilot herself feeling eager to annihilate Steel Vipers.

Horse and his Trinary had just crossed Daemon's city limits. The fury of their combat showed in the damage to the exterior of their 'Mechs, the battle stains, the dents, grooves, and hollows that faded the intense green paint on the metal. They had arrived on Waldorff all shiny and clean, but the sheen had long ago worn off.

Although recharged and ready for battle, they looked like a unit at the end of its tether. The Trinary BattleMechs that had gone into battle tall and powerful-looking now seemed bent and unsteady. Part of the unsteadiness was due to the fact that 'Mechs were not generally suited for combat in an urban setting. 'Mech pilots had the devil of a time picking their way through city streets, especially ones so cluttered with the debris of earlier fighting. Some streets proved impassable. Mounds of rubble formed obstacles that often stretched completely across the street.

The air attacks that Marthe had ordered had been particularly effective, but they had only added to the already considerable amount of debris. The Trinary 'Mechs struggled not to lose their balance as their massive feet crunched down through the piles of rubble.

It is a good thing, Horse thought, *that there are no civilians left in Daemon. They would be flattened like bugs.* He knew there'd be plenty of other bugs to squash, but they would be military ones, Elementals and 'Mech pilots—and maybe even some 'Mechs.

In the moments since they had crossed into Daemon, a heavy rainstorm had developed, sheets of rain pouring down without warning. Streaks of rain began on the outside surface of the cockpit, only to be eliminated by jets of air clearing the moisture away, keeping the cockpit surface dry.

The rain obscured the way ahead. It splashed off buildings and sent small but roiling streams along the street to tubelike devices that were apparently the Inner Sphere method of street-cleaning. As the stream came close to the tube, it was sucked in so hard that the action had the appearance of lifting the waters off the roadway and into the tube. In a storm this devastating, though, the device could not keep up with the heavy flow of water.

Horse was more worried about his warriors than the turbulence of the weather. They had been in the field for more than twelve hours. First, they had gotten cut off from the main Falcon force of the pair of Clusters from Gyrfalcon Galaxy and Turkina Keshik, and then separated from the Falcon Guards. They had fought on here because there was no clear path back to the temporary base on a plain many kilometers away.

Between the Trinary and the plain were the massed Steel Viper BattleMechs of the entire Alpha Galaxy, which had wedged apart the Guards and the Irregulars from the main Jade Falcon force in the first place. More disturbing, however, was the fact that Horse was not aware of any Jade Falcon unit that had yet made contact with the Triasch Keshik, the Steel Viper command unit, led by Khan Perigard Zalman himself. A feeling that the Triasch Keshik was hunting down the Falcon Guards and his Irregulars, and was systematically dividing and then destroying each unit, began to steal its way through him.

But why would the Khan of all the Vipers be hunting a group of freeborns?

A particularly savage gust of wind rocked Horse's *Summoner,* bringing him back to the present. Behind him he heard the sounds of combat. Switching his display to rearview, he saw that one of his Trinary, a MechWarrior named Bello in a *Black Lanner,* was under attack by a Steel Viper *Hankyu.*

Horse called Pegeen over the commline, even as he tried to turn his *Summoner* around on the heavily littered street to go back and help Bello.

"Where'd the *Hankyu* come from, Pegeen?"

"Leaped over one of the rubbled buildings, came down with lasers firing. Bello's taking a lot of punishment."

"I'll help him."

Horse fired a salvo of missiles toward the *Hankyu,* sending a large chunk of armor flying off the enemy 'Mech's back. The plating fell toward the street and immediately became more anonymous rubble atop a high pile of debris. Horse got in no more shots. The *Hankyu* engaged its jump jets and leaped over the shell of the building from which it had come. Horse got on the commline fast and told his Trinary not to pursue.

"Could be a trap," he hollered.

"Almost certainly is," Pegeen echoed.

"Stay in close formation," Horse ordered. "As much as possible in these broken streets anyway. You okay, Bello?"

"Hunky dory, Cap. Took a couple of hits, just scratches."

That drew a smile from Horse as he toggled the commline switch to speak privately to Pegeen. He took Bello's familiarity as a sign of trust. "Pegeen, these Vipers know this terrain. They have the edge on us here. What are the chances of retreat?"

"Retreat? Where to?"

"Good point. Be alert, *quiaff*?"

"Aff."

"We should be hooking up with the others soon. Head toward the beach. They'll be coming in there."

"Aye," Pegeen said, and then, after a precisely timed pause, added, "Cap."

Her affable tone made Horse laugh, and he forced the *Summoner* to a higher speed as it made its way over and around the remains of the city of Daemon.

In the dark skies, pushing her 'Mech forward against the driving rain in the flat, open fields leading to Daemon, Joanna cursed with her accustomed vehemence. It was bad enough that she had to force her *Summoner* through deep mud. Even worse was that she and her Star were being guided by that bantam rooster Star Colonel, Ravill Pryde.

Just where I wanted to be, watching the back of that savrashi! He had to go and get separated from the rest of the Falcon Guards and insist on taking over command of my Star.

Apparently Ravill had gone too far afield in his pursuit of a Viper 'Mech, which he did defeat and, in fact, demolish, but when the Vipers split the Jade Falcons in two, he had found himself separated from most of the Falcon Guards, except for Joanna's Star. With his usual arrogance, he had informed Joanna that he would take over command of her Star. When the Vipers in the city of Daemon were detected and he had also located Horse's Trinary and the other BattleMechs of the Falcon Guards, led by Diana's Star, nearing Daemon Beach, Ravill had taken over the commline and organized the present pincerlike movement, with the three 'Mech groups converging on the city.

The stravag is power-mad. He does not really know the terrain, he is not experienced in urban combat, he cannot even keep his troops together and instead goes off on a mad pursuit of his own—and he has the nerve to risk us with his plan!

Ravill led the Star onto a broken highway leading into the city. Ahead of them was what was once an ornate city gate, announcing the pride of Daemon to all visitors, but it was now in ruins and more like a pile of rubble to be cautiously stepped over.

Abruptly, on the other side of Daemon, near the famous Daemon Beach, lancing beams of bright azure light indicated that a battle had already begun in that area.

"They were ordered to hold fire until we were in place!" Ravill Pryde cried angrily over the commline. "Nobody can be trusted anymore. Especially now that our ranks are riddled with freebirths in this action. We will head that way, to save their precious metal behinds!"

Joanna cursed her position, directly to the rear of Ravill Pryde's *Timber Wolf*'s precious metal behind, and cursed the bantam Star Colonel one more time.

Diana had been following the progress of Horse's Trinary on her secondary display. Their two groups were about half a kilometer apart as she guided her *Nova* through the beach gate and into the city.

And right into the arms of a trio of Steel Viper BattleMechs.

Horse picked up Diana's location just before she came through the gate and detected before she did the threat that lay waiting for her. Ordering his Trinary to pick up speed,

he led them toward the beach gate. As he circumvented a
rubble heap, Horse saw a flash of movement through windows whose frames and glass were, surprisingly, intact in a
wall down the street to his left.

When the *Hankyu,* possibly the same one that had men-
aced Bello, jumped to the top of the wall and began firing
downward, Horse was ready, targeting the *Hankyu*'s torso
with his LRMs. They caught the enemy 'Mech mid-torso
and knocked it backward off the wall. As it fell into the
building, Horse tracked it with his *Summoner*'s right arm,
firing the small laser at the descending *Hankyu* through the
descending row of windows in the building wall. Glass
shattered and frame splintered. Whether or not the missile
salvo or the lasers had together destroyed the *Hankyu,*
Horse felt that, if the Viper 'Mech was still mobile, it was
not revealing itself to him any more.

Pegeen's excited voice came over the commline. "I knew
you were a crack shot, Horse. I thought I was, too, but I
couldn't have done that window trick quite as precisely as
you just did."

"Nothing special," Horse said.

"So you say."

Horse saw on his secondary display that the Viper
'Mechs had begun firing at Diana's *Nova.* He accelerated
the *Summoner.* He needed every gram of piloting skill he
possessed just to keep the 'Mech upright in the wreckage he
ran over, skipped by, hopped on, and jumped across.

The strength of the Viper attack on the torso of Diana's
Nova knocked it against the side of the gate. The impact
caused a ragged crack to form in the gate's stone base. Another hit, this time on the right shoulder, and the *Nova* was
whirled around to face the beach. Diana sensed one of the
enemy 'Mechs heading toward her to try to finish her off.

At that moment there was an explosive sound louder than
any of the noises of battle, and a sudden vibration that
shook the 'Mech. Diana found herself losing control of her
'Mech, and felt the massive machine beginning to fall.

* * *

Simultaneously, as Horse got a visual on Diana's 'Mech, appearing to casually lean against the side of the gate, he found himself struggling to keep his *Summoner* balanced. His body slammed against the restraining belt of his cockpit seat. His brain, similarly, seemed to bounce around inside his head.

"What in the hell was *that*?" Pegeen shouted.

"A tremor, I think. Earthquake. Mild one."

"That's a mild one, then I'd like to see a—"

The major one came before she could finish the sentence. The 'Mechs, Jade Falcon and Steel Viper alike, rocked and swayed. Pegeen's *Hellbringer,* heavy as it was, tilted and bounced off a wall. A moment later the wall itself crumbled, whether from the quake or from contact with the Battle-Mech was not clear. Horse felt the tremor all through his cockpit and, for a moment, a frightening loss of balance. Everything around him blurred, and he momentarily lost the physical feel of his 'Mech through the neurohelmet.

His brain cleared rapidly, just in time for him to regain control. A crashing sound behind him told him that at least one of the Trinary 'Mechs had fallen. He did not have time to check out which one. He noted quickly on his screen that apparently many buildings had crumbled and fallen when the quake hit. High clouds of dust from their impact had not settled yet. Smaller debris was still sailing through the air. One large piece of wall narrowly missed the head of Horse's *Summoner*.

Ahead of him Diana and her *Nova* stumbled close to the attacking Viper 'Mechs. She had the presence of mind to fire steadily at a point on the middle 'Mech's lower torso. Then she used a cloud of armor splitting off in all directions and a cloud of dust caused by the tremor to make significant hits on one of the other 'Mechs. Still, she was outnumbered three to one, and there was some smoke emerging from a small hole that had been opened on the chest of her *Nova*.

Shock over seeing the damage that Diana's *Nova* had taken quickly wore off, as he got his first good look at the Viper 'Mechs she was facing. The strange feeling of being hunted by the Triasch Keshik came back tenfold as the insignia, proudly painted across the torso of the lead Viper 'Mech, suddenly became visible through the pouring rain.

Though unaffected by the first tremor, Joanna's *Summoner* was severely rocked by the newest one. As she fought to regain control, she sensed the 'Mech pitching forward, about to crash into the back of Ravill's *Timber Wolf*. Concentrating with the ferocity she was famous for, Joanna countered the forward movement with a stumble sideways that avoided the *Timber Wolf* but thrust her into the midst of the falling pieces of a building wall. It seemed as if she felt each blow from the fragments, but she was able to maneuver her 'Mech forward and through the hurtling debris.

The *Timber Wolf* also stumbled a bit before Ravill regained balance. He shouted some garbled commands that Joanna interpreted as an order for a charge toward the beach.

That Ravill Pryde! A true leader!

However, with abundant grumbling, she followed the Star Colonel to the battle.

None of the BattleMechs that had accompanied Diana along the beach had gotten into a good position to help her, even before the quake hit. In the bedlam of falling debris from the quake, everything was obscured and the Falcon 'Mechs began to wander around the sands like lost nomads.

As a Viper 'Mech, a *Stormcrow,* came forward to administer the kill to her, Diana momentarily blasted him backward with her PPC, causing little damage but disconcerting the Viper pilot. In that instant of confusion, Horse's *Summoner* seemed to appear out of a dust-cloud, and his furious attack disabled the *Stormcrow* in a haze of flying armor. The Viper 'Mech stood inoperable. Its pilot ejected out toward the beach, where she would at least land softly. The empty 'Mech swayed a bit in the heavy wind and then fell. It hit the side of the beach gate and slid sideways out of view.

Diana went on the commline. "Thanks, Horse."

"Any time, Diana."

"Will you freebirths stop congratulating each other?" Both freeborn warriors were surprised at the sudden blast of words from Ravill Pryde. "I am picking up more of these damn Vipers on their way. We are outnumbered, severely outnumbered!"

Horse checked his own sensor readings. Ravill Pryde was right. The Vipers seemed to be emerging from hidden points in the city rubble. A mass of them were headed toward the city gate.

"They have allowed us to group here," Ravill shouted. "Lured us here maybe."

"Absolutely. This is a trap," Horse said.

"Although I do not doubt it, what makes you so sure it is a trap, freebirth?"

"Have you not noticed the insignias on these Viper 'Mechs?"

"No, stravag! With all this rain, I can hardly see them to shoot, much less attempt to determine what Viper unit I am facing." The fury in Ravill's voice seemed to match the storm outside. "I suppose you have seen what unit we are fighting. Not that it really matters."

"No, Star Colonel, it does matter. The 'Mechs in the city are from the Triasch Keshik. Not a single Falcon unit has yet faced them and suddenly we find ourselves in a trap, sprung by the Keshik. Do you not find that odd, *quiaff*?" Horse said.

"Do not condescend to me, freebirth!" Ravill yelled. "You must be mistaken. There is absolutely no reason the Khan of the Steel Vipers, along with his entire Keshik, would attempt to ambush two Jade Falcon units composed almost entirely of freebirths."

"I cannot answer that question, Star Colonel. But I am positive the city is a trap. Whether a trap for us specifically, or any Jade Falcon unit, I cannot say. Regardless, we cannot fight them in the city. It's a mass of rubble, especially with that last quake."

"You are right," Ravill said. "The beach is safer, more open. Head there. We will fight the Triasch Keshik on the beach."

Horse, who had read a great deal of Terran history, smiled at Ravill's command. The Falcon Guard commander was apparently unaware that he had echoed some famous defiant words from the ancient past.

The Falcon 'Mechs retreated to Daemon Beach through the beach gate. The movement was so swift that many of the enormous fighting machines lopped off chunks of wall simply by brushing against the gate's sides as a mild aftershock rumbled through the city.

33

Viper Valley
Waldorff V
Jade Falcon-Steel Viper Occupation Zone
1 July 3061

Marthe Pryde felt as if she were being swept along in river rapids. The thrill of battle and the elation of every small victory were happening so fast that it was a struggle to keep up with all phases of the current operation. Even now, Samantha Clees and her Gyrfalcon Galaxy had devastated several Viper Trinaries on the far distant side of Viper Valley.

A wise decision, leaving Samantha in command of Gyrfalcon. She is much more valuable to me there than as my exec in the Turkina Keshik. She has commanded them for a decade and needs no orders from me, at least in the field.

Marthe was also glad the battle for Waldorff had turned into a full-scale engagement. The Falcons had already beaten the Vipers off many of the worlds they had taken in their first wave, and Viper resistance elsewhere was scattered and weak. With key units from both sides massed on Waldorff, this could be the deciding battle. The Falcons would do anything to win it, would pay any price. Marthe wondered if the Vipers could pay in the same coin. If she could crush them here, it would be all over. However, the Vipers were putting up a stiff fight.

As yet, the Falcons had still not engaged the Triasch Keshik. *Perhaps they are waiting for me to make a fatal error and then Khan Zalman will pounce.* A fleeting smile touched her lips. *He will be waiting for quite some time.*

The conflict was turning out to be immense, and the Falcons had pulled out all the stops. The Vipers were beginning to take heavy losses here in the valley, but were making the Falcons fight for every centimeter of ground. All around her immediate vicinity, Marthe saw downed and disabled Viper 'Mechs. Most of her own Keshik had already been dispatched to other locations, as reinforcements.

Samantha came online. "We need to push them harder, Marthe. Although they are being hard hit, our own forces are starting to incur losses that I consider unacceptable. We have destroyed most of the Second Viper Guards and have the 400th Assault Cluster in full retreat, but my Gyrfalcon Clusters have sustained significant damage. There is no doubt that we will take this world, but if we do not vanquish the Vipers soon, it will be a pyrrhic victory. How is it over on your side of the valley?"

"Looks good. We handed the First and Fourth Viper Guards a resounding defeat, but they both retreated with most of their numbers in good order. Have you made contact with the Triasch Keshik yet?"

"Negative. You?"

"Neg. And this will not be over until Khan Zalman is brought to heel. We should drive to link up our other units. With the First and Fourth Viper Guards in ordered withdrawals, we need to shatter them before they shore up the

400th or Second Clusters. Not to mention before Perigard and his Keshik decide to show themselves."

"Agreed," Samantha said.

"What about the units that were separated by the Viper wedge?"

"Lost all contact with them. I am sure they are acquitting themselves well, even your Irregulars."

"Do not slight my Irregulars. They all have solid combat experience."

"No insult intended. Just supplying information."

"Where are there problems that will prevent us linking up?"

"The fighting is fierce on the north side of the valley. Right now my First Falcon Striker Cluster and Gamma Galaxy's Falcon Hussars are pinned down at the foot of the cliffs. Uvin Buhallin reports that both units are taking casualties. Apparently there is one particular Viper warrior who is taking on all comers and winning. I am regrouping to proceed there."

Marthe called up the location on her map-screen. "I am closer to it than you are. We will meet up there."

"But—"

Marthe switched off the commline so that she would not have to hear Samantha's objections. It was true that she should follow her own troops. However, the battle thrill she was feeling demanded more action.

She quickly reached the area where the Striker Cluster and the Falcon Hussars were battling valiantly but losing ground. The Falcon 'Mechs kept striking out away from the cliffs, then were brutally pushed back again by the Vipers.

Marthe spotted the Viper warrior Samantha had mentioned, right in the middle of the fray. In a *Crossbow,* the pilot was currently working on the legs of a *Mad Dog,* shooting away more and more armor, exposing more and more of the myomer muscle structure beneath, rapidly shifting attention from one 'Mech to another and sending them reeling.

Marthe flicked on the general commline to address the enemy pilot.

"This is Khan Marthe Pryde of the Jade Falcons. I would speak to the pilot of the Viper *Crossbow.*"

There was no response. All that could be heard on the commline was a complex pattern of static.

"All right then. I challenge the *Crossbow* warrior to single combat. You against me. The rest, Falcons and Vipers alike, will stand back. Winner take all, for this sector of battle." The Viper pilot might have pointed out that Marthe's challenge was not all that generous, since the Falcons had essentially won the Viper Valley. But a Khan's challenge could not be ignored. "Do you accept the challenge?"

The *Crossbow* pilot remained silent, but ceased its attack on the *Mad Dog* and came forward to a clear patch of ground to face Marthe and her *Summoner*. The battle gradually wound down to nothing around the two 'Mechs as Falcon and Viper warriors became spectators.

Samantha's voice came on the commline. "I have you in sight, Marthe. What is going on?"

Marthe explained. Samantha's subsequent tone was clearly disapproving. "Let me replace you in the challenge. We cannot risk losing you, not now, with victory so close."

Marthe smiled to herself at the words. "You have no confidence in me? After all my victories today? I am the Khan. I will take this fight."

Shutting off communication, Marthe's *Summoner* advanced on the *Crossbow*.

It was a long fight, one that would go down in the lore of both Clans. Somewhere in the middle of the battle, everyone in the valley felt some residual impact of the earthquake kilometers away at Daemon and a few even heard the sounds of buildings falling.

At first Marthe took the offensive. She used her LRMs to keep the *Crossbow* pilot on the defensive, as she moved in closer to work over its center torso with her autocannon. But the *Crossbow* pilot, exhibiting more patience than most warriors would, countered with a devastating LRM barrage enhanced by its Artemis IV fire-control system that seriously slowed down Marthe's attack. For a long while the clash was a standoff, but one interrupted by remarkably accurate use of firepower on both sides.

Finally, Marthe muttered, "The hell with this. I cannot keep the heat down now anyway."

She fired rapidly, attacking with all weapons. Her strategy worked, catching the *Crossbow* pilot offguard. Recovering quickly, the *Crossbow* pilot responded in kind. For another long while, the battle looked more like a free-for-all than a duel.

One of Marthe's last missile hits smashed into a hole already opened up by missile fire only seconds before. The earlier barrage sliced away a wide section of remaining armor, which made the *Crossbow* especially vulnerable there. The impact sent the *Crossbow* reeling backward, and it began to act erratically, an indication of gyro damage.

Marthe followed up the lucky shot with a missile hit that scored just above the *Crossbow* cockpit.

And the battle was suddenly over. Something had happened to the *Crossbow* pilot, for the 'Mech began to wander around the area like a wounded animal, going first one way, then another, then stopping, then dropping its arms as all power was lost, and then the battle was lost.

Gradually, with an agonizing slowness, the *Crossbow* crashed to the ground. The pilot had not ejected, another indication that the warrior was hurt or unconscious or dead.

For a moment Marthe stood over the *Crossbow* and requested that the pilot exit the cockpit. There was no movement and no response on the commline.

"I hope you can hear me, Viper," she whispered over the com. "You fought bravely against the Falcons and against their Khan. I wish to know you, and if you are dead I will see to it that your bravery is known for your Clan's *Remembrance*. As soldiers once used to say to each other, 'I salute you, my brave enemy.' "

Marthe was about to exit her own 'Mech and try to enter the *Crossbow*'s cockpit, when Samantha told her there was another flare-up with the Vipers a couple of kilometers away. Both Khans raced toward the new battle. Neither had much firepower left, but they would use what they had and, in fact, they each had a couple of mighty victories left in their Mechs' arsenals.

$$=====\ \textbf{34}\ =====$$

Daemon Beach, near the city of Daemon
Waldorff V
Jade Falcon-Steel Viper Occupation Zone
1 July 3061

Parts of Daemon were still falling. The sound of crashes onto rubble heaps was currently being counterpointed by the heavy footfalls of Viper BattleMechs heading toward the Jade Falcons on Daemon Beach.

While the storm had subsided to a misty rain, the sea was still turbulent, its waves crashing on the surf with a steady noise that was easily as loud as the sounds coming from the city. Ravill Pryde, his *Timber Wolf* lumbering uncertainly across the sand, was trying to reassemble his troops. He was not having much luck, Horse noted.

He sometimes looks the fool, but he does have courage. Look at him. He's ready to take on all those Vipers by himself.

"We are outnumbered," Joanna said over the commline.

"I noticed," Horse said. "Welcome to the beach, Joanna."

"Do not give me any of your freeborn tone, Horse."

"Joanna. Diana here. How many left in the Guards?"

"Cannot say. We were separated by the Viper wedge. My Star is intact. Ravill Pryde is the only other Guard with us, except for you and whoever is with you."

"My Star is not intact." After Diana's bloodname victory

she had fought a Trial of Position to earn the rank of Star Commander, a command Ravill Pryde had awarded her without enthusiasm out of a need to fill a position. "Three of us, and some other stragglers from a number of units. Horse has the only other intact unit."

"Intact or not, it does not look good for us. We have no place to go."

"Not so, Joanna," Horse said. "There is the sea."

"You want to take your 'Mech into that, you are welcome to it. Your cockpit would be ripped open within minutes. You might survive out there, Horse, you swim well. Others of us do not."

"Agreed. I have seen you swim. An efficient crawl stroke, I admit, but not enough for you to survive out in that roiling sea. Then, there's your age to consider. You just don't have—"

"Shut up, Horse. I would survive. I am meaner than you."

"You're meaner than everybody, Jo—"

"Would you two stop bickering!" Diana shouted. "You are like married freeborn villagers after too many years together, you—"

She was drowned out by the protesting screams from both warriors. When that subsided, Diana said, "Anyway, these Vipers are streaming through the gate."

Ravill Pryde shouted a few instructions through the commline and somehow the Jade Falcons, however dispersed they had been, formed up into a formidable fighting unit.

As the Viper 'Mechs neared, Ravill's voice echoed in everyone's ears. "It would seem you were right, Horse. Those are 'Mechs of the Triasch Keshik."

Different voices exploded onto the commline. Why were they fighting the command Keshik? And if they were fighting the Keshik, would not the Khan of Steel Viper be facing them himself?

"Shut up, freebirths!" Ravill shouted. "If I had the answers, I would tell you. All I know is that we are facing the command Keshik of the Steel Vipers and they wish a fight. I, for one, am going to give them that fight!"

It was an agonizingly slow fight. The mist interfered with

line of sight and, with battle-inflicted damage to their 'Mechs, pilots tended to hold back until they found the rare clear target. A couple of 'Mechs from opposing sides even crashed into one another, and each had to struggle comically to keep upright. In neither case was the pilot able to take advantage of the situation to land a telling shot on the other's 'Mech.

Horse was startled to hear a familiar enemy voice on the commline. "Star Captain Horse—and how poisonous that title is on my tongue—I want you for myself."

"Ivan Sinclair, is it?"

Horse deliberately did not address Sinclair as Star Colonel. Omitting the rank was insulting from the lips of any warrior, but Horse knew that Sinclair would be seething at a freeborn deliberately refusing to speak it.

"Yes, it is Star Colonel Ivan Sinclair, and you will not be able to use any of your freebirth tricks on me this time. We have our own private war to resolve, with no one else around. Meet me two kilometers to the north. There is an outcropping of rock there that stretches out over the sea. I intend to kill you this time. Do you accept the challenge, Star Captain Horse?"

Somehow the way he used the rank sounded abusive.

"Let us settle the battle here first, Sinclair. I will not desert my companions just for—"

"Kill him, Horse," Joanna interrupted. "You have to fight him now. Go where he says."

"I agree, Horse," Diana chimed in. "Go."

"Very well, Sinclair. I will follow you there."

"I trust you to maintain Clan honor and not take a shot at my back, Star Captain."

As Horse left the present engagement, he was shocked that so many Vipers seemed to be pouring out of the beach gate and heading toward the Falcons formed up near the tumultuous shore.

A gentle slope led up to the outcropping, which was narrow and stretched, it seemed, a long way over the sea. It was a good choice for a showdown, Horse decided. Neither 'Mech could maneuver much to left and right, and it could be fatal to use jump jets to come down behind your opponent, especially since the outcropping got narrower beyond where Sinclair's *Stormcrow* now stood.

"I do not know what firepower you have left, Horse," Sinclair said quietly. "I propose that we simply go at it, to the finish. I hope to send you to the sea below."

"You begin, Sinclair. Take your best shot."

Sinclair was ready and fired his laser, tearing armor off the torso and legs of Horse's *Summoner.* Horse responded in kind and, for several minutes, the mist that threatened to engulf them was streaked with bursts of red. The colors were distorted by the mist and, to an onlooker, might have seemed like some abstract picture of a 'Mech battle, with unreal stabs of light discharging between oddly painted BattleMechs.

The two were evenly matched. For every hit Sinclair scored, Horse sent him one back. This lasted until Sinclair's laserfire disabled the *Summoner*'s right arm. Horse frantically tried to fire the lasers, small and medium, on that arm, but nothing happened.

Out of some complicated Viper custom, Sinclair halted the attack, apparently to savor his victory.

"I will allow you to retreat, Star Captain," Sinclair said over the commline, with an oily edge to his voice.

"You said this was a fight to the death."

"I hate to admit it, but you are a tough opponent, Horse, and I am willing to—"

"Stravag! I will not accept mercy from you, Sinclair."

"So be it."

The only weapon remaining to Horse was the *Summoner*'s left-arm autocannon, and an earlier weapons check had indicated it was running into problems with ammunition, as was common with this particular configuration, so he had held it back during the battle. Nothing else was active now. Since Horse had not used the autocannon recently, he was sure Sinclair assumed he was out of ammo long ago, even as he steadied his aim now to administer the final barrage, the one that could conceivably send Horse to a watery death.

Horse almost surreptitiously adjusted the aim of the *Summoner*'s left arm. There was no time to do any more. He fired the last burst of shells left in it.

Time slowed down so much that, at first, he thought the burst had gone awry. Then the explosion on the front of Sinclair's cockpit showed that Horse's last-ditch shot had succeeded. A moment later Sinclair, to Horse's surprise, crawled out of the cockpit wreckage. The way he made his way down the outer rungs of the 'Mech surface showed that he was not much the worse for wear.

Horse sighed. A systems check showed that the *Summoner* must have been hit by a final shot that he had not felt, and had been itself disabled. He shut off all other systems, and then also left his cockpit to make his way down his own 'Mech. In the area between the two 'Mechs the warriors met. Sinclair stared at Horse, disgust in his eyes. Horse countered with a half-smile, as sardonic as he could make it.

"You are crafty, Star Captain, I will give you that."

"I, too, honor your abilities, Star Colonel Sinclair."

"I was not particularly honoring you, you son of a bitch!"

Sinclair swung at Horse and caught him on the side of face. He was wearing the thin metallic gloves that some warriors favored and so the blow stung.

But Horse had known stronger blows in his time, and he had reacted quickly. They were two exhausted warriors, and their fistfight had no skill to it. Each just hit the other as hard as he could, and the other struck back. Sometimes one of them managed a combination, and sometimes they just fell into a clinch in each other's arms. Sinclair muttered curses about Horse's freebirth status in those moments.

When neither could fight further, they left their 'Mechs on the outcropping. Later, it was discovered that both 'Mechs had been blown over by the violence of subsequent winds or perhaps some more tremors. The *Stormcrow* apparently fell into the sea and was washed away, but Horse's *Summoner* was discovered on its back in the shallow offshore waters.

They walked back up the beach without speaking, each steering well clear of the other. However, the one in the lead at any given moment tended to look back to make sure the other was not sneaking up to attack.

Before they reached the others, Sinclair shouted to Horse, "We will meet again, freebirth!"

And, frustratingly for Sinclair, Horse did not respond.

35

Daemon Beach, near the city of Daemon
Waldorff V
Jade Falcon-Steel Viper Occupation Zone
1 July 3061

The mist, the tremors, and the 'Mechs winding down all played a part in the Battle of Daemon Beach, as it would come to be known. The heavy mist made visuals difficult, although most MechWarriors depended little on visuals, relying on their instruments and computer displays. Still, once in a while it was useful to get an accurate, or even distorted physical image. However, all the warriors whose 'Mechs were still standing—and, if standing, still operable—realized that night was coming on and the visuals would be too unreliable. A further obstacle in this disrupted battle was trying to avoid the 'Mechs that had fallen, most of which were being buried by sand. The sand was treacherous enough to 'Mech footing. Having to stumble over their fellow 'Mechs was an added insult.

Soon there were only five Jade Falcon 'Mechs still in the fray. Diana in her *Nova*, Joanna in her *Summoner*, Ravill in his *Timber Wolf*, and two warriors from the Khan's Irregulars,

Star Commander Pegeen in a *Hellbringer* and another named Bello, who fought admirably in his *Black Lanner.*

Twice as many Vipers were attacking the Falcons from the front and sides and gradually began to close in on them. Their crossfire made it all the more difficult for the Falcons to react.

"Retreat two steps and edge in closer together," cried Ravill Pryde—who was, after all, the ranking officer.

"There's only the damn sea in back of us!" Joanna shouted.

"That is where we will make our stand," Ravill said.

The Falcon warriors, so used to one-on-one engagements, still were not accustomed to the tactics of these Viper warriors. With the ritual courtesies of Clan combat no longer in force, brutal annihilation was the goal.

The Jade Falcon 'Mechs grouped together, the roaring sea behind them, ten Viper BattleMechs in front of them. One false step and they would plunge off the high terrace into the sea.

Suddenly an unfamiliar masculine voice came over the commline. "Your bodies will be drowned in the sea, freebirths! Did you Falcons really believe you could get away with assigning freebirths to command units and to earn bloodname honors? Star Colonel Ivan Sinclair is disposing of the freebirth Falcon Star Captain Horse right now, and I intend to eliminate the warrior in your midst who has desecrated the Aidan Pryde bloodname!"

The sheer menace in the voice sent a shiver of fear down Diana's spine.

"Who are you and by what right do you attempt to chastise the Falcons?" Diana defiantly shot back, suppressing the fear.

"Aye, stravag!" Ravill's yell drowned out Diana's next retort. "Freebirth she may be, but you have no right. We are Jade Falcon and you—"

"I have the right that every warrior of Kerensky has; that of might. I am here to prove that this freebirth does not have the right to the bloodname she has defiled. A Trial of Refusal is the battle I wage here. As for who I am, should it not be obvious?" Khan Perigard Zalman laughed as the Viper 'Mechs suddenly launched a new barrage of laser and missile fire.

While Diana was still reeling from the sudden news that the Khan of the Steel Vipers had come specifically to kill her, the lucky shot came against Joanna.

She never even knew which 'Mech had made the hit—a hip strike by an SRM that sent her *Summoner* spinning sideways. Another shot that would have done minimal damage to the 'Mech's torso sheared off large chunks of armor and ripped off a piece of the cockpit shield. Cold air rushed in on Joanna. Her restraining belt kept her in the seat, even though she felt the seat itself begin to dislodge itself from its moorings.

The *Summoner* began to lose balance. Its jump jets had been ruined by earlier hits. She had to abandon the 'Mech. It was teetering on the edge of the high sand terrace as she carefully released the restraining belt, noted quickly that her sensors were going haywire, felt the sting of sand and mist rushing in through the cockpit hole, heard faintly Diana's screaming voice on the commline, and struggled toward the hatch.

Pegeen and Bello had worked out a crossfire pattern that confused the Viper BattleMechs in their sector of the skirmish. In moments they had downed two of the opposing 'Mechs but at some cost. A *Nova* fell heavily right in front of them, landing at the feet of Bello's *Black Lanner*.

Pegeen, whose *Hellbringer* was closest to the sand terrace, felt the result of the impact first. The *Hellbringer*'s feet seemed to tilt backward, and she realized the edge of the terrace was collapsing. She struggled to take a step forward, but the step brought the 'Mech foot down on the shoulder of the fallen *Hunchback,* and Pegeen could not get good footing. As the sand shifted toward the sea and the edge of the terrace crumbled, the *Hellbringer* fell forward, raising an enormous cloud of sand. As she struggled to keep her 'Mech from falling into the sea, Pegeen was vaguely aware of Diana's voice shouting to both Joanna and her over the commline.

Ravill Pryde knew that he could not last much longer. He had expended his ammunition and used his lasers recklessly. The heat of his *Timber Wolf* was just short of the dangerous shut-down level, which did not matter much since he did not have much fight left to offer anyway. Additionally, although he hated Diana for a freebirth and for her taking of a bloodname, he was incensed that the Steel Viper Khan had dared to censure the Falcons.

Instead of being cautious, he resolved to charge forward against the Viper 'Mechs directly in front of him and do whatever damage he could with his remaining firepower. He did not bother to inform anyone of his intentions, but merely set the *Timber Wolf* into a run. Although heat had robbed his 'Mech of most of its speed, his *Timber Wolf* still managed a shambling trot, and Ravill took advantage of the surprise he was causing to do severe damage to a *Crossbow* in his path. He narrowly passed the Viper 'Mech, which was now giving off clouds of smoke. One of Ravill's hits had been severe, maybe vital.

Past the line of Viper 'Mechs, Ravill saw that his heat levels had risen further, but he thought he could make one more run back toward the sea, to unload the rest of his firepower. He had to go toward the city gate in order to make the arc of the turn on the treacherous sand.

He was aware of Diana's voice on the commline, but his concentration on the combat was so fierce, none of what she said registered. However, he could not help but register the aftershock that came as he resumed his assault on the Vipers.

Diana did not know which way to turn her *Nova,* what with Pegeen's *Hellbringer* sliding toward the turbulent sea on her left, Joanna's *Summoner* falling sideways on the edge of the sand terrace on her right, and Ravill making his insane charge in front of her. Bello could not help Pegeen, for his *Black Lanner* was involved in a violent exchange of fire with a *Stormcrow*. Diana felt responsible for them all. Hers was the only 'Mech in good maneuvering position, and her skills kept the *Nova* fighting off the Viper assaults.

Even the aftershock did not especially faze her, as she maintained balance and, more importantly, a clear perspective on all the disaster going on around her.

Pegeen raised her *Hellbringer*'s arms to dig into the sand and stop its backward slide. The heavy weight of the PPCs at the end of each arm dug deep ruts into the sand that stopped the 'Mech's slide toward watery disaster. The *Hellbringer* came to a halt with its legs dangling precariously over the edge of the sand terrace and all of its controls coming to the same kind of halt.

"Are you all right, Pegeen?" Bello shouted over the commline. At least the commline was working.

"I am fine. Down, but fine. You?"

"I have about a half-minute of combat left in me. But I just finished off a *Stormcrow*."

Pegeen was about to reply, but the aftershock caused her *Hellbringer* to shift and slide a bit further, and she decided she better get out of the cockpit.

Joanna pulled at the hatch lever. It did not even give. It was jammed shut. Cursing, she whirled around and began to crawl, upward, to the hole the Viper 'Mech had made in the cockpit shield. At the same time the aftershock made her *Summoner* give up the ghost and begin to fall, making her struggle to climb more difficult. She used the pilot seat to thrust herself upward. Standing on its back, she reached for the ragged edge of the hole in the cockpit. Painful sand seemed to pit her face.

Grabbing the edge of the hole, bloodying her hands, she pulled herself upward.

Ravill Pryde might have made it back through the Viper line, but a warrior in a *Crossbow* was ready for him and made a direct missile hit on Ravill's already ravaged center torso, and disabled the *Timber Wolf* completely. The aftershock finished it off, and the 'Mech fell awkwardly to the sand. Ravill sensed a pair of Viper 'Mechs moving toward him for the kill.

On her main screen Diana watched Joanna's *Summoner* fall off the edge of the sand terrace and plunge, left side first, toward the roaring surf below. There was nothing she could do.

Joanna always said she wanted to die in battle.

Turning back to the fighting, she saw Ravill Pryde's *Timber Wolf* land on the sand with what would have been a loud crashing sound, if she could have heard it over the sounds of combat, the sea, the storm, the falling debris in the city, and the diminishing rumble of the aftershock.

She realized her *Nova* and Bello's *Black Lanner* were the only Falcon BattleMechs left standing.

Two of the Viper 'Mechs were shooting down at Ravill Pryde's fallen *Timber Wolf*. Not Clan etiquette, but this was a war to the finish, and the Steel Vipers' perfidious tactics were apparently acceptable.

"Bello!"

"Aff, Star Commander."

"Forward. We have to help the Star Colonel."

"Neg, Star Commander. I am done, disabled. Can't fire, can't move, trying not to look like an easy target."

"Good luck, Bello!" Diana shouted as she moved her *Nova* forward. She was on her way to help the Star Colonel who despised her, by defeating the Khan who had come to kill her.

Joanna almost extricated herself from the 'Mech before its plunge accelerated. One leg was outside the cockpit hole, and she was trying to thrust the rest of her body out as the *Summoner* hit the sand below. She was knocked back into the cockpit and her head careened off the hard cockpit seat.

The rush of pain through her head and her body nearly

knocked her out. It probably should have. But Joanna could not lose control, she did not know how.

The left side of her body was becoming numb, but she could move. She managed to stand, even with her left leg threatening to collapse under her. Standing was difficult as the surging waters of the sea made the 'Mech, heavy as it was, rock slightly where it lay, on its left side. If she did not act quickly, the 'Mech might tip over and land on its face, burying the cockpit in sand. Hopping on her right leg, she maneuvered her body into a roll toward the edge of the cockpit hole. In a show of strength that she had not managed since she was a falconer and had to be stronger than the best of her cadets, she pulled her body out of the hole and for a moment dangled on the edge of the cockpit opening. In place, she felt her body drain of strength. She could go no further using either arm. Instead, she dragged herself forward and slowly, arduously, fell off the 'Mech body and onto the wet sand.

Crawling away from the 'Mech and pulling herself to a sitting position with her back against the hard-packed sand of the terrace, she blearily watched the *Summoner* being pulled, a short distance at a time, into the turbulent sea. She passed out before she saw it disappear under the waves.

Diana blasted the Viper 'Mechs attacking Ravill Pryde out of position, then stood over the fallen *Timber Wolf*.

"You alive, Ravill?" she said, as she scanned the terrain and saw that all of the remaining Vipers, six of them, had turned their attention to her.

"Alive. What are you doing?"

"I am not sure. I am the last Jade Falcon 'Mech standing and I intend to remain that way."

"How many against you?"

"Six, including Perigard Zalman."

"Too many, especially considering they have specific orders to see you dead. Get out of the way."

"Look. You are down, Joanna might be drowning in the sea, Pegeen is stubbornly remaining in her BattleMech while it dangles over the waters, and Bello—though still

upright—is a sitting duck for any Viper 'Mech who cares to
finish him off. I figure not only do I draw off enemy fire, but
there is a chance some of the others may survive, including
you, Star Colonel. So you get out of the way."

"I would, freeborn. But my whole console is off its moorings and on top of me, and I can just barely move. It will
take me a few minutes to escape my cockpit."

"No problem. You work at it and I will cover for you."

"That is insane."

"Probably. Excuse me, I am being fired at."

A *Hankyu* was firing wildly at the *Nova*.

"But it is only a *Hankyu*," Diana muttered and, with a single burst of laser fire, she managed to make it spin around.
Another burst at its left knee and the whole leg collapsed.
The *Hankyu* went down on one knee and was tilted to the
left as it tried to get traction in the sand with its right leg. Diana realized that, for the next few minutes at least, the *Hankyu* would not be a threat.

Hovering over the fallen *Timber Wolf*, ignoring the mutterings of Ravill Pryde, some of them curses directed at Diana, she faced the remaining five Viper 'Mechs. Rotating
her *Nova*'s torso, she countered the Viper attack as well as
she could. She found it surprising that she could not tell
which 'Mech was piloted by Perigard Zalman. She kept her
right-arm PPC busy, since the arm had already taken some
damage and she was not sure how long she could use it. One
azure bolt of lightning demolished the cockpit of a *Battle
Corbra,* and it came to a grinding stop.

Diana moved her *Nova* around the fallen *Timber Wolf* so
that her 'Mech acted as a barrier between the four remaining
Viper 'Mechs and Ravill's 'Mech.

*What am I doing? Ravill Pryde has vowed to challenge
me on the bloodname. I should just leave him to die. If I do,
then there will be no challenge. If I save his life, he will
hardly be grateful to be rescued by a freeborn. Him and
Leif, what is it about these truebirths that make them so
stubborn about accepting aid from a freeborn?*

She did not have time to mull over the problem, as a blast

of missiles exploded against the *Nova*'s chest. The hit nearly toppled her, and the irony of her falling onto Ravill's 'Mech was not lost on her. Whatever other damage was done, the salvo had knocked out some of her sensors. Her scanner screen was showing abstract patterns. Lights flicked on and off. She tried to locate the remaining Viper 'Mechs, but she got only blips and streaks on her screens.

She would have to go visual. She cleared the cockpit shield so that she could see out.

Night had fallen and the mist was heavy. She could see the enemy 'Mechs as the darkest of shadows against the darkness.

As she began firing at shadows, she could not help but think of the death of Aidan Pryde. It was night then, too, and he had lost most of his life support and sensors. And he too had stood by a fallen comrade as he fended off a heavy force of ComStar 'Mechs. Diana herself had been the fallen warrior in that piece of history, while she had Ravill Pryde—who disliked freebirths, who disliked Diana—to protect. Aidan Pryde had dispatched many more 'Mechs than this, and he had more skill than she could ever hope for.

But she *was* his daughter.

And she had his tenacity.

And his recklessness.

And, stravag, another Viper 'Mech, a *Crossbow,* was thrown back and out of action by another blast from the Nova's right-arm PPC. She did not even remember shooting it.

And one thing kept coming into her mind. Aidan Pryde had died in similar circumstances. But Diana did not intend to die. After all, it was less than a year since she had won the Pryde bloodname and she planned to bring it honor for years to come.

She was suddenly shocked out of her reverie by the fact that the remaining three Viper 'Mechs were pulling back. Confused, she opened a commline to Ravill Pryde.

"What is going on? They still have us outnumbered three to one and yet they are retreating. Clansmen almost never retreat and certainly not from what should be an assured victory."

"How should I know?" Ravill's voice sounded as grating as ever. "I had a thought, though. It came after you dispatched that last 'Mech. Is it possible . . ." Ravill's voice trailed off into thoughtful silence.

"What?" Diana demanded.

"I find it hard to even contemplate, but you may have not only defended yourself while outnumbered six to one, destroying three 'Mechs in the process, but I believe you may have actually defeated Khan Zalman. Freebirth!" he cursed, incredulous.

Dumbfounded, Diana sat stunned, unable to move. Could it be true? It seemed she had done the impossible. Willing to die defending a man who hated her, she had triumphed against impossible odds, not only stealing victory from the jaws of defeat, but ripping those jaws apart by defeating the Khan of the Steel Vipers himself. Now it made sense.

"That is why they are retreating," Ravill said, echoing her own thoughts. "The fact that their Khan was defeated in battle by a freeborn has broken their flagging spirits. I believe the battle for this planet is done and so is this war."

36

Daemon Beach, near the city of Daemon
Waldorff V
Jade Falcon-Steel Viper Occupation Zone
1 July 3061

With the Steel Vipers in sudden retreat, Marthe and Samantha easily disrupted the wedge that had separated the Falcon troops. Without further intel, it was impossible to tell what had finally broken the Steel Viper, but both Khans had the feeling the answers would be found at Daemon Beach.

Quickly, the two of them, with the Turkina Keshik and the First Falcon Striker Cluster, headed there. As they approached, Marthe's sensors told her that the fight had been devastating. A lone *Nova* stood protectively over a fallen *Timber Wolf,* with what appeared to be an army of defeated Steel Vipers lying toppled and scattered all around the single standing 'Mech.

As Marthe and the others headed up the beach in their 'Mechs, their electronics occasionally distorted by severe weather conditions, she detected that the lone Falcon 'Mech belonged to Diana Pryde and that the fallen one was Ravill Pryde's.

"I raised Diana on the commline," Samantha reported. "I asked her if she might have an explanation for the sudden Steel Viper retreat."

"And did she?"

"Oh, yes."

"What was it?"

"She told me that she not only deprived them of an easy victory by defeating them while outnumbered, but that seeing their Khan defeated by a freebirth was probably more than any trueborn could bear."

The moment released all that Marthe had held back as the brutal battle for Waldorff had raged. She laughed. She was not one to laugh often, but the laughter released her battle tension, and she relaxed.

The Jade Falcons had broken and smashed the Steel Vipers. Khan Zalman had also suffered a personal defeat when he lost in battle to a freeborn. Unless Zalman wanted to see his forces totally obliterated, he would have to cease fighting. Marthe would offer them the honorable withdrawal of *hegira,* but shame would follow them nevertheless. The war was over. The Jade Falcons had won.

And a newly bloodnamed, freeborn warrior had been instrumental in that victory. *Many Clansmen will have to start rethinking their beliefs concerning those they have always cursed as freebirths.* A slow smile began to spread over the face of the Khan of the Jade Falcons.

As it turned out, Samantha happened to overhear a brief transmission between Diana and Ravill Pryde.

"Why save me?" he demanded.

"I am a warrior. It is my duty, *quiaff*?"

"The odds were against you."

"As Star Commander Joanna says so often and so annoyingly, I am Jade Falcon, *quiaff*?"

The transmission then became garbled. Samantha tried to contact Diana again, but there was no response. The next thing Samantha saw was that Diana had scrambled down the *Nova* and was presently racing toward the sand terrace that was beginning to erode under the effects of an incoming tide.

Marthe saw to it that Ravill would be pried out of his cockpit, while she dispatched others to deal with the warriors in the two remaining Falcon 'Mechs, one standing still and the other dangling off the crumbling sand terrace, about to fall off at any moment. Both pilots were rescued, and the endangered *Hellbringer* was subsequently pulled to a safe place.

Although she could get no visuals on the beach devastation, she could work it out through the diagrammatics on her scanner. She saw that the beach was littered with BattleMechs from both sides, many of them downed and becoming covered with sand. For all she knew, there were more already buried under some of the sand mounds.

Marthe knew that this victory was impressive within the overall rout of the Vipers on Waldorff. What her warriors had achieved here at Daemon Beach, especially the defeat of the Steel Viper Khan by Diana, would surely be worth some lines in the *Remembrance*. Stravag, she thought, the entire Waldorff campaign would take up a passage of its own.

If Marthe had ever doubted some of her own decisions over the last few years, those doubts could now be put to rest. Driving the Vipers out of the corridor proved that the proud Falcons had returned to their former glory, justifying everything Marthe had tried to do as Khan. She had been forced to find her own path at times, when the traditional wisdom could not save them. Yet, she had remained true, in her heart, to the way of the Clans.

Marthe also noticed Diana running across the beach, and wondered what she was up to now. The *Remembrance* would note the heroism of this freeborn warrior with a bloodname. Like her father before her, it would seem that Diana would also find herself immortalized in the Jade Falcon *Remembrance*. That she was the daughter of Aidan Pryde would not go unremarked either. Marthe wondered what Aidan would say if he were here. *Ah, let it go. Let Aidan go. He cannot be my secret conscience any more.*

Later, when she heard about Horse's defeat of Ivan Sinclair and of the heroic actions of the entire freeborn Trinary, the Khan's Irregulars, Marthe realized that their victories, combined with Diana's victory over Khan Zalman, had truly defeated the Steel Vipers concerning freeborns. The freeborn issue had been fought in the council chambers and on the field, and none could dispute the matter now. It would be a long while before any Khan dared question the Jade Falcon use of freeborns.

Arriving at the battle site, Horse was as awed by the devastation as Marthe Pryde had been, except he saw it up close and could smell the rank odors of warfare. Behind him, Ivan Sinclair cursed and ran over to one of his fallen comrades, who lay wounded next to his *Crossbow*.

In a light being cast over the sands from Samantha's 'Mech, Horse saw Diana running across the sand toward the terrace. Looking to his right, he saw that the waves of the incoming tide were high and that the roar that had been deafening his ears was the pounding of the waters against the surf.

He broke into a run and chased after Diana.

* * *

Diana scrambled down the sand terrace toward Joanna. The turbulent waters had reached her and she was lying flat with them surging around her. As Diana watched, Joanna's body was pulled out several meters by an undertow. Calling up all the swim training that had been part of her cadet years and underutilized since, she ran into the water and dove forward.

The water was freezing and it seemed as if her skin went numb immediately. She began to swim toward where she thought Joanna was. Or was it illusion? Was that Joanna's head bobbing up above a level area between the high waves?

Diana fought the incoming waves and was frequently pushed backward. All the way swimming toward Joanna was a matter of two steps forward and one step back.

But then she reached the nearly-drowning warrior. Pulling at her collar, she brought Joanna's face toward her own. Joanna's eyes were confused and she tried to pull out of Diana's grasp. In a wild punch Diana hit Joanna on the jaw. There was no stamina left in Joanna and she went limp, unconscious.

Turning toward shore, Diana wondered if she could make it back. The sand terrace seemed kilometers away now. A wave carried her several meters toward the shore but nearly drowned her in the process.

She continued to pull Joanna by the collar. There was no time to get a better hold and the waves were too powerful.

For a moment Diana wanted to just close her eyes and give up. Then she saw the other figure swimming efficiently and strongly toward her. Strong, muscular arms sliced in and out of the water. The sight gave Diana renewed energy and she swam toward the swimmer.

As they all reached the shore and were able to stand, Diana was startled to find that it was Horse who had helped them. He continued to help her drag Joanna up to safety on the beach.

Marthe Pryde observed the rescue with satisfaction. She had not realized that Joanna was among the missing.

It would have been a sorry note if we had lost that old bird.

At the same time, she saw something that Diana and Horse had yet to notice—that Joanna's body was twisted unnaturally. She was injured.

Marthe ordered that someone with a medkit get to that fallen warrior and administer help. Then she returned her attention to supervising the cleanup of the Battle of Daemon Beach.

37

Jade Falcon Field Headquarters
Viper Valley, Waldorff V
Jade Falcon-Steel Viper Occupation Zone
2 July 3061

After the triumph over the Steel Vipers, Marthe should have felt exultant. And she almost did. But there was one more decision for her to make, one that she did not particularly savor, one that gave her serious pause in thinking about her role as Khan.

The dilemma involved the stubborn *Crossbow* warrior she had defeated the day before. Marthe had returned to where the *Crossbow* still lay in the field and been told that the pilot had not yet emerged from the cockpit, though many hours had passed since the battle. There were so many Jade Falcon casualties that no one had attended to the warrior. Marthe climbed up onto the *Crossbow* and ripped open the cockpit's entry hatch.

"Steel Viper warrior," she cried into the darkness. "Are you conscious?"

No answer.

"We will help you if you are hurt. Are you alive?"

The question made the other warrior laugh, a short guffaw.

"See?" Marthe said. "You cannot be completely silent. Do you need help?"

"I will kill you if you try to enter my cockpit."

Marthe who already had her hand on the hilt of the knife in her belt, smiled. She had no intention of entering an enemy cockpit unarmed.

"If you are not able to come out, I can send techs to—"

"I will not be touched by techs. I can move. I am only slightly wounded. I just do not choose to come out yet. I will come out when night falls."

The voice sounded familiar.

"Identify yourself, Viper."

"I am surprised you do not know who I am, although we have not talked directly in some time."

"Natalie Breen?"

Breen's laughter told Marthe she was right.

"I did not know you were among the Viper forces."

"Few Steel Viper warriors even knew I was here. I was attached to the Khan's unit, and nobody questioned. I stayed out of the way, except for combat. Someone might recognize my voice if I spoke over the commline, so I maintained silence. You fought me well, Marthe Pryde. I am glad that it was at least a Khan responsible for adding to my shame. Perhaps I will stay in this cockpit until I die."

"We will pry you out if we have to."

"No, I will come out my own. Leave a guard who can bring me to you later. Oh, and make sure the guard is a trueborn, and not one of those freebirths you favor so much."

Marthe, conscious that she should be the one dictating terms, nevertheless acceded to Natalie's commands. One Khan should respect another, she thought, even a former one. Even one who puts obstacles in the way of the respect she deserves.

* * *

The issue of proper respect was very much on Marthe's mind as she awaited the arrival of Natalie Breen in her field headquarters. Thinking about the interview to come, she found it difficult to breathe in the dank odor of dampness that accompanied the malodorous smells of yesterday's battles that inevitably seeped into the porous temporary dome.

Natalie Breen entered the dome squinting, as if unused to the bright light inside, especially after the heavily overcast day outside. She rubbed her eyes with one finger.

"Does the light bother you, Natalie?" Marthe asked.

"A bit. I . . . do not much like bright light."

Marthe dimmed the lights.

"We are much alike, Marthe," Natalie said, abruptly. "Except of course that you are a victorious Khan and I am a disgraced former one."

She spoke the words matter-of-factly, Marthe noticed, without any hint of self-pity.

"Perhaps you will think it odd for me to say, Natalie Breen, but I do not consider you disgraced. As Khan of the Vipers, you ordered your warriors to withdraw from Tukayyid, true, but had you not made that decision, the Vipers might have been destroyed. Your Clan could come back after Tukayyid because enough of them had survived. Perigard Zalman is the one who has earned the true disgrace here."

Natalie's eyes widened for a moment. She seemed about to protest, but then closed her eyes and said calmly, "You are out of line, Marthe Pryde. It is your right as the victor, but I respectfully request you refrain from further commentary on this subject, or any other that judges Clan Steel Viper."

A number of disparaging remarks went through Marthe's mind. The warrior in her might have spoken them, but she was Khan and determined to respect a former Khan's wishes.

"It is my right to make you my bondsman, Natalie Breen, *quiaff*?"

"Aff. It is my duty to accept that, Marthe Pryde."

Marthe noted the defiant undertone in what was apparently a calm acceptance.

"Perigard Zalman has requested that you be returned to the Vipers before they debark from Waldorff. Does he do so to alleviate his own disgrace at losing the whole corridor and being forced to accept *hegira,* or is it a display of honor for you?"

"I cannot speak for what Khan Zalman has done."

"Or is it because you still have influence among the Vipers?"

"I do not know. Perigard Zalman is the Khan, and that is all. He keeps his own counsel."

"He is not Khan for long, I suspect. If I were the Steel Vipers, faced with such serious damage to the Clan and with the task of rebuilding it, not to mention his personal loss in battle to a freeborn, I would remove Zalman and replace him with a warrior worthy of the position."

Another brief flicker of anger from Natalie Breen, then another calm response. "You may think as you wish. I find your comments to me condescending. You are Jade Falcon and in no position to judge the acts of the Steel Vipers."

"Perhaps, perhaps not. Still, if I kept you as my bondsman, that would put a crimp in the plans of the Vipers, *quiaff*?"

"Not at all. I would be just another captured warrior claimed as bondsman and that would be all."

"I wonder. At any rate, you might be a good bondsman for me, Natalie. A reminder of how careful a Khan must be to hold power."

"I have been told that power is not important to you, that you claim you are Khan only because it best allows you to serve your Clan."

"That is just another way of saying I do have to hold power."

"No trouble there. You have just earned a significant victory, *quiaff*?"

"But the Clans have lost. You know the old saying about winning the battle but losing the war. The Clans have lost the war. Conflicts like this are five-finger exercises for us. You talk about shame, disgrace. I may have collected some honor with victories here and in the Strana Mechty Trial, might even have earned some lines in the Jade Falcon *Remembrance,* but I still feel the shame of the Clans losing to the Inner Sphere. And I vow before you, Natalie Breen, that I intend to wipe out that shame in the coming days, weeks, years."

Natalie Breen did something quite rare. She smiled. "Vows like that might make me a willing bondsman to you, Marthe Pryde."

"Perhaps. But I have decided otherwise. I would not disrespect you, Natalie, by having you serve me."

"Marthe—"

"No more. Maybe we will meet again in battle, Khan Natalie Breen."

Marthe gestured that the interview was ended, and Natalie left the dome. Marthe mentally wished her well as the other warrior returned to a dispirited and defeated Clan. She would not have wanted to trade places with Natalie Breen, who had been doubly disgraced with her defeat here.

Marthe smiled, thinking how many Jade Falcons, and Steel Vipers for that matter, would have liked to be a fly on the wall for the little chat that had just taken place. They might have expected the two warriors to fight like Battle-Mechs, raging at each other, blasting away with verbal weapons.

But Marthe could not be angry with her. Not Natalie Breen. She was what Marthe could become, if she should fail. Breen's experience was a warning. Khans fall from power. An object lesson in the dangers of being Khan. Marthe would never want to become the "dark knight" on a battlefield, masquerading as a warrior in a futile attempt to purge shame.

I will remember Natalie Breen, she promised herself, but I will also remember the glorious victory here on Waldorff, the heroic victory over the whole invasion corridor. All that is just the beginning for Khan Marthe Pryde.

38

Sibko Training Center 111
Kerensky Forest, Ironhold
Kerensky Cluster, Clan Space
6 July 3061

Peri had glanced over her shoulder all the way to the Science Center building. The past few times she had sneaked into its rooms and their computers she knew Naiad had followed her. She had not confronted the child. Naiad was stubborn and headstrong, so Peri believed it was better to let her think her spying was working. If she was right, Naiad was lurking behind some bushes off to the left. Peri relaxed and entered the headquarters.

Naiad did indeed feel confident in her tracking abilities. Watching Peri go into the building now, she wondered if she should bother to spy further. All this Peri ever did was play around with the computers. It was boring to watch.

She was about to give up when she noticed a movement on the side of the building. A dark shadow crept toward windows to look in.

Someone else was watching Peri.

Naiad thrilled inside at the new complication. She started tracking the new tracker.

Peri had discovered many new documents indicating the extent of the conspiracy of the scientist castes throughout so many Clans. All of the documents were protected against copying and all of Peri's computer skills could not bypass whatever complex program the caste used. Unfortunately, none of her past experience with file protection helped her to crack the code on this one.

She had memorized relevant information and entered some of it into a noteputer of her own, coding it her own way, with a quadruple-number shifting code that could be decoded by others only with painstaking, time-consuming methods. The information would be enough, although breaking the power of Etienne Balzac might require more actual proof.

On this foray into Harvey's files, she finally discovered the disposition of the copies of Aidan Pryde genetic materials. She gasped when she saw the extent of it.

Nearly every Clan has a copy. This must be Balzac's major project, to infuse the sibkos he is bringing up for his own purposes with Aidan genetics. What a race of warriors this can be! It would excite me, if not for the unethical uses to which it is being put. I have to stop him because of that, but I would like to see the results. This sibko here is enough for me to get excited. Naiad and the rest, they are so far along in skills and combativeness it is hard to believe they are as young as they are.

A noise behind her made Peri whirl around. She expected to see Naiad there and was startled at the tall figure standing in the doorway. The man looked familiar at first. Then, suddenly, memories flooded in and in a flash she relived the incident of the attack more clearly than ever before. This was the man who had led her to it. What had Marthe said his name was? Olan.

"Hello, Peri."

"What are you doing here?"

"I have had operatives here for months, watching you. We have monitored your activities and even know what you know. We have been, in a way, looking over your shoulder every time you turned on a computer in this room. Lately you have been getting too close."

Peri stood up, her body tense, her hand casually behind her back, edging toward the knife she kept there. "I assume that since you tried to kill me last time and failed that the solution has not changed, *quiaff*?"

"Not much. I just have to make sure you disappear this time. Here in the outback, that should not be too difficult."

He raised his left hand and snapped his fingers. Two other men entered the room. She recognized both. One was a janitor for this building, the other a clerical tech to the scientists. Now that she knew they were Olan's operatives, they looked sinister in a way they never had before. Her hand went around the handle of her knife, and she edged it slowly out of her belt. The odds were against her, but these three were bandits, not warriors, and she had at least trained as a warrior.

The janitor came toward her. When he got close, she pivoted on her left foot and slammed her right foot into his face. She felt the satisfactory snap of a bone crunching. The janitor reeled backward, both hands covering his nose, trying to staunch the blood.

"You are agile, Peri Watson," Olan said. "But surprise only works once."

"Not necessarily," Peri said as she rushed at the clerical tech who was jumping toward her and caught him in the neck with her knife. His blood spurted over her hands before he fell unconscious and, from the way it was pouring, he would probably die.

Olan's eyebrows raised. "Impressive, but not enough."

He stepped forward, a knife in his own hand. Its blade was thin and long. She lunged at the hand holding the knife, but Olan caught her arm with his other hand and twisted it. Pain ran up her arm. She dropped her knife. Olan flung her away.

Leaning down to pick up the knife, he said, "I applaud your trickery, but I have years of trickery behind me."

He flung the knife away, toward the door through which he and his cohorts had come.

His mistake.

Naiad had easily located the new tracker's two companions, watched them come together, and listened at an open window as they had confronted Peri. Hearing Olan's threat to kill Peri and seeing his henchmen come menacingly into the room, Naiad had worked the window open enough for her to ease herself through it. Her feet softly touched the floor at the moment when Peri drop-kicked one of the bandits in the nose. She had crept up to a position behind Olan as Peri had lunged at the other attacker and slashed his throat.

Standing behind Olan, not sure what to do, she watched the arc of the knife as it spun handle over blade toward her. As it came down, she shot out her hand and caught the knife by its handle. She was not quite sure how she did it, although she was sure that all the practice Octavian put the sibko through in working with wooden staffs must have helped.

Olan walked toward Peri, wielding his own knife threateningly. Peri took a couple of steps backward, her eyes darting around the room, looking either for an escape route or another weapon. On the other side of the room the thug with the smashed nose was straightening up and glaring at Peri.

Naiad raced at Olan and, using the knife with the kind of fierceness Octavian encouraged, slashed the back of the tall bandit's right leg. Her blow was efficient and given with the strength sibko training furnished. Blood spouted out of the wound as Olan's leg collapsed, bringing his head down to Naiad's level. She lashed out again with the knife and cut the side of his face with a stroke that struck bone.

Olan's eyes became enraged, and he muttered something about a filthy child as he raised his knife to strike at Naiad. Peri grabbed at his arm and held it back with all of her strength.

Naiad raised the knife to attack Olan again, but Peri cried, "No, Naiad, no!"

The scream made Naiad hesitate and gave Peri enough time to take the knife from Naiad's hands. She shoved it into Olan's chest, while continuing to hold onto his knife hand. Olan dropped suddenly, his body slamming to the floor.

Peri quickly worked Olan's knife out of his hand. She had a knife in each of her own as she turned to face the last bandit, the one who had posed as a janitor. The man's eyes widened considerably and he rushed out the door.

Naiad looked down at Olan.

"Is he . . . is he dead?"

"I think so. I could not let you kill him. You are too young for that, even if you will be a warrior some day."

"You think so?"

For a moment, in the midst of the carnage of the two dead bandits, Naiad reverted to being a child again, reacting to Peri's compliment as if it were some kind of award.

"Thank you for saving me, Naiad."

"I saved you?"

"I think it is fair to say that, yes."

Praise followed by gratitude raised Naiad's childish elation another notch.

"What now?" Naiad asked.

"I think I have overspent my time here. I have to take what I have found out and leave."

"What have you found out?"

"I will tell you that some day, when I can. Now, you get out of here. There is no reason to connect you to any of this."

"But they should know how I—"

"No, they should not. Save it for some night years from now, around a campfire, when it is time for stories."

Outside there was some commotion. Glancing through a window, Peri saw the third bandit running back toward the building with Octavian.

"Get out of here now, Naiad!"

Naiad scampered to the window and scrambled through the opening. A moment after, she stuck her head back through. "Goodbye, Peri Watson."

"Goodbye, Naiad."

Peri used a window at the back of the building. When she reached the outside, she was grateful to remember the opening in the fence through which she had first gone with Naiad more than a year and a half ago.

39

During the entire time of the Jade Falcon presence on Waldorff there had not been a single bright day. The generally strong Waldorff sun had remained behind dark, thick clouds, while a series of stormy and often strange weather patterns assaulted the troops camped in Viper Valley.

Now that the battle was over, it was a bad time for warriors, who did not like to be idle. Most of the Steel Vipers had already lifted off the planet as part of a general exodus from the corridor.

Marthe Pryde had known a special satisfaction as Perigard Zalman came to meet with her so that she could grant the *hegira*. She had shown no emotion as she stared into his eyes and spoke the traditional words, the ritual by which a victorious Clan could allow the defeated one an honorable exit from the field of battle. In this case the *hegira* was corridor-wide.

It was satisfying to affirm the victory, but Marthe also took a secret pleasure in Zalman's reluctance to deal with her that she read in the slight droop to his shoulders as he left her field headquarters after the formalities. The haunted look in his eyes, residual shock at the defeat by Diana Pryde, was also plain to see.

During the meeting, however, she suppressed the insults

she could have uttered to her defeated enemy. Marthe may have departed at times from the traditions of the Clans, but in her heart she had never forsworn the ideal of honor. The Steel Vipers had been an enemy worth defeating, and that was enough. The Falcons had won, the Vipers had lost. Her talk with Natalie Breen had made her realize that she did not want to rub the disgrace of defeat into the face of the proud and resilient Steel Vipers.

Marthe and Samantha had recently returned from a tour of former Viper worlds to make sure that the withdrawal went smoothly and to assess the damage the war had done to military facilities in the corridor. Neither spoke for a time as they strolled through the encampment and enjoyed the brightness and warmth of the first sunny day they had experienced on Waldorff.

Marthe took a deep breath and said, "I needed this."

"What?" Samantha said. "The warmth, the sun?"

"No, this feels good, but I mean victory. I mean the resurgence of the Jade Falcon Clan. I mean that, even if the Clans have capitulated to the Inner Sphere, we remain a hold-out. We will bide our time and one day we shall yet fulfill our goal of taking Terra for the Clans. We may not be able to conquer the Inner Sphere on our own, but—whatever else—we will continue to control this sector of space."

"We cannot trust the Inner Sphere to let us do that," Samantha warned.

"I know that. In the meantime, we will continue to build up our forces here, concentrate our power, stay out of Clan-type squabbles, and wait out developments."

"Very good. I would endorse that. You can feel it everywhere. The Falcon is reborn. We are back."

The two walked on, heading toward the medical domes where they would pay a visit to one of their most heroic warriors.

Ravill Pryde watched his Falcon Guards perform their basic calisthenics drill. The warriors grumbled a lot about the resumption of routine that he had ordered, but he knew that, in the aftermath of war when the length of the peaceful time was unknown, it was crucial to return immediately to routine. Skills must stay sharp, stamina high.

There was also the matter of respect for their commanding officer contributing to Ravill's order. He knew he had lost a notch or two of respect at being saved by Diana in the Daemon Beach battle. There had been some mutterings about the taint of being rescued by a freebirth with a bloodname. But what was a taint on his reputation? He was still the ranking officer for a battle that would forever be a glorious page in Clan history. And even he had to admit that credit for the victory at Daemon Beach, and possibly the victory for all of Waldorff, did go to Star Commander Diana Pryde. It was a grudging admission, but her acts had won praise for her, for the Falcon Guards, and the Clan itself. When Marthe Pryde had requested that he formally withdraw his challenge for a Trial of Refusal over Diana's bloodname, Ravill had agreed without protest. Her heroism had validated her right to the bloodname.

He stared at Diana in the front row of the exercising warriors. She performed with more fierceness and grace than any of the others. She had done well, this daughter of Aidan Pryde. Ravill wondered if she would be considered a ristar now. How far could they let a freebirth go in the Clan, after all? Perhaps she and he would be end up being ristars together, perhaps rivals. *Well,* thought Ravill, *it is a challenge I welcome. Diana Pryde would be a worthy opponent in any contest.*

After the calisthenics, Horse and his Trinary went to the makeshift simulation chambers to test their piloting. Horse noted with satisfaction that his warriors posted fine numbers in the onscreen evaluations. In the Waldorff campaign they had really come together as a fighting unit, suffering few casualties even as they inflicted many.

"You are looking smug, Horse," Diana said. She had sneaked up behind him, and he was startled by her voice.

He turned to look at her. As she often did since Daemon Beach, she was smiling.

"You look quite pleased with yourself, Diana."

"And why not? We have proven something, Horse, you and I. The trueborns are treating us freeborns differently these days, *quiaff*? Even Ravill Pryde told me he had withdrawn his challenge for a Trial, and—although his voice choked a bit—he praised me for heroism at Daemon Beach."

"Seems wonders never cease."

"Aff. It is good to be alive and even better to be a living Jade Falcon warrior."

"There you go, getting carried away. But I would not get too happy about everything. I would wager that this new-found recognition is temporary, part of the elation of victory. I would not be surprised if things returned to normal down the line. But that does not mean you have not achieved a significant victory—besides Daemon Beach, I mean. We free-borns will be more arrogant. You can be, especially, and I see a new self-respect among my Trinary. The bloodname gives you and us advantages we have not yet begun to explore."

"And I will explore them. You can count on that."

"I believe you, Diana Pryde. You *are* different. I would not like to be the first trueborn who calls you a freebirth."

Diana laughed and hugged Horse. Hugging, although common enough among freeborns, was not popular among warriors. Horse was sure that some of the trueborns in the area took note of their embrace with some distaste, and he hugged Diana all the harder.

Nearly a month in a hospital bed had not improved Joanna's temperament. She was driving the medtechs wild with her rages and, among the medical center staff, lotteries were regularly held where the winners were actually losers who had to draw duty with Joanna for their next shift. Care was taken to ensure that nothing she could throw was placed anywhere near her reach and that the restraining straps were locked so she would not succeed in her many attempts to get out of the bed.

She was raging at a medtech as Marthe Pryde came into

the room. Joanna noted her presence, but did not let up on screaming at the tech. Amused, Marthe tapped the medtech on the shoulder and gestured for him to leave the room, which he did only too eagerly.

"Well, Star Commander Joanna," Marthe said, "have you thought about what we discussed last week?"

"Reassignment?"

"Yes."

"I do not wish to go anywhere. I will adapt a 'Mech to accommodate my injuries, I will—"

"Negative. I will not allow it. I might not have allowed it even had you accepted the prosthetic replacement for your leg."

"I have seen prosthetics. They have turned Kael Pershaw into a walking mass of metal and plastic and synthskin. No, I will keep my leg in its shattered state. I am comfortable with that."

"Then we cannot put you in a 'Mech cockpit again, Joanna."

"You are my Khan and I must accept your decision, but I ask you again to—"

"Do not even say it, Joanna. Even without your injury, I might still have been forced to end your combat career."

"Make a solahma out of me?"

"That was possible and you would have accepted it, *quiaff*?"

"Aff." Joanna spoke the affirmative, in a voice that could only be described as sullen.

"But I think you would be wasted in the solahma ranks, Joanna. And you know how we abhor waste in the Clans. So, I have just the assignment for you."

After Marthe had given the order for Joanna's new assignment and Joanna had endured the discussion calmly, the Khan left and Joanna renewed her anger at the medtechs with even more fervor—and frustration.

Later in the day, Marthe stood alone at the point where Natalie Breen's *Crossbow* had lain for days before being removed by the Vipers. There was still a slight depression in the ground forming a rough outline of the 'Mech.

Although the day remained sunny, the breeze in this part of the valley was cold and blustery. Marthe wrapped her cloak more tightly around her shoulders.

Near her, two Jade Falcon BattleMechs, their metal surfaces shining brilliantly, were engaged in a training maneuver. Both were testing the running capability of their 'Mechs, ritualizing it through races of relatively short distance.

In the bright day the two 'Mechs, a *Nova* and a *Summoner,* gleamed with near-blinding rays of sunlight, and they ran with an almost ambling grace side by side. Marthe recognized them as the 'Mechs of Diana Pryde and Horse.

In her *Nova,* Diana felt exultant. She felt completely in sync with her 'Mech, completely in sync with herself.

"Beat you that time, Horse!"

"Not next time, eyass!"

"We'll see about that, won't we?"

"Drop the contractions. You sound too much like a freeborn, Diana Pryde!"

Diana laughed as her *Nova* got a good jump on the *Summoner* for the next heat of their race.

Marthe felt good as she walked back to her hovercraft. All over the field the Jade Falcons were engaged in intense activity—racing, exercising, shooting targets, screaming orders and insults at each other.

She felt optimism for the future—for her own and that of her Clan. The legacy of Aidan Pryde had, she thought, been fulfilled here on Waldorff. Samantha Clees had put it best earlier, when she had said, "We are back."

Looking around her, Marthe Pryde could see that, in the wake of the splendid victories over the Vipers, in the revival of hopes for future victories, the falcon was, indeed, rising.

Epilogue

Coming back to the Sibko Training Center for the first time since her abrupt and rushed departure, Peri felt a bit apprehensive. She had nearly been killed in this place and that memory did not make her feel comfortable about re-entering its gates.

It had been a busy time, the last nine months. Marthe had reacted quickly after receiving the report on the scientist caste that Peri had dispatched to the Khan's headquarters on Waldorff last July. Although light years away, Marthe maintained a close watch over her Strana Mechty staff as they implemented her orders to dissolve and reorganize the scientist caste on Ironhold. Etienne Balzac had put up a clever resistance, using the bureaucracy and his own crafty mind to construct roadblocks to the Khan's edicts.

During that time, Peri had to hide out in the tech sector. She had tried to locate Nomad just for his company, but the crusty old tech was nowhere to be found, nor had anybody apparently ever heard of him.

Marthe had informed Peri in a secret dispatch that there was no way she could stop the experimentation of the scientists throughout the Clans. As she explained, she could not be sure how much other Clan leaderships were involved in the secret projects. There was no way she could know even what Khans might already be aware of the projects and condone them. She doubted whether most Khans would approve, but in the present political environment within the Clans, she could not be sure. She vowed to Peri that at least the Jade Falcon scientist caste would be revamped.

True to Marthe's word, Etienne Balzac's regime was eventually toppled and the smug, bloated Scientist-General was removed from office and assigned to some backwater research station, much like the one on Falcon Eyrie to which Peri had been relegated for so long. She hoped he was festering there, but knew that he had to be kept under constant recognizance, since the man by his very nature would never stop plotting.

Marthe had offered the post of Scientist-General to Peri, but Peri declined on the grounds that some scientists loyal to Balzac but valuable to the caste remained in place and would resent her too much. A fairly innocuous bureaucrat named Renata Salk had been awarded the post.

Peri was reassigned to the Sibko Training Center at her own request. Before returning, she oversaw the restructuring of the Training Center. All of the Balzac loyalists had been removed from the camp and replaced with people she could trust.

After identifying herself to the guards at the gate, Peri saw Naiad standing in the roadway, clearly waiting for her.

She had grown more than Peri would have expected for a nine-month period. She looked stronger, taller, more precocious than ever. Her feet were spread apart in a defiant stance.

"I heard you were coming today," she said. "Taking over the whole place, *quiaff*?"

"That is right. You are no longer on an easy ride here."

It was true. Marthe had specifically instructed that the sibko training should be intense and geared to create the kind of warriors the Jade Falcons would need in the future.

"I never thought of it as an easy ride before, but you are right. Everything is already harder."

"Good."

"Octavian is gone."

Peri nodded. Octavian was closely allied to Etienne Balzac and had been his own choice to supervise the Aidan sibko.

"Yes. Do you miss him?"

"Not much. But the new one, I don't like her so much either."

Star Commander Joanna gave Peri a fierce look when she entered the barracks where Joanna was currently running a housekeeping drill with several members of the sibko. They were making up beds, apparently for the sole purpose of Joanna cursing them out and ripping their work apart.

Peri stood silently while Joanna finished the routine, then turned and limped toward her. Her leg seemed unnaturally bent and she had to drag her foot slightly. Joanna saw Peri taking note of the limp and remarked, "I think they are calling me Gimpy behind my back. First one I catch saying it will get a solid beating, I promise."

"How are you, Joanna?"

"The usual. Angry. Disgusted."

"I was sorry to hear of your injury."

"That? That is not much. They will not let me into a BattleMech any more, that is all. But I am satisfied. I was not pushed out or forced to solahma duty. I stayed a warrior as long as I could. It took years to get rid of me, after all."

"You are quite the legend, Joanna. You will be a famous warrior for a long time to come."

Joanna snorted. "Fame. Stravag. I am in the *Remembrance* even now, I am told."

"Told?"

"I will not read it."

"We will work together, Joanna, from here on in. I am glad to have you to supervise the day-to-day activities of the sibko. They will be ready for warrior training when you are through with them, *quiaff*?"

"You can be sure of that."

* * *

Outside, the sibko gathered, talking excitedly of the new arrival. They had all been aware of Peri during her earlier tour of duty, but none had suspected she would return triumphantly, as the new director of the Training Center. And word had gotten out about her toppling Etienne Balzac's regime. But when they discovered her connection to the Battle of Waldorff, they became even more intrigued by her.

"She is the mother of Diana Pryde," Idania said. "The hero of Waldorff."

"She knew Aidan Pryde, they say," Andi said. He was smiling, as usual. "Trained with him. She must have fine stories."

"I like the way she walks," Nadia said. "Did you see it? Proud and tough."

"She is only a scientist," Naiad said. "She is no warrior. She is no hero, like you say."

"I thought you liked her," Andi said.

Naiad fumed for a second, then said, "I do like her, kind of. But she is no hero. You are an idiot to think so."

"You are the idiot."

"Not me."

"You."

Naiad rushed at the smiling Andi and knocked him to the ground. He got up quickly and started jabbing at her face. The others formed into a circle to watch them. More of their cheers were in Andi's favor than Naiad's.

"Diana did well on Waldorff," Joanna said. "They are calling her hero."

"I am glad to hear it," Peri answered.

"I suppose you know she saved me from drowning, she and Horse."

"I know."

"Should have left me alone. Then I would not have to be here. I would have died in some kind of glory, as a warrior at Daemon Beach, even if it was by drowning and not the explosion of my 'Mech."

"You will be useful here."

"At least she also saved Ravill Pryde. I heard he was embarrassed. I would like to have seen that, but I was passed out at the time."

Joanna became quiet, her eyes unusually calm.

"We will work together, Joanna, you and I?"

Joanna stared at Peri for a long while. "Do not count on it," she finally said.

Outside there was a commotion. Joanna limped to the window to see what it was.

"They are fighting, the little surats," she said.

Looking over her shoulder, Peri was struck by the sight of the dozen or so children milling around the fight. She had forgotten, during her nine months away from the center, how strongly each of them resembled Aidan Pryde. The realization saddened her a bit. She thought of Aidan as individual, and was not sure she liked the idea of so many genetic copies of him. *Will there be another Aidan Pryde among this bunch?*

"One of the ugly little surats battling out there is Naiad," Joanna said angrily, "a troublemaker if I ever saw one. I expect nothing but grief from her."

"I know her. She reminds me of you, Joanna."

Joanna growled her response. "I would kill you for that— if it was not true."

She limped—quite nimbly—out of the barracks. Peri stared after her, wondering if Joanna really hated her new life as much as she said.

As soon as the limping Joanna was out of the door, she let loose a string of curses that, while rich and imaginative, only foreshadowed the verbal and physical torture that this sibko would experience from Star Commander Joanna during the next few years.

ABOUT THE AUTHOR

Falcon Rising is Robert Thurston's sixth BattleTech® novel and his twenty-first overall. His previous novels in the line were the *Legend of the Jade Phoenix Trilogy, I Am Jade Falcon,* and *Freebirth.* His published work also includes eight books in the Battlestar Galactica series, *Alicia II, A Set of Wheels, Q Colony,* plus novelizations of the movies *1492: Conquest of Paradise* and *Robot Jox.* His career in science fiction dates from his attendance at the Clarion Science Fiction Writers Workshop, where he won first Clarion Award for best story. He has published more than 40 short stories, several critical essays, and historical articles for a volume in the Reader's Digest Books series. He works as an administrator and instructor of Humanities at the same New Jersey university where his wife, Rosemary, is a history professor.

**Don't Miss the Next Exciting
BattleTech Adventure!**

Threads Of Ambition

Book One of *The Capellan Solution*

by Loren L. Coleman

Sun-Tzu Liao, First Lord of the Star League, has a dream to rebuild the Capellan Confederation at any cost. His first victim: his aunt, Candace Liao, who deserted the Confederation during the Fourth Succession War.

As border skirmishes between BattleMechs turn bloody, military units rally to Candace Liao's call to hold the line. Both sides are unyielding, and as Capellan fights Capellan, the high price of glory will be paid in full.

Coming in May 1999 from Roc!

Summoner

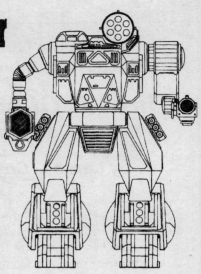

Nova

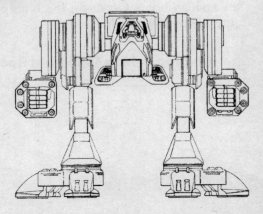

Black Lanner

Timber Wolf

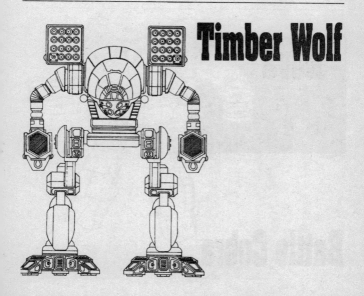

Crossbow

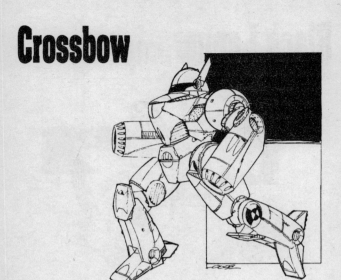

Battle Cobra

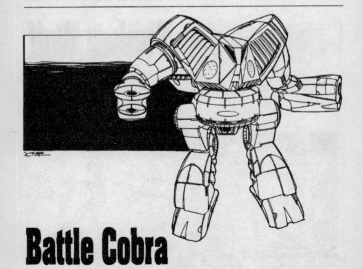

Union-C Class DropShip

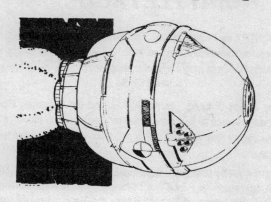

Cameron Class Battlecruiser

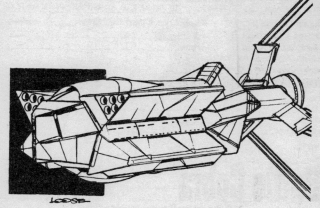